To

Hot"
03/13/23

Both Banks of Life

Forty Short Stories
Revised Edition

Hanna A. Saadah

Copyright © 2016 Hanna A. Saadah
All Rights Reserved

To Judy

Cover Art: Judith Saadah
Photoshop Art: Mackenzie Ford

Disclaimer

All these forty, semi-autobiographical, historical stories derive their essence from personal memory. The dates, names, and places, however, have been changed beyond recognition. The narratives have been radically embellished and rewritten to render this work entirely fictional. Any resemblance to real people or situations in unintentional and should be disregarded.

Prologue
Author's Note

This work reveals my passion for short stories—stories that were once autobiographical, but which I have rewritten to render them fictional. I have plucked these stories out of my memory because they pecked at me like a flock of caged birds, wanting release. I have camouflaged them to protect certain characters, embellished them to make them interesting, and set them free into the world where they will have to fend for themselves in order to survive.

They span about sixty-four years of my life—from 1950 when I was four years old, till 2014, when I retired from the practice of medicine at the age of sixty-eight. They tell tales about epochs that made indelible imprints on my inner being and helped reshape my character. They have occurred on both banks of my life's river, the *Eastern Bank*, representing Lebanon, and the *Western Bank*, representing the United States. Life forward flows, but the banks remain. That is why I called this book, *Both Banks Of Life*.

Being bicultural is tantamount to having two souls in one body. My *Eastern* and my *Western* souls have finally learned to cohabitate peacefully, but achieving that amicable balance took many, soul-searching years. In some stories, one can smell the *East*, in others, the *West*, but in most of them, both *East* and *West* vie for attention by wafting their earthen aromas.

Telling all forty of stories gave me great peace, the unique peace that arises from the soul's catharsis at having finished its life's work and at liberating its imprisoned messengers of good will.

I hope you can enjoy reading them as much as I have enjoyed penning them.

Introduction
Editor's Note

When I was a child, I used to love the stories my grandparents would tell, and retell. I would beg my grandfather: "Tell me again about the time when you met Geronimo in the stockade at Fort Sill." or "What about the great blizzard of 1888 in Iowa when you were stranded at school but managed to make it home with frost-bitten toes?"

I was hooked, captivated by tales of a generation gone by. We all have stories to tell that strike us as exciting, glamorous, adventurous, or merely special because they are about everyday life. Most of us, although we have much to tell, are not good at relaying stories in an inviting way. Hanna, on the other hand, has enchanted me with tales from his life that I, and so many others, have found thought provoking and intriguing.

Poetry was Hanna's first love, and he is a gifted and prolific poet who has produced five books of verse. Next, came the novels and there are four now. His fourth novel, *Twenty Lost Years,* published in Lebanon as *The Diary of Aziz Al Mitfi,* is a historical work and my favorite because it is based on actual events that chronicle the life and loves of Aziz. It also explores the storyteller himself as he weaves the events into lessons of forgiveness, kindness, and generosity, while promenading us through the fecund olive plains and snow-crowned mountains of Lebanon, through the souks of Tripoli and Beirut, and into the hearts and souls of the book's main characters.

I have heard from well-meaning friends that my husband was born with a silver spoon in his mouth. I assume this is because he came from an affluent family: his parents were both physicians, his education was paid for, etc. While these things are true, he has had anything but an easy life.

At age fourteen, his life was turned upside down and changed forever when his father attempted to overthrow the government. The *coup d'état* failed. His father was captured and put in solitary confinement with a death sentence looming over his head. His mother, who was uninvolved, was jailed without a trial. Isolated from his friends and family, and everything that he had known and loved, he was exiled to a boarding school. Add to that the worry about his father's fate and you can imagine how difficult life became for that adolescent boy.

Fortunately, during his father's seven-year imprisonment, he was blessed to always have love in his life, and to have many role models and mentors. You will discover in these stories the many people that have influenced him and helped shape and mold him into the man he is today.

After my repeated pleadings, asking him to share his stories with others, he has, over the past ten years, penned forty of them. While editing this book, I had an epiphany. The stories were arranged in the order in which they were written, but, if they were to be rearranged chronologically, they would read like the story of his life. Although fictionalized and embellished, these now chronologically rearranged stories are based on the historical facts and truths as he remembers them. Many of the names or places have been changed to protect the innocent, or the guilty, whichever the case may be.

We named the book, *Both Banks of Life,* to symbolize the East where he was born and the West where he has been since 1971. I hope you will enjoy *Both Banks of Life*, which chronicles the life of the man I love, the best man I know, a man of faith, of kindness, of goodness, of generosity, and of overflowing love—my husband, Hanna Saadah.

Judy Saadah
Editor

Table Of Contents

1. The Red Spell - 1 -
2. Three Arabian Tales - 10 -
3. Hasseen the Savior - 18 -
4. James Dean's Blue Jeans - 30 -
5. Amioun's Colorful Thief - 37 -
6. The Municipal Elections - 45 -
7. An Evening with Beethoven - 59 -
8. Chopin in Beirut - 70 -
9. Seven Years - 82 -

10. The Eye of the Needle - 86 -
11. The Quack Dr. Blackpill - 94 -
12. Abdominal Fire - 102 -
13. The Doctor Harrison - 109 -
14. Shooing Hallucinations - 115 -
15. Search Behind the Disease - 122 -
16. Professor Ley How - 127 -
17. Pilot Error - 138 -
18. Good Morning Professor Columbam - 145 -
19. Suda<u>a</u> - 182 -

20. Fatherland - Miss Fatima Hussein - 188 -
21. The Clandestine Stone - 211 -
22. Amiss - 218 -
23. A Dying Man Tells - 237 -
24. The Nun's Tale - 244 -
25. The Letter - 257 -
26. Murder in the OR - 262 -
27. Arthur VanChef - 272 -
28. Two Miracles - 280 -
29. Life from Under the Knife - 292 -

30. Frédéric Chopin's Four Ballades - 298 -
31. Love's River - 306 -
32. The Holy Quakes of Malula - 316 -
33. Crisis - 343 -
34. Odysseus - 351 -
35. Easter in Naxos - 360 -
36. The Wedding - 373 -
37. The Curly Black Hair - 379 -
38. Forbidden Fire - 387 -
39. Batman Kindness - 398 -
40. Valediction - 408 -

Books by Author - 420 -

The Red Spell

Sahara Bedouin Land, untouched by the Second World War, was a yawning expanse of sand that stretched between two war-torn continents, its wind-swept dunes bobbing like breasts in the vast silence. The only landmarks upon that golden tapestry, whose intimate pebbles huddled like unheard whispers, were the stars by night and the sun by day. But somewhere, in the middle of that peaceful nothingness, strode a small caravan on its way to the Big City.

The tribe, at the caravan's departure, shared daybreak coffee, held morning prayers, and wished the chieftain, Sheikh Hisham, a miraculous recovery at the hands of American science. During that past year, the sheikh had accompanied three of his wives—who could not be cured by the tribal doctors—to the American Hospital. The first wife rode off among tearful wailings and came back to gleeful ululations. The second was sent off with propitious *well-wishings* and returned to festive *welcomings*. By the time the third wife went, the tribe had gotten so accustomed to the success stories that she left with but a few good-byes and returned to just a few hellos. All three were brought back to health by Dr. Abdullah, the American-trained hospital surgeon who spoke the tribal language.

When other members of the tribe came to similar results at Dr. Abdullah's hands, it became widely believed that he held the secrets to all the tribe's incurable ailments—a belief that visibly angered the tribal doctors. Indeed, it was soon after that belief took hold of the tribe's mind that Sheikh Hisham began to feel ill. At first there were more good days than bad ones, but as time stomped its hoofs among the dunes, the good days grew fewer in number and finally ceased. For an entire month before his departure, Sheikh Hisham was attended by his favorite wives, but none of them ever succeeded in making him smile.

It was Magda, the third wife cured by Dr. Abdullah, who came to him one night. While he squatted among the dunes watching the moon, she sat by his side and whispered, "You need to get out of here before you die. Go to Dr. Abdullah and see if he can cure you."

"Why do you think that I'm about to die?"

"Because I can feel death growing stronger."

"Growing stronger? What is your meaning, Magda?"

"One of the tribe's doctors has put a spell on you because you took us to Dr. Abdullah after none of them could cure us. And after we were cured, others have followed suit and have also been cured. The tribe has lost its faith in its doctors and you have angered them even more when you refused to let them try to cure you."

Sheikh Hisham gazed at the moon without responding. Magda left him to his moonlit silence and went back to her tent. He remained in his squatted position, gazing, motionless, transfixed by the moon's rays, and unable to make up his mind as to what he should do. A scorpion crept beside him and hurried on its way. The moon crept across the sky, looking like a melon slice. A chill slowly crept up his spine and lingered in his head. His mind sparked:

The moon, the chill, and the scorpion are all creepers. What could that mean? What? Creepers bring death. Their bites are poisonous. Indeed, Magda was right. I must leave at sunrise before I die. I'll leave after the Morning Prayer. I'll take Magda with me. I'll sleep in her tent tonight.

At the gates of the Big City, the sheikh's caravan pitched tent. Except for Magda, Sheikh Hisham refused to let any other wife accompany him on his quest. He walked to the hospital along the same road he had traveled before, with Magda trailing close behind. At the hospital, he asked the gatekeeper to tell Dr. Abdullah that he had come on a most urgent matter. The gatekeeper brought back word that the doctor would see him as soon as he was finished with his surgeries. In Dr. Abdullah's waiting room, the sheikh and his wife sat in silence and hardly stirred. They were both pondering the very same question: *"What was it that Dr. Abdullah would have to cut this time in order to amputate the spell?"*

Midafternoon, Nurse Salama appeared and asked the sheikh and his wife to follow her. She showed them into Dr. Abdullah's office and told them that he would be with them shortly. The clock on the wall chimed two as they sat down on the two seats facing the desk. At Dr. Abdullah's desk sat a skull with a black scorpion painted on its cap. On the wall behind the desk were anatomical drawings showing severed parts, dissected to great detail. On Magda's left hung a skeleton with vacant eye sockets, clenched jaw, long, dangling limbs, and digits like creepy spiders. Sheikh Hisham's heart sank to his loins. He grew suddenly pale and sweat began to form upon his brow. That was when Dr. Abdullah, still in his scrubs, walked in.

He was tall, handsome, redheaded, and freckled. Everyone thought he was American until he spoke. Many hundreds of years ago, blond European seeds had sprouted here and there in the Levant and Dr. Abdullah was one of their offshoots. From behind a bright-eyed smile, he extended his hand and greeted, *"Assalamu alaykuma, Sheikh Hisham and Sit Magda*—Peace upon both of you, Sheikh Hisham and Lady Magda."

"Wa alaykum assalam, Hakeem—And peace upon you, Doctor," replied the sheikh, as he shook Doctor Abdullah's hand with his sweaty palm.

"Is Sit Magda having colon trouble again?"

"No, no, Doctor. She has done well ever since you cut off her infected segment. I am the one who needs your help today."

"In God's name, Sheikh Hisham, what's the matter?"

Sheikh Hisham sat down and lowered his head. Then, after a moment's silence, he raised his moist eyes to the doctor, and with a hoarse voice whispered, "I think that I'm dying."

Hearing that, Dr. Abdullah sank in his chair, fixed his blue eyes on the sheikh's face, and with a concerned voice, replied, "God forbid it, Sheikh Hisham. God forbid it, but tell me why you think that you are dying."

"One of the tribe's doctors has cast a deadly spell on me. Magda sensed it before I did. I have been sick for over a month."

Here, Magda intervened and told the doctor that the sheikh had been lethargic, eating very little, sleeping poorly, losing weight, hardly doing anything, and not even visiting his wives' tents. As she talked, the sheikh silently nodded with eyes downcast, shoulders drooped, and death's pallor shading his face. The depth and gravity of the situation did not escape Dr. Abdullah's atavistic vision.

With a frowning face, he took the sheikh into the examination room, drew blood, performed a thorough physical examination, and told him to return the next day for the conclusion. Tailed by Magda, the sheikh left the hospital and walked back to his camp. The sun was on the horizon and the call for prayer echoed from the minarets over the skyline of the Big City. Sick with worry, Sheikh Hisham sat all night and watched Magda toss in her sleep, say a few unintelligible words, sigh, whimper, moan, and occasionally snore.

To his next appointment, Sheikh Hisham arrived unaccompanied. He did not wish anyone to see him decompensate upon hearing the bad news. To breakdown under Dr. Abdullah's merciful gaze was acceptable, but to do it with anyone else in sight was unthinkable. The sheikh lived by his Bedouin precepts of staunch fortitude and fierce independence. If his time to meet Allah had come, he wanted to comport himself bravely. He wanted to have enough time to compose himself after hearing the bad news. The walk back to camp was about two hours, which would allow him enough time to calm himself down. These were Sheikh Hisham's thoughts as he anxiously waited in Dr. Abdullah's waiting room.

Soon, Nurse Salama appeared again and ushered the sheikh into Dr. Abdullah's office. The *scorpioned* skull on the desk, the anatomical dissections on the wall, and the hanging skeleton on the left formed a creepy ensemble around Sheikh Hisham, piquing his anxiety as he awaited his verdict. The seconds from the hanging clock ticked across the room like a dripping faucet, adding to the mounting suspense an air of rhythmic finality. Sheikh Hisham could hear his own heartbeats racing against the clock. He pacified himself by counting the beats between the ticks: lub,lub,tick—lub,lub,tick. It never occurred to him that his heart was pulsating at 120 beats per minute.

Again, Dr. Abdullah walked in wearing his operating room scrubs and holding a small bottle of medicine, which he carefully placed on his desk with an intentional tap that caused its contents to rattle. He then greeted the sheikh, who stood at attention as soon as the doctor walked in. Only this time, the doctor asked the sheikh to please sit down and did not offer to shake his hand. Compared to the day before, the doctor's voice and demeanor seemed ominous to the sheikh. Observing the marked transformation in the doctor's persona, the sheikh resignedly fell back into his chair and awaited the verdict to fall upon his hapless soul.

Dr. Abdullah, in a most solemn but compassionate tone, began his address, looking the sheikh straight in the eyes.

"I have completed your tests, Sheikh Hisham, and have concluded that you and your wife are correct in suspecting that an evil spell had been cast on you. My tests have confirmed the spell and have given me insight as to its nature and its impact. Medically, we recognize three kinds of spells. Those that are cast with air last but one lunar month and resolve when the new moon shows its first thumbnail. The ones cast with water last an entire season, usually about three months, and then they slowly dissipate. Those cast with fire, however, take their energy from the sun and last a lifetime. Your tests have confirmed that you have the fire spell in your blood."

The sheikh grew paler and his chin began to quiver. He wanted to ask if the fire spell was deadly or if it could be treated, but he could not even articulate the words. His tongue stuck to the roof of his dry mouth and he had a hard time dislodging it. Finally, when the long pause became unsustainable, he cleared his throat and whispered with a hoarse, almost inaudible voice, "Can you cure me?"

"I'm not sure, Sheikh. The fire spell is the most deadly of all."

"Deadly?"

"Hardly anyone survives it."

"But some do?"

"Only those lucky ones on whom the treatment works."

"Well, why can't you try it on me then?"

"I am planning to."

"And what do I have to do?"

"You'll have to take these seven capsules and eat three unpeeled lemons all together at bedtime today."

As he uttered *"these seven capsules,"* Dr. Abdullah picked up the medicine bottle, rattled it in the air, and put it back on his desk.

"What's the downside, Doctor? Are these pills dangerous when taken with unpeeled lemons?"

"If they don't work, they might hasten your death."

The sheikh's eyes bobbed out of their sockets as he gazed at the skull before him. He took off his headdress and scratched his bald scalp as if to make sure that there was not a scorpion crawling on it. Then with an unexpected, bold, determined expression he asserted, "I'll take the pills. Dying quickly is better than lingering on like this."

Dr. Abdullah sighed as he handed the capsules to the sheikh. Then he carefully explained the details of the treatment:

"At midnight, cut the lemons into thin slices and eat them slowly, one by one, to dilute the bitterness in their skins. Then take all seven capsules with one cup of water, say your prayers, and go to bed. When you awaken in the morning, face the east and pass urine. If it comes out red, you are cured because the spell is being discharged out of your blood. If it comes out yellow, say your morning prayers and head back home to your tribe because it would mean that your end is eminent."

Dr. Abdullah walked the sheikh to the hospital gate, wished him God's blessings, and followed his stooped figure until it disappeared around the corner. Nurse Salama, seeing the deep concern on Dr. Abdullah's face as he walked back to his office, approached him and inquired, "Is he going to be all right?"

"His condition is beyond science. If he makes it, it would be because of his faith in science and not because of what science could do for him."

"What do you mean, Doctor?"

"His malady is deeply rooted in his belief system and it's unresponsive to reason."

"You mean it's all in his mind?"

"Do not underestimate the powers of our minds, Salama. We are our minds, and we live inside our minds. What we believe to be true is true to us, regardless of reality. For thousands of years, humanity believed that the earth was flat and to them it was flat. Now, you and I believe that after we die we will go to heaven and that is our truth. The sheikh believes that one of the tribe's doctors has cast an evil spell on him and because of this truth he is living in a deadly state of depression."

"If that's his truth, Doctor, then no one can help him except God Almighty. Right?"

"But, didn't God give us our brains in order help others? Would you or I have been able to help the many patients we have already helped and continue to help were it not for our brains?"

"I see what you mean. You really think that you can help him then."

"I do."

"What did you give him?"

"Seven capsules full of dye."

"What dye?"

"Neutral Red."

"That's not a medicine."

"I had our pharmacist concoct them for me."

"What does Neutral Red do?"

"It's a harmless water-soluble indicator that turns red in acid."

"What acid?"

"The urine is acidic. Remember your renal physiology?"
"Oh, I think I understand. Or, maybe I don't."
"You will understand it better, tomorrow."

The next day, while Dr. Abdullah was operating, nurse Salama charged the operating room. She was panting and her face was dimpled with surprise.

"Doctor, he is back with a bottle of red liquid in his hand and is insisting on seeing you. Because of his excitement, I can't tell if he's angry or elated. He's pacing like a maniac, holding the bottle of red liquid above his head, shouting at the top of his voice, 'It's out. It's out.' and paying no attention to all the other patients in the waiting room who sincerely believe that he has gone mad."

Dr. Abdullah smiled from behind his surgical mask and a visible gleam rose into his eyes as he turned his head toward Nurse Salama and said, "Show him to my office and tell him that I'll be with him as soon as I finish this case."

In the office, Sheikh Hisham sat in his usual chair facing the doctor's desk, and placed the bottle of red urine next to the *scorpioned* skull with unambiguous defiance. He was neither bothered by the anatomical drawings on the wall nor by the hanging skeleton on his left. The ticking sounds of the clock were drowned by the noisy heartbeats that rang loud in his ears. His eyes were gazing far away, upon his awaiting tribe, rehearsing his triumphant reentry among women's gleeful ululations and men dancing with swords. It mattered not that the surgery took far too long and that Dr. Abdullah could not join him until two hours had passed. Sheikh Hisham's mind was occupied with his future, his wives, and his grandchildren.

When Dr. Abdullah finally walked in, he found the sheikh sitting calmly, smiling like a sun, with face full of gratitude and awe. He said nothing as he watched the doctor sit down and gaze with astonishment at the hundred golden dinars piled on his desk.

"What's this money for, Sheikh Hisham?" came the doctor's surprised words. "You have already paid your bill and you owe me nothing."

"This money is not a payment, Doctor."

"That's a great deal of money, Sheikh Hisham. Why are you giving it to me?"

"So you can tell me the name of the tribal doctor who cast the spell on me."

Dr. Abdullah understood the lethal seriousness behind the sheikh's response. He paused a moment and then fixated his eyes on the sheikh's as he inquired, "What is my profession's calling, Sheikh Hisham?"

"To heal the sick."

"And to do what else?"

The sheikh hesitated a bit and then replied, "To save lives."

"And what would you do to your tribal doctor if I were to reveal his name to you?"

"I would slit his throat as soon as I return."

"And wouldn't that also mean that I would have helped you kill him?"

Sheikh Hisham lowered his eyes and soon tears began to drip into his lap. The silence groaned with both men's heavy breaths. The clock chimed once. Nurse Salama knocked at the door and stuck her head in to tell the doctor that his next case was ready. With head still bowed, Sheikh Hisham slowly stood up. He collected his golden dinars and put them back inside his pocketed leather belt. He then picked up his red urine bottle and walked toward the door. At the door, with Nurse Salama standing by his side, he turned back to Dr. Abdullah and intoned with a moist, tremulous voice, "May Allah bless you, Doctor," and then walked out with the bottle of red urine swinging from his hand.

Three Arabian Tales
Harked With Little Ears

Children love stories and ask, with innocent curiosity, questions, which adults can seldom answer. As a schoolboy, my mind teemed with beehives of questions, which when I asked, earned me risible rebuke. During the early nineteen-fifties, teachers and parents were a lot less tolerant of children's incessant inquisitiveness.

"Stop asking senseless questions," snapped my aunt.
"I have no time for silliness," sighed my mother. *"Ask me something intelligent instead, something that I can answer."*
"Stick to your schoolwork," admonished my teachers, *"and stop flapping all over the classroom with your imagination."*

My *Three Arabian Tales* transpired before 1954, before I turned eight, and before I knew to feel intimidated by adult company. During those formative years, my father worked in Saudi Arabia and came home once a year, loaded with Bedouin stories and anecdotes, which, sitting among adults, I listened to with buoyant fascination. During that juvenile stretch of life, I perceived the adults who *audienced* my father as merely big people—big people who laughed loudly, smoked cigarettes, sat too long after meals sipping coffee, and entertained themselves with convoluted conversations instead of colorful toys.

Of all the conversations I sat through as a little boy, my father's were the most memorable because he was a gifted storyteller. He could turn a simple incident into an anecdote, a fool's remark into a profound message, a chance encounter into a propitious omen, and an unpleasant event into a divine intervention sent to avert a lurking evil. He embellished, I am certain, as all story tellers do, for the object of telling stories is to entertain rather than to render the desiccated truth. As

Dostoyevsky once said, *"We must embellish the truth to make it believable."*

At that nascent stage of my life, I half understood what he said and left the other half to wander aimlessly in my elephant memory. With relentless curiosity, and in spite of ridicule and rebuke, I continued, unabashed, to intercept those abstruse, adult conversations. Something about unraveling what adults were saying challenged me. I kept those unintelligible conversation snippets in the tenebrous recesses of my mind, holding them hostage until that time, when as an adult, I would be able to decipher their arcane remains. And it is from this latent, childhood memory of mine that now, sixty-two years later, I have re-composed these tales.

*

When my father related the story of an Arabian poet who, watching a caravan from atop his horse, regaled, with an impromptu verse, a veiled princess as she passed him on her camel:

With the light from your eyes
I shall light my fire.

When they heard this couplet, all the adults in the room cooed with enchantment. I, on the other hand, unable to restrain my curiosity, asked with a bleating voice, "So? Did he really light his fire from her eyes?"

Instead of an answer, a hum of polite laughter fluttered about the room, which further teased my mind and left my inquisitiveness un-satiated. And, as my father continued with his story, my growing incomprehension continued to feed my fascination.

In those days, he explained, flirting with a princess could have earned that meddlesome poet a swift beheading. The princess, however, noting the curved scimitars gleaming out of her guards' scabbards, stopped the caravan with a swift wave of her hand.

"Re-sheath your scimitars," she commanded her retinue with a cold, piercing voice. And then, turning toward them, she recited:

> *Poets, when inspired, turn officious*
> *That is why our Prophet disliked poets.*

In spite the chagrin of her enraged guards, she then turned toward the poet and added:

> *You cannot see my eyes through this dark veil*
> *What demons conjured your curt flamboyance?*

Unperturbed by the princess's fuming guards, but utterly enthralled by her poetic extempore, he cadenced back, holding the same meter:

> *Imagination sees deeper than eyes*
> *Nothing can stop excursions of the mind.*

Hearing that, the princess ordered her entire retinue to turn away and then, facing the poet, lifted up her veil for one brief moment and titillated:

> *Behold my unveiled face and thrill your sight*
> *Then, with a poem, fire up the night.*

The room rang with poetry as the strophes were reiterated like a song's refrain, enthralling everyone except me. I sat wandering what that poetry meant and what happened at the end, but no denouement was revealed. Over the years, I have dreamed up so many ends to that story but none of them healed my wounded curiosity. A story without an end is like a wound that does not heal.

*

When my father told the story about the King of Arabia, the room choked on golden silence, unblinking eyes went dry, cigarettes grew long ashes, and a cloud of wonder hovered like a halo in midair:

When, after the Second Great War, the King was invited by the young Queen Elizabeth to a royal banquet at Buckingham Palace, the world watched with keen interest, began my father. The table, set with strict royal etiquette, glimmered like the Milky Way on a dark desert night. Seats were arranged according to rank and the King presided at one head of that very long table, opposite the Queen. Alcohol, a traditional accouterment in royal banquets, was omitted out of respect for the King's Muslim faith.

The Bedouin King, who had been expertly coached in the formalities of royal manners for that special occasion, comported himself with regal grace, initiating each course with slow, small, calculated bites, and gaining the admiration of all the blonde, powdered faces, scrutinizing him. When, at last, the food was cleared and the grapes were brought in, little golden bowls filled with cool water were placed before the King, the Queen, and the rest of the invitees for the purpose of dipping the grapes before mouthing them.

The King, desert-born and reared where there was little water to spare, through some unfortunate faux pas, had not been coached in the particular nuances of the golden bowl use. Naturally, he perceived the glittering bowl of cool, clear, water as a God-sent gift. While the rest of the table, including the Queen, eyed the King, awaiting his first move, reverently, he lifted the golden bowl to his lips, and with sibilant mirth, emptied its lucent contents into his desert mouth.

The table froze. The invitees struggled to recompose their faces. The King licked his lips with succulent insouciance. The Queen, with a pallid smile and a feigned cough, quickly held everyone's attention. Then, with musical grace and royal dignity, she lifted her own bowl to her still smiling lips and slowly savored its entire contents.

Seconds thudded like drums, eyes vacillated in their sockets, and all breathing ceased. The Queen gently laid her emptied bowl down and, with a tacit tilt of her crowned head, ushered the invitees who, in unison, lifted up their bowls and drank them to the lees.

Hearing that story, the listeners burst the room with loud, exclamatory acclaim followed by flaps of laughter, as if a flock of birds had been abruptly startled into flight. Then, after the roars had died and the silence of astonishment supervened, the group, with amused eyes, beckoned my father for one, final, summary remark. Seizing that moment's lull, I inquired, "Do golden bowls make water taste better?"

Murmuring smiles lit the smoke-filled room, but neither comment nor explanation was offered to fill my gaps.

*

It would take another time and place for the apricot incident to be related. My father returned to his hospital in Jeddah, gone for yet another year. When he came back the next fall, I was as eager to spend as much time listening to his stories as were so many of his friends. Being a year older made me feel more confident, but also more inquisitive. Again, it happened after lunch, during one, long, coffee-sipping, cigarette-smoking, October afternoon.

Dropped by the school bus at the head of our dead-end street, I walked home and rang the doorbell. The living room was foggy with cigarette-smoking adults, listening attentively to my father discourse on the upcoming elections, for he was both surgeon and politician. He saddled me onto his knee, and went on with his exposition, of which I understood nothing.

Then, again, the doorbell rang and in stepped a tall man from Akkar—a fertile mountain region famed for its fruits—bearing a gift of dried apricots.

"Mr. Bitar," chimed my father, standing up and giving the man a huge hug. Then, turning to the guests, he added, "This nice man sent me a case of fresh apricots all the way to Jeddah. His son, who works at our hospital, brought it with him in mid August."

*

After the customary handshakes, which *dominoed* around the room, and after the man was seated, handed a demitasse of Arabic coffee, and offered a cigarette from the cigarette tray, my father saddled me back onto his knee and began his apricot story with this prologue:

I love Bedouins, he began, and I love their Saharan wisdom. For millennia they have survived the Arabian Desert and have thrived in spite of intolerable conditions, vast emptiness, and scarce water. From their Arabian Peninsula, they have spawned a magnificent language with inimitable literature, founded a formidable religion, and carved a vast empire.

Of all the Sahara's nomadic tribes, many of whose members I've come to know as patients, not one has accepted the government's invitation to urbanize. They prefer the arid, serenity of the desert to the boisterous, obtrusiveness of the city. The Red Sea is their bathtub and the sand, their master bedroom. From them, among other things, I have learned endurance, cheerfulness, insouciance, contentment, patience, simplicity, and joie de vivre.

One day, in the heat of August, I came to lunch after a long, operating schedule. As I sat down, my nurse came in to tell me that a Sheikh Hussein from an inland tribe had travelled several days on camelback to see me. I asked her to usher him in and invited him to share my lunch, which he declined by placing his hand upon his chest and uttering a polite *thank you*. Then, sitting across the table, he told me of his medical problems, and I agreed to examine him right after lunch. After the food was removed, the cook, with a sly smile, came in with a bowl of cold, perspiring apricots, which he placed before me.

"Mr. Bitar brought them with him from Lebanon last night," he announced, relishing my surprised face.

Sheikh Hussein studied the fruits with delectable curiosity. To a Bedouin, the cold, succulent, red-and-yellow cheeks of those plump, Lebanese apricots must have flaunted a tantalizing spectacle because he couldn't stop eyeing them. Even in the plush souks of Jeddah, apricots were a rarity because they travel poorly and have a short shelf life. Noting his covetous curiosity, I invited him to try some.

"What are they?" he asked, from a parched throat.

"They come from Lebanon. They arrived last night." I encouraged, and then pushed the bowel toward him.

He hesitated. Then, with two, long, sand-blown fingers, he picked up one and, very carefully, put it in his mouth.

"There's a seed inside," I cautioned, as he began to chew.

A smile rose into his eyes as he spit the seed into his hand, reached for another, and another, and another, consuming the fruits with dizzy enchantment. A thrill shivered through my bones as I watched his mouth, savoring one apricot at a time with profound, sumptuous reflection. And when he stopped, it was not because of satiety, but rather because of propriety, for he had eaten about half a dozen by then.

All this time, I said nothing, but watched with a hospitable smile the son-of-the-desert compose himself, put the apricot seeds into his *djellaba's* pocket, wipe his bearded mouth with his sun-parched hand, take in a deep sigh, and then utter with Koranic solemnity his culinary epiphany.

"Doctor," he proclaimed, pointing at the apricots with his long, trembling, index finger. "They say that the *bath* is heaven upon earth. For the fear of Allah, is this the *bath*?"

*

In Lebanon, as in the rest of the Levant, fathers often worked abroad, in the oil-rich countries, and saw their families only once or twice a year. Having private time with my father was rare. I learned to share him with endless visitors and, in spite of such cultural incursions, I managed to derive great satisfaction from his stories. As an adult, when I think of my father, I hear his stories, and it is these stories that keep aglow, my memories of him.

As Nassim Taleb said in *The Black Swan*, "Ideas come and go; stories stay."

Stories told of yesteryears
Come to us through little ears
Hold us captive in their spheres.

When the years will disappear
Only stories keep them near
For our little ears to hear.

Arabian Tales (Heard With Little Ears), First Edition, Al-Jadid, Vol.19, No.68 (2015) Pages 36-37. Second Edition completed in October of 2016.

Hasseen the Savior

"The Red Sea is our oasis;" explained Hasseen, the Bedouin. "It's Allah's gift to us who have nothing else but desert."

"We have a boat but we don't know where to go," said my father as he pointed to the open motorboat he had purchased that morning.

"I'll be happy to guide you," answered Hasseen, as he stood surrounded by his five little children while his wives took cover in their tents.

"Have you ever been in a boat?" came my dad's circumspect query.

"No, we fish from the shore with nets."

"Well, so how can you be our guide if you've never been in a boat?"

"The Red Sea is our oasis, Sir, and Allah is our guide," answered Hasseen with a confident smile. Then, reading my dad's hesitant aspect, he reassured, pointing to his kids, "I've walked these shores all of my life and I know them as well as I know my five children. We could not get lost as long as we keep the shore in sight."

"How much will you charge us for a day of fishing?" asked my father as he looked at the vast desert, lipping the long, languid sea."

"Allah commands us not to charge our guests," he whispered with a shy, avoidant gaze. "*Hatim Tayy* slaughtered his only camel to feed some drop-in guests who were lost in the desert. You have dropped in upon our little tribe and, therefore, you have become our honored guests. *Dthiyafah* (hospitality) is our creed."

I was ten in 1956 when my brothers and I took our first flight to Jeddah in order to spend Christmas with my father: my mother had joined him two weeks earlier. Aunt Maha accompanied us to the airport and before we left, gave me a small, brown-paper sack and asked me to give it to my dad as soon as we arrive.

"Be careful with it; it has fruits that can be easily damaged."

"What kind of fruits?" I inquired as I opened the bag to take a peek.

"They're individually wrapped apricots, ripened in my cellar."

"Apricots in winter?" I asked, intrigued.

"I have my secret method," she answered with a smug smile.

"What secret method?" I queried with raised eyebrows.

"I pick them green, from the tree on the south side of the house because it bears late. Then I individually wrap them with fruit paper, put them in a deep pot, cover them with green grape leaves, and put them in my underground cellar."

"Wow," I exclaimed with awe. "Who taught you all that?"

"Your grandmother. In her days, they did that to save fruits for the long, cold winters."

Sitting on the runway at the Beirut International Airport, we marveled as our Douglas DC 7 airplane started its four engines one at a time until all four propellers seemed to have transformed their spinning blades into invisible noise. Too young for fear, I watched everything below us diminish to miniscule size as we levitated among the sunny, blue smiles of heaven. By the time we landed at the Jeddah Airport, I was feeling like a seasoned traveler who was taking his two younger brothers along to see the Arabian Desert.

My dad's Christmas gift to us was a day of fishing in his new boat, which he had purchased for that occasion. It was a white, open, wooden boat with an outboard motor hanging from its rear. There were benches on each side with life jackets tucked underneath. I had just learned to swim but had never been in a boat or gone fishing before. My excitement was so overwhelming that I was unable to sit still as we drove from our hotel in Jeddah, traversing about an hour of *roadless* desert before we saw the group of tents where Hasseen's tribe lived. A friend of my dad had recommended Hasseen as a guide and given us directions to his tribe's location by the sea.

Standing by my dad as he made arrangements with Hasseen, I continued to feel excited and overwhelmed because of the so many firsts that we had experienced or were about to experience. We had already had our first flight, our first Christmas away from home, our first desert drive, and we were about to experience our first family fishing trip, our first boat ride, and our first unforgettable adventure.

The new boat, full of fishing equipment, food, and water was unhinged from our 1954 Desoto, floated into the water, and off we went deep into the blue unknown with my father at the motor in the rear, Hasseen in the fore, and the rest of us balancing on the sides. Hasseen kept his eyes on the shore and directed my dad northward towards the Barracudas.

After about an hour of seafaring, he told my dad that he could start trolling and that's when the excitement began. Even though I was beginning to feel seasick, I held my rod as my dad tied me down, then he and I, one on each side of the boat, began trolling while my mother held the motor handle. My excitement grew as I began to feel some nibbles, but my seasickness out grew my excitement when the wind began to roughen the surface and the waves began to force their dance upon our little boat. I tried to look away so that my father would not notice my puckered expression, but the more we trolled the more I realized that I was but one or two waves away from violent vomiting. It was at this most inopportune moment that I felt a sudden, deep force try to jerk my rod away. I screamed with a throttled voice and began vomiting, but did not let go of my rod until my dad came to my rescue, grasped the rod, and held me while I continued my retching over the side.

As I watched my dad reel in the fish and saw that it was longer than I was tall, I began to feel utterly helpless, trapped between my deep sense of nausea and the tantalizing joy of having caught my first fish. Struggling to force a smile into the moment's excitement and, at the same time, struggling against the visceral displeasure of my seasickness, my head began to spin uncontrollably and I fell face down at my father's feet. My violent, relentless, retching alarmed my parents who, having no idea how to deal with the situation, looked to our Bedouin guide for suggestions.

Calmly, Hasseen informed my father that we were at least 90 minutes away from our embarkation point but only ten minutes away from shore. By that time, it had also become obvious to everyone that I could not possibly endure another 90 minutes of dehydrating torture underneath a full December sun. The only sensible solution was to drop me ashore and come back for me by car, two-to-three hours later.

My father's first idea was to drop my mother and me ashore, but Hasseen protested.

"No, Sir, you cannot leave a woman alone without a man's protection. The desert is not safe for unaccompanied women and our customs prohibit it."

"But, I cannot stay ashore with my boy because I'm the only one who can manage the motor, nor can I leave you with him because I wouldn't be able to trace my way back to camp, and of course, I cannot leave him ashore all by himself."

"Oh, yes you can," came Hasseen's surprising reply. "The desert would be safer for him alone than it would be if his mother were with him."

"And why is that?" asked my father with exasperated tone?

"Because Bedouins would protect the boy if they were to find him alone. It is part of our noble hospitality, our *dthiyafah*, which dictates that we treat those lost in the desert better than we treat ourselves or our own families."

"And your *dthiyafah* does not extend to women?" asked my dad with unconcealed annoyance.

"No, Sir. Bedouins lose their minds when they see a woman alone. If a woman is caught without her man, she becomes the property of whosoever finds her first."

As my father cautiously drove the boat toward the shore, Hasseen stood at the fore, directing him with hand motions and occasionally screaming, "Rock to your right, turn left, slow down, go back a bit, come around this reef…"

Thanks to Hasseen we made it to shore without a scratch. The sun was hot and there was no cover. My father put his shirt over my head, laid my exhausted body on the sand with a bottle of water next to me, and before taking off said, "No matter what happens, do not leave this spot. If you do we would have a hard time finding you. If all goes well, we'll be coming back for you by car in a couple of hours."

Lying on the shore, I watched the boat maneuver back into the sea and slowly diminish into the frothing blue. My mother's incredulous, silent tears and my brothers' waving hands kept me company long after the boat disappeared into the steaming haze. It was then, with no one around and nothing in sight except sand and sea that my nausea began to fade and life's curious humors started to creep back into my desiccated veins. Within an hour I had gulped the entire contents of my large water bottle and, feeling refreshed, got up and began exploring.

I walked inland up the sandy incline until I was in good view of the vast expanse of desert that stretched beyond the farthest reaches of my imagination. It was a soft, smooth, undulating carpet of gold that rolled before my eyes like an infinite prayer echoing with Koranic chants. The wafting desert wind hissed in the peaceful emptiness and danced in the sunny silence with whirling ghosts of sand. I skipped among the dunes, burst into song, and watched the desert wind carry off my tunes into the pristine emptiness. A sense of blithe freedom overtook my soul as I skipped with tireless abandon and soared the un-scaled peaks of my fearless imagination.

When I had collected enough sand in my shoes, I decided to head back towards the sea for a dip. I was feeling hot and needed the sea to cool me off. Standing with my feet in the shallow waters, I became acutely aware of two realities that should have been obvious to me from the start. The first was that for the first time in my entire ten years of life I was truly alone with no human sign in sight. The second was that the desert had no roads for cars to drive on. As I slowly made my way into the sea, I started to wonder how on earth were they going to find me with no roads and no landmarks to guide them. I even wondered if they would be able to find the car because, after launching the boat, my dad parked it inland, far away from the shore, in order to avoid the tide. But in spite of these realities I had no sense of fear. Some mysterious force, emanating from that vast expanse of peaceful emptiness, must have filled my soul with faith and reassured me that everything was going to be fine.

I reasoned as I trod deeper into the water that Hasseen, who knew the shore as well as his five children, would not only be able to guide my father back to the car but would also be able to guide the car to where I was waiting. No doubt percolated in my mind as I played around with water to my waist. I was even tempted to go in deeper because the water felt so refreshing to my skin. Cautiously, I advanced until I was neck deep and then turned around to look at the shore. It seemed so far away and the desert beyond it seemed even deeper than before. There was no car in sight, no motion except the water's, and no sign of life except for the fish, which swam around me with fearless disregard.

Slowly, I made my way back to shore, climbed up the sandy hill, and gazed at the shimmering mirage in the distance. Utter emptiness—silent, motionless, and indifferent—glared back at me as if I were violating the sanctity of its solitude. Feeling a bit intimidated, I went back to shore, began collecting tiny seashells, and played at setting them in strategic piles by the water's edge. The sand, soft and fine like silk, had neither pebbles nor stones nor anything else that one could collect except those tiny seashells. Each time the tide would advance, I would move my seashell piles deeper inland. After this went on for a while, I became intrigued with the speed at which the tide moved in and tried to measure it against my walking distance. Each time I walked to where my strip of shore curved in-and-out, it was time to move my seashell piles one more step inland.

The afternoon stretched its long fingers and yawned, as everything around me seemed to be taking a siesta. The wind quieted down, the waves stopped barking at the shore, and even the tide slowed its advance against my seashell piles. I could walk to where my strip of shore curved in-and-out twice before I had to move my seashell piles away. The whispering tranquility began to entice me back to sea and I offered it no resistance. If Hasseen knew how to find me, he would find me just as well if I were in the water or on land. Given the hilly incline that surrounded the shoreline, I reasoned that I would be even more visible if I were in the water than on land.

Advancing my prized seashell piles four steps inland to allow me ample time, I delved back into the water and slowly made my way until I was waist deep, a level at which I thought I would be most visible from land. There I splashed and daydreamed until I was awakened from my reverie by the sounding horn of a distant car. I turned around and saw nothing but a corridor of dust advancing towards the shore. It had to be Hasseen and my dad but the shore's topography with its surrounding cliffs obstructed my view. Nevertheless, I stood in my place and gazed at the dust file until it stopped right behind the cliff that framed the shore.

Soon after that, Hasseen and my dad emerged, galloped down the cliff, took one look at my little body waist deep in sea water, and froze in their tracks. As I started to make my way back towards them, they both waved back at me with agitated motions, screaming as if in unison, "Don't move. Don't move at all. Stay where you are."

Relieved that they were not mad at me for wading alone into the sea but bemused as to why they did not want me to come ashore, I watched my dad and Hasseen grasp handfuls of my prized seashell piles and charge toward me with alarming speed, frothing and parting the water with their scurrying legs. Standing in my place, I began surveying my surroundings, hoping to discover the reason behind their frantic charge. There was nothing but calm waters and several high tails, hoisted up like sails, swimming around me in a wide, perpetual circle. I spent as much time admiring the hoisted, beautiful tails of these circling fish as I did watching my dad and Hasseen's thundering charge. The notion that the two spectacles were somehow connected never came to my mind.

To my disillusionment and surprise, when Dad and Hasseen reached the outskirts of the circling tails, they discharged their fistfuls of my prized seashells at the peacefully circling fish and then, with a roaring, battle cry, charged the circle. Stunned, I watched my seashells surprise the calm waters with their tiny bubbles and then watched the high, hoisted, circling tails brake form, and in single file, whisk back into the sea.

Soon I was in my father's arms, held high above the water, being hastily carried back to shore. My piles of prized seashells with which I marked the tide were all gone and I was not even given the chance to find some more. My dad said that we needed to hurry back to camp because my mother and brothers were anxiously awaiting us. When I asked him why they did not bring them along, he simply said that it was safer to leave them with Hasseen's wives than to subject them to a dangerous desert drive.

Back into the Desoto, with my dad and Hasseen in the front and I in the back seat, we drove into the desert leaving my little shore strip behind. Soon we were surrounded by sand from all directions and the only one who seemed to know where we were going was Hasseen, who periodically directed my dad this way or that in order to avoid sand traps. It was during this long drive among the smooth sand hills and lonesome dunes that I asked my father why he and Hasseen used my prized seashells to chase the beautiful fish away.

"They were sharks, Son," replied my father, hoping to end the conversation with his brief answer.

"But, why did you chase them away using my seashells?"

"Well, because the red-sea sharks can be dangerous to swimmers."

"What do you mean, dangerous?"

"Well, they can attack swimmers at a whim."

"Oh, you mean that they can eat swimmers?"

"Yes, Son, they have been known to do that."

Back at camp, after my mother had shed grateful tears and my brothers had asked me all kinds of questions about what was it like to be all alone in the middle of the desert, my father tried to pay Hasseen, but Hasseen refused and kept saying that it was his code of honor to help guests that happen upon him in the desert.

"It's our Arabian hospitality, Sir, our *dthiyafah*, our ordinance from Allah to all our desert guests."

"But, Hasseen, you have saved my son's life thrice. First, I would not have dared to drop him ashore in order to save him from certain dehydration. Second, I would not have been able to find where I had dropped him. Third, if you had not told me that the sharks would run away if we just throw some pebbles at them, I would not have known what to do at that horrifying moment."

"Oh, no Sir," said Hasseen with a calm smile. "Allah was the one who saved your son's life. It was all written in heaven, long before it happened. I'm just a Bedouin who knows his desert and his shores, but Allah was the one who directed you to me."

"But, please, allow me to give you something as a token of our gratitude."

"There is nothing that I need, Sir," came Hasseen's meek reply. "Allah has given me all that I deserve."

Before driving back to Jeddah, one by one, we all shook Hasseen's hand, as he stood surrounded by his children. Then, after driving just a few yards, my father suddenly stopped the car and asked my mother, "Did you remember to bring the fresh apricots along?"

"Yes, they're still in the ice chest in the trunk," came my mother's astonished reply.

"Good," said my dad as he stopped the car, got the little brown bag out of the trunk, and walked back with it toward Hasseen and his kids, with me trailing close behind him.

"Hasseen, would you allow me to offer you and your family something very special and very difficult to come by at this time of year, especially on these shores?"

"Our honor code forbids us from refusing a personal gift when it is given as a gesture of good will," said Hasseen with a smile. "It would be my honor to accept whatever you wish me to have, Sir."

"With a smile, my father presented Hasseen with my aunt's individually-wrapped, red-cheeked apricots."

Hasseen looked with curiosity at the blushing, yellow fruits coated with soft, cool fuzz and asked, "What is this, Sir?"

"Try one and you'll know," replied my dad with a smile.

Hasseen took one apricot, placed it cautiously in his mouth, and began to chew with deliberate slowness. As soon as the sweet, moist juice burst in his mouth, his eyes lit up with surprise and his lips protruded as if preparing for a kiss. Then, after spitting out the seed, he began nodding his head while continuing to chew with savoring intensity. He then gave one apricot to each of his children, put a second one in his mouth, and then followed it by a third. The surprise on his face never faded away. Rather, it turned into a blithe expression as he held the sack of apricots to his chest as if it were a newborn babe. Then, with a smug, all knowing grin, he peered into my dad's smiling eyes and inquired with serious reverence, "What do you call this Allah-blessed fruit?"

"*Mushmush*," replied my dad.

"May Allah grant you and your family a life as sweet as this *mushmush*," was the last thing he said as he walked back toward his tent with his five children tailing him.

On the way back to Jeddah, my father explained to us that the only desert fruits available to Bedouins were dates, and that nomadic Bedouins like Hasseen were seldom exposed to fresh fruits. And when I asked him how do the Bedouins wash he said that they used seawater because potable water was extremely precious and too scarce to be wasted on washing.

Twenty-seven years later, I took my ten-year-old, American-born son on his first fishing trip and watched him reel in his first fish. We were on Padre Island and fished from a shore strip by our hotel. There were no Bedouin tents around, no sharks in the water, and no vast desert to get lost in. Nevertheless, and in spite of our secure surroundings, the mere notion of leaving my son alone at shore was unthinkable. Only then did I comprehend the unimaginable torture and anxiety that my father and mother must have endured when they had to leave me all alone ashore with no certainty that they would be able to find me a few hours later.

Powerful experiences reshape our lives with fear and with faith. It was fear and faith that reshaped the rest of my parents' lives because they never mentioned that story to anyone, including my brothers and me. They needed to forget how close I came to dying of dehydration under the burning sun of Arabia, or as shark food while daydreaming all alone amidst the jaws of the Red-Sea waters.

I, on the other hand, was too young for fear and for faith. Instead, the experience slowly grew with me, transforming me into a better person, a person who idolized and emulated the noble souls of the proverbial Bedouins of Arabia.

And for the rest of my life, every time I would see apricots, I would remember Hasseen, my savior, who knew the desert and the shores like he knew his own children, and who first learned about *mushmush* one December day, under the hot sun, by the Red Sea.

And for the rest of my days, I would try to live by Hasseen's noble code and extend my hospitality to those strangers who had lost their way in the vast desert of life and happened upon my door.

And for the rest of my days, I would remind myself of the many miracles of Allah that protect us from our daily dangers and guide our destinies. I would also remind myself of Hasseen's proverbial answer when he refused to take credit for thrice saving my life by saying: *"Allah was the one who saved your son's life. It was all written in heaven, long before it happened. I'm just a Bedouin who knows his desert and his shores but Allah was the one who directed you to me."*

And for the rest of my days, I would be guided by Hasseen's exemplary sense of peace and contentment as he politely declined reward: *"There is nothing that I need, Sir; Allah has given me all that I deserve."*

James Dean's Blue Jeans

When early adolescence sent its testosterone emissaries into my unsuspecting brain, I found myself transmuted within a short period of time to a self-aware, girl-gazing stripling. My hair, my clothes, my mannerisms, and how the girls perceived me dominated my preteen mind. Life was all about style and popularity in 1958, which is the year blue jeans, began to adorn the elegant Lebanese youth. I was twelve then; James Dean had died three years earlier; Elvis Presley, the Rock & Roll monarch, was inducted into the US Army as U.S. private #53310761; and I wanted blue jeans more than anything else in the world. The problem was how to convince my austere mother—who had no idea who James Dean and Elvis Presley were— that I was ready for my first pair.

As soon as the summer vacation began, I started my campaign by inviting Ziad—my classmate who was the first in school to don a pair of Levi's jeans—to play. It was crucial for my mother, who thought that pressed pants were the only outfit becoming of tidy youth, to see that blue jeans possessed a charm of their own. My hopes, however, were dashed upon the unyielding rocks of tradition when, after Ziad left, she told me that his unpressed blue pants made him look like he had no mother. That was when I realized that I had some serious convincing to do.

At dinner, it was mother who gave me my best idea. Sitting around the table with my two brothers and me, she announced that in the morning she was planning to go to school to pick up our grades and have a talk with our teachers. It was at that most propitious moment that I inquired, "And if our grades are good, are you going to reward us with something?"

"I'll reward whoever makes the honor list," came her brisk answer.

"And what would that reward be?" I quizzed with a sly mind.

"I'll let each of you choose his own reward, as long as it's reasonable and affordable."

"Can we tell you now what rewards we would like?" I pleaded as I looked at my two younger brothers, hoping to solicit their participation.

"No." She blurted. "Think about it real hard tonight, write down what reward you would like on a piece of paper, and stuff it inside an envelope. Tomorrow, at lunch, I will tell you who made the honor list and then you can hand me your envelopes for consideration."

"So, there's no guarantee that what we write will be granted?" I asked with a melancholy drone.

"As I said," she firmly replied, "it has to be reasonable and affordable for me to consider it."

After dinner, my brothers and I had a serious meeting. Being the eldest, I hoped to influence their choices in order to further mine.

"How about if we all choose blue jeans for our rewards?" I enticed, hoping that, faced with three similar requests, my mother would have trouble declining.

"I'm not going to make the honor list," said my younger brother Nadir, "so why should I bother choosing?"

"Because, knowing mother, she would want to know what you chose, anyway," I explained.

"I don't see the point," he insisted. "I'm not going to make the honor list and I'm not going to scribble anything down."

I looked to Samir, my youngest brother, for support but he was only nine and wanted a new bicycle to replace his old one. *"My chances are meager,"* I thought, but still I wrote down: *"A pair of Levi's blue jeans,"* stuffed the paper inside an envelope, and tucked it underneath my pillow.

Lunch was tense with trepidation and the ambiance grew tenser as time *snailed* among the plates du jour across the dining table. My mother deliberately avoided the subject of grades and the three of us were reticent about broaching the topic. It was only when we had finished eating that she coughed, pulled our grades out of her purse, handed them to each of us with a smile, and said, "May I have your envelopes, please."

As my youngest brother and I handed her our envelopes, Nadir excused himself, ran to his room, and hastily returned with his own envelope, which, judging by the little time it took him to produce, had to have been written the night before. Opening one envelope at a time, my mother eyed each of us in silence and then, after what seemed like a long, smoldering pause, she spoke.

"I have only one reasonable request at hand," Nadir's. He wants a volleyball and that's fine. But Samir, you want a new bicycle while your old bicycle is still in good condition? I don't see the point; you can wait another year, right?"

"Oh, no Mom. My old bicycle has only foot brakes and these are considered unsafe because they cause skidding. I need the safer model with real hand brakes instead."

"Who told you all this nonsense?" she queried with suspicion.

"All my classmates have bicycles with hand brakes and they all say that they are so much safer."

"Hum," she nodded, ignoring his pathetic argument. Then, looking at me with raised eyebrows, she asked, "And how about you, Salem? You want these shabby, un-pressed, blue pants that make you look like you have no mother? I don't understand why as you grow older you wish to look shabbier. It should be the other way round, right?"

I tried to defend my position but to no avail. Neither my brothers nor my mother could see the merit of my request. I had to come up with a more convincing argument than *"It's the fashion,"* but lunch was over and it was already too late. I retired to my room, defeated and inconsolable. I wanted so desperately to look like James Dean or Elvis Presley, but without a pair of Levi's blue jeans that seemed like an impossible feat. *"How could I impress the girls with my pressed pants,"* I pondered while mired in pitiful melancholy. *"They love the American look and that means blue jeans. Pressed pants and the honor roll make me into a nerd. Oh, Mother, why can't you be a bit more modern?"*

As the summer dripped like a steaming faucet, we spent our time at the nearby Tripoli beaches, leaving home after lunch and not returning till sundown. In the evenings, we dined on the cool veranda and listened to the radio. The Arab world was ablaze with hostilities causing us to feel helpless, without ever understanding what was happening. Day after day, we listened to news of escalating tensions, which finally burst like an abscess during that one, ominous week of July 1958. On July 14, the Iraqi revolution overthrew the monarchy, murdered King Faisal II, and dragged his body through the streets of Baghdad. The very next day, on July 15, in Operation Blue Bat, President Eisenhower landed about 14,000 men in Beirut to quell a revolution fomented by the United Arab Republic of Egypt and Syria under the leadership of Jamal Abdul Nasser. Two days later, on July 17, British paratroopers arrived in Jordan, invited by King Hussein who felt threatened by the new, hostile Iraqi regime.

It was hard for us to understand the significance of these violent transactions, but my mother helped with simplified explanations. Day after day, after listening to the news, she would comment on the history behind the happenings. I don't think that my brothers ever understood much or even cared to understand, but I thought I did. I vaguely understood that the origin of our turmoil began two years earlier in 1956 when England, France, and Israel, began what became known as the Tripartite Aggression against Egypt in an attempt to repossess the Suez Canal, which had been nationalized by Egypt's Nasser. That bloody military aggression destabilized the Arab world, cost Egypt a great many lives, and would have all but wrecked the economy of that country were it not for President Dwight Eisenhower, who forced all parties to withdraw, and reestablished peace in the region. Knowing all that made it easier for me to place the current happenings into context, and also to understand my mother's ominous sense of alarm.

During one particular bad-news-day, we sat with Mother in pensive silence, more out of respect for her own concern than out of our own appreciation of what was really transpiring. After a long pause, she took in a deep breath and said, "I'm really concerned about our fate as a tiny Christian oasis in this desert of dissent."

"Don't worry, Mom," I hurriedly reassured. "Lebanon will always be there for us."

"I wish I had your faith, Son," she replied with a headshake. "You're far too young to understand and perhaps that's a good thing."

Before I had a chance to think of some other comforting comment, the radio broadcasted a new poem by the renowned Said Akl, sung by the equally renowned Fairouz, whose cadenced lines challenged the pervasive hypocrisy of the time. Powerful music, especially when accompanied by powerful words, can draw tears out of rocks and smiles out of the angry frowns of tenebrous clouds. We listened with downcast eyes as the piercing words, laced with Byzantine tunes, stole into our weary ears and rained down onto our throbbing hearts.

> *We are our thoughts, no more*
> *We are what's on our mind*
> *Like storms we spark and roar*
> *But seem so kind and tame*
> *To souls, all eyes are blind*
> *Pretense is our game.*

After the song came another long, reverent pause. The poem 'We Are What's On Our Mind' pushed Mother into deep thought and none of us dared stir or break the sanctity of her silence. I kept my gaze to the ground while my two brothers gazed at the orange trees calmly sleeping in our garden. The morose moment stretched and yawned like a long night on the gates of a cloudy day. It was her sullen voice that finally cracked our reverie. She dolefully repeated into the night air the first two lines of the poem, "We are our thoughts, no more / We are what's on our mind..." and then she looked me in the eye and asked, "What's on your mind, Son?"

"Blue jeans," I blurted out and then hastily covered my lips with my hand.

She looked at me with startled eyes and then started laughing uncontrollably until tears rolled down her cheeks. Not understanding the humor, we were afraid to laugh along. Instead, we fidgeted in our seats and began to look rather uncomfortable, which made her laugh even harder. Then, with a big smile over her wet face, she looked at Samir and asked, "And what's on your mind, Son."

"A bicycle," he dutifully answered, which caused Nadir and me to brake out with uninhibited laughter. It was a most merciful catharsis.

The next day, Mother took Samir to the bicycle shop and gave me enough money to go buy my first pair of blue jeans. When I returned, Samir was already on his new bike riding merrily down the street and Nadir was playing volleyball with his neighborhood friends. I walked into the house with a smile that I could not conceal and a bag in my hand. I found Mother in the living room, having afternoon coffee with two of her lady friends. I kissed her on the cheek, thanked her with a most grateful heart, and then shook the hands of her two friends.

"Let me see it," she said, as she looked at me with expectation.

I handed her the bag and was surprised when she handed it back to me saying, "Let me see it on you, Silly."

I went into my room, slipped on my very tight blue jeans, checked my form in the mirror from all four angles, and then pranced back into the living room for the viewing.

"Oh, no, it's too tight, Son. You'll outgrow it in no time. No, no, go back and get a bigger size."

Her two lady friends readily agreed. One said that they would shrink with each wash and the other said that they would look like shorts by next year. I was outnumbered three to one and was not allowed to argue my point. I retreated into my room, put the blue jeans back into the bag, and raced to the *American Styles* shop for a larger size. When I tried the next size up, it looked baggy and seemed like a poor fit. I knew in my heart that the girls would snicker at me if they were to see me in them and that I would not dare to wear them before at least another year. I felt crushed and dizzy with disillusionment until the last two lines of the song began to replay inside my head, *"To souls, all eyes are blind / Pretense is our game."*

I went back home with the original blue jeans in the bag, walked into the living room, greeted, went into my bedroom, slipped on the same, tight blue jeans, and then pranced into the living room with a smug smile and paraded. As I walked back and forth like a model with the three pairs of eyes locked onto me, the song began to play again in my head, *"To souls, all eyes are blind / Pretense is our game,"* which, for some contorted reason, replaced my smug smile with a wry grin. It was only after seeing my grin that my mother clapped her hands and triumphantly proclaimed, "Now, that's a decent pair of pants." Immediately, her two lady friends agreed.

Perhaps, that was the most shameless and triumphant moment of my life. It was also the time when I developed high respect for the power of suggestion and the illusion of presentation.

Rightfully so, in *Macbeth,* Shakespeare declares that, "There's no art to find the mind's construction in the face," and in *Hamlet* that, "The apparel oft proclaims the man."

Amioun's Colorful Thief

Amioun, my hometown in Lebanon, stretches like a serpentine smile atop a rocky ridge that arches like a whale in the mist of a vast sea of olive trees. The name is not strictly Semitic (*Ammun—tough and firm fortress*) nor is the Aramaic alternative (*'Am 'Yuwn—Greek people*) its basic original. According to the historian Condor, this *Amia,* none other than the present-day Amioun, may be considered one of the oldest towns in North Lebanon. It's the capital town of the predominantly Greek-Orthodox Christian district of Al-Kourah, which comprises more than fifty villages and derives its name from the Greek word (χωριά—*villages*).

Commanding the highest point of Amioun's rocky ridge is St. John's Church-on-the-Cliff (*Mar Hanna El-Sheer*), which was built on the ruins of a pre-Christian temple. It connects through a secret tunnel to 28 man-made crypts, carved into the rocky cliff beneath it, and each crypt has a small window that overlooks the olive plain below. Carbon dating of these crypts suggests that they were carved some 15,000—24,000 years ago, placing them in the Upper Paleolithic period of the Stone Age, which also means that they were carved out of rock with nothing but stone tools. The town of Amioun has been continuously inhabited since or before the second millennium B.C., which makes it more than four thousand years old.

That such an ancient capital with such a dignifying history should become the site of theft and murder was inconceivable to my idealistic, thirteen-year-old mind. To me Amioun was heaven upon earth and the fairyland from whose soil all of our childhood friendships sprouted. It was the playground of our youth, the repository of our memories, and the sanctuary of all our secret dreams.

Nevertheless, 1959 was an exceptional year in many regards. The vines were blighted, which threatened that year's produce of *arak*: our traditional, distilled grape wine that families competed at making. The olive trees had borne poorly for the preceding three years and that year's olive harvest vied for being the worst in memory. The almond trees were scantily adorned with their fuzzy nuts and even the fig trees seemed barren in comparison to prior years. The economy of the region was under threat, and no one knew what to do about it.

Uncle Ibraheem, the farmer, apprised my father of the dire situation at the Beirut International Airport. My father, who had just arrived from Saudi Arabia for his summer vacation, lost his smile as soon as he heard the news. I listened to their deliberations during our car ride to Amioun. My father seemed impatient when we arrived and would not postpone walking the land until after lunch. The house was full of relatives, friends, neighbors, onlookers, and political supporters who had gathered for my dad's arrival. My grandmother had laboriously prepared lamb chitterlings, my dad's favorite dish. The long dining table was spread with numerous mini plates of our traditional hors d'oeuvres (*maza*) and the *arak* bottles stood among the plates like minarets, calling the faithful to prayer.

"Let's take a look," announced my father to his diverse audience of *welcomers*.

"But, why don't you eat first. The food will get cold if we wait any longer," came my grandmother's plea.

"Keep it warm for us, Mama," replied my father as he walked out of the house with his formal suit and polished shoes, followed by all those who were still young enough to walk the land during the summer's noon heat.

Several cars in single file drove us to *Kahloon*, the olive grove where the family lands bask. Leaving the cars by the roadside, we walked the land in a crowd with my father at the helm. The heat became less and less bearable the longer we walked, causing my father to loosen his necktie, take off his jacket, and sling it over his shoulder. It took us about an hour to survey enough of the land to satisfy my dad's curiosity. Before we turned back, we bucketed water from my grandfather's collection-well by the grand oak tree and quenched our thirsts with last winter's cool rainwaters. On the way back, I heard my father tell Uncle Ibraheem that he was going to consult an agricultural engineer in Beirut and arrange for him to make a site visit. The plan satisfied my worried uncle and everyone else agreed that it was a good idea. That being settled, the cars took us back to my grandmother's home for the awaiting meal with its featured, labor-intensive, lamb chitterlings.

Sitting around the long, lush, dining table, my father offered the prayer of thanks and gratitude, toasted my octogenarian grandmother, and remembered his father, Amioun's *Khoury Nichoola* (*Priest Nicholas*), who had died forty years before, during his eighty-second year, when my father was only three years old. Then food was partaken and the conversation branched out like a bird-laden tree, full of spring gossip. After the fruits were served, I saw my father reach into his pockets for cigarettes. Then, looking a bit bewildered, he asked, "Has anyone seen my jacket?"

"You left with it but came home without it," replied my circumspect grandmother.

"Oh, now I remember. I handed it to Samir Salloum while we walked the land."

"You handed it to whom?" came several astonished voices in unison.

"Samir Salloum, the son of Fadwa and Dumeet," replied my father with a feigned, innocent look.

"You've been gone too long, Son, to know that in your absence Samir Salloum has become Amioun's most famous thief."

"Samir Salloum, our neighbor, the son of Fadwa and Dumeet, a thief?" exclaimed my father with a held-back smirk.

My father's exclamation sparked many stories that competed for his ears. Aunt Catherine said that Samir Salloum stole her brass caldron and sold it in the brass market in Tripoli. Aunt Salam said that he stole all her bed sheets, which she had hung on her clothesline to dry in the sun. Aunt Victoria said that he stole her goat and sold it to the butcher on the other side of town. Aunt Jenefyef said that he stole her pomegranates and sold them in Kfarhazeer. Uncle Gibran said that he stole his donkey, rode it to Kfarhazeer in order to sell Aunt Jenefyef's pomegranates, and returned it the following day. Finally, my circumspect grandmother interrupted the flow of stories by asking my dad the question that caused our hair to stand on end.

"Was your wallet in your jacket, Son?"

"Ah," my father gasped as he checked his back pockets with a bewildered look that slowly faded into a subdued smile.

"And, how much money did you have in it?" echoed my grandmother against the stunned silence.

"All my vacation money," came dad's curt reply.

"And, how much money was that?" she insisted.

"Three thousand dollars, all in one-hundred-dollar bills," replied my dad with downcast eyes.

"Well, you'd better kiss it good-bye," came Grandmother's miffed answer as she rose from the table with some empty plates in her hand and started toward the kitchen.

"I'm sure he needs it more than we do," mumbled my dad as he handed Grandma his empty plate.

For coffee, the family gathered in the large, cool, living room framed by high, stone arches that met in the center of the ceiling. Instead of chairs, the entire circumference of the room was lined with wooden benches covered with straw mats. As more visitors joined the circular crowd, whispers about my father's lost jacket and wallet circulated into the ears of newcomers provoking unconcealed expressions of consternation. At some point during that afternoon melee, Aunt Catherine who was standing by the front door let out a loud scream, causing many to make a sudden rush toward her. Then, with a crowd trailing behind him, Samir Salloum walked into the living room and handed the jacket to my father.

My father stood up, put his arm around Samir Salloum's shoulder, and walked with him into the bedroom. They were gone a while after which my dad escorted Samir Salloum out and returned to the living room with the jacket on his back and a big smile on his face. At that point, Grandma appeared and ordered, "Check your wallet."

My father reached into his jacket's breast pocket, pulled out his fat wallet, and slowly counted 30 one-hundred-dollar bills under the incredulous gaze of all the spectators. Then, with a smug smile, he returned the wallet to his back pocket, stood up, and said, "It's late. We need to go to Tripoli before it gets dark."

On the way back to our Tripoli home, I asked my father, "Why didn't Samir Salloum steal the money?"

My mother immediately answered, "He was afraid of retribution. He's a petty thief who steals things too little for prosecution. But three thousand dollars is a big theft that could have put him in jail for many years."

My father did not answer me until we were alone the next morning. My mother was taking her shower and I was sitting with him on the veranda overlooking the garden when I asked him again, "Why didn't he take the money?"

"I asked him that very question when we were together in your grandmother's bedroom," teased my father.

"And what did he say?"

"He said that I was the only one in Amioun who trusted him, and because of that he would never steal from me."

"Well, did you give him some money as a reward for bringing the jacket back?"

"I tried to, but he wouldn't take any."

"Why wouldn't he?"

"He told me that he enjoyed being honest for a change and that joy was his reward."

"Did you not know that he was a thief when you handed him your jacket?"

"Of course I knew, Son," replied my dad with a smirk. "I may not live in Amioun anymore, but I do know what goes on."

"So how come you trusted him with your jacket?"

"Well, he was the one who offered to carry it for me and saying 'no thank you' would have meant that I did not trust him, and that would have broken his heart."

"But then, why is it that you're the only one who dared to trust him?"

"Because I believe that it's far better to trust everyone and be swindled by a few than to be suspicious of everyone in order to avoid a few thieves."

Later on, I learned from Grandmother that my grandfather, *Khoury Nichoola*, the town's priest, had preached those very same words in one of his sermons long before my father was even born and had backed up his assertion by pointing out that Jesus had never treated anyone with suspicion even though he knew what was in everyone's heart.

"Your father is just like his father," she added with a disapproving shake of the head, "and keeps saying to me that when he retires from medicine and politics he's going to become a good priest, just like his dad."

The next summer, I was fourteen when we met Father at the Beirut International Airport again. When we arrived in Amioun, Uncle Ibraheem and my dad took me along to walk the land and see the results of the agricultural consultation, which had transpired during my dad's absence. The agricultural engineer had ordered more fertilizer for the olive trees and had used a fungicide to clean up the vines. The results were very good, judging by the robustness of the olives on the trees and the grapes on the vines.

On the way back to Grandmother's, as if last year's memory was rekindled by this year's land walk, my father asked Uncle Ibraheem if Samir Salloum was still petty-thieving in Amioun. My uncle simply said no and then tried to change the topic, but my father pressed him with, "Well, do you think that he has been reformed?"

"No, he'll never be reformed."

"Well then, why isn't he thieving anymore?"

"Because he's in jail."

"In jail? You mean someone finally reported him to the authorities."

"No, no one here would. Amioun has tolerated him ever since he was old enough to steal."

"So what happened then?"

"He was at a political rally and heard someone badmouthing you. He defended you by slapping the fellow and telling him that you were the only honest candidate in the region. Soon, a fight broke out between your supporters and those of the opposition. Samir, in a fit of anger, pulled out his gun, shot the man in the heart, and disappeared. Two days later, he surrendered to the authorities and was sentenced to life in prison. Half of Amioun attended his sentencing; some were angry, some cried bitter tears, and some stared without saying a word. He was Amioun's only colorful thief and now, with him gone, nothing really happens for the old women to gossip about."

*

Fifty years later, at the age sixty-four, my accountant of thirty-three years, James Howard Jr., informed me that he was planning to retire. I was deeply saddened by the news and during our good-bye conversation I asked him what did he think of our time together.

"To tell you the truth, I didn't think that you would last very long in practice."

"And why's that," I responded, a bit surprised."

"I thought you'd surely go broke during your first year because of the way you do business."

"What do I do that's so irregular?" I queried with a perturbed smile.

"Well, you don't collect your fees at the time of service, you trust all your patients by sending them monthly statements, you never use a collector, and if people don't pay you within a year you write their balances off. No one does business like that and gets away with it except you."

"You mean that I violate all the sane accounting principles of the day?"

"Yes, you do, but somehow, you manage to get away with it. Whoever taught you this crazy notion?"

"Amioun's priest, *Khoury Nichoola,* in a sermon he delivered in 1919," I answered with a held back smirk.

James Howard's eyes peered into mine as if questioning my sanity. I held the moment as long as I could while he fidgeted in search of a polite response. Finally, in a most reserved manner, he said, "I'm not familiar with this preacher nor with his country. What was his sermon about?"

"He was a small-town-priest who reminded us that Jesus had never treated anyone with suspicion even though he knew what was in everyone's heart and, based on that insight, he preached that it's far better to trust everyone and be swindled by a few than be suspicious of everyone in order to avoid a few thieves."

The Municipal Elections

"Your mother is here to take you home," said the school principal, Mr. Donald Dublin, as he pulled me out of chemistry class.

"But, my mother is in jail, Sir," was my startled response as I scurried beside him through the long corridor.

"Calm down, Son. She shouldn't see you like that," he admonished.

"But, are you sure, Sir, that she's been released?" I quizzed, quivering with disbelief and held-back tears.

"She's waiting in my office and your two younger brothers are already with her."

"You pulled them out of class too?"

"You wouldn't want her to go home alone, would you? You and your brothers will just have to start your Easter break two days ahead of the rest of us."

My mother struggled to stand up when we walked in but fell back into her chair and opened her arms instead. She was pale and frail but her tearless eyes brimmed with joy at seeing us well, after her four-month confinement. I was fifteen then, she was forty-five, and the year was the fateful 1961 when my father's political party attempted a coup d'état against the Lebanese government and failed. Soon after that, my mother was apprehended, my father and his comrades were incarcerated and it was rumored that they were going to get the death sentence. My two younger brothers and I were taken in an army truck to our Tripoli Boys School, where we were boarded and ordered not to leave the premises. We had no news of our mother or father during these four, loveless months. Rumors grew more painful as time elapsed, causing us to become more reclusive until isolation became our refuge.

My brothers and I packed the few clothes we had into a big laundry bag and left the dormitory without saying good-bye to our roommates who were still in class. There was a taxi waiting at the school gate, the same taxi that had brought my mother from where she was sequestered at the government hospital to where we were sequestered at our school. Although we would have preferred to run out of the mighty, iron gate screaming, we walked out slowly instead, holding mother by the arms. The taxi driver was a man from our hometown, Amioun, who updated us on what had happened to our friends and relatives during the past four months and related the significant political developments that had transpired in our absence. Officiously, he painted a grim, frightful scene and broadcasted it into our un-questing ears. It was most merciful that the drive home took only twenty minutes.

When we arrived, we found the house door broken, nailed back together by a nice neighbor and held shut with a rope. We had to break into our own home and once in, held the door shut with a chair. The house looked like a battleground with toppled furniture, broken glass, and the contents of drawers, cabinets, and closets chaotically crowding the floor of each room where they had been spilled. Walking among the rubble and unable to find a suitable space to sit in, we made our way to the library, piled all the strewn books into one corner, and dropped down onto the oval sofa with faltering limbs and wax faces.

"I was told that they had thoroughly searched the house," whispered my mother as if talking to herself.
"We can help you Mom," I volunteered.
"Our bank accounts have been frozen. We need money to get started," she muttered as she shook her head.
"I have money, Mom. I've been saving my allowance for the past year."
"You have it on you?"
"No. It's hidden in my room."
"There's nothing left son; they've opened and searched everything and everywhere."
"But I had it hidden in my closet."
"Oh, well, it's surely gone then because the contents of your closet are all on the floor."

"But the shelves are still in place."

"The shelves? What do you mean by that silly answer?"

"I've pried open the front strip of the second shelf and hid the money in the space between the shelf's two layers."

"These shelves are solid wood. What layers are you talking about?"

"They're fake, Mom. They're like our doors, empty on the inside, and I've used that space as a hiding place."

A faint smile colored her gray face and her eyes widened with surprise as she realized that her firstborn had his own little secrets. Refusing my help, she pulled herself up by leaning forward and pressing down on her knees. Then motioning to the three of us standing at attention around her, she commanded, "Let's have a look."

With smug confidence, I negotiated through the piled chaos and led the family into my bedroom. My closet doors were ajar and its shelves were empty but were still in their places. With nimble fingers, I pushed on one end of the wooden strip, causing the other end to protrude, and then I pulled the strip out. My mother and brother's eyes glared with amazement as they peered in between the shelf layers into my secret space. Taking the wad of money out, I handed it to my mother with a triumphant air and said, "Three hundred and eighty-six liras."

She slowly counted the cash, equivalent to about $125, and inquired with utter disbelief, "Where did all this money come from? Your pocket money was three liras a week. This doesn't add up."

"My father used to let me keep the change whenever he sent me to the store to buy him cigarettes."

"And he was a chain smoker," she added. Then, peering inside the shelf again, she asked, "And what's this notebook?"

"That's my secret notebook," I confessed as I carefully delivered the notebook out and handed it to her.

She flipped through the pages with a mother's circumspect suspicion of her teenager, frowned at me with discomposure, and then exclaimed in front of my brothers' glaring eyes, "It's gibberish."

"Well, it's written in my secret language that no one else can read," I sheepishly confessed, enjoying my brothers' startled aspects and my mother's surprised look.

"You've invented a secret language?" She gasped with consternation.

"No, Mom. I just made up my own secret alphabet."

She handed the notebook back to me with a sigh and said, "You're growing up too fast my son, which is a good thing. You can take your father's role as the man of the house, as long as he's gone."

I was stung by her statement: *as long as he's gone,* and wondered why she didn't say: *until he returns,* instead? *"Did she think that my father was never coming back?"* I wondered, but was afraid to ask.

Later that day, I went to the store and purchased food for my family from my own saved money. On the way back, with bags under my arms, I walked tall as if I were my father, big, strong, confident, and indomitable. I could feel the neighbors' eyes spying me from behind curtains and some even came out on their verandas for a closer look, but no one said hello or waved. We all breathed carefully then, secret policemen were everywhere, there was fear in the atmosphere, and talking to us was tantamount to treason.

By Easter, thanks to my aunts and the few relatives who were out of jail by then, our home was restored to order and we received some money from a business partnership my father had in Kuwait. My mother, a gynecologist, reopened her clinic but very few of her patients came. It was rumored that the death sentence was soon to be handed down to many of the party leaders, and no one wanted to face a woman whose husband was on death row. Moreover, secret service men were posted at her clinic door and at our home entrance, and they took down the names of all who visited. Consequently, it took many months before her practice could eke out a living. What helped matters most was that Tripoli, being a conservative Muslim town, favored female gynecologists, especially when they were Christian, because the Koran described in poetic detail the glorious birth of Christ from Mary's womb.

When summer came, we all relocated to our mountain town, Amioun, to escape the humid Tripoli heat. My brothers and I never went to the beach that year because it wasn't safe for us to be in the public eye. Tensions were brewing underneath the surface between the two major political factions, those who supported the government and the death penalty for the insurgents, and those who opposed the police state and demanded that the incarcerated be treated as political prisoners rather than as common criminals. The air hissed as people argued their positions, and intimations of armed conflict during the upcoming municipal elections bit our ears like winter frost. It was a summer of discontent fomenting political unrest and reeking of violence.

My best friend Nizom and I took long walks in the olive groves, wandered among the vineyards, and had our deep political discussions far away from adult ears. The grapes would soon be ready for the picking and wine making was but a few weeks away. Except, that year, fear was on everyone's mind because the municipal elections were to take place just before the winemaking season. Our peaceful hometown, Amioun, was destined to become embroiled in bloody conflict because the weaker pro-government faction was plotting to use its political muscle to rig the elections in its favor. Every able-bodied person was armed to the hilt and the stench of un-spilt blood was already in the air.

One day, while sitting under the shade of a large oak tree, cracking almonds between two stones, Nizom threw a pebble far away into the blue air and exclaimed, "Many a life will be thrown away just like that if the elections were to take place as scheduled."

"But, surely, they're doing something about it," I reassured.

"Who's doing something about it?" he smirked.

"The adults of course," I replied with smug confidence.

"Salem," he said, as he looked into my eyes. "The adults are too scared to act. We're the town's only hope."

"What are you talking about? Two fifteen-year-old-kids are Amioun's only hope? I think you've eaten too many almonds."

"I didn't mean to say that you and I are Amioun's only hope," he said with exasperation. "What I really meant was that you, Salem Hakeem Hawi, are Amioun's only hope."

"No more almonds for you," I snapped and confiscated the pile of un-cracked almonds sitting between us.

Nizom got up and walked away without saying a word, leaving me wondering if he had suddenly gone insane. We had been friends since infancy and he was the only one who dared travel alone to Tripoli to visit us when we were boarded at our American Evangelical School for Boys, better known as Tripoli Boys School. He had always been brave, smart, and sensible but what he said that day made little sense. Knowing that he would return, I waited for him in the shade, worried, confused, and a bit frightened.

When after a very long hour he did not return, I started my walk back home with a thousand questions buzzing in my mind. As I approached the main road, I found him waiting for me by the brook. He appeared calm, reclining by the purring waters, whittling a stick with his pocketknife. I sat on a nearby stone and waited for him to say something but he didn't, forcing me to fuel the conversation.

"Why did you walk away without saying a word?" I asked with obvious irritation.

"Because you refused to take on the responsibility of saving Amioun from bloodshed."

"Nizom, this is paranoid talk."

"No, you are blind to reality."

"What reality?"

"The reality that you alone can prevent this massacre."

After saying that, Nizom's face became contorted with distress. Seeing how dead serious he was caused me to become even more alarmed. I still had no idea what was on his mind, but by then I was willing to listen. And so, to break down the ice that had jelled between us, I whispered with a resigned, mellow voice, "Okay. Tell me what's on your mind?"

He took one long look at my face, and feeling reassured by my transparent sincerity, opened up his heart to me.

"Look, Salem," he began. "Your dad is not only on death row, he is also on every lip and in all the daily papers. This, by default, makes you noticeable. Anyone who hears your name, Salem Hakeem Hawi, will know that you are the son of the political prisoner, Dr. Hakeem Hawi, and this notoriety should allow you access into the Ministry of Interior Affairs."

In Lebanon, as in most of the Arab world, the middle name of all siblings, boys and girls, is always the father's first name. That much I understood, but still I had no idea where he was going with his scheme, and I was afraid to ask. I remained silent and waited for him to continue.

"All we have to do is go to Beirut, find the Ministry of Internal Affairs, ask to see the minister, and implore him to cancel the elections."

"Drop in on Minister Pierre Jumayyell, the busiest minister in the country, just like that? Are you insane? What about all the guards, secret service men, and secretaries that one has to go through in order to get to him? How do we get through all of them?"

"That's where your name will be our passport. At every stop, you will show them your identity card and tell them that you need to see the minister on very urgent business. No one will suspect a meek-faced teenager like you of mischief."

"And what about you? Why should they let you through?"

"Because I am with you and together we represent the Amioun Youth."

"But we haven't consulted with any of the Amioun youth," I exclaimed.

"It doesn't matter," he growled. "For God's sake, Salem, grow up. It's something we can say if questioned and it happens to be believable."

"So it's all up to me, basically. Is that right?" I asked as the heavy weight of responsibility began to stoop my shoulders.

"It's all up to you, Salem Hakeem Hawi," he repeated. "Trying cannot harm, but not trying could cause so many senseless deaths and might split the town into vindictive factions for generations to come."

I paused as tears dripped from my eyes onto the ground between my feet. Then, with an interrupted sigh, I capitulated.

"Well, what the heck, lets give it a try. If it works, we would feel like heroes, and if it doesn't we would feel like the two fools we already are."

We spent the rest of the afternoon discussing some important details. The cars from Amioun to the Martyrs' Square in Beirut charged two liras per passenger and the cabs from the Martyrs' Square to the Ministry of Interior Affairs charged half a lira per passenger. Then if we would add half a lira for a soft drink and a sandwich each, we would need a total of ten liras for the trip. Between us, we only had three liras, and that presented a big problem. Besides, our parents would never allow us to go unaccompanied to Beirut and hence it was futile to ask them for the balance because they would want to know what it was for.

Walking back to Amioun, we became morose as our plans were seriously threatened by pecuniary realities. If we had the money, we could leave in the morning and be back before sunset. We could say that we were going on a picnic and that wouldn't be a lie—and as long as we return home by dinner, no one would miss us. All we needed was the large sum of seven liras, but we couldn't tell anyone why we needed the money because that trip was our secret. If we were ever found out, we would be severely chastised by both political sides that were intent on fighting it out no matter what the consequences.

Despair is the father of hope because from its desperate, dark alleys new ideas sprout. At dinner, sitting around the table with my mother and two brothers, I suddenly remembered that my mother had never reimbursed me for the money I had given her when we first returned home. I waited until my two brothers left the table before I asked, "Mom, were you planning to give me back some of the money I gave you?"

"What money are you talking about, Son?" came her surprised question.

"The money that I had hidden inside my closet shelf," I replied with a meek voice because I understood how horribly tight things were at the time.

"Surely, you don't need all of it now, do you?"

"Oh, no Mom, of course not. I just need about seven liras because my friends and I are going on a picnic tomorrow and we need to buy a few things."

"Oh, well then, that's reasonable. How about if I give you ten liras a week until you are paid off?"

After dinner, with the money in my pocket, I ran to Nizom's home and informed him that we had become solvent. That night I did not sleep. My mind was performing all kinds of acrobatic stunts, as I lay, open-eyed, blue with worry and stiff with dread. The next morning, after my mother left for Tripoli, Nizom and I left for Beirut, full of foolish hopes and in total denial of the farce we were living. We arrived at the Martyrs' Square a little before ten-thirty and found our way among the human hordes to the cab stop. We took the two remaining seats in the service cab, which took us to the Ministry of Interior Affairs, and dropped us there at eleven o'clock.

The building was a stone edifice built during the eighteenth century while Lebanon was under Ottoman rule. Although in slight disrepair, it stood dignified like an old lion, surveying the roaring throngs that swarmed its gates. At the front door, forty steps above street level, stood two armed guards checking the identification cards of all comers, and at the lobby entrance stood another two guards who frisked all visitors before allowing them in. The lobby was a beehive with scores of people scurrying in and out, carrying folders, large envelopes, paper scrolls, and fat briefcases.

Servants were running about, carrying trays loaded with Turkish coffee, freshly squeezed orange, carrot, and tomato juices, and hot coals for the purring water pipes, or *argeelees*. The human hum, in spite of the high ceilings, echoed like an organ out of tune into the hot, stuffy air.

After clearing the guards, we stood stunned, lost amidst this shuffling rush of humanity where everyone—except for the two of us—seemed to know exactly where he or she was going. We wanted to ask someone, anyone, where was the office of the Minister of Interior Affairs, Mr. Pierre Jumayyell, but no one noticed our pleading faces and gesticulating arms. Desperate for direction, with no signs or name lists to help us, we climbed up the wide, winding, marble stairs to the third floor where there were less people and we could converse with one another without having to shout.

"There's an open door where we might find someone who could answer our question," whispered Nizom, trying not to be too obvious.

"Well, should I just walk in and ask where's the Minister's office?"

"I think you should. There's a cute secretary sitting behind a desk; I bet she would be glad to tell you."

"Are you sure?" I hesitated.

"It's the only way," he insisted. "Come on, what are you waiting for?"

I hesitated, crossed myself thrice, and then walked in.

"Yes, may I help you?" came her clear voice as she eyed me.

"Oh, yes, please," I replied as I gazed at her kind, beautiful face with teenage enthrallment.

"Well, how may I help you then?" she repeated with a kind smirk.

"Oh, yes, I'm, we're looking for the Minister's office."

"Minister's office?" she echoed with surprise.

"Yes ma'am, you know, the Minister of Interior Affairs, Mr. Pierre Jumayyell."

"Oh, I see, you're here to visit his highness, Minister Jumayyell," she droned with a playful, supercilious tone.

"Oh, yes ma'am. It's a very urgent matter."

"And do you have an appointment?"

"No, ma'am, but it's such an important matter that I don't think he would mind seeing us."

"Well, in that case, if you'll tell me your name, I'll call it in and see if he'll see you."

"My name is Salem Hakeem Hawi."

"Salem Hakeem Hawi," she repeated as she gazed at me with renewed curiosity.

I nodded without speaking.

"You're not the son of Dr. Hakeem Hawi who tried to topple our government, are you?"

"Yes ma'am, I am. I'm his oldest son."

"May I see your identification card, please?" she asked with a crisp, demanding tone.

I handed it to her and watched her examine it carefully. Then, becoming overtly suspicious, she asked, "And who's with you?"

"My friend, Nizom AbuHabib."

"Call him in," she commanded with scrutinizing eyes.

I walked out, came back in with Nizom, and we stood at attention before her desk awaiting her verdict.

"May I see your identification card, young man," she said as she put out her hand to Nizom.

Without saying a word, Nizom handed her his ID card, which she studied with equal scrutiny. Then she walked off with both ID cards and disappeared into the adjoining room. I looked at Nizom, who had grown pale with anxiety, and whispered, "Do you think they're going to arrest us?"

"I don't like how she walked away with our ID cards," he said as he shook his head.

"If they confiscate them, we wouldn't be able to get back home. No check point would let us through without ID cards."

"I'm starting to feel clammy and sick at my stomach," was the last thing Nizom said before he fainted at my feet. Feeling equally sick but not to the point of fainting, I knelt beside him and started to fan his face. It was at that most unpropitious moment that I felt a hand tap me on the head. I looked up and froze. Towering above us stood his highness, the Minister of Interior Affairs, Mr. Pierre Jumayyell.

"What happened to your friend?" he asked with a calm smile.

"He fainted, your Highness," I quickly responded as I stood at attention.

"Why don't you come with me then and we'll let Miss Selma take care of him," said Minister Jumayyell as he put his arm around my shoulder and led me into his office.

It was a modest room with a big desk and bookshelves all around. The Lebanese flag stood by the window, which overlooked the throngs below.

"Sit down, Son," he commanded as he pointed to one of the chairs facing his desk. "If you're coming to request permission to see your father, I can't give it because he is in solitary confinement."

"No sir," I quickly replied. "I'm here to ask you to cancel the municipal elections in Amioun because we think that there's going to be a massacre.

"Massacre? That's a very strong word, Son. Our sources have not given us such information."

"Oh, but Sir, I live there and I have heard the adults talk. It's very bad, Sir. They all have ready weapons and they hate each other with passion."

"And which side are you on, Son?" he asked as he eyed me with penetrating curiosity.

"I, Sir, am on the side of life. No one deserves to die for such a silly cause," I said before my voice broke.

"Who sent you here, Son?"

"No one knows I'm here, Sir, no one except my friend, Nizom AbuHabib who represents the Amioun youth. He's the one who fainted in the other room."

"Does your mother know you're here?"

"Oh, no Sir. She'd kill me if she ever found out."

"Fine, Son. Go on back home and keep this secret between us. I'll check with our sources and see what I can do."

When I walked out, the secretary was at her desk but Nizom was not in the room. Noticing my roaming eyes, she simply pointed to the door and said, "He's all right but must have needed some fresh air. He said he'd wait for you outside."

I found him sitting on the long steps holding his head between his hands. Feeling equally drained, I sat beside him, and as calmly as I could fake it, asked, "What happened to you?"

"I think I fainted," came his curt, reply.

"You think you fainted? Do you also think that you're Nizom AbuHabib?"

"Don't make fun of me, please."

"Well, tell me then why did you faint?"

"My mind played tricks on me," he said with a pale frown. "When I saw her walk away with our ID cards, I knew that they were going to take us to jail and interrogate us until we confess who was behind our visit. But, since there's no one behind our visit but us, they would find it hard to believe and they would begin torturing us until we came up with some adult names. I was thinking of what names I should give them to avoid being tortured and that's when I began feeling clammy and sick at my stomach."

We arrived back at Amioun before sunset and each of us went to his own home as if nothing had happened. We told everyone that we had walked all the way to the spring of Dillah, had lunch in the café by the waterfall, and then walked all the way back. Our shoes were quite dusty from having walked all over downtown Beirut and that, plus our exhausted personas, made our story believable enough that even our suspicious mothers believed it.

Three days later, one week before the elections, it appeared in all the Sunday morning papers. *"The municipal elections in Amioun have been cancelled by orders of his highness, the Minister of Interior Affairs, Mr. Pierre Jumayyell. The ministry gave no other explanation except that it would reschedule the elections at a later date."*

The next day, I accompanied my mother to Tripoli. While she saw patients at her clinic, I opened my secret shelf, took out my notebook, and with my secret alphabet wrote:

Nizom and I dropped in on his Highness, the Minister of Internal Affairs, Mr. Pierre Jumayyell, at his offices in the Ministry of Internal Affairs. We explained that due to the rising tensions, the upcoming municipal elections were going to cause a massacre if they were allowed to take place. He checked with his resources and, after due consideration, cancelled the elections.

No one suspected that we were the ones who did it and his Highness asked us to keep it a secret. The town's people are baffled. The anti-government faction is saying that the government was afraid to lose and so they cancelled the elections. The pro-government faction is saying that the government did not wish to humiliate Amioun with one more devastating defeat.

No one will ever know what really happened except the three of us—Nizom, his Highness, Minister Pierre Jumayyell, and I.

An Evening with Beethoven

What makes an indelible impact on one's memory becomes a part of one's self. We are but the living offspring of our genes, times, environments, and experiences. And what conducts these four formative forces, which direct our destinies, is mother coincidence, the invisible puppeteer of all outcomes and expectations.

For Baby Boomers in post-Second-World-War Lebanon, it was normal for most of us to grow up fatherless. Fathers travelled to wherever work summoned, which meant that children wrote letters to their fathers, but only saw them a few weeks per year. My story transpired during one of those paternal sojourns, which *Ammu* George had made from Kuwait to Lebanon in 1966, when I was a first-year medical student at the American University of Beirut.

Serendipity had located for me a flat on Joan d'Arc Street, in the same building where *Ammu* George's family lived. *Ammu*, the Arabic word for uncle, is an endearing title that children use to address the dearest friends of their parents. The relationship between my family and *Ammu* George's, although interrupted by the errant lives of the fathers, was nonetheless interlaced with long threads of friendship. As an adolescent, I was fascinated by *Ammu* George's lightening wit, caricature charisma, biting humor, and irreverent mystique. In some unsettling way, I had always felt that I needed to know him better and was, therefore, ever eager for his company.

At the elevator, his daughter, Micha, who had just finished her last final exam, asked, "Are you though with your finals?"
"Thank God, yes," I chortled. "They left the worst for the last, cadaver anatomy; that's why I smell of formalin."
"Any plans this weekend?"

"Yes. I plan to sleep."

"What a waste of time," She smirked. "Why don't you take a nap and then drop by for a drink. My father has just arrived from Kuwait and he'd love to see you."

"*Ammu* George is here?" I gasped, my sleepless face quivering with startled excitement. "Oh, dear," I scratched my head with my moist, formalin fingers. "How long is he staying?"

"He's leaving next year," she smirked again, "which means we will have him for a full fortnight."

"Christmas and New Year's Eve with your dad? How fortunate," I sighed. "The last half-Christmas I spent with my father was six years ago, just before he went to jail."

"Don't nap too long, then. We're expecting you," she grinned, exiting the elevator on the third floor.

Sleep refused to shut my eyes in spite of a long, warm shower, a darkened room, and a downy bed. My mind spun as I tumbled from side to side, listening to the incessant honking of hurried cars five stories below. Exhaustion, when it doesn't usher sleep, ushers more exhaustion. I lay unable to rest, unwilling to rise, and incapable of steadying my mind.

The evening crept in by stealth, like a cat. I had done all I could to rest, but all my efforts failed. Un-rejuvenated, but expectant, I rang *Ammu's* door.

"You didn't sleep, did you?" smiled Micha, as she ushered me into the sitting room.

Ammu stood up, gave me a gregarious hug, and immediately asked, "How's your father?"

I gazed at *Ammu's* tall, lean figure, his irreverent gray-black mustache, his aquiline nose, his piercing, brilliant eyes, his warm, all welcoming aspect, his halo of indiscriminate kindness, and answered, "They only allow me to see him for 10 minutes, once a week. I'll be seeing him tomorrow."

He put his arm around my shoulder and, with a kind smile, ushered me toward the sofa by the window.

"Come, sit here, next to me. I'm having a drink and you need one."

He poured me a whisky, placed an LP on the record player, and we sat in momentary silence, listening to the honking and clonking sounds arising from the congested street below.

"When you visit your father, would you give him our love, please?" he began.

I took a sip of whisky and whispered, "He would be thrilled to know that we are, again, neighbors."

My chest was set aflame by the whisky gulp I had accidentally imbibed and my face became contorted, perhaps more from the image of my father behind bars than from the gulp of whisky, which had set my insides on fire.

"You can at least see your father once a week," he consoled, while I recomposed myself. "I saw mine for the first time when I was thirty-five."

"How come?" I asked with disbelief.

"He immigrated to Detroit when I was two months old and forgot to return until 35 years later. I was raised by my mother, as you are now being raised by yours."

I took a smaller sip of whisky as Beethoven's Ninth Symphony began to soften and agitate.

"Did you know that my mother and your mother's mother were both named *Malakeh* [Queen] and that they both lived up to their names?" Then, after a small sigh, he added, "Mothers raise us and fathers braise us."

"*Thus Spake Zarathustra,*" I pontificated, trying to match his philosophic wit.

"I see that you have read Nietzsche, one of my favorite authors," he remarked with raised eyebrows.

"I have, but he wasn't kind to women."

"What do you mean by that?" he protested with a knowing smile.

"Well, he said: *'Thou goest to women? Do not forget the whip.'*"

"No, Son," he corrected with the kindness of a good teacher. "It was the old woman who spat this little truth into Nietzsche's ear and asked him to hold its mouth lest it should scream too loudly."

"So that wasn't Nietzsche's opinion then?"

"It wasn't, but it remains a widely held misconception. Notice, though, that he did not say *do not forget thy whip*, but rather, *do not forget the whip*, a tacit indicator that women are the ones who whip us," he giggled.

Another sip of whisky was followed by an interlude of silence as the symphony's first movement began announcing its end.

"You know that Beethoven's mother, Maria Magdalena, was also a good and capable mother, who saved the lives of her three children, when the Rhine flooded, by marching them across the roofs of neighboring houses."

"How about Beethoven's father?"

"Johann van Beethoven was a no good alcoholic and a musical mediocre. Maria Magdalena described her marriage to him as a *chain of sorrows*."

"So Beethoven's genius came from his mother then?"

"Indeed it did. She was first married at 16, lost her first born in infancy, and by age 18 she had become widowed."

"Was Beethoven her oldest child?"

"Twice he was," he smiled teasingly.

"Twice? That's an oxymoron."

"She named her first born Ludwig, but he died when he was six days old. So, she named her second born Ludwig, and he was the one who survived to become the genius we are listening to now."

I sipped on my whisky and waited to hear his comments on the second movement, which was then playing, but instead, he said, "This scherzo reminds me of a poem by Hilaire Belloc."

I did not know what a *scherzo* was nor had I ever heard of Hilaire Belloc, but I refrained from revealing my ignorance by holding tightly to my glass of whisky and to my silence. He looked at me with soft, comprehending eyes and explained, "A *scherzo* is a lighthearted musical movement. Hilaire Belloc was a French born British writer (1870-1953) who wrote, among other things, lighthearted poetry. The introduction to one of his books reads," and he quoted:

> *Before I'm dead*
> *I hope it will be said*
> *His nights were scarlet*
> *But his books were read.*

I laughed when he said that, and he giggled like an adolescent, relishing my joyful distraction. Then his eyes wandered toward a piece of pottery sitting on a side table, which I had noticed when I first came in. It was unique and did not seem like a piece that one could buy anywhere. So, without knowing, I ventured, "Who made this piece?"

"Dora, my daughter. She's an artist like her mother. She's the one who insists on having fresh flowers in the house at all times. Micha, on the other hand, fills the house with smiles that are more beautiful than Dora's bouquets. I am the luckiest king with three rare jewels in my crown, and my only son, Omar, is my scepter."

Another sip of whisky was followed by yet another moment of silence, which made the noise, bellowing from the street, seem even louder. Then the entire building vibrated when a commercial jet passed above us on its way to the Beirut International Airport, prolonging our silence. When that noise died down, I probed *Ammu* because I wanted to hear more poetry.

"So, you were saying that this scherzo reminds you of the lighthearted poetry of Hilaire Belloc."

"Indeed, this second movement reminds me of his *Tarentella*."

"*Tarentella?*" I flushed with the embarrassment of ignorance.

He lit a French Gitanes cigarette, took in a long draw, and with the smoke still suffusing his irreverent mustache, recited, beating with his words the tempo of the scherzo:

Do you remember an inn, Miranda
Do you remember an inn
And the tedding and the spreading
Of the straw for a bedding
And the fleas that tease in the high Pyrenees
And the wine that tasted of tar
And the ting, tong, tang, of the guitar?

And the cheers and the jeers of the young muleteers
Under the vine of the dark verandah?
Do you remember an inn, Miranda?
Do you remember an inn?

I gasped with awe at this sensual arrangement, recited with equally sensual passion. I loved the way *Ammu* connected things that seemed disconnected. *"How can he remember so much?"* I thought, and craved more of his connections, associations, interpretations, and depth.

I loved Beethoven, but loved him like people loved music or like schoolboys loved soccer. However, after hearing Ammu discourse, I wanted to love Beethoven with heart, with passion, and with the probing profundity of a *musicophile*. *"This man's brain is a classical herb garden,"* I surmised as the slow, lyrical third movement pronounced its beginnings. Here, *Ammu's* face began to evince melancholy and his gaze floated past me to a pastoral painting on the wall.

"Art is proof that life is not enough," he suddenly proclaimed, and he then surprised me by inserting a cadenza I had written into the cascading music:

Biology limits us
Art liberates us
Society shackles us

Imagination releases us
Our bodies imprison us
Our minds deceive us
Our biases diminish us
Our hates impoverish us
Our loves enrich us
Our lives judge us
Our deaths ennoble us.

I shall go smiling into death.

Foolishly, I asked, "Who said that?"

"You wrote it in your last letter to me, remember? You have your mother's gift for verse. I only added the last line, *I shall go smiling into death,* because I have a fearless love and an insatiable curiosity for the unknown," he stated with a half smile behind his eyes.

I remained silent and waited for his knowing, half smile to die down. Then, I summoned courage and framed my ideas in a rhetorical question.

"Are you agreeing, then, that biology limits us and art liberates us, because art is of the imagination, and imagination is our metaphysical realm, our liberating force from the merciless shackles of society?"

"From a medical student's view, that's a heartfelt realization. With medicine, you cure our mortal parts, which ultimately die, whereas with art, in all its forms from music to sculptor to painting to writing to beautifying, we not only liberate our spirits, we also immortalize our souls."

Then, as the third movement was nearing its end, he recited:

But words are things, and a small drop of ink
Falling like dew, upon a thought, produces
That which makes thousands, perhaps millions, think
'Tis strange, the shortest letter which man uses
Instead of speech, may form a lasting link

Of ages; to what straits old Time reduces
Frail man, when paper - even a rag like this
Survives himself, his tomb, and all that's his."

"Who said that?" I cheered and clapped, forgetting that I was holding a glass of whisky in my hand. Laughing at my oblivious *indexterity*, he leaned forward, inspected the Persian carpet under his feet, and very carefully, replenished the whisky I had spilled.

"Who said that?" I asked again.

"It comes from Lord Byron's *Don Juan*."

Holding on to our second whiskey as the fourth movement marched in, we visited sundry topics, tacitly avoiding some painful ones. He always had a quotation to mark whatever topic we promenaded into, as if his mind were a magazine of firecrackers ready to deploy at the slightest spark.

"*Ammu*. How come you know so much?" I sheepishly asked.

Evasively, he answered me with a quotation from (I found out later) Alfred North Whitehead: " 'Knowledge shrinks as wisdom grows.' "

I pressed him on because I craved to be like him, one day. I had watched doctors become so mired in the science of medicine that they became oblivious to life's artistic dimensions. I repeated, "So, *Ammu*, really, how come you know so much?"

"It's my job to know everything," he giggled. "I'm a *jassoos*," he giggled again as he saw surprise rise into my eyes.

"*Jassoos*?" I gasped. "A spy? You're pulling my leg? Come on. What on earth would you spy on?"

"I'm a newspaper spy. I cull the daily newspapers and report on topics, which are of interest to my employers."

At that point, the *choral* suddenly burst into the room and *Ammu* began beating the tempo with his closed fist, oblivious, absorbed, and entirely transcended into the Elysian realm. I watched but dared not interrupt this ethereal moment. Instead, my heartbeats joined his fisted march and began pounding with him.

This hammering intensity endured, in spite of mounting exhaustion, until the finale.

    He sighed, wiped the sweat off his brow, gleamed at me and said, "What a tortured soul."
    "Tortured?" I protested.
    "Tortured indeed," he admonished.
    "But it's Schiller's *Ode to Joy*."
    "I know, I know, but it's a misconception," he retorted and then promptly quoted from Schiller's Ode:

> *Oh friends, not these sounds*
> *Let us instead strike up more pleasing*
> *And more joyful ones*
> *Joy, joy*
> *Freude, freude.*

    "Misconception?" I protested again. "But this choral, with its uplifting music became a famous hymn, which you and I sang in the chapel of Brummana High School when we were students."
    "Yes, yes, I know. It was the American, Presbyterian pastor, Henry van Dyke, who, in 1907, wrote the famous hymn, *Joyful, joyful, we adore thee*. But he was just as mistaken as all the other interpreters of the choral."
    At this point, *Ammu* got up and played the fourth movement again. But, this time, he did not bang the table with his fist. Instead, he coined his own words against Schiller's *Ode to Joy*. Instead of *freude, freude,* (joy, joy) he chanted, *anger, anger.*
    "Listen," he instructed. "A tortured, angry Beethoven is banging, banging upon the gates of heaven, which refuse to open, refuse, refuse to let him in."
    "But why was he tortured and angry?" I asked with disbelief. "How can anyone who is that tortured and that angry compose such heavenly music?"
    "He was angry because music was his life, his entire life, but he could no longer hear it because he had grown totally deaf by the time he composed his ninth symphony. That was why he was

banging, banging upon the gates of heaven. He wanted heaven to reverse his sentence and restore his hearing so he could hear his opus magnum, his life's finale."

*

Fifty years later, my memory still holds that evening with *Ammu* George as sacred. I remember his humor, his kindness, his wit, his vast repertoire of knowledge, but, above all, I remember the fearless intensity with which he lived life. And when his time came to die, he did *go gentle into that good night*, as he said he would, with a smile behind his eyes.

*

Enlightened men do not die. They live in our memory like a rainbow that never loses colors, like a river that never stops flowing, like *freude-freude*, like an ode of joy:

> *To excitedly float the river time.*
> *To turn one page only to be enthralled*
> *by yet another and all the chapters*
> *and books that follow. To toss aloft the*
> *blazing torch for youth to catch the flame and*
> *with it rise. To flow with life's currents, nor*
> *struggle against its implacable sweeps.*
>
> *To know when to stop and where next to go.*
> *To embrace life's bounty with gratitude*
> *and life's verdicts with gleeful attitude*
> *nor beg nor grovel for more when the oil*
> *in the lamp runs dry. To feel ennobled*
> *by having had the chance to do our best.*

*To make room for the future by bowing
out. To cheer on change and progress, and watch
them skyrocket beyond our eyes and minds.
To view our destined recyclement as
a glorious reunion with earth and heaven.*

Blithe are the graces of enlightenment.

Chopin in Beirut

Beirut, today's tearful eye of the Mediterranean, was once the merriest port on its azure shores. That once-gleeful polis, history's fiancé after the twin wars, began its life as a seductive maiden with the birth of Lebanon. Lebanon, that mountainous region of greater Syria, had spent four hundred years laboring under the Ottoman's yoke. When, after the First World War, the victorious Allies dismantled the Ottoman Empire, Lebanon was mandated to France; and after the Second World War, Lebanon was granted independence. For the first time in history, in 1943, a sectarian, feudal democracy was established, which planted the seeds for civil unrest and internecine strife.

With her newfound freedoms, Beirut donned western fashions, espoused European post-war ideas, and vested itself in modern fineries. Western educational institutions like the American University of Beirut (AUB) and the Jesuit University (Université Saint-Joseph) flourished. Tourists flocked in, the economy swelled, radios filled the night air with song, and Western movies flooded the theaters. Soon after, operas, philharmonics, and masterful classical recordings made their debut among the Beirut elite. On the other side of this acute modernization, poverty spread among the less fortunate and the less educated. It was during this imported, westernized era that I, a baby boomer, came to fruition.

But, given that rosy cheeks do not crimson long, that the smiling face of peace is heir to the acne of war, and that history allows hindsight but not foresight—political strife fomented revolutions and my family fell victim. My father was incarcerated, tortured, sentenced to death, and spent seven years in a Beirut Bastille, before he was released, stooped and maimed. At fourteen, I was sent to a boarding school, and when I graduated, I left my native Tripoli and matriculated in the American University of Beirut.

It was in that Beirut, with my father's tower prison less than a mile away from my dormitory, that I spent the last eight years of my university life before immigrating to the United States.

While a third year medical student, my father fell ill and needed surgery. Under heavy guard, he was transferred to the AUB Hospital and, by divine serendipity, was assigned a room on my floor. For the first time, visiting my father no longer required a special permit from the Ministry of Internal Affairs.

With my white gown and stethoscope as irrefutable passports, I could pass through the checkpoint at his door, round on him twice daily, and spend as much time in his room as I wished. Although my morning visits were brief, because I had other patients to attend to, my evening stops were prolonged because I made sure he was the last one on my rounds. It was during one of those late evening sojourns in 1969 that I met Chopin.

That eventful evening, when I walked into my father's room, I found him was with a visitor. She must have obtained a special permit through some connection of hers, I surmised, as I introduced myself. She was in her forties, plainly dressed, but had a peculiarly charming face. Her hand, which I briefly shook, left a lingering impression on my palm. Her fingers were long, tapered, warm, refined. I gazed while she talked to my father with rhythmic voice and words that flowed like rhymes, accented by delicate hand motions. She was telling him about her mother. When their conversation ended, my father said to me, "You know who Dunia is, don't you?"

I half-smiled as my eyes gleamed with the embarrassment of ignorance. During that momentary suspense, I spied a blush steal into Dunia's cheeks. Uncomfortable, we both sat and awaited my father's exposé.

"Her father was a major writer of novels, plays, essays, and short stories," came my dad's long-awaited intimation.

I searched the recesses of my memory but no name surfaced. I knew that I should know who her father was; otherwise my dad would not have teased me with his question. Dunia coughed and blushed again. My dad smiled. I tried to appear focused, but having lost my focal point, my eyes roamed around without purpose.

"Dunia is the daughter of one of your favorite authors, Sayed Tayyar," explained my dad with a smug smile.

"Oh," I gasped, and involuntarily stood up. "I've read all your father's books and, whenever I can bend my friends' ears, I read to them my favorite short story, *Odysseus*. I must have read and re-read *Odysseus* one hundred times."

Dunia and my father exchanged knowing glances while they waited for me to compose myself. I sat down, and after some awkward reflection, I asked Dunia, "Are you a writer, too?"

She laughed and said, "No, but I'm a personal interpreter of writings."

I was stumped by her response and looked to my dad for an explanation, which he did not provide. He merely smiled and nodded approvingly. My feelings of awkwardness lingered on and did not begin to ease until she stood up to take her leave.

"I need to go rescue my mother," she smiled as she embraced my father.

"Son. It's getting late. Why don't you walk Dunia home?" came my dad's unanticipated request.

"I'd love to," I gasped as I stood up. "Let me go drop my gown and stethoscope off, put on my coat, and I'll be back in just a few minutes."

"The guards won't let you in without your doctor's garb," reminded my father. "Walk out with Dunia and she can wait for you in the lobby while you visit your locker."

We walked out together in amiable silence, and when I returned to the lobby, there was a small crowd surrounding her. I stood aside and watched her autograph whatever they handed her, notebooks, cards, handkerchiefs, and loose papers. When she was finished, she walked up to me, hooked her arm into mine, and said, "Take me home, Doctor, before I am accosted again."

As we exited the hospital into the chilly night, an epiphany drenched my skin with a clammy drizzle. Her expression, "I'm a personal interpreter of writings," assailed me with bitter embarrassment as I suddenly realized that, Dunia, our most celebrated Lebanese concert pianist, was on my arm. Embarrassed, because I did not recognize her and because it took a crowd of fans to alert me to her artistic identity, I failed to come up with any sensible talk as we walked, and was most relieved when she opened the conversation gates with, "So, did you choose medicine because your parents are doctors?"

"I wanted to become a farmer," I sighed, and watched my foggy breath dissipate into the crowded street.

"So, what changed your mind?" she giggled.

"My parents wouldn't hear of it," I croaked, inhaling a waft of pipe smoke from a passerby.

"So, do you regret your decision?"

"Not anymore. I have fallen in love with medicine and plan to spend the rest of my life married to her."

"You personify medicine? How poetic." She grinned.

"I stole that line from Chekhov."

"Who's Chekhov?"

"A nineteenth century Russian physician who, like your father, wrote short stories and plays. But, when asked if he favored writing over medicine, he famously answered, *'Medicine is my lawful wedded wife and literature is my mistress. When I get fed up with one, I spend the night with the other.'*"

Dunia laughed and pulled me into the static traffic, layered as if the street were a parking lot. "We need to cross to the other side," she said, as we negotiated the maze of mired cars and glaring lights. On the other side, the aroma of roasted peanuts titillated our nostrils. A lean, tall, Sudanese vendor stood facing us with coals glowing underneath his steel drum and a neat pile of warm peanuts on top. Dunia gave him a lira and said, "Two, please."

Out of magazine papers, he fashioned two cones, and with a wooden spoon, he filled them up with his warm, wafting peanuts.

Then, smiling with a golden tooth, he handed each of us a cone and said to her, *"Allah yawwid alaiki."* (May God reimburse you.)

Munching on peanuts, we walked down the shopping side of Hamra Street, lined with plush vitrines, while busy throngs loitered around the bustling café-bars on the other side.

"Tell me more about Chekhov," she suddenly asked, cracking the peanut silence.

"I didn't think that a classical pianist would be interested in Russian literature," I countered.

"I was raised by a writer, remember?" she teased. "So, how other writers treat their wives and daughters interests me."

"Oh, perhaps I shouldn't tell you then."

"Tell me what?" She smiled and took my arm again, after crumbling her emptied cone of peanuts and tossing it into a trashcan.

"Tell you that he felt wives were inconveniences, and resisted marriage as long as he could."

"Really?"

"This is what he said to his friend, Souvorin, who was pressuring him to marry: *'Give me a wife who, like the moon, won't appear in my sky every day.'*"

Dunia became solemn and her arm slowly relinquished mine. She seemed transported out of our nice *now* to some sad yesterday. I walked by her side and waited for her to return. Cars honked at the traffic jam ahead. A roasted chestnut vendor offered us a taste, which I declined. I felt responsible for her change of mood and wished I could take back Chekhov's quote, which must have exhumed some long-interred emotion, deep in her soul.

"My father felt the same way about marriage," she abruptly declared with a moist, muttering voice. "Perhaps, for writers, marriages are distracting inconveniences."

"Does that also apply to the interpreters of writings?"

"How do you mean?" she asked, not knowing what's on my mind.

"In my father's room, you referred to yourself as a personal interpreter of writings?"

Dunia paused, looked at the half-moon suspended between the rows of tall buildings, and paraphrased, as if talking to herself, "Give me a man, who like the moon, won't appear in my sky every day."

"Does this mean that, like Chekhov, you also resist marriage?"

"Music was my way of getting closer to my father, of becoming less of an inconvenience to him," she sighed. "And just like you and your medicine, I ended up falling in love with my piano and planned to spend the rest of my life with him."

A reflective, peripatetic pause ensued. A faint smile surfaced on her lips, followed by an approving nod.

"You are a perceptive young man," she declared. "A husband would be an inconvenience," she acknowledged. "Indeed, that's why the idea has never appealed to me."

I was touched by her transparency, which came so naturally, and left me feeling more like a friend than a stranger. I wanted to counter with a confession of mine, but could not find something as meaningful to reflect upon. Still, I felt it was my turn to add wood to the smoldering conversation fire, and so I philosophized.

"You cannot compare my love for medicine to your love for the piano. Music is an art, and medicine, a science, which means that you and I love differently."

"*Au contraire*, my dear young doctor. There is as much science in music as there is art in medicine. Wait a while and life will make that clear to you."

At that point we had approached the end of Hamra Street where the aroma of sizzling gyros assailed my nostrils and reminded me that, except for the cone of peanuts, I had not eaten all day. I wanted to stop for a sandwich, but I did not dare disturb the night's magic. She must have noticed my hesitation because she asked, "Are you hungry?"

"Ah, yes. I've not eaten all day."

"You must like gyros because I can hear you sniffing."

"Do you mind if we stop for a moment?"

"Yes, I do." she smiled, and retook my arm with firm intent. "I need to get back to my mother. She's not well and she is all alone at home."

"Is your home far?"

"No. It's just around the corner. I'll fix you a sandwich when we get there."

Stunned by her generous hospitality, I mumbled, "You need not do that. I'll eat when I get to my apartment."

"You are a young, hungry doctor who took the time to walk me home, and I do intend to feed you."

"What's wrong with your mother?" I asked, hoping to redirect the conversation away from my stomach.

"She has dementia and requires a lot of attention."

I regretted asking when I saw Dunia's eyes brim with concern. During that muted pause, her lips turned pale with pain. I recalled that she was an only child and surmised that, after her father's sudden death from a heart attack, she became the sole caregiver of her demented mother. As I pondered these issues, Dunia let go of my arm, reached into her purse, and pulled out her keys.

"We have arrived," she said, opening the iron gate to the building.

"I better let you go take care of your mother," I said, apologetically.

"Nonsense," she retorted. "You're coming up with me and I'm going to feed you."

Before I could respond, she took me by the elbow, marched me in, and closed the gate.

"We live on the third floor and the elevator is not working."

She turned on the stair lights and we walked up to the first landing.

"The owner of the building has promised to fix it but a month has already passed and we still have no elevator, which means that my mother has not been able to take her walks for an entire month," she grumbled.

"Lebanese talk?" I quipped.

"Worse," she huffed as we reached the second landing. "He's a miser, prompt in collecting rent, but a procrastinator when it comes to upkeep."

When we reached the third floor, she was wheezing and coughing, which robbed her of speech. We stood before her door until she caught her breath, and then, looking embarrassed, she whispered, "I know I need to lose weight but I'm constituted like my father. He was overweight and a chain smoker. I'm just overweight and, thanks to my asthma, I've never smoked."

When Dunia opened her door, her mother, tall, lean, and gray, ghosted before us wearing a long, flannel nightgown. With blank eyes and expressionless face, she gazed as we walked in, but gazed not at us. Dunia took her by the hand, led her to a chair in the living room, helped her sit down, and said, "We have a visitor and, while you sit with him, I'm going to make him a sandwich."

The living room was dominated by a Steinway grand piano and there were three chairs arranged in a semicircle around it. Several Farroukh paintings of Lebanese mountain scenes hung on the walls, lending the room a historic, rural flare, which contrasted comfortably with the classical concert piece. Twice, I looked at the mother, hoping to arouse some reaction but, like a statuette, she continued to stare, unaware. When Dunia walked in with my sandwich, I was gazing at the middle painting, a pine-tree scene with red roofs in the background.

"Do you like Farroukh?" she asked as she laid down the plate and gazed at the scene with me.

"These are originals, aren't they?"

"Yes. My father bought them in the early fifties, when Farroukh was teaching art at the AUB."

"They must be worth a fortune, now."

"To me they are priceless because they represent my father's relationship with a great Lebanese painter. I can't help but believe that some of my father's rural short stories must have been born when he was gazing at some of these Farroukh scenes."

Here, Dunia turned around, sat down, and pointed to my sandwich, sitting on the side table. I sat, glanced at her mother who was still frozen in a stare, and took my first bite. It was a delicious wrap of *labni* (yogurt cheese), pickled cucumbers, and olives.

Dunia smiled as she watched me consume the entire sandwich in just a few bites, and then said, "I make my own *labni*, because I like it fresh. You're still hungry, I can tell. Would you like another sandwich?"

"No, thanks," I said, placing my palm upon my chest to indicate satiety. "But, I'd love one more helping of something else, if you don't mind."

"I have fruits, and some *baklava* for dessert."

"Oh, no, that's not what I meant."

"So, what did you have in mind then?"

Pointing to the grand piano, I murmured, "dessert for my soul."

Dunia's eyes shone with a melancholy gleam. She looked at her staring mother, sitting among us but not sitting with us. Then, she placed her palm upon her chest, as I had done earlier, but to indicate overwhelming emotion instead of satiety. Her downcast eyes brimmed and it took her a while to regain composure.

"How did you know about that?" she then asked, wiping off a tear that hung from her blinking eyelash.

"About what?" I sheepishly asked, suspecting that I had unwittingly offended her.

"Oh. So you don't know and that makes it even eerier."

I must have looked bewildered and discombobulated because she forced a tender smile and then reflected, "My father used to say that to me whenever he wanted me to play. 'How about some dessert for my soul, darling?' he would ask, lighting a cigarette and sitting opposite the piano with expectant eyes. I miss him terribly. He was my most adoring admirer."

I watched the pain crawl inconsolably over Dunia's face. She hid her eyes behind her slender hands and softly sobbed. My impromptu expression *'dessert for my soul'* exhumed her father and placed him in the chair where I was sitting. I was no longer the medical student who had walked her home on his dad's behest. I was the resurrected soul of Sayed Tayyar (1903-1961) who died four years after Farroukh died.

"What would you like to hear?" she whimpered, regaining her emotional calm.
"Chopin's Ballads."
"All four of them?" she half-smiled.
"No, just the first one will do."
"How so?"
"It is filled with tragic undertones and discord, and I love it because it speaks to my life as a struggling medical student with father on death row."
"For a non-musician, you seem to know your Chopin rather well."
"He speaks to me through his sweet melancholy."
"How come you know him so well?"
"Through T. S. Eliot's *Portrait of a Lady*."
"T. S. Eliot? How's he connected to Chopin?" she asked intrigued.
Without answering her question, I quoted:

"So intimate, this Chopin, that I think his soul
Should be resurrected only among friends
Some two or three, who will not touch the bloom
That is rubbed and questioned in the concert room."

Her eyes kindled as she rose to her piano, sat down, and without opening a notebook, splashed the first seven bars onto the room's solemn silence. Her mother peered, focusing her gaze at Dunia with reawakened intent, as if that seven-bar introduction had descended into the cryptic recesses of her memory then rose up into her hibernating mind.

"He wrote only for the piano," she instructed, "and published his first Polonaise in G minor at age seven. Franz Liszt said, *"he confided those inexpressible sorrows to which the pious give vent in their communication with their Maker. What they never say except upon their knees, he said in his palpitating compositions."*

"So why did he fall in love with Amandine Aurore Dupin, an unappealing French Novelist who called herself George Sand, wore men's clothes, and smoked cigars?" I asked, hoping for some inside information.

Dunia played the seven introductory bars again and explained, "She was one of the most brilliant women of her generation, and her powerfully dynamic masculinity answered some vital need in his effeminate personality. But, the liaison ended up with a sad disaster," she lamented. "She broke his heart when she abruptly left him. He asked that Mozart's Requiem be played at his funeral. He was only thirty-nine when he died. He was and still is the saddest pianistic composer in history."

After a silent pause, the room assumed a somber air when Dunia, like a supplicating oracle, lifted up her arms and eyes, and buoyed up herself to some surreal realm before commencing her performance. Then, like merciful rain, her long, slender fingers dripped down upon the grand piano keys, issuing forth susurrus tunes that eloquently recited all the known and forgotten poems in all the languages of humanity. Obliviously, her hands, like ballerinas, danced the ivory stage, rising, falling, pirouetting, and flying wingless in a sonorous sky of their own creation. Time fell off the quivering edges of moments, leaving no footprints behind. Notes whirled around our senses and suffused our brains with vertiginous feelings. Tears ran down the cheeks of Dunia's mother and her staring eyes blinked rhythmically like wings in flight. And when Dunia played the final note, we all heaved, as if rising out of deep water to take our first breath.

The ensuing silence, which felt like fog, held us hostage in its suffocating fumes. Dunia on the piano, I in my chair, and Dunia's mother behind her stare—all sat motionless, awaiting the fog to dissipate. It was her mother who was the first to move. She stood up. Then, with festinating steps, came to my side and laid her frail, quivering hand upon my head, as if blessing me. Dunia, with a stunned face, cautiously approached, took her mother's hand, and led her away to her room. When she returned, she told me that her mother had not exhibited any emotion for over three years, and that when she put her to bed, her mother closed her blinking eyes and said, "Chopin." She had not spoken in years.

    I never saw Dunia again, although I looked for her each time I walked down Hamra Street or smelled roasted peanuts. A twenty-year civil war was soon to follow, destroying most of Beirut and devastating all of Lebanon. When I was told that she had fled to the US, after her mother died, I did not try to look her up because I did not wish to disturb the vista of that magical night, the night when Frédéric Chopin (1810-1849) rose from his tomb at Père Lachaise Cemetery in Paris and personally played his first ballad for the three of us in a private Beirut home.

    Fifty years later, the memory of that room, where I had witnessed resurrection from the catacombs of dementia, has never left my eyes nor has faith ever blazoned brighter in my soul. Music, humankind's most ancient alphabet and earth's only true international language, apprehended by all regardless of education, enjoyed by all regardless of culture, and hallowed by all regardless of faith, is how God communicates with his long-suffering humanity from behind her tears.

Seven Years

I was surprised when he said: "I have to go back to Beirut tonight." Having said that, he gave me a long warm embrace and drove into the night. I gazed into my mother's worried eyes as we watched the car lights blink and vanish down the street, and then I asked, "Mother, why is he leaving us on New Year's Eve? Why are there armed men in the garden?"

"He will be back tomorrow for lunch, God willing. You are fourteen years old, dearest, and I expect you to behave like a brave young man. Get ready, we're going up to the village for the night."

In the yawning fog, the village lights stretched like a smile along the hilltop. And as soon as it was polite to leave the family gathering, I stole away in search of my best friend, Nizom, whom I found at home playing cards. When he saw me approach he immediately excused himself, gave his hand to a friend, and walked away with me.

"What is going on, Salem? There are armed men all over the town. Where is your dad?"

"He went back to Beirut. There were armed men at our home in Tripoli, inside the house and in the garden."

All night, we sat by the radio and listened to the news, while our minds weaved a thousand tales. At 6 a.m., after the national anthem, the announcer began the broadcast with: *"A band of militants involved in antigovernment conspiracy were intercepted and captured."*

Within a few days, my mother was apprehended, my father was sentenced to death, my little sister went to live with my aunt, and my two younger brothers and I were taken in an army truck to a boarding school and ordered never to leave the premises.

Later on that year, my mother was released from jail and for the first time we were allowed to visit my father. He limped, had missing teeth, pale sunken cheeks, and stooped at half his normal height. Each month, we brought him food and clothes, and when they took him out of solitary confinement two years later, they even allowed us to bring him one book. We brought him the family Bible.

When I graduated from high school, I brought him pictures; when I fell in love, I brought him my girlfriend; when I was accepted into medical school, I slipped him a poem through the narrow bars which ended with: *"Never worry about the little river; it will always find its way to the sea."* That was the only time I saw his tears.

For seven years I lived at half-mast in the shade between darkness and light, in the anguish between love and hate, in the tears between smiles and frowns. Then, a new president was elected and it was rumored that he might clear the jails of political prisoners. Rumors fly to wherever they are needed, and that one nested in my heart. It would take off, roam around, and return, like a white pigeon, full of good tidings that I needed to believe. This went on for a year or two and still, the white pigeon would not tire.

One day I was paged while making rounds at the hospital. It was my mother's voice, vibrant, hesitant, and moist.
"Dearest, you'd better go to the jail right now. They might release all of them this afternoon, and because of the traffic between Tripoli and Beirut, I might not be able to make it in time. I'd hate for him to walk out and find no one to greet him."

I took off like a frantic pheasant, still in my white gown, which I did not notice until friends in front of the jail pointed it out to me. I waited and stared at the iron-gate; it did not move. Then, I heard motion, orders, footsteps, and the heavy gate creaked as it slowly rolled.
One by one, all remaining fifty prisoners walked out: seven years ago, there were two hundred. I stood by the gate waiting for the last one to emerge. When he did not, I jumped inside to find him saying goodbye to the warden, serene, with a shimmering smile

in his eyes. I kissed his cheeks and walked behind him to the gate, proud, with head flying at full mast.

After we were out, I hurried back into the jail and gave the warden one long, silent embrace. He was the only one who was kind to my father and allowed me to smuggle him medicine and books.

On the way to Amioun, our hometown, we rode together. Instead of rushing to Beirut, my mother decided to wait for us at my grandmother's home in Amioun. We said little as we drove because his eyes were absorbing seven years of change. He gazed as if amazed at the landscape's transformation, and then announced, "I have been absent too long. Imprisonment is a dying that never ends. Merciful death is barred from assuaging those behind bars."

At the gates of Amioun, people lined the streets, waved flower bouquets, and shouted welcoming cries. Before we arrived at my grandmother's home, my father told the driver, "Stop here. I have to see Bahije."

"But, Doctor, they're all waiting for you at your mother's home," cried the driver.

"Bahije lost his only son just a few days ago. I must stop to offer him my condolences before I am consumed by the welcoming crowd."

Bahije was waiting at the door because he had heard the honking of the cars that joined us along the way. We all waited outside while he and my father walked in and sat by the window. We could see them talk with lowered gazes, scratch their heads, wipe their cheeks, stand up, sit back down, cover their faces with trembling fingers, and then bow their heads as if in prayer.

When my father walked out, he was unescorted. Bahije remained inside and closed the window shutters. The cars left dark dust in their wake as they hurried to my grandmother's home.

The crowd was jubilant. My nonagenarian grandmother held on to my father's neck and would not let go. Smiles danced with tears upon the welcoming faces. Then, after a long embrace, my grandmother relinquished my father's neck and whispered, "Go to your guests. They have waited a long time for this moment."

After the crowd dissipated, and we made it home, we had our first family dinner in seven years. Everyone was exhausted, but no one wanted to let go of the evening, of our first supper, of our first breaking bread, of our gathered diaspora.

When my father and mother retired to their bedroom, relief waltzed throughout my body, dancing to the moist tunes of love, love that had traversed the seven-year desert to reunite at the oasis.

For the first time in seven years, my father slept in a bed with clean sheets. For the first time, he slept with my mother. For the first time, he did not have to rise at daybreak for inspection. For the first time, he had a clean, private bathroom. And for the first time, he was home with his family.

I slept like a child that night. At daybreak, I heard noise in the kitchen. I tiptoed and peered. My father and mother were making Turkish coffee, standing with their backs to me, facing the gas stove. He was holding the coffee pot with his right hand. She was stirring it with her left hand. And in between them, their free hands were clutched like a mighty cable, suspending a seven-year-long bridge.

Seven Years, First Edition, AL-JADEED: VOL. 12, Nos. 56/57, Summer/Fall 2006, and released winter 2007. Revised edition was completed in October of 2016.

The Eye of the Needle

<u>1970</u>

"Why are you blushing?" I asked, as her blue eyes gazed obliviously into the tepid afternoon.

"I'm just worried," she sighed, and said no more.

"Are you worried about the king or the paupers," I teased.

"What king and paupers? What on earth are you talking about?"

"King Hussein, of course, and the Palestinian resistance fighters, whom he has just evicted."

"I'm not concerned about the fate of the PLO right now; all I'm concerned about is my own little fate."

"Is that why you're blushing like a sunset?"

"Please, Salem, drive on and pay attention to the road. I may be setting but I'm not blushing."

I had just returned from Jordan, part of a medical team that was dispatched by the American University of Beirut to assess casualties in the Palestinian refugee camps around Amman. Earlier that week, at the A.U.B Emergency department, we had received loads of injured Palestinians who brought with them stories more horrific than their wounds. Because of that, our parents endured great worries while we were gone and welcomed us as unsung heroes when we returned, unharmed.

My parents organized a reception for me at their home in Tripoli and invited our friends and relatives who came, toasted, and departed, leaving behind Aunt Catherine, who needed to consult my mother regarding an urgent matter. I had volunteered to drive her back to Amioun, our mountain hometown, after the consultation, and then head back to Beirut to resume my medical duties on the busy wards of the American University Medical Center. The drive from Tripoli to Amioun took half an hour, during which some seeds were sown in a little patch of time and watered with bitter tears.

"We're almost halfway to Amioun and you're still blushing," I insisted. "Why don't you tell me what's blushing you?"

Un-wiped tears began to drip down from Aunt Catherine's cheeks as she attempted to ignore my question. I handed her my handkerchief and waited. The setting sun made her look more morose and she grew more taciturn the longer I drove. In the distance, Amioun stretched like a sleeping cat atop the ridge that towered over the olive plain. *"We're almost there,"* I thought, *"and still, she hasn't said a word."*

"Could you at least tell me why you're crying?" I pleaded.

"Because your mother slapped me smack on the face," she abruptly screamed, no longer able to compose herself.

"My mother smacked you? What on earth did you do to deserve that?"

Aunt Catherine went silent again as darkness dropped its veil upon the valley. I turned my headlights on and drove quietly toward the rocky ridge that held Amioun as its crown.

"Why did my mother slap you?" I begged. "She seldom slapped us when we were growing up, even when we deserved it."

"What hurts me most is that she shamed me first and then she slapped me," came her sniffling reply.

"Shamed you? How did she shame you? What did she say that hurt your feelings so much?

"First she said that only arrogant atheists reject God's gifts, and then she slapped me when I continued to beg her for an abortion."

"Abortion? You're pregnant?"

"Yes, and I am also forty years old and the mother of four little children."

"Weren't you using some form of birth control?"

"As a nurse I should have known better," she sighed, shaking her head and wiping off her tears with the handkerchief I had given her. "It was too tiny a hole and I wasn't thinking. But it was obviously big enough to admit your uncle's *trouts*."

I pulled the car to the side, turned off the engine, and stared at her with livid consternation.

"What hole are you talking about?"

"The hole in my diaphragm, the same diaphragm I had used for several years without incident."

I wanted to say: *"Why didn't you think to change your ancient diaphragm?"* But, I decided not to add fuel to her already fuming fire.

"When I was your mother's nurse, I was the one who used to do the sperm counts on the microscope. I should have known better, but passion must have enthralled my intellect. I'm doubly ashamed, one, to have gotten pregnant, and two, to have asked for an abortion."

1971

Before I left to the US for my medical residency, I drove to Amioun to bid my grandmother, my aunts, and my uncles, farewell. My last stop was at Aunt Catherine's, who met me with the baby on her breast.

"I'm too old for this," she sighed, forcing a pale smile.

Her four little children rushed in, hugged me, and we began exchanging idle talk.

"Are you a real doctor now?" asked the youngest.

"How long will you be gone?" asked the oldest.

"Leave him alone and go play," ordered Aunt Catherine.

They hovered around, of course, as Aunt Catherine and I talked.

"She's a healthy girl," I reassured.

"Thank God for that, but will she be smart? They say that *lateborns* grow up to be problems."

"My mother had me at forty and I'm not a problem," I teased.

"Did you like her name? The kids wanted to name her Catherine but I stood my grounds. One Catherine in the house is enough, I said, and so we named her Kate."

1973

I returned from the US for a visit after the Syrian-Egyptian-Israeli war had ended. Beirut and Tripoli were still in turmoil and so I stayed in Amioun with my Aunt Catherine and got to hold Kate on my lap. She had exploring eyes, a scouting personality, and an indomitable sense of independence.

"What do you think?" asked Aunt Catherine, having watched me interact with Kate for a while.

"I think she is precious."

"But is she smart?"

"I see genius behind her eyes," I replied with authority.

"I'll be content if she's just normal. Amira, our next door neighbor, had a Down syndrome baby at forty."

"Has Kate seen her father yet?"

"He came from Kuwait for a visit last year and is coming back in July to spend a whole month with us."

"Have you thought about getting a new diaphragm?" I jested.

"I had my tubes tied," she murmured with pursed lips, "and when your uncle returned from Kuwait last year and saw how exhausted I was with our five little ones, he made the mistake of asking me if he could do anything else for me before going back to his work."

She smirked when she said that, and then waited while my curiosity burned.

"Is that how you got your new washer and dryer?" I snickered.

"No, my dear young doctor, that's how your uncle got his vasectomy."

1977

I finished my residency and fellowship and was getting ready to return home when my father called.

"I hear you sold your car, your furniture, and bought your return tickets."

"Yes, Dad. I should be home by the end of July."

"Stay where you are for now, Son. We have a raging civil war that's going to take a long time to die. At present, Lebanon is not a place to start a career or raise a family."

1981

Amioun was invaded by opposing civil-war factions and its evicted inhabitants all became refugees. Our extended family congregated at our large home in Tripoli and Aunt Catherine became the house manager for the duration of the exodus, which lasted nine months. When the invading armies left Amioun, the inhabitants returned to find their homes demolished and all their belongings stolen. No one had money to rebuild. In time, however, small shacks and dugouts were fashioned around or underneath the demolished homes and Amioun began to show some feeble signs of life. Very slowly, schools opened their doors, businesses returned, and rescue money from the Lebanese immigrants started to pour into the region.

When I visited Aunt Catherine that year, she, my uncle, and their five children were living in three storage rooms underneath their demolished home. Our eyes met when Kate pranced by with a bunch of books under her arm.

"Is she good in school?" I quizzed.

"She's bored with her classes and studies on her own."

"Is she passing?" I teased.

"She has all A's and asks the teachers questions they cannot answer."

"What kind of questions?" I teased again.

"Questions about things above my head. Whey don't you let her ask you some and you can find out for yourself.

1987

I returned for my father's funeral, two years after the invading Israeli Army had withdrawn from Lebanon.

"Will you go with us?" asked Aunt Catherine after the conclusion of our customary condolences.

"Go where?"

"Kate's graduation. She's the valedictorian."

"Your mean she is that smart?" I grinned.

"Why don't you come and see for yourself."

The graduation was held at the American Evangelical School in Tripoli. I remember most of Kate's speech:

We should not take credit for our beauty or our intelligence because they were given not earned. We should not take credit for our achievements for they are the products of the bows that, as Gibran says, shot us as living arrows up into the skies of life. We should not take credit for our characters for they are parts, like Tennyson said, of everything we've met. We should, instead of being concerned with our own credits, be concerned with those who are less endowed, nor have credits that they can call their own, and we should spend our life's labors insuring that they, the less fortunate, would have us as guardians of their welfares. And we should, for the rest of our lives, nurture an attitude of gratitude for all the gifts that we have received, and should endeavor to honor these gifts by using them for the betterment of humanity. And we should be ashamed to die, when our turns come, without having won, as the Antioch College motto enjoins, some victory for humanity.

*

2000

I returned to find Amioun totally rebuilt. My aunt and uncle were back in their home, the storage rooms under the house were full of olives and olive oil, and the fecund garden was pregnant with vegetables and fruits.

"Where is Kate?" I asked as we sat on the large veranda, sipping Arabic coffee.

"She's in Dubai."

"Doing what?"

"She's the Managing Director of an investment company," announced Aunt Catherine with pride.

"Is she successful?" I winked.

"Who do you think paid the money to rebuild our house?"

"So, can we conclude then that she is both smart and successful?" I asked, rubbing it in.

"You never forget, do you?"

2002

Kate came to visit us at our home in Amioun. I asked her if anyone had ever told her the story of how she came to be.

"I was an accident," she asserted.

"What kind of accident?" I pried.

"My mother was forty with four kids and I was unplanned."

I gleamed and, very cautiously, told her the entire story to the minutest detail, omitting nothing. She blushed and said, "So, it was your mother who saved my life."

"No, it was your mother who saved your life," I affirmed. "She could have gone to another gynecologist and gotten an abortion, but she didn't." Then, as an after thought, I added, "And she also breast-fed you for two full years."

She smiled with eyes, brimming with deep love for her mother, and said, "By the way, I'm going to be on Dubai Television next week."

"Why?"

"They are interviewing me because I am considered a good role model for Arab women, and because I'm a vital economic force in their society."

"How wonderful. I wish I could watch it."

"Why can't you?"

"I'll be in back in the US by then."

2005

"Kate is on television again, and all of Amioun is watching Al-Jazira," announced Aunt Catherine as I walked in. "Come, come, sit down, and let's watch the interview together."

The interviewer asked questions about the economy, about society, and about education, all of which were answered most eloquently by Kate, who had just started her own investment company to further empower youth and women in the region. Then the interviewer startled us all with, "You are one of the wealthiest women in the Arab world and you are also a Christian. Prophet Muhammad, prayers be upon him, admonishes us to give a percent of our earnings to the poor. Jesus, on the other hand, says that it is easier for a camel to go through the eye of a needle than for a rich person to enter the kingdom of heaven. How do you reconcile your wealth with your faith?"

Kate flushed, and with a wink that only her mother and I understood, replied, "I entered heaven through the eye of a needle long before I became rich."

The Eye Of The Needle, First Edition, Al-Jadid Magazine, Volume 17, No. 65 (2011) Released in August 2013. Revised Edition completed in October 2016.

The Quack
Doctor Blackpill

We can only think from within our time-space cocoons, a constraint that hinders understanding of predecessors. However, looking back across wide generational gaps may vouchsafe us enough hindsight to bridge past with present. In spite of that, what our predecessors did may still seem unethical to us now, as might what we are doing now seem unethical to those who will succeed us.

I was an intern in 1970 when Dr. Blackpill died. None of our professors went to his funeral, but my father and his friend, Dr. Elias, did. They were medical students when Dr. Blackpill was in his prime and both had apprenticed with him during their third year, in 1942. Having travelled far to come to his funeral, they dropped by my hospital as I was getting off my shift.

"How about dinner at Al-Ajami?" invited my father.
"Certainly," I replied. "Interns are ever hungry critters."

Al-Ajami, established in 1770, was the oldest and best restaurant in Beirut. Tucked deep in the Beirut souks inside a convoluted, stone-arched edifice, it attracted *connoisseurs* of the international, culinary world. Frequented by Ottoman pashas until 1918, French Mandate officers until 1943, and dignitaries from North Africa, Europe, and the Levant since independence, it was the socio-political hub of Lebanon. Its thick stonewalls resounding with bubbling hookahs, whispered conversations, and high-pitched utensil clanks filled its tenebrous dungeons with a sense of sober suspense and mouth-watering expectations.

Greeted at the door by the *maître d'hôtel,* Abu Ahmad, we were seated in a quiet alcove, removed from the busy hum of men. It was then, among the comings and goings of white-uniformed waiters and laden plates that I inquired about the funeral.

"It was massive," replied my father. "Only the privileged made it into the church; the rest amassed in the church plaza, flooded the surrounding streets, and sardined the balconies overlooking the spectacle."

"It was more becoming of a statesman than a physician," added Dr. Elias.

"How come I've never heard of Dr. Blackpill?" I inquired.

When my question provoked polite laughter, I reciprocated with a muffled giggle, but my eyes retained their curiosity. Seeing my embarrassment, Dr. Elias and my dad exchanged knowing glances and then came to my rescue.

"He was highly regarded and loved by his patients, but not by his colleagues, especially our professors," began Dr. Elias.

"They called him *The Quack*," interjected my father.

"We had to request a special permission to rotate at his clinic," continued Dr. Elias. "Our professors were against it, but they had to submit to our wishes because he was on the volunteer faculty of the American University Hospital.

"Your dad and I shadowed him for two months. With hawk eyes he would survey the crowded waiting room and ask the sickest looking patient to come in first. His histories were brief and to the point. His examinations were limited to the body areas highlighted by his history. His treatments were simple and direct. And his medical notes were intelligent and terse. He saw about fifty patients a day, and everyone paid cash and left happy."

"Talk about authoritarian medicine," added my dad. "No one had the audacity to question his decisions, and no patient dared not recover."

"You mean that he helped all his patients get well?" I quizzed with doubtful tone.

"Almost," smiled Dr. Elias. "He was a magician of sorts and we never quite understood how he did it."

A salad bowl of *fattouch (salad with toasted bread crumbs)* arrived and the waiter, scooping with two spoons, served each of us a generous portion of the starter, left the earthenware on the table, said *bon appétit*, bowed, and backed away.

"Well, did you learn a lot?" I quizzed, eager to restart the conversation.

"He was a master interpreter of facial expressions and a scrupulous decipherer of complaints," explained Dr. Elias. "One time, a man came in complaining of headache. He quizzed him and brought out the facts that the headache, which began after Christmas, always started soon after the man left home in the morning and resolved soon after he returned home in the evening. We watched with awe as Dr. Blackpill stood up, grabbed the man's hat out of his lap, and told him to return in two days.

" 'What about my hat?' asked the man.

" 'Come see me in two days and I will give you back your hat,' replied Dr. Blackpill.

" 'But, what about treatment?' asked the bewildered man. 'I've already paid you and you're sending me home with nothing.'

" 'As I said, come see me in two days,' replied the doctor, and then called the next patient in.

"Your dad and I were afraid to ask for an explanation and played along as if we had understood. Two days later, when the man returned, the doctor sat him down, looked him in the eyes, and asked, 'Do you still have your headache?'

" 'No,' replied the surprised man. 'It went away after I left your clinic and it is still gone.'

" 'The hat was your Christmas present, wasn't it?' inquired the doctor with a smile.

" 'Yes, sir,' replied the doubly surprised man.

" 'Well, here it is, but do not wear it if you don't want your headache to return.'

"The man picked up his hat and, looking dumbfounded, said, 'My wife, who gifted me the hat for Christmas, wanted me to look like a modern Frenchman. Wait till I tell her that, instead, I ended up looking like a pain-in-the-head Lebanese.' "

A grinning silence lingered among the plates as we took time to savor the *plat du jour* of okra stew served on a bed of rice, topped with *sautéed* pine nuts. After we savored the *home-cooked* food and dishes were cleared, I asked, "So, why do you call him Dr. Blackpill? Surely, that is not his real name."

"For his adoring patients, his name was Dr. Nabeel Saleem, but at the American University Hospital he was known as Dr. Blackpill," giggled my dad.

"Remember the blonde, middle-aged schoolteacher who came to him for nausea?" reminded Dr. Elias.

My father nodded with smiling eyes.

"Go ahead," I pleaded, overflowing with curiosity.

"Well, she was about 45 and had been nauseated for almost two months. Dr. Blackpill asked and asked, shook his head, examined her belly, checked her fingernails, looked at her tongue with a bright flash light, listened to her heart and abdomen, and then asked, 'Do you still live with your parents?'

" 'No. I moved out at the beginning of the school year.'

" 'When do you vomit?'

" 'Only on certain mornings,' she replied.

" 'And what do you teach?'

" 'I teach French at the Lycée,'

" 'Have you added any new teachers?'

" 'Well yes,' she gulped and blushed. 'A nice Frenchman has joined our faculty and the students love him.'

" 'And how long have you been doing it?'

" 'Doing what?' she blushed again.

" 'Doing it with the French teacher.'

" 'I don't know what you're talking about, Doctor,' she stuttered, looking at us with gaping eyes.

" 'You're pregnant my dear. I doubt that the Frenchman will marry you. So the issue here is: what are you planning to do with the baby?'

"The teacher burst into tears and hid her face behind her long, smooth fingers. The doctor held her hand and whispered, 'I'll give you a medical leave of absence, saying that you have tuberculosis and that you need to spend six months at the Bhannis Sanatorium. The school will be glad to let you off and no one will know. My sister manages the sanatorium and you can stay with her until you deliver. I'll go up to Bhannis and deliver the baby, after which you can go back to your old life.'

" 'But, I can't keep the baby, can I?'

" 'You can, but then you'll lose your job. French Lycées do not allow unwed mothers among their faculty.'

" 'I can't lose my job,' she gasped. 'I support my elderly parents, who depend on me for everything. They would die of shame if the word were to get out.'

" 'I know a couple who want to adopt. They live in Cyprus now, but want to repatriate. We can arrange for them to come for the baby and I can give them the necessary papers saying that I delivered the wife of the new child.'

"Unable to make up her mind, the teacher looked at us with pleading eyes. The doctor, pressed for time, scribbled a few lines on a prescription pad, handed it to her, and said, 'Go home, take one of these black pills when you wake up to prevent morning sickness, think about consequences, and come see me tomorrow.' When she returned, she had a suitcase in her hand.

"After the teacher left, we asked him about legal issues. He sneered and said, 'the law is a mule. If I had to get the law's permission, I wouldn't be able to help half my patients. I do whatever my conscience dictates and to hell with *the law's delay and insolence of office,* as Shakespeare so aptly put it.' "

At this point, a bowl of blushing apples, smiling oranges, and fat, yellow bananas was set as a centerpiece. I reached for the banana, Dr. Elias peeled an orange, and my father bit an apple with such succulent crunch that it caused eyes to glare at us. Then, with exuberant mouth, he said to Dr. Elias, "Do you remember that blue-eyed woman who had a discharge?"

"I will never forget that one," replied Dr. Elias with a wry grin.

When nothing else was said, I realized that my dad and his friend were teasing me. The intrigue in their avoidant eyes as they attended to the fruits in their hands told me that I should call their bluff. I ate my banana, reached for another, and began peeling it with deliberate care, expecting that one of them would soon succumb to the telling urge.

"So, Son. Are you tired of us telling old stories?" resumed my dad.

"Not at all," I replied with feigned indifference. "I was merely focused on my fruit as you were on yours."

"Let me tell it," interjected Dr. Elias, and my father, taking another bite of his apple, acquiesced. "It was a grand piece of detective work. This woman comes in with her husband, complaining of an odorous discharge for about a month. Dr. Blackpill asked the husband if he had a discharge and then asked the woman if she itched. With *no* to both answers, he asked how long they had been married. They both fumbled for an answer and finally agreed on two years. On pelvic examination, the doctor retrieved a foreign body, put it in a kidney basin, and walked out with it, giving the woman time to get dressed. We watched him wash the retrieved clump and separate it into fifteen *Lira* notes, worth about ten dollars at the time. With a poker face, back in the examination room, the doctor handed the money to the fretful woman and said, 'This tip belongs to you; do not surrender it to the pimp in the waiting room.' With glimmering tears, the blue-eyed woman tucked the money deep inside her purse, hugged the doctor, and left."

None of us laughed when the story ended. Before it was told, it seemed to wear a humorous mask. But, afterword, it reeked with the proverbial sadness of *'he who is without sin, let him cast the first stone.'* Ending on that sad note, we paid and walked out amongst the honking cars and peddling vendors. We walked a while in silence before we waved a taxi. The driver struck a conversation with us when he found out that we were physicians. His mother was dying of lung cancer, and he was having trouble dealing with the situation.

"How old is your mother?" asked my dad.
"She's eighty five."

"That's the same age of that elegant man who came to see Dr. Blackpill," volunteered Dr. Elias.

"I remember that man well," added my father.

"Should I take her to see Dr. Blackpill?" cried the driver.

"No, sir," replied my dad. "Dr. Blackpill's funeral was today. But, I will tell you the story because it might help you cope better. When that well-dressed gentleman came to see Dr. Blackpill for his lung cancer, he looked desperate and terrified. He had heard of the doctor's black pills and wanted to try them."

"And both my mother and I are desperate and afraid," stuttered the driver.

"Well, Dr. Blackpill held the man's hand and asked him, 'What scares you more than death?' The man, who had been a high-school mathematics teacher, pondered the matter a while and then replied, 'dementia, infirmity, indignity, loss of a child, dishonor, poverty, and loss of independence.' Dr. Blackpill looked the man in the eyes and with a kind tone whispered, 'You have had a good life. Be thankful that God is calling you now so that he can spare you these seven misfortunes that frighten aging humanity.' Then, handing the elegant man a prescription, he added, 'These black pills will help you sleep better. Take one before you go to bed.' The man relinquished his frown, shook the doctor's hand with both hands, and walked away with a pacified face."

When the taxi driver dropped us at the hospital, he got out of his car, shook Dr. Elias and my father's hands, refused payment, and drove away.

One question still burned on my lips as we stood in the hospital lobby, saying a protracted good-bye.

"Did his patients call him Dr. Blackpill or Dr. Saleem?" I asked, half embarrassed.

Both Dr. Elias and my dad welcomed my comic relief and reassured me that he was, indeed, hallowed by his patients.

"No one called him Dr. Blackpill except his colleagues at the hospital," reassured my father, "but they never called him that to his face. To his patients, he was the very revered Dr. Nabeel Saleem."

"But where did that name come from?" I pressured.

"From us," replied Dr. Elias with a smirk. "Your father and I dubbed him *Dr. Blackpill* and the name stuck. For all kinds of colds, headaches, insomnias, functional pains, and many other complaints, he would hand his patients a carefully inscribed prescription, which read: {*Pilluli Mica Panis 1000mg/tablet, take one twice daily with food for seven days, # 14 tablets.*}

"We watched as patient after patient got well, but were afraid to ask what *Pilluli Mica Panis* was. When we asked our other teachers, they had no idea. But, on our last day with him, he invited us to lunch and that was when your father summoned his courage to inquire about Dr. Blackpill's magic cure.

"He was happy to explain that *pilluli mica panis* is Latin for *pills made of bread crumbs*. He explained that patients needed placebos to recover and his was a benign, cheap medicine. The surrounding pharmacies all knew what it meant and compressed bread pills especially for him. Over the years, he found that white or brown bread pills failed to help some patients, but when he had the pharmacists concoct the pills from dense, pumpernickel rye bread and double the size and price, the heavier, more expensive black pills had greater impacts on the patients' minds and the cure rates skyrocketed.

"His final words to us were: 'I am a scientist and a placebologist. I know when to give a real medicine and when to give a placebo. The law says that I am cheating my patients, but my conscience says that I am helping them. As I told you before, the law is a mule, slow, stubborn, powerful, unintelligent, and insolent. I, on the other hand, am held to higher standards by my God-given conscience and by my love for my patients.' "

Submitted to the Journal of the Oklahoma State Medical Association in Marsh, 2016. Accepted for publication in November, 2016.

Abdominal Fire

Chief Resident: "If you report it, I'll burn your house with you in it."

Intern: "But, it's a great teaching case."

Chief Resident: "It'll ruin my career and my future."

Intern: "But if we don't report it, how can others learn from it?"

Chief Resident: "Let them learn from other cases."

Intern: "But isn't it our responsibility to share our medical discoveries?"

Chief Resident: "You can publish it after I am dead but be sure to use fake names, fake dates, and fake places. I'd shudder in my grave if my children or grandchildren were to find out."

Intern: "You're not serious."

Chief Resident: "Promise me. Promise me on your father's grave."

Intern: "Okay, okay. If my silence means that much to you, I promise it until death do us part."

Chief Resident: "Such a deadly expression. Why did you have to put it that way?"

This conversation took place forty years ago at the Southern Government Hospital (SGH) where Dr. Ibraheem Assaf was our chief surgical resident and I was the intern who assisted him on the case. Soon after that fateful interlocution, the year ended, we lost contact, and we built our medical lives apart, around different specialties and in different countries. Nonetheless, I kept my promise and never told a soul.

The operating room (OR) crew was also sworn to secrecy by Dr. Ibraheem. The way he did it was most delicate. When we were finished, he asked me to close the abdomen and, while I worked, he addressed the three OR nurses with downcast eyes.

"You know how embarrassing this would be if word should ever get out. So, I have to ask you not to tell anyone because telling would not only hurt our image for letting such a disaster happen—it would also hurt the image of the hospital and destroy the community's confidence in its staff."

"Of course, Dr. Ibraheem," said Nuha.

"Not a soul will ever find out," said Muna.

"I promise you, Doctor," said Rabeeah, the nurse anesthetist who was also the most beautiful woman in the hospital and the one that all the new interns fell in love with. She walked like a poem, which rhymed at the hips, and she never noticed the wanton looks that tracked her path as she made her anesthesia rounds.

The entire surgical staff of the SGH admired Doctor Ibraheem and loved him dearly for his gregarious spirit and absolute dedication to his patients. Indeed, he was the hospital's icon and the mentor after which we all modeled ourselves. That was a time when respect was the whitest gown a doctor could wear and Dr. Ibraheem's gown was, indeed, the whitest of all.

Last month, I received the Alumni Magazine and in the obituaries there was a picture of Dr. Ibraheem—handsome, commanding, gray haired, and wearing the same smirk that had always belied his sky-full heart. I was sickened by the news and felt a strong urge to communicate with his widow, listed as Mrs. Linda Assaf. Donations were to go to the Surgery Department, Ibraheem Assaf Chair, Calgary Foot Hills Hospital, Alberta, Canada. With my check, I sent a handwritten note to his widow in which I expressed my long-held feelings of love, friendship, and gratitude toward her late husband. Before the month was over, I received a handwritten note from Mrs. Assaf thanking me and asking me to be one of the speakers at a memorial ceremony to be held in his honor at the Foot Hills Hospital the following month.

I prepared a ten-minute speech and flew to Calgary. The Foot Hills Hospital stood atop a hill overlooking the Bow River, which trickled down from the Bow Glacier in the Rockies and snaked through Calgary on its way to the Hudson Bay. At the auditorium, I was given my nametag and ushered to the front row where I sat among people I did not know. Soon, Mrs. Assaf greeted me and took the seat beside me. Then, realizing that I did not recognize her, she added, "You don't remember me? I am Rabeeah Arees, the nurse anesthetist at the SGH. I changed my name to Linda because Canadians had trouble saying Rabeeah."

    I gasped at the gleam in her eyes, which resurrected all my fond memories of the SGH. She was still beautiful and I caught myself gazing at her as I had done forty years earlier when I was one among many rotating interns who had fallen in love with her. I surprised myself, however, when instead of saying something courteous, I blurted out, "Did you know that all the rotating interns were in love with you?"

    She blushed, her eyes giggled with adolescent glee, and then, fumbling for words, she *reparteed* "You're still as silly as you were forty years ago."

    After the memorial service ended, we gathered for coffee in the Ibraheem Assaf Reception Hall. It was there that I mustered enough courage to stutter the question, "Have you, have you told, ever told anyone?"

    "Of course not. We were sworn to secrecy, remember? And how about you? Have you told anyone?"

    "I haven't either."

    On the way back to Oklahoma City, I penned the story and sent it to the Medical Digest because that monthly bulletin had a special section for unique medical experiences. It appeared in print a few months later under the title, *From One Best Friend To Another*, and I did not forget to send a copy to Rabeeah.

*

From One Best Friend To Another

The third case of the day was Abu Youssef, a man in his fifties whose liver was studded with hydatid cysts. Hydatid disease was rampant in the region, causing major morbidity and mortality. The inhabitants got infected because their garden vegetables, which they used to make *Tabbuli* and other salads, were contaminated with tapeworm eggs from dog feces. The ingested eggs hatched *oncospheres*, which penetrated the intestinal walls, migrated to the various organs, and developed into cysts. In the region served by the SGH, the dog, man's best friend, was also man's worst enemy.

Dr. Ibraheem was an experienced hydatid surgeon who had operated on numerous cases and was renown for his successes against this treacherous disease. Things seemed to go well at first as he successfully dissected one liver cyst after another while I held the retractors and obeyed his detailed instructions. However, while dissecting the last cyst, which was also the largest, he accidentally nicked the wall, spilling the entire cyst contents—with thousands of *protoscolices*—into the peritoneal cavity. This kind of accident was tantamount to a death sentence because the thousands of *protoscolices* would grow into thousands of cysts in a matter of months, presenting a situation that was neither operable nor treatable.

We hastily suctioned as much of the cyst fluid as we could, full knowing that no matter how hard we suctioned we would still leave enough *protoscolices* to kill Abu Youssef within the coming year.

The operating room ambiance shifted from hopefulness to gloom, and silence swallowed all our words before they could even reach our throats. It was at that most dark of moments that lightning sparked in my head. I cleared my throat and said, "This month there was an article in the Journal of Abdominal Surgery, which advocated washing the abdominal cavity with 70% Ethyl Alcohol after a hydatid spill."

"Were the results good?" growled Dr. Ibraheem with eyes gaping from above his surgical mask.

"They reported a total of twelve cases."

"And, what was the outcome?"

"Two survived, one after two and the other after three subsequent surgeries."

"So, it didn't work, right?"

"Well, two out of twelve is about 17%, which is better than zero."

"Okay, please Muna, hurry up and get us a gallon of 70% Ethyl Alcohol from the pharmacy."

While Muna and Nuha retracted, giving us good exposure, I poured the alcohol into the belly cavity and Dr. Ibraheem suctioned it out. Caught in the moment's enthusiasm, and about half way into the gallon, the suction tip nicked a small intestinal vessel, causing a minor bleed. Without much thought, as if moved by habit's well-established automatism, Dr. Ibraheem put out his hand and commanded, "Cautery, please."

Without hesitation, Nuha handed him the tool, which he used to cauterize the bleeding vessel. At the first spark, with the abdomen full of un-suctioned alcohol, a sudden conflagration exploded, cinched our eyebrows, and melted our gloves. Instinctively, we all pulled away from the operating table, leaving the anesthetized patient to his blue abdominal fire.

Seized by an overwhelming sense of helpless confusion, and suffering from the sharp pains of our burns, none of us could think clearly to know what to do. None of us, that is, except Rabeeah, the nurse anesthetist, who shouted at the top of her voice while still holding the anesthetic reins, "Get some blankets and put out the fire before we all burn to death."

Startled from their shock, Muna and Nuha rushed to the side cupboard and threw blankets to us. It was only then that Dr. Ibraheem and I managed to put out the fire. Amazingly, the abdominal skin was not charred and, after changing gloves, I was able to close the skin with relative ease.

The next day at rounds, Abu Youssef looked like he was feeling quite well. Dr. Ibraheem cautiously approached the bed with chart in hand and queried.

"Abu Youssef, how do you feel today?"

"Oh, fine, fine, Doctor. Thank you. Thank you so very much."

After checking Abu Youssef's wound and listening to his heart, Dr. Ibraheem queried again, "Do you have any complaints?"

"Oh, no, no, Doctor, my wound burns a bit, but I feel good."

"Well then, I'll see you tomorrow."

"Oh, well Doctor, I do have some strange feelings but I'm sure they will soon pass."

"What kind of strange feelings?"

"Well, I feel like I've had too much to drink. I used to get that way when I would drink too much *arak*."

"Ah, surely, this feeling would be gone by tomorrow."

"And, Doctor, I also have this strange smell in my nose."

"What smell?"

"Almost like the smell of *shish kabab* roasting on coals."

Abu Youssef was discharged a week later, having suffered no complications. At two weeks, the wound had healed well and I removed all his 33 sutures without incident. At three months, six months, nine months, and one year, Abu Youssef showed no sign of recurrence. In fact, he was as grateful to Dr. Ibraheem for having saved his life, as were all the other hydatid disease patients that Dr. Ibraheem had successfully operated on that year.

When Dr. Ibraheem's term ended and he was preparing to leave SGH, the hospital had a good-bye party for him and posted an open invitation to all his patients. Among the many who came, Abu Youssef showed up to pay his respects and brought a gift of homemade *Tabbuli* with him.

After the party was over, I tried to convince Dr. Ibraheem to let me report the case. I even had the title ready: *The Cure of a Hydatid Spill with Abdominal Fire*. Dr. Ibraheem declined. He neither ate Abu Youssef's *Tabbuli* nor gave me permission to publish the case. His last words to me were: *"You can publish it after I am dead but be sure to use fake names, fake dates, and fake places. I'd shudder in my grave if my children or grandchildren were to find out."*

Abdominal Fire, First Edition, Al-HAKEEM, Journal of the Arab American Medical Association, Spring Issue of 2010. Revised edition was completed in October of 2016.

"The" Doctor Harrison
Muskogee VAH, 1971

No matter how meticulously we plan and plot our lives, if we survive long enough, we will come to realize that our precious lives have been, almost entirely, shaped and sharpened by the wild winds of coincidence. We are the products of our times, places, genes, and happenstances, all of which are naught but coincidences beyond our control. However, forging opportunities out of happenstances is within our power and those forged opportunities might grant us novel means to reshape our otherwise immutable destinies.

"While we speak, envious time will have already fled: carpe diem, seize the day, trusting as little as possible in the next day," urges Ovid in his *Odes*. Balance that with Louis Pasteur's adage, *"In the fields of observation, coincidence does not favor except the prepared minds,"* and one can begin to apprehend the intricate clockworks of destiny.

At the medical school of The American University of Beirut, three *bibles* were, and continue to be, in perpetual circulation. I use the word, *bible*, un-capitalized, to mean tome, and to point out its root, Byblos, the Phoenician-Lebanese city from whose shore papyrus was exported, and which gave its name to the Greek nouns: *biblion*-book, and *byblos*-books.

The three *bibles* that shaped our lives as medical students were the Old & New Testaments, the Koran, and Harrison's Principles of Internal Medicine.

*

When, in 1971, I came to Oklahoma, my Arabic Bible and Harrison's tome accompanied me all the way from Beirut to Muskogee (circa 11,000 kilometers) for it was at the Muskogee VAH that I was to begin my internal medicine residency. During those B-C years, meaning those *Before-Computer years*, Harrison's tome was my life, especially during the first few months of residency when my medical confidence was thinner than rain. I still remember the conversation I had with our chief of medicine, Dr. Phipps, in September of that year. We had just finished rounds when he said, "This patient would be interesting to present at our upcoming grand rounds."

"He had an uneventful myocardial infarction," I protested. "What makes him so special?"

"Because Dr. Harrison will be our speaker, and his main interest is cardiovascular disease."

"Dr. Harrison?" I inquired. "Have you recruited a new cardiologist?"

"No," he smirked. "I'm talking about Dr. Tinsley Randolph Harrison. Does this name ring a bell?"

"Am I supposed to know him?" I asked with a sheepish voice.

"He's the founder and editor of *Harrison's Principles of Internal Medicine*, the book which never leaves your side."

"Oh," I gasped, with awe stricken face.

"Start working on your case presentation for next week's grand rounds. You will have ten minutes."

I spent that evening in our two-bed intensive care unit reviewing Mr. Morgan's chart. He came in the night before with a small inferior myocardial infarction, but had good vital signs. Nitroglycerine and Lidocaine took care of his chest pain and arrhythmias, and he quickly stabilized. Dr. Phipps favored keeping him monitored in the ICU for two more days before moving him to a regular room. We planned his discharge for the day after grand rounds, just in case Dr. Harrison would want to see him.

During that apprehension-riddled week, I lost my appetite, and my hyperbolic anxiety deprived me of restorative sleep. I spent my nights rehearsing Mr. Morgan's medical details, re-editing my ten-minute presentation, reading about arteriosclerosis, and preparing my mind to respond with confidence to questions, which Dr. Harrison might hurl at me.

*

At grand rounds, Dr. Morley and I were the only two medicine residents present. There were no other residents, no interns, and no students during those *lean years* because the Muskogee VAH had just started functioning as a teaching hospital. The rest of the meager audience in the conference room was made up of staff physicians, physician associates, nurses, and the librarian.

Dr. Harrison—lean, cheerful, unassuming, and simply dressed—sat with Dr. Phipps in the front row. Dr. Phipps opened with a brief exposé of Dr. Tinsley Randolph Harrison's legacy: his birth in Alabama in 1900, his medical education at Johns Hopkins, his chief residency at Vanderbilt, his consummate interest in cardiovascular disease, and his innumerable research and teaching activities. He then ended with this panegyric: "Professor, dean, chairman, holder of the torch of Osler, founding editor of the most influential, most international, best selling textbook of medicine in history—he has and continues to spend his life in the indomitable pursuit of knowledge, excellence, and patient care." Then, before our agape eyes, he held up for all to see, the first edition of *Harrison's Principles of Internal Medicine* published in 1950, and read the first paragraph from the first page:

No greater opportunity, responsibility, or obligation can fall to the lot of a human being than to become a physician. In the care of the suffering he needs technical skill, scientific knowledge, and human understanding. He who uses these with courage, with humility, and with wisdom will provide a unique service for his fellow man, and will build an enduring edifice of character within himself. The physician should ask of his destiny no more than this: he should be content with no less.

As I stood up, after this awe-inspiring encomium, to present my case, Dr. Harrison smiled at me and lit a cigarette. Dr. Phipps followed suit and so did several in the audience. In 1971, smoking was a *de rigueur* accouterment of medical and intellectual personae.

When my presentation ended, leaving me with wet palms and a thudding chest, Dr. Harrison stood up and, with a shimmering Georgian accent, asked, "Did you do a rectal examination on this 60 year-old man with an inferior myocardial infarction?"

"No, Sir," I replied with confidence.

"Why not?" He grinned. "It is a necessary part of the complete physical examination."

"It is contraindicated during acute myocardial infarction, Sir, because it can trigger bradyarrhythmias."

"Good answer." He grinned again. "But, don't forget to do it before discharge," he forewarned.

Then, with utter humility, this great doctor, author, researcher, and mentor, began his discussion about the risk factors of arteriosclerosis. He discoursed on hypertension, diabetes, obesity, hyperlipidemia, sedentariness, stress, and—as he lit one more cigarette—smoking. When, after an erudite presentation, he opened the floor for discussion, my hand went up first.

"Yes, young man," he grinned, looking at me with questing eyebrows.

"Sir," I began with a scattered voice. "If smoking causes arteriosclerosis, how come you are still smoking?"

"Young man," he grinned again, looking at the cigarette, pluming in his hand. "How old are you?"

"I'm 25 Sir," I answered with a blush.

"Well, I'm 71 and the best thing that can happen to me at this point would be a heart attack. I have little to lose and much to gain by dying with unscathed dignity. He then quoted from Shakespeare's *As You Like It:*

> *Last scene of all*
> *That ends this strange eventful history*
> *Is second childishness and mere oblivion*

Sans teeth, sans eyes, sans taste, sans everything.

Then, looking intently into my eyes, he admonished with fatherly kindness. "You, on the other hand, have a whole life to lose. Don't start because, once you begin smoking, you'll find it very hard to quit."

I did not know if I should smile or frown. The smokers in the room chuckled, and nodded their approval. Dr. Phipps saved the moment when he stood up, thanked Dr. Harrison, and concluded the conference with this question:

"What is the single, most valuable advice you can give our doctors in training?"

Without a hint of hesitation, Dr. Harrison replied, "Be thorough. Be thorough at any cost. Never resort to shortcuts to save time. Saving time, at the expense of quality, can prove deadly to your patients and to your reputations."

*

Before I discharged Mr. Morgan, I told him that I needed to do a rectal exam to complete his admission medical examination. He refused. I insisted and informed him that if he did not allow me to complete my medical examination, I would have to discharge him against medical advice, which could have dire health consequences. After tense debate, he acquiesced, and upon preforming the examination, I discovered a rectal mass, which surprised both him and me, and radically changed our tendentious views. We both felt like we had just dodged a sniper's bullet. A sudden friendship brimmed in our eyes, the friendship that binds strangers when, together, they narrowly escape death.

His rectal cancer was successfully resected at a later date, and at discharge, he thanked me for being more stubborn than he was.

"Your stubbornness has saved my life, Doc," he intoned as he shook my hand.

"You can thank Dr. Harrison for that," I teased.

"Who is this Doctor Harrison?" He asked with a confused aspect.

"He is the author of our medical text."

"And what does he teach in this text of his?"

"He teaches that a doctor should be thorough, thorough at any cost, and should never resort to shortcuts to save time because saving time at the expense of quality can prove deadly to patients."

*

Dr. Harrison's wish of dying-with-dignity-unscathed was granted and he eluded that last scene of *second childishness and mere oblivion.* Fearless, he rejected hospitalization and died peacefully at home, in 1978, from a massive anterior myocardial infarction.* His influence, however, continues to live on through those who had the fortune of knowing him.

"The chief event of life is the day in which we have encountered a mind that startled us," said Ralph Waldo Emerson. I am a living example of this adage.

Dr. Harrison's textbook still ranks uncontested among today's medical tomes and continues to instruct doctors all over the world. As Henry Adams said, *"A teacher affects eternity; he can never tell where his influence stops."*

Tinsley Harrison, M.D., Teacher Of Medicine, by James A. Pittman Jr., M.D., 2015.

The Doctor Harrison at Muskogee VAH, 1971. First Edition, OSMA Journal, Volume 108, Number 12, Pages 593-594, January 2016. Revised Edition completed in October of 2016.

Shooing Hallucinations

It happened unexpectedly, like a lightning bolt in fair weather. But 1971 was that kind of year; the Vietnam War was raging; I was new to America; and I had never heard of DTs.

In Lebanon, we watched the Vietnam conflict explode on the black-and-white screens, but the war remained distant from our hearts and misunderstood by our minds. We had our own social problems then, our own wars to comprehend, and our own defeats to accept. America, on the other hand, was our El Dorado, the open-armed land from whose bosom all knowledge flowed, and from whose breasts all humanity fed. It was the mighty beacon of science to which we all flocked to specialize after finishing our medical training at the American University of Beirut.

Alcoholism in Lebanon was socially contained. Every town had its few *drinkers* who were contained by their families and friends. Moreover, it was legal for families to make their own distilled alcohol, *arak,* and there was plenty of it. It was also sold everywhere, even in the minutest grocery stores, and there was no age limit for buying it. Kids were allowed to drink it and often did so on festive occasions. Because it was so widely available, alcoholics never ran out of drinks, DTs were unheard of, and the term was unfamiliar to my ears.

As a first-year-resident in medicine, I was assigned to the Oklahoma City VA Hospital and my first day on the service was also my first night on call. I was busy admitting two new patients when my pager screamed, "Doctor, you're needed on 5-North. Immediately." I darted out of the emergency department, ran up the stairs, and when I reached 5-North, I found Head-Nurse Stalwart pacing in front of the elevators waiting for me.

"Oh, you used the stairs."
"It sounded urgent."

"You're the resident on call?"

"Yes, ma'am."

"I hope you can handle this situation because we can't."

On the way to Room 505, Nurse Stalwart went over the details and handed me Mr. Bowser's chart.

"He's a Vietnam Veteran who took to heavy drinking after he returned and has been at it for several months. His wife and two daughters finally gave him the ultimatum and told him that if he did not quit, they were going to leave him. He stopped drinking five days ago and started to go crazy on them the day before yesterday. He was admitted at four o'clock today and has all the right PRN orders but we can't get to him to start an IV or to administer his Valium and Thorazine."

"And why can't you get to him?"

"He's in DTs, pretty bad, and thinks that a pack of dogs is after him."

"DTs?"

"Yes!"

"What are DTs?"

Nurse Stalwart rolled back her eyes as she exclaimed, "Oh God, don't tell me..."

"No need for alarm, Ma'am." I interrupted. "I can handle it if you will just tell me what the initials stand for."

"Delirium Tremens."

"What's that?"

Nurse Stalwart lowered her eyeglasses down her nose, took one piercing look at me, and with a patronizing tone inquired, "How old are you, Son?"

"Twenty-five," I mumbled, feeling a bit intimidated.

"And you've never heard of DTs?"

"We must not have them in Lebanon," I sheepishly answered.

"Lebanon? You've no alcoholics over there?"

"Oh, we have some, indeed."

"And what happens to them when they stop drinking?"

"They don't stop drinking. In my hometown, Amioun, there are three *drinkers*—that's what we call them over there—and they're always drunk. I've never known any of them to stop drinking."

My innocent answer must have touched a motherly nerve in Nurse Stalwart's heart. Slowly, her frowns gave way to a faint gleam that glowed underneath her concerned aspect. I could almost hear her heart whisper, *"What's this poor, little man from Lebanon going to do when he sees what awaits him in 505?"* Walking toward 505, she took my arm and began educating me.

"When heavy drinkers stop drinking suddenly, they develop an alcohol-withdrawal syndrome with agitation, confusion, hallucinations, body shakes, rapid heart, high blood pressure, etc. They basically go temporarily mad, but after we hydrate them and sedate them for a few days, they come out of it and go back home."

"What do you sedate them with?"

"His admitting doctor's orders say to give him IV fluids, IV Valium, and IM Thorazine but, in case you didn't hear me say it, we're unable to get close enough to him to treat him."

"And why's that?"

"Because he's combative and thinks that the dogs are after him. That's why I paged you, Doctor."

That was the last thing she said to me before we entered Room 505. In spite of feeling profoundly ignorant, my state of mind when I walked in and surveyed the scene was inappropriately comfortable. It was merciful that youth had endowed me with an exaggerated sense of aptitude. Consequently, I took immediate charge of Operation Dogs without having the necessary knowledge to guide me. All that propelled me at that most strained moment were sheer confidence and blind faith. During my last year in Beirut, I had amputated limbs, injected adrenalin into arrested hearts, intubated lungs, and gone without sleep for 48 hours at a time. Casualties arrived in droves, it seemed, when I was on emergency call. So, what could be worse, I thought.

But here, in America, people are giants. The man stood like a colossus, twice my size, holding the room's corner with his back, thrashing like a bear at anyone who dared come close to him. His eyes were bulging, red, and paranoid. He was drooling at the mouth and barking at the top of his lungs, "Get away from me you bastards. Go away. Go on. Shoo. Shoo."

I had never seen a more massive man in my life. He looked like he could bite a tree in half and use it for toothpicks. Other orderlies and nurses hugged the walls, wearing frightened aspects and serrated lips. Chaos flickered everywhere like the lights of a police car in a crowd.

When I walked in, for some reason, everyone stood still. I must have looked ridiculously minute before that mad giant. Nevertheless, even *he* stood still, as if at attention, and waited for me to say something. At that eerie instant, the last words of my mother echoed in my ears, *"Go on to America, Son. I have prayed for you and know that God will take good care of you. Just listen to him when you are in trouble and he will guide you."*

"God's on my side," I thought, as I approached *Goliath* with not even a sling in my hand. When our eyes met, I could see dread in his and he must have seen kindness in mine because he did not seem to mind the fact that I had gotten too close to him. Stopping at about five feet away, I asked, "What's bothering you, Sir?"

"These damn hounds," he barked, pointing at the empty corner to the left of the door. "They're rabid and aim to bite me. Just don't let them get any closer. Shoo them away. They're mad. Mad dogs. All seven of them."

I surveyed the room. There was an IV pole with a liter of intravenous fluid hanging from it. I looked at all the stunned faces for a hint, a tacit suggestion, but all I saw were the blank looks of astonishment and awe. I was a little man, alone, unarmed, in the middle of an arena, with seven rabid dogs and a mad giant glaring at me. The only thought that came to my mind at that most strained moment was Dr. William Osler's adage, *"Listen to your patients and they will hand you the diagnoses and tell you what to do."* Suddenly, the giant's words came back to me like an epiphany:

"These damn hounds. They're rabid and aim to bite me. Just don't let them get any closer. Shoo them away. They're mad. Mad dogs. All seven of them."

    My external calm and small stature belied the aggression that I was about to evince. With sudden, ostentatious might, I grabbed the tall IV pole, shook off the dangling liter of IV fluid, and charged the rabid pack of dogs like a Roman gladiator with long spear. I thrashed and darted, parried and lunged, emitting fierce battle cries and scoring one fatal stab after another. "One out of seven, two out of seven, three out of seven," I shouted as I battled the rabid pack single handedly, until I had exterminated all seven of them. When I said, "Seven out of seven," I threw the IV pole onto the floor as if it were a bloody sword and, dripping with sweat, looked to the giant for approval.

    He began screaming again, "Doc. Doc. There's one more behind you. One more. Get him. Get him. Get him before he gets you and me."

    I quickly picked up the IV pole and darted again and again at where he was pointing until his screams died down. Then, still holding the IV pole in my hand, I looked to him again for approval. This time, his red eyes were no longer bulging and he had the hint of a smile on his exhausted face. I approached him with an extended hand, which he shook with gratitude. Then, leading him to his bed, I said, "The nurses need to start your IV treatment so that you can get well and go home."

    The next morning, as my team and I were making rounds with our attending physician, Mr. Bowser actually waved at me as we passed Room 505. He looked calm, was eating breakfast, and his eyes were no longer red. Nurses in the halls giggled as we passed them. Our attending, Dr. Neighbor, seemed a bit annoyed and asked, "What's going on? Did something happen that I don't know about?"

    "Nothing of significance, Sir," I reassured. "Last night I had to shoo away a hallucination and Head-Nurse Stalwart must have reported the incident in her nurse's notes."

"How interesting?" he smirked. "Shoo away a hallucination? What on earth do you mean by that?"

"It's nothing but silliness, Sir. Mr. Bowser had DTs last night and believed that rabid dogs were after him."

"And, what did you do?"

"I shooed them away."

"And how did you do that?"

"With an IV pole."

"Shooed them away with an IV pole?" He repeated as he shook his head with disbelief. "Is that what you normally do in Lebanon?"

"No, Sir. In Lebanon our *drinkers* don't have DTs because they never stop drinking."

"Perhaps you could enlighten your team and me as to why the Lebanese drunks don't ever stop drinking."

"Could I do that some other time, Sir?" I pleaded with a blush as I glanced at my watch. "I have six new patients to present to you before the ten o'clock resident's conference begins."

*

The next time I was on call, Head-Nurse Stalwart approached me with a grin and said, "I don't quite understand how you knew what to do when you had never seen DTs before? So many of those who were present are wondering the same thing."

"I really didn't know what to do when I walked into that room. Mr. Bowser was the one who gave me the clue."

"I was there, remember? I heard everything he said and he never said anything sensible."

"Oh, yes he did, but you must have failed to apprehend it."

"And what was it that I had failed to apprehend, Doctor?"

"He said, '*these damn hounds. They're rabid and aim to bite me. Just don't let them get any closer. Shoo them away. They're mad. Mad dogs. All seven of them.*' And so I did exactly as he said."

"He was babbling, Doctor, and you did exactly as he said? What on earth did he exactly say?"

"He said, *'Shoo them away,'* and that's what I did."

Shooing Hallucinations, First Edition, The Bulletin, Oklahoma County Medical Society, November/December 2014. Second Edition completed in October of 2016

Search Behind The Disease

"No matter how bright the physician, illness is always smarter. Like an onion, under every layer lurks yet another and another... We peel and peel but seldom get to the core."

These were Dr. Muchhammer's humbling remarks to us, his internal medicine team at the VA Hospital. On that day in 1972, upon hearing his declaration, we all froze with awe before our attending physician—as if he were the oracle of Delphi, pontificating from the southern slopes of Mount Parnassus.

"To become good doctors you have but to know two things, he declared:

"First, you have to know the patient, who will always remain a half-solved mystery, no matter how much he reveals to you because no patient ever tells everything.

"Second, you must know the disease otherwise you would not be able to ask the key, unlocking questions. And disease will also remain a half-solved mystery, because it continues to change with theory and with discovery."

With these precepts, Dr. Muchhammer led us on rounds, stroked patients' brows, asked infrared questions, peeled layer after layer, and then helped us deepen our shallow analyses. We yearned to learn how did he know to ask the one question, which we never thought to ask, and how did he manage to unveil for us to see—*"And see, no longer blinded by our eyes"**—the inscrutable diagnoses with hardly a test or an x-ray in hand.

One dark winter morning abuzz with admissions, we presented our cases with sleep-deprived eyes and yawning aspects, for we had admitted ten patients during our night shift. Presenting our last elderly patient, I happened to mention that he was a perennial seeker of emergency care.

"Perennial?" He asked with raised eyebrows.

"Yes, Sir. He is admitted through our emergency department about once a month, always with the same complaint, shortness of breath. His blood gases from admission till discharge stay about the same, with no measurable improvement, but he always feels better when he leaves. His emphysema has been rather stable even though he continues to smoke and drink."

"Why, then, does he seek monthly admissions?"

"I don't know, Sir," I sheepishly replied. "I've reviewed his entire chart of five volumes, but could find no clues. He seems ever the same, admission after admission, and his blood gases have never been alarming."

Dr. Muchhammer stood up, placed his palm onto the patient's piled, five-volume-chart, scrutinized our listless aspects with his glittering eyes and asked, "Did you search behind the disease?"

"Behind the disease, Sir? I'm not sure I understand what you mean."

"Search behind the disease," he muttered, and then walked away.

At the dragging tail of that laborious day, my team and I went over the patient's details, re-examined and re-questioned him, but unearthed nothing of value. My intern suggested that we visit his home to look for dust, mold, sick house syndrome, and whatever else might be hiding behind his disease. The patient granted us permission. We called his wife from his room and set our visit for the coming Saturday.

Mrs. Poumon was delightfully hospitable. She gave us a tour of her very clean house and of Mr. Poumon's equally clean woodcarving shop. "That's where he spends all of his time," she announced, pointing to his seat, table, and tidy tools. "Ever since he returned from the war, that's all he wants to do. He was much more sociable before."

Sipping coffee and munching on doughnuts, we asked Mrs. Poumon sundry questions, but uncovered no clues. On our way out, my intern asked her that one last question, which none of us thought to ask.

"Mrs. Poumon. Does the wood dust bother you, and do you cough or wheeze or suffer from any lung problems?"

"No, I feel mighty fine and Harry hardly makes any dust. I just wish he would spend more time with me and less time in his shop," she smiled, holding the doorknob in her hand. "We hardly go anywhere anymore."

Crestfallen, we thanked her and dispersed with the impending Monday morning rounds with our attending, nagging at our brains.

When Dr. Muchhammer walked in that Monday morning, he must have seen capitulation in our eyes because he asked no questions. He half-smiled and said, "Let's start with Mr. Poumon."

Sitting on Mr. Poumon's bed, Dr. Muchhammer greeted, said few words of encouragement, and then abruptly asked, "What war were you in?"

"Pearl Harbor, Sir. We didn't know we were at war when the Japs hailed bombs on us."

"What was your position?"

"We were antiaircraft gunners on the USS Nevada, Sir."

"We?"

"Me and my buddy. James Lovelorn was his name."

"Was?"

"Under the orders of Ensign Joe Taussig Jr. we were returning fire against bombers that were targeting us when we sustained a direct hit from a torpedo. Parts of the ship started to burn, smoke was everywhere, and..."

At this point, Mr. Poumon choked, gulped, and his lips began to quiver. We stood in silence and watched Dr. Muchhammer grasp Mr. Poumon's hand, bow his head as if in prayer, and whisper, "And what happened to James?"

Mr. Poumon collected himself, cleared his throat, adjusted his sniffling nasal prongs, and whispered back, "A shrapnel beheaded him while he sat right next to me, Doc. There he was, sitting without a head, his body twitching, with blood spewing from his neck like a geyser..."

Another moment of silence...
Dr. Muchhammer handed a tissue to Mr. Poumon and waited.

"I began to choke on the bellowing smoke, but continued to return fire until I was blown into the harbor and began to drown. I held on to a floating body, which happened to have its life vest on. *Under water I would drown. Over water I would choke and burn with the burning oil.* That's all I could think about while I clung to that dead man's life vest."

Another moment of silence...

"And who rescued you?"
"I have no idea, Doc. I woke up on a hospital ship with burns all over my body and a horrible heat in my lungs."
"May I see your burns?" Asked Dr. Muchhammer.
Mr. Poumon pulled up his sleeves and uncovered his legs for us to see.
"The burns were superficial, Sir, but what got me was the smoke. I coughed for years and I'm still coughing, but not nearly as bad as before. About once a month, though, when I get into a bad coughing spell, it sends me back to Pearl Harbor and I truly believe that I am choking to death. That's what scares me so bad and makes me rush to the emergency room."

Sweat began to accumulate on our sallow faces, not the sweat of awe or embarrassment, but rather that of epiphany. Dr. Muchhammer was revealing to us, layer by layer, the scorched landscape behind Mr. Poumon's disease.
"So, do you think that re-living your fear is what sends you to the emergency room each month?"
"Yes, Sir. You just hit the nail on the head. I flat out panic and think that I'm choking and dying."

"If we were to take care of your fear, you wouldn't panic, would you?"

"I didn't know there were treatments for fear, Sir, which is why I've never told a soul..."

In the early seventies, even though the Vietnam War was still raging, the posttraumatic stress disorder syndrome, though partially remediable, was not yet a fashionable diagnoses. Nevertheless, under good psychiatric care, Mr. Poumon's *panic* admissions ceased and, in time, he was able to stop drinking and smoking. However, his incessant woodcarving, which was his self-discovered occupational therapy, continued unabated. For a while, I kept in touch with him by phone, calling him occasionally for a friendly chat. At the end of that year, Dr. Muchhammer received a wood-carved *USS Nevada* from Mr. Poumon. On the hull, the following words were inscribed: *To Dr. Muchhammer, with gratitude. Harry Poumon.*

*

When Dr. Muchhammer's rotation ended, we grieved, but his indelible impact never left our medical minds. We spent the rest of our medical careers investigating the triad of patient, disease, and that undiscovered landscape, which always lurks behind the disease.

> *Learn all we lacked before; hear, know, and say*
> *And feel, who have laid our groping hands away;*
> *What this tumultuous body now denies;*
> *And see, no longer blinded by our eyes.*
> *From The South Seas Sonnet by Rupert Brooke (1887-1915)

Search Behind The Disease, First Edition, Page 20-24, The Bulletin, September/October 2015. Revised Edition completed in October of 2016.

Professor Ley Haw

I have been reticent about relating these indecorous happenings because they will be understood and misunderstood, placed in and out of context, eulogized, condemned, and used for both parable and parody. But, in spite of Oscar Wilde's admonition that, *"Truth is rarely pure, and never simple,"* I have resolved to tell my side of the story about my esteemed friend and mentor, Professor Ley Haw, whose name and details I have camouflaged beyond anyone's recognition. *"What's in a name?"* the bard had Juliet say. *"That which we call a rose / By any other name would smell as sweet."*

My intention here is to preserve the sweet memory of these happenings and jettison all the names appended to them as I would the envelope that holds within it, a most secretive letter from a most esteemed friend.

Because I cannot reveal the truth about where Professor Haw was born nor how he was raised, I will merely relate that he was raised by his grandmother who, throughout his formative years, summoned him by the most endearing nickname of *Scheistekopf*. He thought so highly of his sainted grandmother that after her untimely passing he reverently resolved to change his name from Ley to *Scheistekopf*. However, because of certain, unavoidable, bureaucratic delays he could not actuate the name change before he had gone to college. Happenstance would have it that he decided to take German during his freshman year and was surprised when Herr Helmut, his German teacher, upon learning of his nickname, smirked from behind his raised eyebrows and bushy mustache and explained to the unsuspecting student that *Scheistekopf* meant shithead. It took young Ley Haw many a doleful moon before he recovered from his grandmother's posthumous, scatological nomenclature.

I first encountered Professor Haw when I was a surgical intern. He was so famed for his fast, exacting, operative technique that one of our first internship assignments was to watch him operate. I remember watching his fingers move like a sewing machine, placing sutures into the grafted coronary arteries in perfect cadence, exactly one millimeter apart, making them look more like a zipper than a hand-made suture line. His face, hidden behind his operating microscope and mask, remained invisible throughout that two-hour operation, which I was later told would have taken any other cardiac surgeon at least three-and-a-half hours to complete. That was the only time I saw Professor Haw during that surgical rotation, and I was not fortunate enough to spend any more time with him until four years later when I had finished my general surgical training and decided to specialize in cardiovascular surgery.

Rounding with Professor Haw was an electrifying experience because he often shocked us with his lightning wit. He could take the most pressured situation and, by poking fun at it, discharge the compressed voltage with a roaring laugh. We all feared and liked him, as one who fears the mighty aircraft but would, nevertheless, hurry to board it. Indeed, his rounds were flight rounds because he moved as fast as he sutured, and we all scurried behind him enthralled, awed, entertained. Every one of us wanted to become Professor Haw, but deep inside, we all knew that as a man and as a surgeon, he was both inimitable and un-emulate-able.

One morning after rounds, he surprised us by inviting us to dinner at his home. "I'm cooking this coming Saturday," he said, "and you'd better come hungry and be prepared to eat and drink; I don't trust a man who doesn't drink although I do trust a man whose wife doesn't because she can be the designated driver."
"Casual?" I asked.
"Red shirts for all of you budding surgeons," he repartied. "It hides the wine stains."
"What time?" I queried.

"Sunset, and be punctual," he affirmed, wagging his finger at us. "Late comers will be turned back," he added with a smirk and then whiffed away, leaving all four of us wondering when would the sun, set on that Saturday.

Before I had seen him in his social feathers, Professor Haw was an awed academic icon, who inspired excellence, but strode too fast for anyone's supplication. Naturally, my fellow residents and I rang his doorbell at exactly at 6:02 p.m., the posted sunset time of that Saturday. His wife, an aromatic bouquet of smiles, gave us a blithe, alacritous welcome and with a wave of her lean, ballerina arm pointed and said, "He's in the kitchen waiting for you guys."

"Come in boys and have a seat at the counter," he ordered as he stirred and tasted the multiple pots simmering atop his eight-headed gas stove. "I'm cooking *osso bucco* and have been at it all day. You'd better like it otherwise you'll be eating pizza."

"What's *osso bucco*?" I asked, unabashed at my culinary ignorance.

"A dish of veal shanks braised with vegetables, white wine, and seasoned stock. It's the stock reduction that consumes inordinate time."

"And the name? Is it Italian?" I tested.

Inspecting his pots with his back to us, he explained, "Yes, literally, veal shank, a Tuscan rendering of Milanese *òs büs*, from *osso* bone, from Latin *ossum* + *buco* pierced, short past participle of *bucare* to pierce, from *buca* hole. Now, stop asking questions and pour us some wine. Let's start with the 2008 Grgich Hill Violetta."

I raised my eyebrows to my fellow residents as if to inquire if anyone had heard of Violetta wine. Seeing no response, I pulled the chilled bottle out of the sweaty silver cooler and poured. The aroma wafted like the sweet night breeze from an orange orchard, but we dared not raise the glasses to our lips until he looked at us and toasted, "To life, love, and laughter."

"Wonderful, magnificent, delicious, and amazing," were the four adjectives issued by our titillated tongues.

"It's a late-harvest Napa Valley wine blend of Sauvignon Blanc, Riesling, and some Gewurztraminer, which depends on *Botrytis cinerea*, a special fungus that permeates the grapes' skins, concentrating the sugar and flavors. It goes well with this *Gruyère* cheese because they both have a hint of sweetness that is too delicate to savor as dessert and more *à propos comme hors d'œuvres*."

The conversation took off after the second bottle of Violetta was sipped from thin-lipped crystal glasses among witticisms and humor. As we became more discursive, he held back his tongue and let us have the stage. Occasionally he would interject a blue flame or a red spark that would startle us. The one that pierced me because I could not understand what he meant by it was, *"The poor don't know what they're missing."*

I looked to my fellow residents and felt reassured when I saw that they had equally stunned faces. Our silence must have irked him because he gazed at us with consternation before he elaborated, "I was very poor for a very long time and had no idea what I was missing. Some truths are by their very nature shameful, but that should not provide us with an excuse to euphemize. 'Truth, for any man, is that which makes him a man,' said Antoine de Saint-Exupéry. The *osso bucco* is ready. Let's eat."

At dinner, he quoted widely, effortlessly, and shamelessly. Nothing that he said seemed serious at first but after we had time to digest it, it acquired a cupric patina that was unmistakably grave. By the time the evening ended, we felt a formidable web of friendship that tethered us together against the chilling winds of medical life.

"Among friends, one can never have too much wine," was his last remark, "unless one is driving, of course," he giggled. "And one must never drink and drive, without wearing one's seatbelt," he giggled again.

At the door, we found a taxi waiting for us. "Leave your cars here, boys, and come back for them tomorrow. The taxi has already been paid to take you to your homes. Run along now and apologize to your wives for staying out so late. If they're like my wife, they would already be asleep. Make it up to them tomorrow, if you know what I mean, just to be polite."

Another year passed as we all followed Professor Haw around, assisting him on surgeries, and learning as much from him as we could hold. One morning, after a particularly difficult coronary bypass surgery on a patient with bad kyphosis, he smiled while we were changing in the locker room and asked, "Would you like to accompany me to Paris?"

"Paris," I gasped as the words went dry in my throat.

"Paris, France, not Paris, Texas," he teased.

"You mean, Paris, when, what for, eh, I can't think."

"I have an invitation to spend a week with Dr. Carpentier and am allowed to bring one resident along."

"Dr. Alain Carpentier, the father of modern-mitral-valve repair and the head the Department of Cardiovascular Surgery at the Hôpital Européen Georges Pompidou in Paris?" I spewed, as if I had memorized these lines especially for that occasion.

"You know about him?" he smiled again.

"Who doesn't? Besides his innumerable awards, wasn't he the one who published the seminal paper on mitral valve repair entitled *The French Correction*?"

"More important than all of that pomp is the fact that he is one of the foremost medical philanthropists in the world: he has established a premier cardiac center in Vietnam where over 1,000 open-heart cases are now performed annually, and has also founded cardiac surgery programs in 17 French-speaking countries in Africa."

"How much will the trip cost?" I asked.

"It won't cost you anything."

"When do we leave?"

"In two weeks."

"Oh, no, we're expecting our first child in two weeks."

"Well then, I'll take someone else. Your firstborn may prove far more important than Dr. Carpentier. Remember what James

Agee said, *'In every child who is born, under no matter what circumstances, and of no matter what parents, the potentiality of the human race is born again'.*"

"But this is the chance of a lifetime," I lamented.

"Expect less and get it, young man. I'd hate for you to waste your life resuscitating dreams."

Professor Haw returned from Paris with myriad ideas and numerous tales. He told us that after operating all morning, Dr. Carpentier would invite all his visiting associates to a one-hour lunch at a five star restaurant, order a glass of his favorite *Nuits St Georges* wine for everyone including himself, enjoy an exotic meal, and then return to the operating room to operate for the rest of the afternoon. When one of us remarked that if Dr. Carpentier were operating here, he wouldn't dare have a drink before going back to the operating room, Professor Haw nonchalantly retorted, "One has to sin occasionally to feel righteous most of the time."

Our last year of residency was also our best because we became the main operators on most cases while Professor Haw assisted, instructed, and meticulously critiqued our operative techniques. One day we had started with an emergency at 5 a.m., did two more emergency cases at the end of the day, and could not leave the hospital till 10:30 p.m. When Professor Haw's old Mercedes would not start because he had left his morning lights on, I offered him a ride, which he graciously accepted. Feeling exhausted, each of us rehearsed the happenings of that day in utter silence, hardly exchanging a word, until we arrived at his home. Out of polite reverence, I got out of my car and walked with him to his door. He smiled at me as he pulled out his keys and said, "I would ask you in but I'm afraid you would accept."

"Do you need a morning ride?" I laughed. "I'll also bring my jumper cables."

"Pick me up at 6 a.m.," he bowed, and disappeared behind his door.

Next morning, on the way to work, I told him about Mrs. Solomon, whom I had seen in the clinic last week. He listened intently as I related the details of the case. "She is 90, sharp, wealthy, and fit, but is going into rapid heart failure because of severe mitral valve degeneration, which is compounding her severe aortic valve stenosis. I don't think that she has more than a week or two unless we operate. She's our first case this morning."

"You scheduled a 90 year old lady for a double valve replacement without discussing it with me?" He roared.

"She told me that she preferred an operative death to a heart failure death."

"You're resorting to euphemisms again."

"Euphemisms?" I griped, surprised at his word choice.

"Was she the one who told you that she preferred an operative death to a heart failure death, or are these your own word selections."

"Well, I don't recall her exact words, but that's what she meant."

"Since she's wealthy, why didn't you advise her to go to Belgium?"

"Belgium? They're not better than we are, here."

"Euthanasia is legal in Belgium and much cleaner than an operative death."

"Would you like me to cancel her surgery?"

"No, let me talk to her first."

We met Mrs. Solomon in the surgical waiting area. The anesthesiologist had already visited her and there was an intravenous line dripping into her arm. As we approached, she sat up and greeted us with a raspy voice, bright-blue eyes, and a sparkling smile.

"You must be, eh, the famous Dr. Haw," she gasped, extending a shaky hand toward him.

Dr. Haw, in the French tradition, bowed and kissed her hand with slow, regal grace.

"Did you also, eh, learn that from, eh, the famous Dr., eh, Carpentier?" She thrice gasped before she finished her sentence.

"Do you know him?" he smiled.

"I make regular, eh, donations, eh, to his artificial heart, eh, project, and was one, eh, of the invitees, eh, when he received, eh, the 1996 Prix mondial, eh, Cino Del Duca." She replied, gasping repeatedly, and looking exhausted by the time she had finished that long sentence.

Professor Haw waited until she had regained her breath. He then increased her oxygen flow to 6 liters and gently asked, "How did you two get connected?"

"Simone Del Duca, eh, his wife, née Nirouet, eh, is my cousin." She gasped, unimproved by the increased oxygen flow. "I was at her wedding, eh, when she married, eh, Cino Del Duca. My father Armand, eh, and her father Henri, eh, were brothers."

Having said that, her smile languished into an exhausted surrender, but her eyes remained wide open, and bright with light.

Professor Haw smiled, sat by her bed, listened carefully to her heart, and then whispered, *"Êtes-vous vraiment préparé, madame?"*[1]

"Je suis certainement, eh, préparé pour votre, eh, magie Carpentiere,"[2] she whispered and then closed her eyes.

In the locker room and while scrubbing, Professor Haw was silent and remained silent until the anesthesiologist, Dr. Salamander, declared that Mrs. Solomon was ready. Only then, Professor Haw looked at the entire team, standing at attention, and whispered, "She's ninety and frail. The faster we do it, the better her chances. This is not an ordinary operation; this is a race until life or death."

The ensuing four hours were charged with battle fever as we all worked with engine precision like a trained SWAT team executing a mission with fearful speed. Professor Haw's fingers moved with synchronous harmony like a virtuoso pianist playing Franz Liszt's Piano Concerto #1, which calls for its four movements to be performed without a break. He replaced the aortic valve first

---

[1] Are you really ready, Madam?
[2] I am certainly prepared for your Carpentier magic.

and then turned on his *magie Carpentiere*[3], replacing the mitral valve with brisk exactitude and inimitable ease.

When it was all done, we held our breaths as we watched his hands grasp the defibrillator paddles, place them on each side of the arrested heart, and deliver his first shock. Nothing happened. A second shock followed and a third, but the heart would not re-start. Our exhausted eyes were focused on a ninety-year-old mended heart that refused to re-start. For a flash, perhaps wanting to escape the potential irreversibility of that horrifying moment, I thought of Professor Haw's old Mercedes, lying pulseless in the garage, waiting for me to jumpstart it.

"Dr. Salamander, please lighten up the anesthetic a bit; I don't think her heart is going to revive otherwise," commanded Dr. Haw.

Five minutes passed, another three shocks ensued, and then another plea was issued to Dr. Salamander to lighten up the anesthetic even more.

"If I lighten her up any more, she might wake up while her chest is still open," cautioned Dr. Salamander.

"Lighten her up one more time or else we're going to lose her," retorted Professor Haw with a parched voice.

Another five minutes ensued and another three shocks followed, but her nonagenarian heart would not re-start. Dr. Haw laid the defibrillator paddles down over her open chest, looked at me with brimming eyes, and lamented, "One more time, and if it doesn't re-start, we go to lunch."

We all froze in the gravity of that moment. If the heart doesn't re-start, the blood pump will be turned off, she will be extubated, and all her lines will be removed. Then the junior resident will close up her chest with a few steel sutures. After that, the nurses will tidy up her body, cover it with a white shroud, and quietly wheel her to the morgue. Professor Haw and I will go to the family room, tell her children and grandchildren what happened,

---

[3] Carpentier magic.

and then we'll all go to lunch and try to forget that we have lost that morning's battle and that woman's war.

We might remember some things at certain times, but given that our natures tend to readily forget our failures, we would resist remembering the inglorious in order to make room for the glorious. Lines from Robert Frost's *Home Burial* assailed me:

> *No, from the time when one is sick, to death,*
> *One is alone, and dies more alone.*
> *Friends make pretense of following to the grave,*
> *But before one is in it, their minds are turned*
> *And making the best of their way back to life*
> *And living people, and things they understand.*

We all froze as Professor Haw lifted the defibrillator paddles into the air as if he were lifting a fervent prayer. He then placed them carefully on both sides of the heart and pushed the button. Her entire body jerked, no doubt because her muscles had been awakened from their deep anesthetic repose. The heart quivered, then wiggled, then churned, like a car trying to start from a rundown battery. Then we heard a small monitor beep followed by a weak heart contraction, as if a frail fist was attempting one last grasp at life. Slowly, the contractions grew stronger and the beeps more rhythmic. Dr. Salamander bellowed, "She has a pulse." The operating room burst in grateful sighs and gleeful cheers as I began closing up her chest and Professor Haw left to talk to the family.

We did go out to lunch when all was done, but were afraid to order Champagne. "It is unfortunate that what I drank with Dr. Carpentier in Paris would be frowned upon here," he smirked. "Sometimes, a glass of Champagne is necessary to commemorate a triumphant moment."

These were Professor Haw's last words to me before we left the restaurant and plowed back into the operating room to finish our last two cases.

I did jump his car that evening, and it did start after some whining and churning.

"You need a new Mercedes," I quipped.

"Do you have any idea how much they cost these days?"

"I hear that a big one like yours goes for about eighty-five thousand?"

"Well, that's like the ten thousand dollar hooker."

"Ten thousand dollar hooker?" I laughed with surprised eyes. "What on earth does that mean?"

"It means that she might be worth it but I'm not," he giggled as he got into his old Mercedes and drove off.

Three days later, when Mrs. Solomon was extubated and discharged from the ICU, we walked into her private room to find her sitting, her big-blue eyes bright with expectation.

"I can talk now, and am no longer gasping for air," she chirruped. "Your *magie Carpentiere* worked. What a small, intricate world?"

"I am overjoyed, Madam," replied Dr. Haw with a bow. " 'All's well that ends well.' Do you have any questions?"

"No, not really. I knew that you were joking and that's why I never worried."

"Joking? Joking about what, Mrs. Solomon?"

"You know," she chirruped again, "when you said, 'One more time and if it doesn't re-start, we go to lunch.' "

*

When I left Professor Haw's cardiac surgery program, I was an enlightened man who had learned to merge humor with tragedy, grief with play, excellence with independence, and merit with humility. It took four years under his mentorship before I fully understood what Ralph Waldo Emerson meant when he said: *"The chief event of life is the day in which we have encountered a mind that startled us."*

And what Henry Adams meant when he said: *"A teacher affects eternity; he can never tell where his influence stops."*

Pilot Error

"Any consults?" asked Tavşan, my teen-aged daughter, as I walked in after my fifth day as an infectious disease consultant at Mercy Hospital in Oklahoma City.

"None," I grumbled, half kissing her cheek.

"They're about to show the first flight of the space shuttle, Enterprise," she said excitedly. "Let's watch it together?"

"I have work to do, Darling."

"What work? You've just ended your first week with no consults."

"I need to address the announcement cards. It's the first time Mercy Hospital has an infectious disease consultant on its staff."

"Oh, here it is."

"Here's what?"

"The Enterprise," she giggled.

"Friday, August 12, 1977 is a memorable day for America," announced Walter Cronkite on the CBS Evening News.

Having qualified in infectious diseases, I had spent that entire week arranging my office and waiting for phone calls, which never came. Returning home that Friday evening, empty handed, doubled my medical debt and halved my confidence. Worrisome thoughts assailed me as I busied myself addressing the announcement cards. Alone, Tavşan watched the Enterprise take off atop a Boeing 747 on its first, free atmospheric flight.

When the phone rang, later that night, I heard Tavşan say, "Yes, it is. Yes. Sure, let me get him for you."

Her footsteps hurried. I stopped addressing and turned around. When she appeared at my door, her lips glimmered with a smile as three words leapt out together from her excited throat.

"It's the hospital."

I steadied my voice. My pounding chest heaved a deep, stuttering sigh. I picked up the receiver. It was nine o'clock.

"Hello, this is Dr. Hawi."

"Hi, Doc." rang an alacritous voice. "This is Frances, the charge nurse on 3A. Dr. Lapins needs you to see Mr. Lepores in 307. He has pneumonia and is not responding to antibiotics."

"What's he on?"

"He was started on I.V. Cefazolin three days ago, and erythromycin was added yesterday."

"How old is he?"

"Fifty-two."

"Is he very ill?"

"He's on oxygen, but seems stable."

"What does he do?"

"He's a...."

Tavşan listened attentively as Nurse Frances answered my incessant questions. When I stood up to leave, she snuggled her arms around my neck and chortled, "This is the consult you've been waiting for all week long, Daddy."

"I don't know when I'll be back, Dear, but you need to be in bed by ten."

On my way to the hospital, I ruminated over Nurse Frances's details. He works as a commercial pilot for Pan Am, which means that he could have acquired his pneumonia anywhere on earth. My head spun with myriad, far-fetched possibilities, which I had studied during my preparation for the infectious disease board.

Before going up to his room, I reviewed the chest x-rays. The pneumonia was bilateral, patchy, and involved mainly the lower lobes. At the microbiology laboratory, his blood cultures were still negative. When I arrived at the floor, Nurse Frances was waiting for me with the chart in her hand. She was white-haired, fleshy, grandmotherly, and wore an affable smile.

"You must be Dr. Hawi, the infectious disease detective," she quipped, handing me the chart. "Thank you for coming at such a late hour."

I thanked her with a somber bow and sat down with the chart. Besides the high white count and high fever, his chart details were not helpful.

"You know he flew B52s in Vietnam," she volunteered, as I handed back the chart.

"That further complicates matters," I sighed.

"But, that was several years ago?"

"Some bacteria can lie dormant for years," I replied, with ostentatious authority.

When I knocked at room 307's door, it was close to ten. Mr. Lepores was sitting in a chair, looking flushed and uncomfortable. He was tall, gray-headed, and wore a pencil mustache that was conspicuously darker than the rest of his hair.

"Hello. I am Dr. Hawi, the infectious disease specialist."

"It's awful nice of you to come see me this late, Doc," he gasped, and shook my hand. "Excuse me for not standing."

I sat on the bed and, after exchanging a few polite snippets of conversation, I asked, "Can you tell me how it all began?"

"I flew in from Philadelphia two weeks ago and was doing some needed work around the house, when I felt the first chill."

"When was that?"

"Last Monday."

"Had you flown outside the continental US during the past month?"

"Not even during the past year, Doc."

For an entire hour I interrogated him. "Have you been in contact with parrots, rats, old barns, attics, ticks, mosquitoes, excrement, sewage, water towers, etc.? Have you been hunting, fishing, camping, hiking, rafting, spelunking, etc.?"

By the time eleven o'clock struck, we were both exhausted and frustrated, having uncovered no clues. I examined him. He was hot, his breaths and heart were rapid, and his lung bases were moist with rales. His cough was dry and I could not get him to expectorate any sputum. Sputum microscopy was one of my fortes, and without it I felt disarmed.

"Do you have any idea what I have, Doc.?" he asked, sensing my frustration.
"Not yet, but I know that I need to change your antibiotics."
"Good. That already makes me feel better. I'm not allergic to anything.

I left Mr. Lepores's room with a heavy heart. Nurse Frances, who was signing off her shift, looked at me with tired eyes and handed me his chart. I wrote my consultation note, discontinued his antibiotics, ordered intravenous doxycycline, and handed the chart back.

"Why doxycycline?" she quizzed.
"It's good for unusual pneumonias."
"So, is that your diagnosis? Unusual pneumonia?"
"It's my working diagnosis, until I can come up with a better one."

At home, I found Tavşan waiting for me. My tired, disillusioned expression promptly wiped off her smile. She said, "Good night," and retired to her room.

After a restless night, I spent Saturday morning going through my pneumonia files, hoping for an epiphany. By noon, I had half made up my mind to bronchoscope Mr. Lepores if he had not improved on doxycycline. Bronchoalveolar lavage could prove helpful and is not as risky as a lung biopsy.

At lunch, seeing my tired face, Tavşan asked no questions. As we ate in silence, the phone rang, startling us both. It was Nurse Frances again.
"Dr. Hawi. Mr. Lepores just spiked a temperature of 105."

Driving to the hospital, I wondered if he were having a Herxheimer reaction to the doxycycline. *"It could be a good sign or* else he's getting worse," I thought. *"There is no pulmonologist on the hospital staff, which means that I would have to be the one to intubate him and place him on the respirator."*

I raced up to the third floor and rushed to Nurse Frances who, with troubled eyes, handed me the fever chart.

"He seems to have gotten worse since you stopped his antibiotics and started the doxycycline. His blood gases remain about the same but take a look at these vital signs..."

"It could be a Herxheimer reaction to all the bacteria being killed by the doxycycline," I explained. "Sometimes, patients seem worse when they're actually getting better."

I was still panting from having raced up the stairs when, together, we walked into room 307. Mr. Lepores lay quietly in bed, flushed, and listless.

"Mr. Lepores. Are you feeling worse?" I asked, as I sat by his side.

"Yes, Doc, I think I've gotten worse since you changed my antibiotics."

I re-examined him. His heart rate was as high as his fever, 105, and he was breathing 30 times a minute. I doubled his oxygen and, seeing that it hardly made a difference, decided to move him to the intensive care unit.

"Mr. Lepores. I think we can take better care of you in the intensive care unit."

"Oh, no, please," he suddenly screamed, as if awakened from a nightmare. "No ICU for me," he pleaded. "It brings back memories from Nam. I've lost many a buddy in Nam's ICUs."

Seeing the dread in his eyes, I quickly reassured him by saying that we can take care of him equally well in his room, and that the respiratory therapists can bring in the needed equipment and set it up by his bedside. I said all that without knowing if that kind of arrangement was even possible. Then, noting Nurse Frances's disapproving look, I motioned for her to follow me out. At the door, a lean, attractive blonde in her twenties, wearing a white

T-shirt and black denim pants, burst in and, with big, blue eyes, surveyed the scene.

"Hi, I'm his daughter, Bonny. How's he doing?"

"Hi, Bonny," greeted Nurse Frances. "This is Dr. Hawi, the infectious disease specialist."

We shook hands, and then I apprised her of her father's condition, making sure that Mr. Lepores heard every word. She became perturbed, gazed at her flushed, panting father, then looked me straight in the eye and reprimanded, "You mean to tell me that after six days in the hospital y'all still don't know what kind of pneumonia he's got?"

"I'm afraid not," I murmured, avoiding her gaze.

"So, what's next?"

"I am leaning toward looking down his lungs with a scope."

"So why don't you?"

"It's not an easy thing to do on someone who is already air-hungry."

"But, if you wait, he will get air-hungrier, won't he?" She snapped.

I paused, knowing that she was right in concept but wrong in fact. Indeed, I was procrastinating because I doubted that bronchial washings would hand me a prompt diagnosis. What I really needed was a lung biopsy, but getting it would be much riskier although more definitive. By the time I was ready to share these thoughts with her, tears were dripping from her cheeks, her lips were livid with worry, and her hands clenched her little black purse as if her entire life was stashed inside of it. Nurse Frances—trying to help me out of that awkward moment by paraphrasing what I had said earlier about the Herxheimer reaction—unwittingly heightened Bonny's anxiety with, "Sometimes, things have to get worse before they get better."

Appearing defeated, Bonny reached into her purse, pulled out a white tissue, and commenced to nervously blot her tears. Then, as if the white fluff reminded her of something important, she looked askance at her dad and asked, "Did he tell you about the rabbit?"

"Rabbit? What rabbit?" I jumped with unconcealed excitement.

"Oh, honey, I never touched that poor thing," came Mr. Lepores's protestation from across the room.

"But, Daddy," she screamed. "It could be a clue. Why don't you tell the doctor what happened and let him decide?"

I walked back to Mr. Lepores's bedside and pleaded, "Please, do tell us about the rabbit."

He repositioned himself, glared disapprovingly at his daughter, and related the story with a hoarse, embarrassed tone:

"I was on my riding mower in some tall grass. All of a sudden, the blades caught a white rabbit and scattered it all around me. It was too late to stop and so I kept on mowing, but never touched anything."

"Mr. Lepores," I teased. "Do you think a healthy rabbit would let you mow it down?"

"I guess not," he agreed. "I reckon it must have been sick or dead."

"What does that mean, Doc.?" asked Bonny, seeing the relief on my face.

"It means that your dad has rabbit fever, or tularemia pneumonia, which he acquired by inhaling the infected droplets of the scattered rabbit."

"Does this mean that now you know what to do?"

Before I could respond, Nurse Frances handed me the chart on which I added the stat Gentamycin order.

When I arrived home that evening, I found Tavşan in the living room, excitedly watching the first landing of the Enterprise...

"And that's the way it is on Saturday, August 13, 1977," came Walter Cronkite's departing catchphrase. Indeed, that day was memorable for both America and me.

Pilot Error, First Edition, OSMA Journal, Volume 107, Number 11, November 2014, pages 584-586. Second Edition completed in October of 2016.

Good Morning Professor Columbam

<u>1977</u>

"You're too young," she gasped, as I walked into the examination room.

"Good morning, Professor Columbam," I smiled, and then introduced myself.

"Are you sure you're qualified?" she sparred. "I expected a much older doctor."

I smiled again as I shook her upheld, ballerina hand. Delicate, tremulous fingers lingered in my palm as she eyed me with gleaming curiosity. I sat down facing her and readied my fountain pen.

I was thirty then and Professor Edna Columbam was sixty-nine, with hair tightly *doughnutted* over her head and eyeglasses leisurely tethered to a gold chain around her neck. A navy-blue business suit and high-heeled matching shoes framed her lean figure and graceful legs.

In response to my entering the time and date on her chart, she crossed her legs and rearranged her skirt, making sure it lingered a few inches above her knees.

"I hope you are well," I began, feeling a bit intimidated by her commanding elegance.

"Do I look well to you?" she smirked with questing eyes.

"You look strikingly well," I blushed, furtively peering at her swan-like pose.

"Appearances are how we wish to be seen, and are always at variance with who we truly are."

"Who said that?" I asked, with piqued interest.

"Is there anyone else in the room?" she rebuked with roaming eyes.

I was new then to the art of deciphering personas, especially inscrutable ones like Professor Columbam's. My meek response to her rebuke came out as a personal question.

"Are you an English Literature Professor?" I ventured.

"You are either unseasonably perceptive or impudently inquisitive," she replied with pronounced eloquence.

"Your precise and elegant use of language gave you away."

My pronouncement must have strummed her strings because she tilted her head, looked straight into my eyes, rearranged her skirt, and quoted:

> *Appearances to the mind are of four kinds:*
> *Things either are what they appear to be;*
> *Or they neither are, nor appear to be;*
> *Or they are, and do not appear to be;*
> *Or they are not, and yet appear to be.*

"*Rightly to aim in all these cases is the wise man's task,*" I added, finishing the quote.

"I see, you are familiar with Epictetus," she gazed approvingly. "So few these days are dedicated to literature and philosophy, which leaves us, the intellectual few, rather lonesome."

Professor Edna Columbam and I quietly bonded after our initial encounter. To her I was an apprentice member of the intellectual few and to me she represented the fading grace of an insular generation, being submerged under the rising tide of commercialism.

After I finished my examination, she asked with her eyes if I had discovered the answer to her two complaints, deteriorating handwriting and increasing hand tremors.

"Do they interfere with your function as a professor?" I asked, attempting to assess impact.

"I continue to function well and hardly anyone notices, but my hands do compromise my facility."

Her answer stung me because I understood her worry.

"Your condition is still mild," I reassured.

"But is it progressive?" she demanded. "My handwriting has been declining for months and my hand tremors are getting worse. I would hate to age into a quivering wreck of my former self."

"These are strong words, Professor Columbam," I protested.

"I watched the tremors reduce my father to a dependent, helpless, quaking relic. I want to know if you can do something to prevent them from doing the same to me."

I remained silent as her eyes pleaded for my reassuring response and her lips quivered with un-whispered words. I knew I had to tell her the truth, but I found myself unable to say it to her face. Enthralled by her regal poise, I lacked the courage to drop life, lifeless at her feet.

"Your silence portends a pernicious truth, Doctor," she whispered, bowing her neck and shaking her head.

"It will take many years," was the kindest response I could give, "and medicines do help control the symptoms."

"Why do they call it *familial essential tremor*?" she snapped. "I understand *familial* and *tremor*, but what is so *essential* about it?"

"That's not what you have, Professor Columbam."

"Oh, but my father had it when he was about my age and I'm behaving just like him."

"I'm sure your father did not have it either."

"How can you say that without having seen him?"

"Because essential tremor does not reduce one to '*a quivering wreck of his former self*'. These strong words were coined more than a century ago by George Huntington to describe the relentless course of hereditary chorea, the disease which still bears his name; but that's not what you have."

Silence gripped the room like a dark shadow. She sighed and her head began to tremble as she became visibly exasperated at my reticence. Solemnly, she rearranged herself and inquired.

"What is it then that my father had and that I now have?"

"Parkinson's Disease," I blurted, unable to hold back the truth any longer.

"What? That sounds ominous," she exclaimed.

"Parkinson's Disease progresses at different rates in different people, and treatment is quite helpful early on. Would you like me to refer you to a neurologist?"

"Oh, no. It would bring back memories of my father's macabre struggle against this horrible illness."

I paused in thought as I watched her pin-rolling tremor, exaggerated by the rising tension, cause one hand to beat in her lap while the other supported her bobbing chin.

"I want *you* to treat me. Why do I have to see a neurologist? Are you not qualified?" she challenged with circumspect eyebrows.

After I gave Professor Columbam her *carbidopa-levodopa* prescription and took time to explain the potential adverse effects, she stood up and declared, "The adverse effects seem worse than my disease. I shan't fill your prescription, but I would like it if you would keep an eye on me."

An uncomfortable blush rose into her cheeks as she twice folded the prescription and tucked it into her light-blue purse. Perhaps pleading for attention made her uncomfortable, or perhaps taking orders from one who could have been her student presented a preposterous anachronism.

I followed her ballerina figure down the corridor and was glad to see that her gait was yet unaffected by her disease. At the reception desk, she looked at me with softened eyes and whispered, "When shall I return?"

"I leave this decision to you, Professor." I replied with a bow.

As I walked back to my office, I heard her tell Alicia, "Three months, please." When I sat down to write her note, her whispered question resounded in my head. Most patients would have said: "*When would you like me to return?*" instead of "*When shall I return?*" I noted. But Professor Edna Columbam was not willing to relinquish her reins, especially to one less than half her age.

Time hissed, Professor Columbam rescheduled twice, and a new year wafted in.

1978

"I took your medicine," she proudly declared, before I was able to greet her.

"Good morning, Professor Columbam," I smiled.

"It is a good morning, isn't it?" she responded, crossing her legs and pulling her skirt two inches above her knees. "Aren't you going to ask me why I changed my mind?" she queried with raised eyebrows.

"I would love to know why, Professor."

"I dropped a cup of coffee in my lap."

I gasped.

"Don't worry. It wasn't hot. But it hurt my dignity and ruined my dress. Worse, it happened at a university function with students and teachers present."

"And that was when you changed your mind?"

"No. I stopped drinking coffee in public."

I paused to give her a chance to continue, but she didn't. Instead, she grinned at my curiosity and waited.

"So, what was it that made you change your mind, then?"

"I fell twice at home when I couldn't control my steps. I live alone, you know."

"Did you hurt yourself?" I asked with concern.

"No, but it frightened me enough, causing me to give your medicine a chance."

"Did it help?"

"I hate to admit it, but I wish I had taken it before I spilled my coffee."

"Are you experiencing any adverse effects?"

"Not in the least. I move better, walk better, and no longer spill or fall."

"Have your students said anything to you?"

"They wouldn't dare."

"How about your family?"

"I have none. I have remained single by choice, saying no to many a suitor."

"Oh."

"I tried having a roommate in college. It was then that I realized that I wasn't meant to share my living with anyone. I do have a soul mate, though, and we do share a life."

As I escorted Professor Columbam out, I noted that her gait was no longer musical, that her arms had lost their graceful swing, and that her steps had become uncertain. This time, however, she did not ask, "W*hen shall I return?"* She merely told Alicia, "Six months, please."

Back at my desk, Alicia walked in to tell me that Professor Columbam had forgotten to discuss one more issue with me. I walked back to the waiting room to find her still standing at the reception window.

"Please come in Professor," I invited and led her back to my office. "What did you forget?" I probed.

"A rather personal matter, which is most difficult to express. But, it nags at my mind and I need to vent it out."

She paused, gulped, sighed, and was about to speak but didn't. As she sat trying to reshuffle her words, her chin quivered, her eyes blinked with moisture, and her head quaked with anticipation. Then, as if she had had a change of heart, she stood up and said, "I am sorry to have bothered you."

I stood up when she did and was about to walk her down the hall again when she commanded, "Sit down, please. I can escort myself."

I watched her turn around and walk out with slow, hesitating steps and then heard her tell Alicia, "Let's make it three months instead."

1979

I awaited Professor Columbam's return with uncharacteristic impatience and became concerned when Alicia informed me that she had called and rescheduled. *"Perhaps she wanted to delay finding out more,"* I thought, and then asked, "Did she say why?"

"Her department is giving her a retirement party, she said, and she's going to be too busy moving her office to her home."

"So, for when did she reschedule?"

"She changed it to one year."

"One year? That's too long and too unreasonable," I snapped at Alicia as if she were the one behind the delay.

As the days snailed on, I found myself thinking about Professor Columbam whenever time granted me a shady respite. But, later on, I caught myself thinking about her even when I was with other patients. I envisioned her leaving her office with slow, festinating steps and spending the remains of her life at home, without students or academic connections. Then I began seeing her fall down and stay down because she was no longer able to rise or call for help. When that thought refused to leave me, I called her.

"Good morning, Professor Columbam."

"Who is it?"

"It's Dr. Hawi."

"I've paid my bill and the check has already cleared the bank."

"I'm just calling to say hello. How did your retirement party go?"

There was a long pause followed by rapid breaths and a few suppressed sniffles.

"Professor Columbam. Can you hear me?"

"I do hear you, my dear. I'm just not used to having my doctors call me to inquire about my health."

"Think of me as a student calling to say hello. How was your retirement party?"

"They asked me to retire because I had become too slow to be effective. The chairman of the English Department decided to give me a thank-you party for my forty years of teaching. It was painful to say goodbye to all that I have known and loved, but it was a necessary closure."

"You can teach part time, can't you?"

"That disease you call Parkinson's is shaming me just like it shamed my father."

"Is that why you rescheduled?"

A long, stuttering sigh escaped ahead of her words.

"My elegance has absconded and took with it my self-esteem."

Another sigh was followed by a quotation:

This is the state of man: today he puts forth
The tender leaves of hope, tomorrow blossoms,
And bears his blushing honors thick upon him;
The third day comes a frost, a killing frost;
And—when he thinks, good easy man, full surely
His greatness is a-ripening—nips his root,
And then he falls as I do.

"Wolsey's Farewell to His Greatness from Henry VIII," I responded, to her surprise.

She gasped. I waited for her to say more, but she didn't.

"Would you like me to pass you to Alicia so that you can reschedule?"

"I have always trusted those who love Shakespeare," she quipped, and then added:

But I have promises to keep
And miles to go before I sleep
And miles to go before I sleep.

"Is that your *Frostian* way of saying *no*?"

"I'd like to see you sooner but, besides moving my office, I am making new living arrangements and that takes priority over everything else."

My conversation with Professor Columbam hurled me into the dim alleys of vicarious meditation. I imagined losing my elegance, self-esteem, powers, connections, and dignity.

"Nothing prepares youth for the ravages of age and disease," I surmised. *"Betrayed by great expectations, surprised youth is left to make those discoveries with green unpreparedness down the slippery slopes of relentless time."*

1980

"Good morning, Professor Columbam," I greeted, surveying her form, precariously poised on the examining room chair. Her hair was not tightly *doughnutted* over her bobbing head; instead, it lingered, lusterless, around her leaning neck. Her black skirt draped her uncrossed legs, far below the knees. Her hands whisked rhythmically in the bowl of her lap and her enfeebled faculties of expression peered at me with a resigned stare.

"I am taking your illustrious medicine and getting worse," she declared. "Should I stop it to see if I improve?"

"Are you taking your pills on time?"

"One tablet every six hours without fail."

"What happens when you forget a pill?"

"Dr. Parkinson reminds me by quaking my entire body like a storm rocks a tree."

"Have you fallen again?"

"I have learned to stand and wait a while, before I commence stepping." Then, glancing at her cane without turning her head, she added, "And this helps."

"How is your driving?"

"I no longer drive. I have a live-in soul mate who doubles as my chauffeur."

"A relative?" I slipped, forgetting that she has no relatives.

She became reflectively reticent for an awkward patch of time before she responded:

"She was my secretary for thirty years and they retired her with me. Neither she nor I have any family left, but we've always had each other and that's all we've ever cared to have."

Professor Columbam's head bobbing intensified when she said that and a faint blush peered from behind her cheeks.

I swallowed her graceful confession with poise, performed my medical examination, adjusted the medications, and watched her stuttering gait, steadied by the cane, scurry with uncertain steps to the reception desk.

"Dr. Hawi. This is my resolute friend, Roxanna Liebhaber."

I bowed and shook Roxanna's firm grip. Her younger stockiness stood in blatant contrast to Professor Columbam's elegant frailty. *"It's a good match,"* I thought as I watched Professor Columbam hold on to Roxanna's arm and walk out.

Six months later, when Professor Columbam returned, Frau Liebhaber helped her onto the examination table, remained at her side, and participated in the discussion. I was a bit dismayed, however, because her presence robbed us of our intimate time together. Nonetheless, she proved to be a most dedicated caregiver.

"You are losing weight," I remarked, after I greeted.

"She is refusing to eat. I only cook the things she likes, but no matter how hard I try, she takes a few bites then pushes the food away," interjected Frau Liebhaber.

"Is it your appetite?" I quizzed. "I can prescribe an appetite stimulant."

"My appetite is fine, Doctor, and Roxanna is a marvelous cook."

"Why don't you eat, then?"

"I don't eat because I am grieving."

"She never cries," interjected Roxanna.

Professor Columbam's chin started to bob and her eyes assumed a piercing stare directed at some metaphysical realm that was only discernable to her. I looked to Roxanna for an explanation but she intimated that she had none. As the silence grew, we both realized that Professor Columbam's feelings had been deeply hurt for reasons that neither of us could fathom.

"Professor Columbam," I whispered. "I'm sorry to have hurt your feelings."

"Could you please tell me what you're grieving about so that I'll learn how to handle it," broke in Roxanna with intemperate tone.

"I am grieving John Lennon's senseless assassination. I am grieving the forty beautiful, young Americans who have already died of AIDS. And I am grieving the fifty-three American citizens held hostage in Iran."

Having finished her pronouncement, Professor Columbam, avoiding eye contact, lowered her gaze and busied herself with pulling her black skirt further down over her knees. At that point I realized that Roxanna's presence was an impediment.

"Roxanna," I pleaded. "Would you please excuse us for a few minutes."

Frau Liebhaber seemed relieved at my request and marched out without saying a word.

"Thank you, Doctor," sighed Professor Columbam. "How smart of you to have noticed. I love Roxanna and were it not for her, I would be in an extended care facility. But she does get on my nerves with her overbearingness."

"So, now that we are alone, could you tell me why you're refusing to eat?"

"Because when I eat more than a few bites, I start to drool and it embarrasses me. I cannot bear to be seen drooling by the one woman who holds me in the highest regard."

"Do you sometimes cough when you eat?"

"I do that too and it seems to be getting worse. What does that mean?"

"It means that your disease is starting to affect your swallowing muscles, causing you to drool and aspirate."

"Is there anything one can do?"

"Eat little bites, chew them well, swallow them slowly, sip water in between, and make sure Roxanna is not with you when you eat because your heightened anxiety at her presence will make things worse."

Professor Columbam became pensive at my remark. After a brief, reflective pause, she took in a deep breath and half asked, half proclaimed:

"It would be so much easier if I would just stop eating, wouldn't it?"

"You don't mean…"

"You don't have to say it and I don't need to hear it. I'd rather *'go gentle into my good night'* and you must promise me that you will not intervene with tubes or artificial means."

"But, you…"

"Whilst I have my faculties, I shall make all my decisions and I would like you to note them in my chart. Roxanna is far too emotional to be rational. She is already grieving me and I do not wish to intensify her grief."

"There are other treatments, which we have not yet tried."

"No additional treatments please. I have a tireless disease that is robbing my body of its graceful powers and could soon begin to rob my mind of all its learning and memories. I do not relish dying unaware and would rather experience my dying with intact mental faculties."

Professor Columbam's tremulous voice belied her assertive disposition. When I finished noting her directives in the chart, she thanked me and said, "Please call Roxanna back. I have said all I've wanted to say."

When Roxanna came in, she appeared worried and asked with an impatient voice, "What do you think, Doctor?"

"Professor Columbam's disease is progressing rapidly."

"And obdurately," interjected the professor.

"She will not allow additional treatments and wants no further interventions. I have noted her wishes in the chart and it is our duty to do as she wishes."

"I understand," said Roxanna with capitulating tone.

"And she needs to eat alone because being watched while eating makes her nervous and turns off her appetite."

Teary-eyed, Roxanna nodded and lowered her gaze. I pushed Professor Columbam's wheelchair to the reception desk and told Alicia, "Three months please."

"No. I wish to return in six months," countered the professor, disappointing both Roxana and me, but not Alicia, who rolled her eyes and gave her the delayed appointment.

1981

On her next appointment, Professor Columbam had added some weight and looked stronger. She seemed remarkably cheerful, responding to my usual greeting, "Good morning, Professor Columbam," with, "Indeed it is." Even Roxanna smiled, and that was the first time I saw her teeth, strong, in perfect alignment like a white-helmeted police regiment. Professor Columbam's hair was tightly pulled into a *doughnut* over her head and she donned a flowered, blue dress, which resonated with her light blue shoes and purse. Surprised and delighted, I exclaimed, "You look like you're feeling so much better."

"Indeed, I do feel much better, thanks to you. I no longer feel malnourished because Roxanna leaves me to eat alone. It takes me a long time to finish my plate but I do, and I do not choke while eating."

Roxanna nodded approvingly and, flashing her white teeth at me again, added, "She also lets me do her hair and get her dressed each morning. I've outfitted my van with a wheelchair lift and now we go shopping together."

"I don't feel like a prisoner any more because I have mobility," interjected the professor.

"Can you walk without help? I asked.

"Let me show you," she smiled as she put out her hand to stop Roxanna from helping her get out of the wheelchair.

Slowly, hesitantly, carefully, she lifted the foot pedals, dropped her feet to the floor, pushed up with trembling arms, rose to a stooped stance, and shuffled a few steps forward while her head bobbed, like a pigeon's, with every proud step she took.

"Voila," she smiled, slowly turned around, cautiously moved back to her chair, and eased herself in, looking exhausted but triumphant.

"Are you taking your medicines?" I asked.

"Every four hours," she stuttered, her voice trembling with the moment's fatigue.

I examined Professor Columbam in her wheelchair. Her arms and legs had grown more rigid and her tremors had descended to her feet and risen to her face, causing her to tremble rhythmically as if responding to the beat of an inner drummer.

"I need to adjust your medicines," I sighed.

"No you don't," she affirmed. "I have enjoyed watching Dr. Parkinson disable my nervous system with inveterate precision. Every few weeks, I find that I can do fewer things with my body, but that has forced me to do more with my mind. I am dictating my autobiography and Roxanna is typing it. It's a wonderful project for both of us because our lives have been intertwined for more than thirty years."

"When she forgets something important, I remind her," added Roxanna with a smug expression.

"When did you regain your indomitable, inner strength?" I asked, quite amazed at her renaissance.

"When I emerged out of starvation and acquired mobility. I was like a starved prisoner of war who finally gets freed. Starvation and imprisonment, Doctor, take away initiative and replace it with lassitude. *'I feel my heart new-opened,'* said Wolsey in his farewell to his greatness."

In response to her erudite diction, I quoted:

The selfsame moment I could pray;
And from my neck so free
The albatross fell off, and sank
Like lead into the sea.

"I am impressed with your apropos quotation from Coleridge's *Rhyme Of The Ancient Mariner*. You should have been one of my students."

"I feel that I am."

"What a considerate response. I look forward to seeing you in three months then."

Professor Columbam motioned to Roxanna to wheel her out and, looking at me, re-quoted from Frost:

But I have promises to keep
And miles to go before I sleep.

1981 Summer

When Professor Columbam returned three months later, her disease had progressed to the point of near-total dependency. She was no longer able to dress, shower, or visit the bathroom without Roxanna's assistance. But she was still able to feed herself and that meant everything to her.

"It's taking me about an hour to eat my meal and that's the only independent activity that I am still capable of besides intelligible speech."

Professor Columbam's speech was hesitant and slow, but it was still intelligent, precise, and remarkably cheerful. She had succeeded in disassociating herself from her disease and was observing her body's demise as a detached outsider rather than as an affected victim.

"Have you finished dictating your autobiography?" I challenged.

"Indeed I have, and together we are editing it, a few pages a day," she declared, glancing endearingly at Roxanna.

"I volunteer to be your first reader when you finish."

"Can you spare the time?" she teased.

"I never waste time, and that allows me to save time for life's important things," I replied with a soft smile.

"I might bring it with me in three months, if you don't change your mind," she again teased. Then she quoted from Kipling's *IF:*

If you can force your nerve and heart and sinew
To serve your turn long after they are gone
And so hold on when there is nothing in you
Except the will, which says to them, hold on.

"What an apropos motto," I cheered.

"Indeed, it is," she smiled with eyes aglow, and as Roxanna wheeled her out, added, "I should have been your teacher."

1981 Autumn

The fall of that year came in like a child's bedtime story, dreamlike and soporific. I awaited Professor Columbam's October appointment with apprehension. When they arrived, her stooped body was wilted into a wheelchair bouquet and her head was wrapped with a blue scarf, tied under her chin, concealing her thin hair but highlighting her sallow complexion. The scarf's knot was wet with drool.

Next to her, Roxanna stood colossal. No smiles were exchanged as I surveyed the scene. I got down on my knees so that, from her stooped position, she could see my face, and greeted:

"Good morning Professor Columbam."

"It's not a good morning," she snapped. "Have you not heard the news?"

"News," I exclaimed, delighted that she still had her wits.

"President Sadat of Egypt was assassinated."

I gasped and waited for Roxanna to finish wiping off her drool.

"You know what that means, of course, don't you?" she quizzed with quivering lips.

"What does it mean?" I asked.

"It means that peace in the Middle East has been assassinated as well."

It was hard to redirect the conversation towards her health after that portentous declaration. Not willing to mire our precious time in more political discussions, I inquired:

"How's your autobiography coming along?"

"It's almost finished. We are now editing in the last era."

"What era is that?" I asked, a bit bemused.

"Illness, retirement, and death," she enunciated.

"Is there a chapter about love?" I asked, hoping for a more positive discussion.

"Love is in all the chapters. I have loved my work, loved my students, and loved Roxanna with all of my life's powerful passions, and it is these loves, which I shall dearly miss in death."

Roxanna's face lit up with a most mournful smile and she almost said something but didn't. I seized that moment and asked her: "How do you think she's doing?"

"She's happiest when I'm reading and she's editing. I feed her now because her hands have become too shaky. She sleeps well and we both take an after lunch nap. Her bodily functions are well received in diapers and I give her daily sponge baths in bed."

"You are a wonderful nurse, Roxanna," I applauded.

"She's a wonderful mentor, Doctor. Wait till you read her autobiography."

Roxanna's face quivered with reverence as she uttered these few precious words. Professor Columbam, unmoved, merely added, "Without language *Homo sapiens* would have been yet another wild animal species, roaming aimlessly. All their achievements have come through language, and language remains their greatest achievement."

Professor Columbam's cheerful wit and indomitable spirit, in spite of rapid physical decline, was awe-inspiring. She was still the commander in chief of her life and was enjoying every moment with blatant disregard of destiny.

After I finished examining her, I became concerned with how shaky and frail her hands had become. "Are you still able to use the phone?" I asked.

"I have little need to use it, but Roxanna turns the speaker on and leaves the receiver in my lap when she goes shopping. I can dial 911 and can answer her when she calls to check on me. I have a perfectly arranged life, Doctor, and you needn't worry about me."

"Indeed, you are the captain of your fate and the master of your soul."

"Oh, no," she cried as if I had committed a grave sin. "You have just *malaproposed* Henley's *Invectus*. Try it again but, this time, quote him correctly and do not inverse the sequence, please," she pleaded.

"I'm not sure I know what you mean?" I answered sheepishly, while still on my knees.

"The last stanza of that most omnipotent poem is:

It matters not how straight the gate,
How charged with punishments the scroll.
I am the master of my fate:
I am the captain of my soul.

He wrote it after he became a double amputee, you know. Remarkable man, W. E. Henley. Have you read his works?"

"I'm afraid not."

"You should read his poem, *Margaritae Sorori*, Latin for Sister Margaret. He wrote it whilst dying of tuberculosis. The last stanza is most poignant to my present state:

So be my passing!
My task accomplished and the long day done,
My wages taken, and in my heart
Some late lark singing,
Let me be gathered to the quiet west,
The sundown splendid and serene death.

I escorted Professor Columbam and Roxanna to the door with a tear in my heart and a smile in my eye. Later on that day, like a dutiful student, I looked up W. E. Henley and committed both *Invectus* and *Margaritae Sorori* to memory, hoping to show off my erudition on her next visit.

1982

It was on a Thursday in January of that fateful year when Alicia rushed and knocked at the examination room door.

"There's an Officer Gustin on the phone wanting to speak with you," she announced with pressured speech.

I begged my patient's pardon, darted to my office, picked up the receiver, and gasped, "Yes, Officer Gustin. This is Doctor Hawi."

"Doctor, I'm sorry to bother you but do you know a Mrs. Edna Columbam?"

"Yes, she's my patient?"

"And did you know a Mrs. Roxanna Liebhaber?"

"Yes. She's Professor Columbam's live-in caregiver."

"Was she also your patient?"

"No, but she was the one who brought Professor Columbam for her appointments."

"Well, when Professor Columbam awakened this morning, she found Mrs. Liebhaber dead in bed with her."

"Dear Lord," I cried. "How is Professor Columbam handling all of this?"

"She seems to be in shock and the EMT thinks that she ought to be hospitalized, but she's refusing, which is why I'm calling you."

"May I talk to the EMT, please?"

Luckily, my partner, Dr. Hamdon, had taken the day off and his nurse was willing to sit with Professor Columbam while I made suitable arrangements with the home-health services. The medic was kind enough to stay with her until Dr. Hamdon's nurse arrived. After office, I drove to Professor Columbam's home. She was in her wheelchair and when she saw me, she sighed and looked askance at the home-health nurse, sitting by her side. I asked the nurse to give us a private moment, knelt down before her stooped posture to be able to look her in the face, held her trembling hand, and whispered, "I'm so sorry."

She gazed into my eyes with a firm, resolute stare, sighed again, and then with a quivering, lugubrious tone, declared, "You know that Roxanna didn't believe in doctors. I had admonished her repeatedly but she never listened. She was the loveliest and the most stubborn of women. Oh, what an anachronistic demise."

I was stung by how calm and composed Professor Columbam appeared. After my telephone conversation with Officer Gustin, I was expecting to find a shocked, old wreck but was pleasantly surprised to find her still in command of her shrinking world.

"Did you know that Roxanna was ill?" I asked, hoping for a sensible medical explanation.

"Roxanna was never ill, Doctor," she grumbled with pursed lips.

"Had there been any sudden deaths in her family?"

"I *am* her entire family and I haven't died yet," she snapped.

The nurse tiptoed in with a glass of milk and a sandwich on a small tray.

"She's refusing to put any food in her mouth," complained the nurse. "Would you please explain to her the importance of proper nutrition."

"I'm glad you came in, Janet," she addressed the nurse while squeezing my hand. "I'd like you to witness what I'm about to say to Doctor Hawi."

"Professor Columbam," I protested. "This is not a good time to be making important decisions."

The nurse blushed, put the tray down, and stood in awe of what Professor Columbam was about to pronounce.

"I am asking you in the presence of Nurse Janet Johnson," enunciated Professor Columbam with a slow, resolute tone, "to promise that you will never force feed me, invade my body with IVs or tubes, hospitalize me, institutionalize me, or resuscitate me."

"What are you trying to say?" I asked, standing up and letting go of her hand.

"I am saying that it is my God-given right to refuse all supportive measures and I need you to promise me that you will not violate my wishes."

"That's not very reasonable, Professor," interjected Nurse Johnson.

"It may seem unreasonable to you, my dear young nurse," she patronized, "but exercising my human right as a suffering and hopelessly ill individual is my solemn prerogative."

"So, what would you like me to do, then, if you no longer require my medical help?" I retaliated with visible irritation.

"I need you to help me die with dignity and without delay."

"That sounds like a request for euthanasia," I protested.

"I did not ask you to hasten my death, Doctor. I merely asked that you do not delay it. It is my right to choose where, when, and how to die. I do not wish to die of neglect, but I do choose to die of willful starvation. Would you obey my last wish and help me die peacefully, at my own home, and in my own bed? Would you please help me die with unscathed dignity?"

Professor Columbam's words sounded preposterous to my Hippocratic mind. I was trained to save lives, ease pain, and heal disease. Nothing in my training had ever prepared me to help patients die by their own methods, but Professor Columbam was asking me to do just that.

Nurse Johnson picked up the food tray, took it back to the kitchen, and did not return. I swayed under the heft of indecision, with discordant thoughts and dissonant feelings, barking at my conscience. Professor Columbam must have been pleased with my silence because her head tremor diminished as if, having spoken her peace, she was no longer quaked by the moment's tension.

"I need to think about this," I finally said as I prepared to leave.

"But, you have not started your reading assignment yet," she smiled.

"What assignment?" I asked, as if I were a student who had neglected his homework.

"I would like you to read to me from Whitman's *Song of Myself*," she said, pointing with her trembling hand to the bookshelf that held Walt Whitman's poetry volume, *Leaves of Grass*.

Relieved at the change of topic, I fetched the book, sat next to her, and waited.

"Please open to *Song of Myself* and read to me section six, which begins with:

A child said, What is the grass?
fetching it to me with full hands;

As I read, Whitman's words penetrated my being as effortlessly as sunlight penetrates glass. When I reached the line: *"And now it seems to me the beautiful uncut hair of graves,"* I stopped to swallow the dryness in my throat, which Professor Columbam noticed because she tempered the momentary silence with, "What a heavenly image."

The next time I stopped to swallow was at the end of the line: *"The smallest sprout shows there is really no death,"* and that's when Professor Columbam came to my aid with, "Resurrection, indeed. Growth out of the dead dirt is resurrection."

When I reached the last couplet, she intoned it with me as if it were a vesper:

All goes onward and outward... and nothing collapses,
And to die is different from what any one supposed, and luckier.

Feeling overwhelmed, I rose from my seat, closed the book, and returned it to the shelf. Then, hoping to avert further discussion, I took my leave and prepared to make my exit. She thanked me, waited until I was at the door, and then said, "I've had a good life, Doctor, and I am asking you to help me have a good death. Is that too much to ask?"

Friday

I added Professor Columbam to my daily rounds and began calling on her at the end of each day. The home health nurse the following day insisted that I sign the *Do-Not-Resuscitate* order, which I did in the nurse's presence and then we both waited for Professor Columbam to countersign it.

"Get me my fountain pen, please," she smiled at the nurse. "It's in the central drawer of my desk."

Then, holding the pen with her undulating hand, she proclaimed, "I am about to sign the most important fiat of my life."

"Your handwriting is still legible," I complimented as I watched the words *Edna Columbam, PhD* trail behind her fountain pen's nib like a writhing confession.

"Seriousness steadies my hands," she replied with a quivering voice. "I plan to write you a final note before I lose my powers. The nurse will hand it to you after you pronounce me."

"Why not tell it to me now?" I pleaded.

"Written words endure while spoken words turn to air and mutate from mouth to mouth. I wish to leave you something indelible."

"What an honor," I murmured.

"You are my last meaningful contact with this receding world, Doctor."

"How about all your other students? Aren't they meaningful contacts?"

"They were but they are no longer," she lamented. "I prefer they not see me like this. Dancing to Dr. Parkinson's drums is unbecoming of an old professor. I would rather leave my elegant image on their mental screens."

I left Professor Columbam with flailing sentiments. She not only seemed at peace with her decision, she also managed to humor death with joyful relish, which left me intrigued and looking forward to seeing her the next day. There was so much about dying that I did not know and that she was teaching me using great literature, a vehicle unheard of in our traditional medical factories.

Saturday

On the third hunger-strike day, I found her spry and expectant as if fasting had fed her strength instead of robbed it. Because it was a weekend, I was able to visit her after my morning rounds instead of at the day's end.

"Good morning, Professor Columbam," I greeted as I walked into her living room.
"Indeed it is, good Doctor. I have had time to think and the mind is a most magnificent entertainer."
"What did you think about, if I may ask?"
"Many things. I am rearranging my memories according to the intensity of joy they bring me."
"I thought you had already done so in your autobiography."
"My autobiography is for others to read. My personal memories are solely for me and I have arranged them on a spectrum from melancholy to joy with blatant disregard to chronology."
"And which ones are your favorite memories?" I smiled.
"I'm not sure that I have favorites. I seem to value the sad ones as much as the joyous ones, and that realization has occurred to me only today, just after I had finished rearranging them. It was a most unexpected discovery."
"One never stops learning if one keeps an open mind," I affirmed.

"I still feel I have a lot more to learn about *'The undiscovered country from whose bourn no traveler returns,'* and I can't wait to enter that nether kingdom in order to find out," she proclaimed with a wry smile.

I recognized the quote because I had memorized *Hamlet's* soliloquy while my father was dying, and found great solace in recalling it. But the fact that she was taking the quote out of context gave me ammunition, which I did not hesitate to use. To her surprise, I framed the quote in context, and blurted it out to her:

Who would fardels bear,
To grunt and sweat under a weary life,
But that the dread of something after death,
The undiscovered country from whose bourn no traveler returns,
Puzzles the will and makes us rather bear those ills we have
Than fly to others that we know not of?

"But, unlike Hamlet and you, my dear young doctor, I feel no dread. On the contrary, I look forward to life's ultimate reward, eternal peace."

When I prepared to leave Professor Columbam, having had a long discussion about the divergent perceptions of youth and age, a little bit of me wanted to stay behind.

"Are you planning on seeing me tomorrow?" she asked.
"Of course," I asserted.
"But tomorrow is Sunday. Don't you take a day off?"
"I have no off days," I quipped.

Sunday

On Sunday morning, the home health nurse called and said that Mrs. Columbam was having difficulty breathing. When I arrived, her breaths were rapid and labored, she felt hot to touch, and her cough, though feeble, was persistent. After listening to her lungs, I got close to her ear and whispered, "You have pneumonia and I need to treat you with antibiotics and give you oxygen."

"No tubes, no IVs, remember?" she gasped.

"I can manage the antibiotics by mouth but oxygen only comes in a tube."

"No oxygen then," she gasped again.

I made sure she took her first antibiotic dose before I left and called the nurse every two hours for updates. When the nurse informed me that her lips were turning blue, I rushed back.

She greeted me with a panting smile and whispered, "It's - very - good."

"Are you comfortable," I whispered back.

"No. But it's - very - good," she gasped.

"What's very good?" I probed, stroking her hand.

"I can see - my journey's end. And it's - beautiful," she coughed, clasping my fingers.

"Oxygen will help you talk better," I insinuated with a raised voice. "I have a jar in the car."

"No tubes, remember?"

"No tubes," I beguiled. "Just nasal prongs to help you talk."

Her breathing slowed, her livid lips deepened, and she let go of my hand. I ran to my car, rolled in the oxygen jar, strapped the nasal prongs on, opened the valve to five liters, and waited for her ashen complexion to brighten. Before she opened her eyes, she groped for my hand and squeezed. Then, she gazed at me as if I were a distant abstraction. Her lips quivered, struggled, and pronounced:

"Thank - you."

The nurse standing by my side murmured with disbelief, "She's back."

I felt another hand squeeze, a feeble dawn gleamed over her face, and her breaths grew stronger, sucking the oxygen with hissing force. The nurse returned with a glass of water and placed the straw between her lips. Professor Columbam sipped the water, gasping in between gulps. Then, after resting from her drinking effort, she smiled at the nurse and said, "My dry mouth - thanks you."

As the nurse and I exchanged knowing glances, Professor Columbam slept. After a while, when I stood up to leave, she awakened, looked at me with sunset eyes, and implored:

"I've kept you long enough, but could you please stay a little longer?"

"It's Sunday and I can stay as long as you wish," I reassured, sitting back down.

The nurse, sensing that Professor Columbam had something private to share, left the room. I felt another hand squeeze. Professor Columbam cleared her throat.

"You know," she began, "there are three ways to die and I am grateful to have the best."

Not knowing what to say, I squeezed her hand and waited.

"Dying slowly is a wonderful experience. It allows one to take proper leave of life. Dying unprepared, as with a heart attack, is like an assassination. And dying unaware, as with dementia, is like a betrayal. The last two rob one of the dying experience. I am glad to be dying slowly with my faculties intact."

"Are you afraid?" I smiled.

"I'm overjoyed. My dying experience is adding yet another dimension to my life. I have lived well, and thanks to you, I am able to die well."

Professor Columbam's color became a gentle flush. She shifted in her place, had me rearrange her pillow, took in a deep breath, and exclaimed, "Oxygen is a wonderful thing. It will let us talk longer."

"Have you any regrets?" I asked, holding her arm.

"Only two. I should have expounded on them in my autobiography, but I didn't."

"Would you share them with me, then?" I pleaded.

"I should have countered William Shakespeare and Dylan Thomas. No one has dared counter those two giants before. But dying makes one impudent."

"What would you have liked to say to them?" I asked as I offered her another sip of water.

"To old William, I would have liked to say, *'Thus conscious does make heroes of us all. And thus the native hue of resolution is emboldened by the brave cast thought.'* Oh, do recite that last section of Hamlet's soliloquy, please. I'm too dyspneic to do it."

Slowly, I enunciated the last six lines of Shakespeare's most famous soliloquy:

> *Thus conscious does make cowards of us all,*
> *And thus the native hue of resolution*
> *Is sicklied o'er with the pale cast of thought,*
> *And enterprises of great pitch and moment*
> *With this regard their currents turn awry*
> *And lose the name of action.*

"So beautiful yet so untrue," she lamented.

"But he was only talking about suicide," I protested and recited the preceding seven lines:

> *For who'd bear the whips and scorns of time,*
> *The oppressor's wrong, the proud man's contumely,*
> *The pangs of despised love, the law's delay,*
> *The insolence of office, and the spurns*
> *That patient merit of the unworthy takes,*
> *When he himself might his quietus make*
> *With a bare bodkin?*

"And what do you think I'm doing, my dear doctor? By refusing to eat, I am committing slow suicide," she reprimanded and then added, '*To be, or not to be: that is the question*' should be rephrased. To be or to choose not to be: that is the question."

She rested while I tried to find a suitable rebuttal. The silence of her rapid breaths grew. I could tell that she had more to say. I waited until she surprised me with, "Have you read Camus?"

"I read *The Plague*."

"Go to the bookshelf and fetch *The Myth Of Sisyphus*. I'd like you to have it both as a gift and as a reading assignment."

With book in hand, I returned to her side. She labored but managed to explain, "In this essay, Camus poses the existential question, *'Shall I commit suicide?'* If the answer is no, then one has reason to live. If the answer is yes, then one has nothing left to live or struggle for. And that is where I am now, my dear."

I left Professor Columbam and spent the remains of my Sunday reading The *Myth Of Sisyphus*. Sisyphus, the king of Corinth, was punished by Zeus for his avarice, deceit, and violation of the revered Greek hospitality rules, *Xenia*, because he delighted in killing both guests and strangers. His punishment in the underworld was to roll a big boulder uphill, only for the boulder to roll back, causing Sisyphus to endlessly repeat his absurd task. Thus Camus saw Sisyphus as personifying the absurdity of human life. But the essay concludes by asking the reader to imagine Sisyphus happy, because the struggle toward the heights is what fills the heart with joy.

That night, in my dreamful sleep, I began to perceive Professor Columbam's final struggles as, indeed, meaningless, and to understand that after Roxanna Liebhaber's death, she wished to end her Sisyphean condition with the joyful dignity of a conductor, conducting her last symphony all the way to its grand finale.

Monday

When I returned Monday after work, she greeted me with, "I am better. Your antibiotic is working."

"She's only drinking water," interjected the frustrated nurse.

"I think food was making me worse. I don't seem to shake as much since I began my hunger strike," she smiled.

"Your tremors have decreased because your muscles have grown weaker with starvation," I explained. "You have been without food for five days now."

"How long can I last without food?" she asked as she pointed to the chair next to her bed.

As I eased myself next to her, the nurse gave me a confused look and left the room.

"How was your night?" she asked with a concerned tone.

"My night was fine," I replied, surprised. "How was yours?"

"I slept very well. Oxygen is a better soporific than *Papaver somniferum*."

I was not surprised that Professor Columbam knew the Latin name of the opium poppy, but I was surprised that she had improved. Pneumonia and starvation are a deadly couplet in most cases, but Professor Columbam had defied that proverbial wisdom. Her inner strength, fortified by oxygen, was a marvel to witness, and her tenacious capacity for joy in spite of imminent demise was spiritually uplifting.

"I read *The Myth Of Sisyphus* last night," I distracted.

"Well then, since there's nothing medical that you can do for me, I'd like to voice my second rebuttal."

"Rebuttal?" I asked, looking confounded.

"You forgot? Yesterday I countered Shakespeare and today I wish to counter Dylan Thomas. Could you please pull his poetic works from the shelf?"

I had heard of Dylan Thomas but never read him, which disarmed me. I could hold my end of the conversation with Hamlet's soliloquy, but I knew nothing of Dylan Thomas except that he was a heavy-drinking Welch poet who died of alcohol poisoning. Back by her side, I awaited her instructions like a dutiful pupil.

"Find *And Death Shall Have No Dominion* and read it to me, please."

When I had finished reading, she asked, "What do you think this poem is about?"

"Immortality?" I guessed.

"Indeed, and the refrain, *'And Death Shall Have No Dominion'*, is taken from St. Paul's epistle to the Romans (6:9)."

"I see," I said with a nod.

"So what do you think is wrong with the poem then?"

"I don't understand it enough to know what you mean."

"The line, *'Faith in their hands shall snap in two,'* is a blatant contradiction. For death to have no dominion we must have faith, otherwise, death shall have dominion."

"I see," I said, rereading the second stanza. "It is a contradiction."

"I prefer Ghalib's simple honesty to Thomas's vacillating uncertainty. *'This above all: to thine own self be true, And it shall follow, as the night the day, Thou canst not then be false to any man.'* said the Bard. A poet should be true to himself for his verses to echo in the hearts."

I had no idea who Ghalib was but was embarrassed to ask. I knew that the *Bard* meant Shakespeare but was confused by the juxtaposition of his quote to Ghalib and Thomas. To try to understand her meaning, I inquired, "So what did Ghalib say about immortality?"

"Mirza Assadullah Khan Ghalib was a classical Urdu and Persian poet from the Mughal Empire during British colonial rule of India," she instructed. "Here's what he said about death:

I think we have caught sight of the road to death now.
Death is the string that binds together the scattered beads of the universe.

And here's what he said about immortality:

I know that Heaven doesn't exist,
But the idea is one of Ghalib's favorite fantasies.

"Obviously, Thomas did not do his homework; he should have read Ghalib first."

"How can a starved brain so effortlessly retrieve such exacting verse," I wondered, as I sat enthralled, hoping that she wouldn't stop discoursing.

"Now, please read to me Thomas's villanelle, *Do Not Go Gentle Into That Good Night*, and I'll tell you why I disagree with it."

When she said that, I remembered our conversation about her drooling and coughing, and her words to me when I suggested that she eat slowly, using small bites: "It would be so much easier if I would just stop eating," she said. "I'd rather go gentle into my good night."

I surmised what she was about to protest after reading the first stanza:

> *Do not go gentle into that good night,*
> *Old age should burn and rave at close of day;*
> *Rage, rage against the dying of the light.*

"What good does it do to fight implacable death?" she began. "He wrote that villanelle to his dying father. I refuse to desecrate noble death and distort its beautiful emotional bouquet with a meaningless fisticuff. Good dying should not be resisted; it should be venerated and embraced as our last, meaningful living act."

I left Professor Columbam feeling enriched and that night I came to understand that, indeed, I needed her more than she needed me. With this new realization, I became Professor Columbam's last student and relished visiting her for my daily private lessons.

Tuesday

When I returned on that evening, she asked the nurse to come in as a witness and said, "I have instructed my lawyer to liquidate everything I and Roxanna own and to give the entire proceeds to the Jesus House of Oklahoma City. I have further instructed her to put you, Doctor, in charge of donating my entire library to the poorest school in the state of Oklahoma. And like Roxanna, I wish to be cremated and wish my ashes to be added to Roxanna's."

Here, she pointed a shaky hand to a large urn in the corner of the room, smiled, and went on.

"And like Roxanna, I do not want a funeral or a memorial; I wish to fade away with grace, unmentioned by the tidings of the day."

Attempting to dilute the macabre moment, I nodded and asked, "How was your night?"

She answered with an unrelated question. "Do you have a garden?"

"I do, and I love gardening."

"Would you oblige me then by adding our ashes to your soil?" she asked with a smile and then quoted again from Whitman's, *What Is The Grass:*

What do you think has become of the women and children?
They are alive and well somewhere.
The smallest sprouts show there is really no death.
And if ever there was it led forward life,
And does not wait at the end to arrest it.
All goes onward and outward and nothing collapses.
And to die is different from what any one supposed, and luckier.

I smiled because I did not know what else to say. I had never encountered anyone who had embraced dying as a joyful, meaningful experience, laden with hope and beauty. I had many questions, which I would have liked to ask but dared not. Things had turned around and she was the one conducting the visit instead of me. I was not surprised when, after I helped her take a sip of water, she lamented, "You are my last student."

"You still have a lot to teach me," I replied with a smile, "and I am eager to learn."

"Very good then. Would you please bring William Wordsworth's poetry volume from the shelf? There's a certain stanza, which I wish to share with you."

I was relieved because I had read enough of Wordsworth and even knew his *Daffodils* by heart. But what she chose was *Ode On Intimations Of Immortality,* which I had not read.

"Please turn to the last stanza beginning with *'Though nothing can bring back the hour'* and read it to me."

I read slowly, enunciating the important words:

Though nothing can bring back the hour
Of splendor in the grass, of glory in the flower;
We will grieve not, rather find
Strength in what remains behind;
In the primal sympathy, which having been must ever be;
In the soothing thoughts that spring out of human suffering;
In the faith that looks through death,
In the years that bring the philosophic mind.

"Do you hear what he means?" she asked with rekindled eyes.

"It's very wise," I evaded.

"He is teaching us to face death with faith and a philosophical mind. Without faith and philosophy one could stand to ruin a good life with a horrifying death. I have readied myself and look forward to a meaningful finale of an equally meaningful life."

"What do you think is the meaning of life?" I distracted.

"There is no universal meaning, as you must already know. Every one must find a personal meaning and mine is literature."

"Literature?" I gasped.

" *'We die. That may be the meaning of life. But we do language. That may be the measure of our lives,'* said Toni Morrison."

Not knowing anything about Toni Morrison, I asked, "Who's Toni Morrison?"

"Keep an eye on her after I am gone. She's a black novelist, author of *Sula* and *The Song Of Solomon*, and is destined for the Nobel Prize in literature."

Professor Columbam, who preferred literature to food, was feeding her soul while starving her body. The striking contrast between her blithe spirit and her fading form helped me see dying as the living finale of an opus magnum rather than as the tenebrous end of a film noir. As day by day, her voice grew weaker, she would whisper when I would take my leave, "Are you coming back tomorrow?" to which I would answer, "As soon as I finish my evening rounds." When her voice became almost inaudible, I had to read her lips, which never lost their cheer.

On Sunday, her eleventh day of starvation, I asked, "What would you like me to read today?"

She whispered, "Frost's, *Home Burial*."

I pulled Robert Frost's volume from the shelf, opened it to *Home Burial*, and was about to start reading when she whispered, "Just read the six lines, starting with *'No, from the time when one is sick...'*"

I was familiar with the poem. It told of a mother's inconsolable grief at losing her first child, but I couldn't understand why Professor Columbam wanted me to read it until I found the six lines she had referred to:

> *No, from the time when one is sick, to death*
> *One is alone, and dies more alone*
> *Friends make pretense of following to the grave*
> *But before one is in it, their minds are turned*
> *And making the best of their way back to life*
> *And living people, and things they understand.*

When I finished, she sighed and whispered, "Do you see, now?"

"I don't know what you mean?" I whispered back.

"Frost was as wrong as was Dylan Thomas and Shakespeare. When you love literature, your mind is never alone because it's always full of friends who will recite with you all the way to the grave."

I had never thought of literature that way, but I could tell that she wanted me to; and to convert me to that literati ethos, she spent the last remnants of her energies.

The Letter

That was her last lesson because when I returned on Monday evening, she was in a coma. When I returned on Tuesday, her breathing had become agonal, but a knowing smile lingered upon her livid lips. I stayed until she took her leave, smiling at *the undiscovered country from whose bourn no traveler returns.*

Before I left, the nurse handed me a sealed envelope. I did not open it until I was in the quietude of my home. The handwriting was barely legible but, after some deciphering, I was able to read and re-read her last precious words:

*

My Dear Doctor,

My death will free you to pursue literature, which is the intellect's best friend. Please take time to resurrect all the dead poets and fall in love with their works. Read the classics and see how far humanity has regressed. A cultivated mind is life's apotheosis, and the heart is never alone when its mind is full of literature. "To be able to fill leisure intelligently is the last product of civilization," said Bertrand Russell.

Humanity's fear of death is misplaced. Instead, we should be afraid of old age and its accouterments: disease, homeliness, frailty, and dementia. When old age diminishes and demeans us, we become thanatophiles; we pray for death to come liberate and redeem us. This is why I have embraced death with joyful alacrity instead of fearful trepidation, "Like one who wraps the drapery of his couch about him, and lies down to pleasant dreams." These last two lines of *Thanatopsis*, written by the seventeen-year old William Cullen Bryant, have served as my guiding motto.

"It is old age, rather than death, that is to be contrasted with life. Old age is life's parody, whereas death transforms life into a destiny: in a way it preserves it by giving it the absolute dimension. Death does away with time." I wish I had written these lines, instead of Professor Simone de Beauvoir, the icon of French feminist existentialism. You should read her essay *La Vieillesse* (*The Coming of Age*). It's a meditation on the decline and solitude all humans experience if they do not die before they age and decay.

Dying is our last living act and we should endeavor to make it beautiful and meaningful, which you have helped me do and for that I am grateful. Death, in contrast to dying, has nothing to do with life because, as Epictetus once taught, "When we are alive, we are not dead, and when we are dead, we are not alive." Squandering valuable life worrying about irrelevant death is thus preposterous and most unbecoming of an enlightened intellect.

I die grateful that my Parkinson's disease did not erase my memory and abscond with my faculties. I die, as Malcolm said of Cowdor in Macbeth, "Nothing in his life became him like the leaving it; he died as one that had been studied in his death, to throw away the dearest thing he owned, as 'twere a careless trifle."

And whatever your garden grows, Roxanna and I shall be part of it as we shall be part of your memories and the memories of the many language students whom we have touched over the years. As Henry Adams once said, "A teacher affects eternity; he can never tell where his influence stops."

Cheers,

Edna Columbam, PhD

Good Morning Professor Columbam, First Edition, OSMA Journal, Vol. 106, No. 3, March 2013. Revised Edition completed in October 2016.

Sudaa

The story began in 1978, twenty years before the twin loves, *Himeros* and *Eros*—who had greeted *Aphrodite* as she issued from the sea foam—received their third brother *Sildenafil,* better known to us as Viagra. For millennia, *Aphrodite*, the goddess of beauty, love, pleasure, and procreation—aided by her two angelic agents, *Himeros* and *Eros*—ruled the Freudian skies of humanity. It was only when 1998 issued Viagra, which caused a global male uprising, that *Aphrodite* added the Viagra brothers to her aphrodisiac retinue.

In 1978, the year when 43 year-old King Hussein of Jordan married 27 year-old Queen Noor, Mrs. Alhajj—who was young, attractive, bejeweled, and modern looking, but spoke no English—came all the way to Oklahoma to see me. A year earlier, I had helped her student brother—who suffered from hypogonadism, and responded to testosterone—regain his virility. I presumed that she must have heard about me from him, because it was he who had made the appointment.

After the customary greeting of *al-salamu alaiki* and the cultural circumlocution of *keef halik,* I inquired, "How may I help you, Mrs. Alhajj?"
"Oh, Doctor. I have come from far away just to see you," she entreated with solemn eyes.
"But, you have great medical care in your country," I reassured, with a hint of surprise.
"We do, Doctor, we do, but not with this problem," she replied, lowering her gaze.

For what seemed like a long and tedious while, she hovered around the embarrassing topic, utilizing vague, unfocused diction. She used so many words but said so little, as if to say what she had come to say was going to cause her ineffable shame. But, when I firmly informed her that I could not be better than all the highly trained doctors in her country, and that she was probably wasting her time, she looked at me through helpless tears and pleaded, "You helped my brother, Doctor, when no one else could."

"How many doctors did your brother see before he saw me?" I asked, knowingly.

"You were the only doctor he ever saw. He was too proud to see the doctors at home, but, for some reason, when he came here on scholarship, he was not embarrassed to confide in you."

"Are you having sexual problems, *ya ukhti*?" I asked with polite, cultural discretion, referring to her as *my sister*, for I was thirty-two at the time.

"Oh, no, no, Doctor. You misunderstood. I'm so sorry. I feel fine, myself," she half-smiled, covering her mouth with her hand.

Still unable to uncover the purpose behind her long journey, I furrowed my eyebrows and asked with a firm voice, "So, if you feel fine, why did you journey 8000 miles to see me?"

Her face glowed with the deep, crimson flush that heralds painful confessions. She fidgeted in her seat, gulped with a dry mouth, scanned the examination room walls with circumspect eyes, took in a deep sigh, and then whispered, "Oh, Doctor. I have never told a soul."

I said nothing, my calm face belying my mounting impatience.

"Oh, Doctor. It's all about my husband. He wants a boy and..." she hesitated then covered her eyes with both hands.

I rearranged my posture, hid behind my veil of anguish, and clung to my silence.

"Oh, Doctor. On our wedding night, he had chest pain. We rushed him to the hospital. It was a small heart attack. They told him that he was lucky. But they also told him that he had diabetes, high blood pressure, and high cholesterol, which he did not know about because he refused to go to doctors. When he recovered, they sent him to the Cleveland Clinic where they did four bypasses on his heart, gave him more medicines, and told him not to have sex for six weeks. When the six weeks passed, he tried and tried, but nothing... Oh, Doctor, it was so sad; I mean, so embarrassing; I mean, so disappointing. He told me that he felt betrayed by his own body, and that, in turn, he had betrayed me. He swore that he was mighty and fine before his heart attack."

I handed her a tissue and waited while she dried her cheeks and organized her few, remaining, precious words.

"He visited many specialists. Nothing. This is why I came to you. I told him that I wanted to visit my brother and he believed me. Oh, Doctor. If I don't have a boy within a year, I will be out."

"Out?" I cried with disbelief. "What do you mean by out?"

"We had a prenuptial agreement. If I don't give him a son within two years, he will divorce me. But if I do, my son and I will inherit 10% of his fortune. The remaining 90% go to his other wives and children. Many-many millions, Doctor. No one knows how much he's worth. Not even he knows."

"How old is he?" I asked with suspicion.

"He is twenty years older than King Hussein," she said with a subdued voice "He is sixty-three and I am twenty-seven, the same age as Queen Noor. You see, Doctor, neither he nor I have much time left."

Mrs. Alhajj began to sob when I told her that his age, his heart attack, his multiple medical problems, and his numerous medications render untreatable his male dysfunction.

"They told him the same thing at the Cleveland Clinic—when he returned for his checkup after the surgery—and so did our doctors at home. That is why I came to you. If you can't help me, I will be doomed. Doomed and damned, Doctor. Our customs are very harsh. No man will re-marry a divorced woman who did not bear children. I will be shunned by everyone, including my family."

I felt impotent before her suppliant tears, as impotent as a man who could not swim, standing on a bridge, watching a helpless woman drown. Crestfallen, Mrs. Alhajj quietly sobbed and her mascara-tinged tears freely flowed down her cheeks. I handed her more tissue and probed my brain.

"Has your husband considered the possibility of an implant?"

"They offered it to him, but he declined because it was artificial. He wants to have a child God's way."

"How about artificial insemination?"

"Same thing, Doctor. It's not God's way."

"Do you know the names of the medications he takes?"

"Oh, no Doctor. How can I know? He takes so many. Even he doesn't know what he takes."

My mind stormed as she stared at me with big, beseeching pupils. How could I treat a man I have never seen for a disease that has no treatment? Then, a sudden bolt of lightning pierced my brain.

"Does he put a medicine under his tongue when he gets chest pain?" I inquired from behind the dark veil of my idea.

"Oh, yes Doctor. He keeps the glycerin pills with him at all times, but he has never had to use them."

Desperate for a solution, for a most desperate situation, I sighed with relief at the realization that nitroglycerin had already been prescribed. Smiling, I took out my prescription pad and wrote the following note:

Dear Doctor,

Mrs. Alhajj has asked me for a favor, which I could not grant. Perhaps you might extend her dire situation a helping hand by providing her husband with a tube of transdermal nitroglycerin ointment, which he is to employ in a therapeutic trial for his dysfunction. I have explained to Mrs. Alhajj the particular details of its use, but I need you, his home cardiologist, to provide him with the prescription.

"Mrs. Alhajj," I instructed, handing her the note. "I only have one safe idea, but it's untried. Give this note to your husband's cardiologist and if he accepts to provide him with a tube of nitroglycerin, squeeze one centimeter into your palm and massage him with it before you attempt intercourse."

Mrs. Alhajj blushed with aspiration as she folded the note and tucked it deep into her crocodile-skin purse. I walked her to the waiting room, bid her farewell, and returned to my work, bloated with disbelief and denial at what I had just done.

*

One month later, my secretary, Alicia, knocked with urgency on the examination room door.

"Doctor, you have long-distance call from Mrs. Alhajj."

My heart sank. I excused myself and took the call from my office.

"Mrs. Alhajj. What's wrong? Is your husband all right?" I inquired with many morbid ideas in my mind.

"Thank God, Doctor. Nothing is wrong and my husband thanks you. But, I have one little problem."

"Problem? What kind of a problem?" I inquired, squeezing the telephone handle with my grip.

"Each time we have relations, Doctor, I get a bad headache, which lasts several hours."

"Oh, dear," I cried with delight. "It's a nitroglycerin migraine, and it's treatable. Get a pencil and paper and I'll tell you what to do."

I slowly enunciated her anti-migraine prescription: *"Take 25 mg of indomethacin plus 10 mg of propranolol, with a little food, one hour before you have relations*, and that should block your nitroglycerin migraine. Ask your doctor to prescribe them to you. They are effective and safe."

"Thank you, Doctor. Thank you, and thank you, and thank you," she repeated before she hung up.

*

About a year later, again with urgency, Alicia knocked at the examination room door.

"It's Mrs. Alhajj, calling long distance."

Again my heart sank and my mind spun. I excused myself and took the call from my office.

"Mrs. Alhajj. Is everything all right?" I stuttered.

"Oh, yes, Doctor. Everything is very all right. I'm just calling to thank you. We have a baby boy and my husband thinks it's a medical miracle."

"I'm so happy for you," I squealed with relief. "What did you name him?"

"We named him *Sudaa*."

"*Sudaa!*" I giggled with astonishment. "You named your son, *Migraine*?"

"Well Doctor. I hate to tell you this, but the pills you prescribed for me did not work and I continued to have headaches. My husband felt so sorry for me. He was the one who named him *Sudaa*."

Fatherland
Miss Fatima Hussein

<u>The Tripoli Schools</u>

In Tripoli, Lebanon, the American Evangelical Schools recline in the Muslim centers of town, surrounded by resounding minarets that five times a day, call the faithful to prayer. Established by Presbyterian Missionaries in 1873 when the area was under Ottoman rule, they remain the beacon for English-teaching schools in North Lebanon.

I entered the school's kindergarten at age four and in 1963, at the age of seventeen, graduated from their high school. The classes were an amiable mélange of the two monotheisms, but we all went to chapel every morning, sat side-by-side in the pews, joyously chanted together the daily hymns, and listened to the sermons and bible stories with eager ears. The schools closed their gates on Muslim and Christian holidays and we enjoyed double vacation times. Christmas, the Prophet's birthday, Easter, Al-Adha, Lent, and Ramadan were all observed by everyone. On Christian holidays, our *gratulant* Muslim friends visited our homes and we reciprocated on their holidays. At Christmas, we all sang Christmas carols to the sonorous sounds of the magnificent organ, whose fingers reached all the way to the ceiling arches, which framed the chapel's dome.

At the end of third grade, the boys had to leave the Tripoli Girls School branch and were transferred to the branch upon the hill known as the Tripoli Boys School. At that time, the American Evangelical Schools were not integrated beyond the third grade, but that segregation, of course, did not apply to teachers. My favorite teacher during those formative years was our English literature teacher, Miss Fatima Hussein, a *Muslimah* from the heart of Tripoli. A graduate of the American University of Beirut—another American missionary beacon of learning established in 1866—she introduced us to the literary giants of Western culture and inseminated in us the love of classical reading and creative writing. By graduation, we were all in love with Shakespeare, Coleridge, Byron, Keats, Dickenson, Frost, Cummings, Whitman, Elliot, Thoreau, Emerson, and so many others. Also by graduation, my seventeen classmates and I were all desperately in love with Miss Fatima Hussein, who was thirty-seven at the time.

To my eyes, my thoughts, and to my heart, Miss Fatima Hussein embodied the apotheosis of womanhood. She was a magnificent soul condensed into breathtaking beauty with deep-blue eyes, night-black hair, a brilliant mind, a ballerina figure, and a spirit that embraced the entire humanity. Perhaps, among my classmates, I was the one who was the most helplessly smitten with Miss Hussein. It mattered not that she was twenty years older, that we belonged to different monotheisms, that she was well established in a promising career, and that I was an adolescent without skills or resources. All I felt at that time was an irresistible yearning to cling to her even if that meant that I would have to keep repeating my senior year forever. With that inconsolable state of mind—when our open-air graduation ceremony ended—I approached her with tear-filled eyes and said, "Miss, Hussein."

"Yes, Mr. class poet," she quipped.

"Will you wait for me?" I whispered with a hoarse voice, parched with dreadful strain.

"Wait for you? Why? Where? What for?" She asked with embarrassment as she wiped off my shameless tears.

"I'll become a doctor in eight years and then I'll come back for you."

She smiled with a pain worse than mine, wiped off my tears again, pulled me to her chest, and whispered in my ear, "When you become a doctor, come visit me. I would be an old woman then and might need your medical help."

After spending eight years at the American University of Beirut, I did become a doctor, but instead of going back to Tripoli to visit Miss Hussein, I went to America to specialize. Five years later, when I had finished my specializations, I was thirty years old and that year was the fateful 1975. I sold my furniture, bought my Pan Am ticket, and was preparing to return to Lebanon when my father called:

"I hear that you are coming back?"
"I have a job offer at the AUB. I start on July first."
"You can't come back, Son. We're about to suffer a civil war that might last twenty years. Lebanon is no longer safe. The Lebanon you grew up in is gone and won't return. As much as I'd love for you to come home, I think that you should stay in America until things settle down."
"Stay in America? Stay for how long?"
"Until it is safe to return."
"And how long would that be?"
"Only God knows, Son. Stay where you are and pray for us who are stuck here and cannot leave."

The Civil War

Later that year, the civil war broke out and sweet little Lebanon was transformed into a bloody battlefield. It became difficult to communicate because the telephone lines were heavily damaged and the mail service was suspended. In my isolation, I obsessively listened to the news, hoping to understand the daily developments of the socio-political conflicts that were disfiguring my fatherland. But, as the media tailor what they feature to what the public likes to hear, essential details were regularly omitted and happenings were often flaunted out of context, all of which added to my confusion. Occasionally, a visitor from Lebanon would call or mail me a letter entrusted to him by my parents. I felt that I was living in exile, away from my beloved homeland, subsisting entirely on rumors and a few crumbs of facts.

Some nights, I unwittingly kindled my insomnia by wondering about my Tripoli Boys School upon the hill with window-framed views of the Mediterranean Sea, views I soaked in day after day from fourth grade until graduation. I pondered the whereabouts of my classmates, my teachers, and my ardent teenage love, Miss Fatima Hussein, who had become the alphabet of my thoughts. In my isolation, I convinced myself that if I would imagine good things, then bad things could not happen. But being so far away and so out of touch, I found it harder to conjure good scenes. As the weeks hissed across my mind, I began to see happenings in either red or black. The snow-white mountains, the green valleys, and the ancient blue sea, being neither red nor black, tantalized my imagination and began to pull away like a frightened kitten who would not let me hold her long enough to feel her purr against my chest.

A few days before Christmas, one sunless Sunday afternoon, two of my Lebanese friends showed up, uninvited, at my door. My heart sank when I looked at their faces. In their eyes they held all the shades between black and red, between gloom and fear, and between grief and finality. I did not dare ask nor did they dare speak. We just sat in ominous silence, examining the sundry inanimate objects about the room.

"The fighting has gotten very fierce in Beirut," said Samir.
"Snipers are at every building top and they shoot at anything that moves," said Sami.

I knew that they did not drop in just to talk about the civil war but I did not dare force the issue by asking them certain pointed questions such as, 'What happened or what did you come here to tell me?' I wanted to postpone my knowing as long as I could and so did they. The silence groaned awkwardly as the minutes ticked. Samir cleared his throat as if he were about to say something but then he didn't. Sami coughed, sniffled, and then let out a deep sigh. I began to feel breathless under the suffocating tension.

"We heard that there was an explosion next to the lighthouse, close to your Beirut home," said Samir.

"Rumor has it that your brother, Nadir, has been injured," mumbled Sami.

Still, I did not want to ask even though I knew that they had come to tell me something and that they would not be able to hold back their words too much longer. Red and black visions of Nadir, my middle brother, tormented my eyes. He turned twenty-eight on the 10th of December and I couldn't call him to say happy birthday.

"We heard it was a bad injury," said Samir.
"They said that he might not make it," said Sami.
"They have him at the AUB," said Samir.

I looked at their quivering faces and felt sorry for them. They came to tell me something and neither of them was able to say it. To lessen their burden, I interjected, "When did it happen?"
"On his birthday," came their answers in unison.
"Did my father call you and ask you to come tell me?"
"He called us from the Egyptian embassy. They let him use their wireless."
"He was killed by a sniper, wasn't he? Killed on his birthday," I nervously blurted as if talking to myself.

Their silence was their confession. After that, nothing else was said and they soon excused themselves, leaving me to my red imagination and black grief. It was only when my father was able to fly to London that he and I were able to talk at length. He told me about the funeral, my mother's inconsolable grief, and how he was planning to send my little sister and younger brother to study abroad as soon as it became feasible.

"I don't want what happened to Nadir to happen to them," were his last words to me before he said good-bye.

The Invasion

Grief from afar is a dry well full of resounding echoes. I could not cry nor could I feel sadness. All I felt was a deep, painful void, a dry socket that I could only distract by day, but which kept me awake at night. It was then, in my exiled loneliness, that Miss Fatima Hussein's words came to my rescue:

"When you are sad, if you cannot find words that assuage your loss, you may not be able to get over your grief. Be creative in expressing your emotions and make use of literature; it is the balsam of broken hearts."

That was when I began writing poetry about my fatherland's 1975 deadly autumn and my brother's blue face. The verses scrolled out of me, one or two stanzas at a time, but I had no need to write them down. Once they had descended upon my mind, they became indelible and I could retrieve them at will, especially when I felt overcome by grief. The first two stanzas of *Fatherland* descended upon me after midnight on New Year's Eve, when the rest of the world was in frenzy:

I watch the trees undress in autumn sun
Reveal their private branches, one by one
Unmindful of my gaze, no blush no cry
Embrace the humming wind and mark the sky.

These clouds of misty perfume and the breeze
Bring back your face amidst the naked trees
And tipsy violins and all the sins
Of gushing youth, and ah—the memories.

In July of 1976, six months after my brother's death, our Christian hometown, Amioun, was invaded and ransacked by upper-mountain Christian forces. The invaders were Catholic Christians while the invaded were Greek Orthodox Christians. Amioun's evicted inhabitants took refuge in Tripoli, an overwhelmingly Muslim city, where they were well received and given shelter and food until they were allowed to return to their homes six months later. During that dark half-year, I felt like a quadruple orphan who had lost his brother, his hometown, his country, and his history. I received word that my extended family with all my aunts, uncles, and cousins were living with my mother and father at our large

Tripoli house. Following Miss Fatima Hussein's advice, I held on to my sanity by writing poetry. The biblical injunction, *"With sorrow thou shalt bring forth a child,"* came to mind as I realized that birth was the antidote of death, creation, the antidote of destruction, and both antidotes were within my power, thanks to Miss Fatima Hussein. That's when the third and fourth stanzas of *Fatherland* were born:

> *Where mighty, melancholy mountains peak*
> *And olive branches meditate and speak*
> *Unto the earth, who is so old and noble*
> *And the vine, invites the birds to gossip on her cheek.*

> *Fatherland, oh, fatherland*
> *If only I could hold your hand and stand upon your shore*
> *Behold your hoary mountains dive into the sea and snore*
> *With mystifying grace*
> *Implore the endless waves to wash your ancient face.*

The Visit

In 1978, during a lull in the war, I flew back to Beirut. To get to Tripoli, I had to drive across two mountain ranges because the seashore road was blocked by warring militias. An otherwise easy, 90-minute drive turned into an arduous, eight-hour journey. Arriving before dark, I was surprised to find my extended family still living with us. After tear-laced kisses and whimpering embraces, I sat down and listened to all their tales. All their homes were demolished during the invasion, stripped to the bone, and rendered uninhabitable. All the able men had gone to the oil countries to work and were sending money to support their *homeless* families. The homes would take years to rebuild.

The next morning, I asked my father to drive me to Amioun to visit my brother's grave. The town was hard to recognize with all the disfiguring rubble scarring its beautiful face. Places where I had grown up and played were no longer discernable, their original images preserved only in my memory. Painfully, I became aware that my mind was being transformed into an archive of old photographs of places that had molted out of recognition. The home of my grandfather, the town's priest, was being used as a trash dump, and its stone arches, like fossils, lay buried in the dirt. Around it, the few natives who were able to return to the village walked about with lowered gazes and stooped backs. I waved hello to some and they waved back, but without recognizing me. I had been gone too long and too much had happened during my absence.

    The cemetery lay atop a rocky cliff overlooking the vast olive plain beneath, connected to the main road by a long, narrow bridge. The iron-gate squeaked as we slipped in and began our amble across the long, narrow link between life and death, and between present and past. My father limped from back injuries sustained while a political prisoner ten years earlier. I walked beside him in the thin air that wafted from the graves, smelling of morning rain. At the family's gravesite, there was a tattered wreath over a gravestone engraved with his name, Nadir (1947-1975).

    The rain-drenched silence groaned under the heft of memories as we stood there and stared. My heart clawed incessantly at my chest, scuttled across the flesh within, and caused a hemorrhage of tears to explode out of my charged sockets. My sobbing convulsions alarmed my father who steadied my shoulders and watched me discharge my three-year-old debt of grief with a flood of held-back tears. My tears and I became the suspending bridge between present and past, between life and death, and between red and black memories whose colors were faded by the acid rains.

    "Enough, Son. Let's go back home. Your mother will start worrying if we stay any longer."

    "No," came my gasping reply. "I have three years of tears that I need to shed before I leave. I don't want to carry them back with me to America."

Silence was our conversation on the way back from the grave. My eyes had dried up by then but my father's were still shimmering with recall. I remembered the last line in my mother's letter, which arrived to America two months after Nadir's death:

"Everything has been taken away from us; the only thing we have left is poetry."

The fifth stanza of my unfinished poem scrolled out of my mind as I watched the sun blush at the Mediterranean Sea and the rising moon smile from behind the Cedar Mountains:

Fatherland, before I gray, I will be back
I will be back one misty autumn day
To hug your loving dirt against my chest
And plant a garden on your ruddy breast
Loiter together in the timid afternoon
Until the sun begins to blush before the moon.

The High School

The next morning, I felt an urge to visit my high school and check if Miss Fatima Hussein was still teaching there. I was thirty-two then, which meant that she would be fifty-two. I remembered her words to me after graduation: *"When you become a doctor, come visit me. I would be an old woman then and might need your medical help."*

The walk from home to school when I was a student used to take me 45 minutes and since I was most eager to see what changes had taken place during the past fifteen years, I decided to go on foot. I passed through the town's center where, when I was a child, the only taxis were horse-pulled carriages, and where the sidewalk photographers snapped shots of passersby, offering each photograph for just one Lira. The change that shook me the most was noise. In contrast to the rhythmic gallop of the horse-pulled carriages, there was a chaotic congestion of cars flooding the streets and honking their horns in frustration. Armed men and vehicles were posted at every corner, and cars were parked on the sidewalks, leaving little room for pedestrians who spilled into the roads, crisscrossed between the honking cars, and slowed down the already stifled traffic.

When I got close to the Tripoli Girls School—where I had gone till third grade—nostalgic soap aromas filled my nostrils as I passed the small soap factories along the way. I stood by the school gate and was surprised to see boys and girls of all ages frolicking in the schoolyard. They still looked about the same as when I was among them, but the supervising teachers seemed much younger than they used to be. It took me a while to realize that, at thirty-two, I was already older than many of the teachers standing among the kids. *"Relativity must not be an attribute of the human mind,"* I thought, as I turned to leave.

Leaving the Tripoli Girls School, I passed through the commercial parts of town where all the groceries, grains, and meats arrive to be distributed by the wholesalers. There were trucks loaded with chicken, goats, sheep, vegetables, fruits, nuts, charcoal, gas jars, and fresh-water bottles from the mountain springs. Ironsmiths were welding and cutting their ironworks and copper artisans were hammering their wares into pots and trays. The Friday flea market was busting with all imaginable items and the stench of animal dung, human throngs, and fresh agricultural products caused me to hurry on through and begin my ascent up the residential hill where the air was cleaner and the traffic was more domestic. I used the long, winding stairs, my usual short cut, and arrived at my high school just before noon.

The high iron-gate with *'Tripoli Boys School'* emblazoned on it was closed shut and there was a soldier with a machine-gun standing guard. I cautiously approached and greeted him with, "Good morning, Sir."

"Good morning to you," he replied with a smile.

"May I go in for a look? I graduated from this school fifteen years ago."

He smiled at me as if I were a foreigner and then added, "Where do you live now?"

"In America."

"And how long have you been gone?"

"Seven years."

"So you really don't know what happened to your school?"

My heart stood still as I imagined some catastrophic massacre that befell my teachers. I must have turned pale because he did not wait for my reply and simply added, "Your school was turned into barracks when the Syrian army came in two years ago to enforce the peace."

"Barracks?" I gasped. "You mean there are no teachers or students inside?"

"They all went to the Girls School down town."

"Oh!" I exclaimed. "So that's why it was full of boys and girls of all ages."

I thanked him and began my long descent back, resolving to stop at what used to be the Tripoli Girls School to see if they would let me take a peek. *"Surely, the teachers would know if Miss Fatima Hussein is still there,"* I thought. As I approached, my heart began to pound as if it were dreading what it was about to hear. *"Something could have happened to her. She could have been killed in an explosion or kidnapped for ransom or sniped like my brother. She could have gotten married and left town."* I thought of all possible scenarios and could not settle down my mind until I reached the school gate and greeted the guard with, "Good afternoon, Sir."

"Good afternoon to you," smiled the middle aged, plump man.

"I just found out that the Tripoli Boys School was turned into barracks. I graduated from there in 1963. I was wondering if any of my old teachers could still be here?"

"Fifteen years is a long time, Sir. I think the only one remaining is Mr. Sansour. He is the principal now."

"Oh, good. Could I see him, please?"

"Sure, his office is in that building on the ground floor. He should be there now."

As I walked, I tried to remember how everything used to look when I was in third grade. So much had been renovated, which blurred the original views, but there was still a déjà vu familiarity to the surroundings, a nostalgic remembrance perceivable through the mind's recalling eye. As I mused, time scurried, unnoticed, and before I realized it, I found myself at the principal's office. The door was open wide, there was no secretary, and Mr. Sansour was at his desk working on papers. He had grown white with years, but was still in good form. I knocked. He peered at me through his eyeglasses and said, "Yes. May I help you?"

I walked up to his desk, put out my hand, and smiled, "I'm one of your students from long ago, Sir. You taught me chemistry."

His knowing eyes studied me as his mind strained to recall my name. "Ssss. Salem. Salem Hawi. How good of you to stop by. You're a doctor, I hear," he said as he stood up and warmly shook my hand. "Are you going to stay in America or have you decided to return to us? We need you here a lot more than they need you there. You know that most of our doctors have left because of the war."

"It's not safe, Sir. This is my first visit in seven years and a lot has changed."

"Changed for the worse, unfortunately. Please sit down and tell me about you. I'm sorry about your brother Nadir. He was my student too. What a senseless death. How are your parents handling it?"

We talked for a long while, and several times I attempted to ask him about Miss Fatima Hussein, but could never bring myself to phrase the question. I had to overcome my fear of bad news, first. We talked about our 1963 class: I told him what I knew of the whereabouts of some of my classmates and he told me that Mahmoud had died a few years earlier of pancreatic cancer. I found myself becoming more and more disturbed as more bad news about people I knew unfolded. Dr. Rowda became a double amputee when a missile exploded between his legs while he was having a drink on his balcony last summer. I could sense that he had more to tell me but, seeing the weariness on my face, he paused as if to give me a chance to change the topic. It was during that lull that I summoned up the courage, took in a deep breath as if I were preparing to dive from a high cliff, and asked him with downcast eyes, "Is Miss Fatima Hussein still unmarried?"

He eyed me with amazement as he tried to decipher my meaning. Perhaps he understood that I was avoiding one question by asking another, or perhaps he realized that I was afraid to ask, but was eager to know. In response, he lowered his gaze and began: "She was married to her students, which left no room for a man in her life. She had many suitors but never gave any of them a chance. School was her only life and that's how she lived until her house was hit during a night battle. No one dared move till the next morning because there was a curfew. It took them all of the following day to find her buried under the rubble. They took her to the hospital where she stayed a few days and all the while refused to open her eyes. We all visited her but she never looked at us nor said a word. We all thought that she had become deaf and blind from the explosion, but the doctors assured us that her ears and eyes were fine. When she was released, she had no place to go because her parents had died and she was an only child with no living relatives. She was sent to the Bakhour Psychiatric Hospital on Mount Turbol. Many of us have gone to visit her, but she still keeps her eyes shut when we visit and will not speak to any of us. She has been there about a year now and there are no signs that she cares to leave. She seems quite content in her solitude. What a great waste. She was the best teacher we've ever had and everyone loved her."

"Does she open her eyes for the help?" I asked.

"We are told that she does and sometimes even talks to them. She just won't talk to or open her eyes for visitors. You're the doctor; what does all that mean?"

"Perhaps it means that she does not want to see or hear any more bad news or maybe that's her way of dealing with disillusionments. She may also be clinging to her beliefs."

"Beliefs? What do you mean by that?"

"Well, you know what an idealist she was and you have seen how war forces us all to become realists. Perhaps she has decided to preserve her idealism by keeping her soul quarantined."

"That's the best explanation I've heard so far. I'd like to share it with the other teachers, if you don't mind."

"Just tell them that Miss Fatima Hussein is afraid to lose her faith in the human race and that's why she cloisters herself."

The Mountain Hospital

When I arrived home, I was greeted by my parents' worried looks and an outburst of unintelligible words. I had to ask them to speak one at a time before I understood that they were worried to death about me. Apparently, things were not as safe as they appeared to be and they thought that I shouldn't have ventured that far away from home. Having already lost one son to snipers, I could understand their agitated state of mind. It did not count that I had spent the first seventeen years of my life in Tripoli. What mattered was that I had spent the last seven years abroad and that fact transmuted me into a naive foreigner.

I slept poorly that night and my mind conjured a web of disturbing images. I saw firestorms, bloody rivers, and a rough sea frothing with angry waves. But the most disturbing image of all was that of the snow-mountains crying steaming-hot tears. The image was so real that I got out of bed and gazed at the moonlit mountains to see if they were on fire. Sleep refused to come until I had written the sixth and seventh stanzas of *Fatherland*.

> *Some weary nights I wonder if you sleep*
> *I see the worry on your mountain face*
> *And frowning furrows run so dark and steep*
> *And little soldiers run about the place.*
>
> *Hoary mountain land, repose, un-frown your brow*
> *Forget the little soldiers now*
> *Look back a thousand scores, recount*

The many times some little soldiers ran about your mount.
What do the little soldiers know?
So they come and so they go
And you will have their dust, and mine
And every year there will be snow.

The next morning I took a taxi to the Bakhour Psychiatric Hospital on Mount Turbol. We passed through multiple armed checkpoints, demolished quarters, shanty camps, angry crowds burning tires in the middle of the road, and long traffic lines manically honking their horns. An hour's trip took us three-and-a-half hours so that by the time I climbed the hospital steps, my eyes, heavy with sights of mass misery, had dried up in their sockets, and my knees had stiffened with sudden aging. My mind, on the other hand, overflowed with questions. *"What if she refuses to open her eyes or talk to me? What if she does not remember who I am? What if she asks me to leave? Should I carefully prepare my words or should I be natural?"*

As I weighed these questions while approaching the reception desk, one thought burst into flame and set my brain on fire. *"There had not been a day during the past fifteen years that I had not thought of Miss Fatima Hussein."*

The realization, that ever since I graduated I had been longing for this very moment, stunned me into a daze. I must have appeared sick because the lady at the reception desk stared at me with gaping eyes.

"Are you alright, Sir?"

"Oh, alright, yes ma'am. It just took us too long to get here."

"Where from did you come?"

"Tripoli."

"Oh, they are experiencing riots."

"Riots, burning tires, armed check points, and impossible traffic. It took us more than three hours."

"Well, it's still clean and peaceful up here. How may I help you?"

"I came to visit Miss Fatima Hussein."

"Oh, she no longer allows visitors. You should have called us first."

"I'm Doctor Salem Hawi."

"Oh, I'm so sorry, Doctor. I'll call one of our nurses to take you to her."

While nurse Latifa and I walked the long corridor to room 303, I made some inquires.

"How's she doing?"

"She seems fine but says very little and prefers to remain in her room. We have to bring the food to her because she refuses to go the dining room. She never gives us any trouble, though, and spends all her time reading. Every time she finishes one book, she goes to the library and gets another. She talks to the librarian more than she talks to anyone else. They both like poetry and literature."

"Does she talk about her past life?"

"She never talks about herself or about anyone else. She has no relatives and no one comes to visit her anymore. She's going to be with us for life, I am told."

Miss Fatima Hussein

Nurse Latifa knocked softly on Miss Hussein's door, stuck her neck in, and announced me by saying, "Doctor Salem Hawi from Tripoli is here to see you."

Her faint voice repeated Nurse Latifa's words with unconcealed astonishment, "Doctor Salem Hawi from Tripoli is here to see me?"

"Yes, Miss Fatima. It took him three and a half hours to get here because there were riots along the way."

"Oh, well. Can you just give me a few minutes to tidy up the room and ready myself?"

My heart throbbed with joy and my eyes overflowed with un-concealed moisture. *"She's willing to see me and still remembers my name after fifteen years,"* I thought from behind my tears. I felt an overwhelming sense of relief because a great fear had been lifted off my heart, the stifling fear of rejection. Nurse Latifa was most amused by Miss Hussein's excitement and exclaimed with surprise, "I've never heard so much enthusiasm in her voice. You must be very dear to her, Doctor. Maybe you can influence her to start going to the dining room and socializing a bit. Her self-imposed isolation can't be good."

While nurse Latifa and I waited in the corridor, she told me that the hospital was full, that the war had caused an epidemic of mental illness, and that most of their patients were actually normal before the war. She talked about the inmates' inconsolable grief caused by so many senseless deaths, property losses, humiliations, and displacements. "The whole country is mentally ill, Doctor," were her last words when the door of Room 303 cracked open and a faint voice whispered, "Come in please."

Miss Fatima Hussein stood in the middle of the room facing the door, just like she used to stand in class as her students scrolled in. She had grown whiter with confinement but her welcoming smile was unchanged and her wide-open eyes shimmered like blue flames. A youthful visage and a model's figure belied the fifty-two years that had left their dust upon her heart. Like an obedient student, I stood at a distance and waited for her to ask me to take a seat. She didn't. She merely stood there, expectant, smiling, and utterly silent.

"It's good to see you, Miss Hussein," I mumbled, unable to find better words.
She gleamed in her stance but said nothing.
"Miss Hussein, I'm so sorry about what happened. I visited Mr. Sansour yesterday and he was the one who told me."
Slowly, her smile relinquished her face, her figure slumped into a stoop, and her deep, blue gaze drooped to the floor. My mouth went dry at her sudden metamorphosis that made me feel like a meddlesome intruder.

"Miss Hussein, I'm sorry to have upset you. Would you like me to leave and perhaps return at some other time?"

She shook her head and pointed to a straw chair by the window.

"Would you like me to sit down?"

She pointed again to the chair, waited till I had sat in it, and then eased herself into the matching chair on the other side of the window. There was a side table between us with a pile of books on it, but the spines were all turned toward her so I couldn't see the titles. I fidgeted in my seat and held my breath as if I were in the principal's office.

"You kept your promise," she whispered.

"What promise?" I gasped, astonished to hear her speak.

"Have you forgotten?"

"You mean at graduation when I said—will you wait for me—and you wiped off my tears and then I said—I'll become a doctor in eight years and then I'll come back for you—and you said—when you become a doctor, come visit me. I would be an old woman then and might need your medical help."

I blurted all that without stopping as if I had rehearsed it a thousand times before coming to see her.

She nodded as a faint gleam briefly rose into her face and then vanished away into the silence. That was her last emotion before her face turned to wax and an oblivious stare terminated all further hopes of conversation.

I was at a loss for what to do. I wanted to say something or do something but nothing meaningful came to mind except my Fatherland poem, which was missing its last stanza. As the lines began to scribble themselves before my eyes, I stood up, took in a deep sigh, walked to the door, turned around for one last look, and with an obo voice recited the finish of my *Fatherland* ode:

Fatherland,
The footsteps of the Lord stood once upon your sand
And the sea amid a storm stood still
And there are little soldiers under every hill

And the cedar trees upon the mount command:
Thou shalt not kill
And quietly pray for peace
In the land of the Lord our Father
In the Fatherland.

The Return

The next time I visited Lebanon was nine years later, for my father's funeral. I was forty then, Miss Fatima Hussein was sixty, and my father had died at the age of sixty-nine of pancreatic cancer. The funeral procession passed in front of my grandfather's home where my father, the priest's son, had grown up. It was still being used as a trash-dump, an eyesore that tormented my father during the last twelve years of his life. We crossed the bridge from the road to the cemetery—the same bridge that my father and I had crossed nine years earlier to visit my brother's grave—and we interred my father right next to my brother underneath the same dirt that held our ancestral dust.

Things were not any safer that July of 1987 but, nevertheless, and in spite of my mother's pleadings, I took a taxi to the Bakhour Psychiatric Hospital on Mount Turbol. We passed by Tripoli Boys School, my high school upon the hill, which was still being used as barracks. The road up the mountain was littered with burned vehicles; there were piles of plastic bags here and there because trash was not being picked up; shanties that housed the homeless were scattered all along the way; and the cars on the road rattled with age.

The once peaceful and clean mountain hospital, after eleven years of war, had become dilapidated. One corner was demolished, the hospital entrance was littered with plastic bags, the reception desk looked mutilated, and piles of debris were scattered all over the lobby. I walked up to the receptionist and said, "I'm doctor Salem Hawi here to see Miss Fatima Hussein."

"Oh, Doctor, I'm sorry but she's no longer with us."

"What do you mean, no longer with us?" I snapped with perturbed voice.

The receptionist became agitated at my tone. Hesitantly, she picked up the phone and called for Head Nurse Latifa. As I paced in the foyer, awaiting Nurse Latifa's arrival, muffled whispers erupted here and there and many an inquisitive eye spied my every move. Then, from behind my back, I heard, "Dr. Hawi?"

"Nurse Latifa, you still remember my name after nine years," I exclaimed as I extended a friendly hand.

"Oh, Doctor, how could I forget it. She talked about you all the time."

"And where is she now?"

"She's no longer with us, Doctor."

"That's what the receptionist said, so where is she then," I asked with trepidation.

Nurse Latifa's face became contorted and a blue stare overtook her brown eyes. Holding my arm, she walked with me to a side room and closed the door.

"Would you like to sit down, Doctor?" she said as she pointed to an old, dusty couch.

I did not resist because my knees were about to buckle. She sat next to me and waited for me to say something. That endless moment brought back to my mind the time when Samir and Sami came to tell me of my brother's death, and my heart sank when I looked at their faces, and I dared not ask nor dared they speak, and we just sat there in ominous silence.

"The corner of the east wing was demolished by a stray bomb during a night battle one week ago. It took us all the next day to get to her because she was buried deep under the rubble. No one claimed her body because she had no relatives. We had to take her to the Orphan's Cemetery down in the valley. The ambulance driver and I were the only ones present at her funeral. She was a Muslimah but the priest in charge of the cemetery was the one who conducted the graveside service. He was most kind and ended the service by reciting verses from the Koran."

"Did anyone else get hurt?"

"Only her room received a direct hit. The other patients were scared to death by the explosion, but none of them was physically harmed."

"How about her belongings?"

"She had no belongings, Doctor. Everything in her room including her clothes belonged to the hospital and the explosion destroyed them all."

Then, as if she had forgotten something important, Nurse Latifa suddenly excused herself, said that she would be back in a minute, and asked me to please wait for her. When she returned, she held an envelope with my name on it, inscribed with Miss Fatima Hussein's handwriting.

"About a month ago, she gave me this envelope and told me to give it to you when you came for her. She must have known that she was going to die and that you would be coming back to check on her."

On the way back, while the taxi negotiated the steep mountain road, I opened the envelope. In it, there was a short, handwritten letter addressed to me:

*

Dr. Salem Hawi
Bakhour Psychiatric Hospital
Mount Turbol
Lebanon

My Dear Salem,

When you visited me, I said but little even though I knew a lot. I knew that you would come back for me and that you would find me dead. I also knew that you thought about me every day. You need to know that I also thought about you every day. You have not left my mind since graduation day when you said, with tears in your eyes, "Will you wait for me?" I could not answer you then but now I can. Yes, I will wait for you. But do not hurry and do as much good as you can for as long as you can. I know that, when your time comes, you will come back for me one last time.

I love you,
Fatima.

*

The Unshed Tears

In mid air, on my way back to America, I wondered if destiny and coincidence had contrived to cause Miss Fatima Hussein to die on the same day that my father died. I also wondered why was I unable to shed any tears either during my father's funeral or during my descent from Mount Turbol Psychiatric Hospital with Miss Fatima Hussein's last letter in my hand.

Perhaps, unlike the three years of tears that I shed at my brother's grave, I was destined to carry my father and Miss Fatima Hussein's tears back with me to America. Unshed tears are how our souls hold onto loves that have been lost. They are the griefs that become parts of what we become, the indelible memories that send us thoughts from our lost loves, and what our souls need to reunite after they are released.

These were my musings as I floated above the clouds across the Atlantic Ocean, suspended between East and West, past and future, love and death, reality and dreams, and between language and thought. Sweet melancholy would comfort me for the rest of my days and poems would become my prayers, which I would raise to God whenever I felt the need to talk to my brother, my father, or to Miss Fatima Hussein.

> *Because I have two hearts*
> *Because I straddle oceans*
> *Because I am both banks of life*
> *The froth and currents in between*
> *The dissonant emotions*
> *I see beyond the mighty walls of time*
> *Beyond the eyes, the made-up lips and faces*
> *Beyond the borrowed sentiments and faint laces;*
> *Because I have two hearts*
> *My soul is vagabond*
> *It camps in many places.*

The Clandestine Stone

Stories told by common folks echo their unsung histories, and unless these stories are chronicled, they will forever be lost.

That political events can influence medical verdicts is as self-evident today as it has been for centuries. Juries, like voters, are prone to choose with their emotions, which derive from the prevailing temperaments of their times. This First World War story, told to me by a doctor who had suffered the irrevocable verdicts of emotional injustice, is as pertinent now as it was in 1915.

I was thirty-five years old when I returned to Lebanon to visit my family during a reprieve in 1981. The Lebanese Civil War, which had started in 1975 and lasted about twenty years, was in détente then, and many immigrants like me seized that opportunity to reconnect with their torn roots.

Soon after arriving, my mother of sixty-five urged me to accompany her to visit her grand mentor, Dr. Niqula, who was celebrating his ninety-sixth birthday. I demurred, certain that I would feel uncomfortable among the geriatric crowd, but in her peculiar kind firmness she prevailed.

"Youth, because it cannot visualize its eminent old age, feels out of place among the aged," she smiled as she took my arm and marched toward the door.

"Dr. Niqula means a lot to you, Mother, because he mentored you. I hardly know him. Besides, internal medicine has little to do with general surgery."

"Have you read Santayana?" She quizzed with wry intonation, certain that I hadn't.

I sighed—for we were already down the street by then—lowered my head, and murmured, "What did Santayana say?"

"George Santayana famously said, *'Those who cannot remember the past are condemned to repeat it.'* He also said, *'The young man who has not wept is a savage, and the old man who will not laugh is a fool.'* You came all the way from America to reconnect with your war-torn roots and you are refusing an opportunity that will not come again."

Walking to Dr. Niqula's home, my mother instructed, hoping to kindle my interest. "Dr. Niqula," she said, "was the foremost general surgeon in Tripoli during the Ottoman Empire rule, during the French Mandate rule, and remained at the helm of general surgery after Lebanon's independence in 1943 until he retired in 1965 at the age of eighty."

"How's his memory?" I smirked.

"As sharp as yours, my smug, young Son," she retorted. "He retired because his hands became unsteady. I was assisting him during his last surgery when he addressed me from behind his mask. *'I have been operating for fifty years, Mai. I think my time has come to lay down the knife.'* Pity how the razor-sharp edge of an instant can end a life-long career."

Contrary to the geriatric crowd I had anticipated, Dr. Niqula's home was abuzz with people of all ages. His only daughter welcomed us in, for he had by then lost his wife and son, one to age and the other to disease.

Lean, small, and stooped, he sat on a sofa, conversing with his guests. When he saw my mother, his eyes sparkled and he half-stood as he extended a trembling hand.

"Is this your American-doctor-son?" he asked, as I bowed to shake his hand.

"Indeed, he is," she replied.

"You are brave to come while our civil war rages, and braver still to visit a centennial man."

"You visit our family conversations often, Doctor Niqula," I responded, "and it is high time I reciprocate."

"You possess a noble trait, young man, politeness, which seems less prevalent among our younger colleagues. Do you think that science and technology are eroding the polish of our profession?"

I stood stunned before his acuteness. However, my befuddlement was not lost on him because he motioned for me to sit next to him, which pleased and released my mother. As she meandered among the guests, doctor Niqula and I conversed as if we were the only two in the room. I asked him about the old times and he asked me about the current times. As we talked, I felt as though we were peering at each other from the opposite ends of a telescope, spanning a sixty-five-year distance.

He was interested in American medicine, partly because he was French educated, and partly because his grandson had just finished a cardiac surgery fellowship at the Cleveland Clinic. At that point in the conversation, the happy smile, which had not left his face, turned into a sad gleam as he cleared his throat and whispered, "Can you believe that he has already been sued?"

"Your grandson sued?" I gasped. "What on earth for?"

"He did an emergency resection of an aortic aneurysm on an elderly lady who later sued him, claiming that the chest tube he inserted damaged her breast implant."

I did not know how to respond to his disillusionment. The pause grew awkward. I cleared my throat, and in an effort to lift the veil of silence, whispered back, "Have you ever been sued?"

People came and left, he shook many a hand, and exchanged deferential snippets of conversation with his guests until the room, which was replete with *wellwishers*, held only his daughter, my mother, and me. It was then, still un-fatigued and spry, that he called my mother into the conversation.

"Come join us, Mai. Your son is a good listener and we have enjoyed exchanging stories. I have one more story to share and I want you to hear it"

Dr. Niqula smiled as my mother joined us and then surprised us both with, "Getting old is letting go of the idea of youth."

"You are still young," chimed my mother.

"The reason I grew old, Mai, was because I got tired of being young."

"How so?" I politely inquired with a hint of disbelief.

"We spend half our lives climbing our mountains and looking forward to reaching the peaks, and the other half descending cautiously and looking forward to reaching the base, the very same base from where we had started."

Then, to my astonishment, he quoted from T. S. Eliot's *Little Gidding*:

> *We shall not cease from exploration*
> *And the end of all our exploring*
> *Will be to arrive where we started*
> *And know the place for the first time.*

I was struck by his profound honesty and looked to my mother for help.

"Old age also trades physical pleasures for intellectual ones, and explores emotional dimensions unfathomable to youth," added my mother with a high-pitched tone.

"Indeed," he nodded, "but do not forgot that one more important thing. Old age makes us better storytellers and hands us more stories to tell."

"That is so true." I nodded, remembering the great pleasures I had as a child, listening to my grandmother tell her old stories, which I have never forgotten. Then, as an afterthought, I interjected, "Stories heard in childhood remain etched on our memories and keep us connected to our parents and grandparents long after they are gone."

"All history, Son, is naught but a string of stories, which ties the past to the present and tethers death to life," he declared. Then, after a brief pause, he added, "Unlike us, our stories are immortal. Ghalib, the renowned Urdu poet, framed it best when he said: '*I think we have caught sight of the road to death now. Death is the string that binds together the scattered beads of the universe.*' What Ghalib was really talking about was not death, but rather the immortal stories of the dead."

After a few reflective moments, Dr. Niqula slid back to 1915, the year when he had started his surgical career in Tripoli. He had returned from France, sold some family land, equipped a small hospital, and began doing surgery when Lebanon was under Ottoman rule.

A year earlier, with the outbreak of World War I, an Ottoman land-and-sea blockade had starved the Lebanese mountain, killing about a third of its Christian inhabitants. Moreover, the Ottomans abolished Lebanon's semiautonomous status and appointed the brutal Djemal Pasha as commander in chief who, with an iron hand, ruthlessly ruled the region. It was during that unpropitious period that Dr. Niqula's story transpired:

"An important Tripoli man came to the hospital at midnight. He was in severe pain and I hurried from home to see him. He was writhing with the pain of a renal colic when I arrived. I promptly gave him some morphine, which was hard to procure at the time, but which I was able to buy on the black market from Ottoman officers.

"For three days, the renal colic persevered, unabated, in spite of morphine and intravenous fluids. The man and his family urged me to operate. I removed the wedged stone from his right kidney. He awoke without pain and went home in a few days.

"Six months later, he presented again at midnight with a similar pain, but this time the pain was on the left side. Again, for three days, I gave him morphine and intravenous fluids. When he could not pass the stone, he and his family again urged me to operate. This time, I removed the stone that was wedged in his left kidney and he awoke without pain and went home shortly thereafter.

"A week later, an Ottoman officer with six soldiers showed up at my hospital and asked me to follow them to the *Serai*, where I was interrogated, roughed up, and thrown in jail.

" '*You will remain in jail until your trial next week,*' said the officer as he locked my cell's door and disappeared. I was given bread and water once per day and allowed to go to the toilet twice a day. On my trial day, the lawyer representing my patient told the judge that I had conspired against his client by taking the stone out of the right side and implanting it in the left side, full knowing that he would have to return for a second surgery.

"The judge nodded in approval in spite of my lawyer's scientific defense, which showed with anatomical pictures that it would have been impossible for me to implant the stone on the other side. *'Doctors are devils,'* said the judge. *'If the doctor was not conspiring, he would have given the man his first stone, but he couldn't, could he? And even if he had given the man the first stone, how do we know that it was the man's stone and not the stone of some other poor man. Doctors are devils and it is hard to outsmart them at their trade.'* He then ordered me to pay back my patient all the money he had paid me and an equal sum for all the pains I had caused him."

I did not know if I should seem amused or bemused. I merely stared at this noble man's setting eyes and waited until he had journeyed back from 1915 to 1981. Then, when his eyes regained their luster, my mother came into the conversation with, "Lord Acton famously said in a letter to Bishop Creighton: *'Power tends to corrupt, and absolute power corrupts absolutely. Great men are almost always bad men.'* "

Dr. Niqula smiled with satisfaction at his student's adage and then, as if condensing the wisdom of his entire ninety-six years on earth, he reflected, "What you really mean by power is the freedom to exercise power. The real power, then, is freedom. And freedom is a lovely maiden. If you entrust her to the honorable, she will be treated with adoration and respect. But, if you entrust her to the ignoramuses, she will be raped."

*

On our way back home, my mother had to rub it in with, "Aren't you glad you accompanied me."

"Yes, Mother. I am, indeed, very glad."

"And what would you have done with your valuable time if you hadn't accompanied me?" she interrogated with a knowing smile.

"I would have read my book."

"Which you would have soon forgotten," she interrupted. "But you will never forget this visit to Dr. Niqula, will you?"

*

Dr. Niqula died a year later with only his daughter by his side, but his story still pulsates with my heartbeats each time I see or hear of legal injustice being levied against the innocent.

And each time I think of him and of my aging mother across the ocean, the words of Mohandas Gandhi play over and over in my mind:

It is nonsense for you to talk of old age as long as you outrun young men in the race for service and in the midst of anxious times fill rooms with your laughter and inspire youth with hope when they are on the brink of despair.

The Clandestine Stone, First Edition, The Bulletin, Oklahoma County Medical Society, January/February 2016. Revised Edition completed in October of 2016.

Amiss

He was seventy-five when first I met him in the emergency department, as stiff as a broken branch, face cratered with the crevices of time, he lay on the gurney, holding his abdomen with crooked hands. His skin crawled around his cavernous eyes and hung like a wet garment from his drooped shoulders. His voice rasped and stuttered as he answered my questions with spit-words and sputtered phrases. I helped him disrobe because his gnarled fingers were too stiff to pinch the buttons. At last, he lay cringed on the examination table with eyes tightly shut and face closed-in as if expecting a slap. Like an afternoon shadow, his stooped wife stood in the corner of the room, looking at her feet, and never said a word.

As I talked to them after the examination, he listened with eager eyes, nodded approvingly, interacted, and asked questions, whereas his little wife held the corner spot like a statuette, taciturn and expressionless.

That was my very first encounter with Uncle Otis.

For two years I labored, trying to improve his *eaten-up-with-ulcers* feelings, but his condition proved resistant to modern medicine. He continued to lose weight in spite of all my efforts and there were times when he was sure that his ulcers bled, even though I could never find blood in his stools. Over time, his relentless *nervous-stomach* continued to enfeeble him. After losing what little body fat he had, he began wasting his muscles until his cachexia reached a point that rendered even more uncertain his already wavering gait. I will never forget his frightened aspect and frail voice as he tried to respond to my concerned queries.

"Why don't you eat, Uncle Otis?"
"I'm too nervous, I giss. Jist can't eat, Doc. Jist can't do it."

To temper my failure at re-nourishing him and bringing him back to health, I began to entertain the idea that he might be deliberately starving himself towards his rendezvous with death and wished that I would not interfere.

After exhausting my therapeutic repertoire, I decided to treat his severe anxiety, even though, at his age, the ensuing sedation from anti-anxiety medications might promote falls and deadly fractures. Cautiously, I started with small doses, which I gently escalated. Nothing touched him; he continued to lose weight and get weaker. Urged by the pressure of rapid deterioration, I added a strong anti-depressant and waited another while. He lost more weight and looked as if he were ready to turn to dust. Out of sheer despair, I added *Stellazine*, a major tranquilizer used for agitated psychosis and contraindicated in the elderly. When he returned a month later, he had added six pounds and no longer looked like a scarecrow.

"Uncle Otis," I cried, my voice resonant with the delight of long-awaited relief. "You must be feeling better."
"Of late, I've been able to eat Doc. My throat and stomach don't clamp down on me like they used to."

As he said that, a faint smile gleamed behind his sunken eyes and triumphantly lingered upon his sallow face, like an after-sunset blush on the horizon. Instead of being swept downstream, Uncle Otis was climbing up the banks of life again.

He slowly regained strength on his three medications but always seemed as though, deep within his soul, he lacked something essential. His aspect betrayed an old, sad discontent with life, which I blamed on his advancing age. He was a wealthy man with good children and lived comfortably with his wife in their large country home on their vast estate. I saw him frequently and helped him through the usual undulations that accompany chronic illnesses. When he would take his medications, his health would stabilize, but when on his own, he would stop taking his pills, he would be promptly reclaimed by his abdominal pain and weight loss.

"I jist hate to take them pills Doc," he would sigh as he pleaded with me, "but I giss I got to. Nothin I can do about it. Nothin."

In response, I would nod, pat him on the shoulder, and politely agree.

"Nothing we can do about it, Uncle Otis. It's nature's way."

One morning, I received word that his seventy-five year old wife had suddenly died from a blood clot. I called him after the last patient had left.

"Old men do not handle widowhood well," I thought as I placed the call, *"and most follow their wives within a short time."*

"Uncle Otis," I began. "I'm so sorry. What happened?"

"Oh Doc," he panted. "She told me that her right leg was swellin and botherin her, so I offered to take her to the doctor. No, no, she says, let's wait and see. Well, two days later while at the commode, she suddenly grabbed her chest and fell forward. I called the boys and we made it to the hospital all right, but she died that night. The doctor said it was a blood clot to her lungs that killed her, a clot that came out of her sick leg."

"Uncle Otis, how are you going to manage living all alone in that big house of yours? Shouldn't you consider moving in with one of your boys?"

"I'll be all right, Doc. My kids ain't that far from me."

"Well, make sure to stay on your medicines. You know how sick you get when you stop them."

"Don't worry Doc. I'll be all right."

Something about his voice was different. Perhaps it was a bit steadier and a trifle stronger than before. But it was his manner that gave me pause because it no longer conjured sympathy. After months of pathetic suffering, Uncle Otis sounded assertive, as if he were in control.

Two months later, when Uncle Otis came for his appointment, he looked sprightly well. I even noticed a faint, mischievous grin, gleaming through his no-longer-cavernous eyes.

"Uncle Otis, you look robust," I encouraged. "You seem to have grown younger, stronger, and happier."

"I'm feelin fine Doc. Over my grief. Real fine."

"Well, let's go over your pills; I need to make sure you're taking them the right way."

"Pills? I ain't takin any, Doc."

"Now, Uncle Otis, you know what happens when you quit taking your pills."

"Doc," he smiled triumphantly. "I haven't taken my pills since the day she died, and I feel mighty fine."

"Well." I said, grasping for something intelligent to say. "Well, how do you know that you won't get sick again, like you had so many times before?"

"I won't Doc. I know it. I jist won't."

We sat in silence while I studied his chart. Then I looked him in the eye and chided.

"Uncle Otis, you should have called me when you decided to quit your pills. It was dangerous to stop them abruptly."

"It was *her*, Doc."

I looked at him with bewilderment but was afraid to ask what he really meant by, *"It was her, Doc."* Gradually, his face re-donned its old, contorted aspect and he assumed that tortured look, which he had come with when first I saw him.

"You mean that she was the one who wanted you to stop your medicines?" I sheepishly asked.

"It was her Doc, all along. I hate to say it, but it *was* her. It jist was."

Having said that, his lips wrinkled with recalled tensions, and moist stories welled into his red eyes. I lowered my gaze and listened.

"You see Doc, she was always after me, naggin, naggin, naggin all the time. Drove my nerves crazy. I hated bein around her, but she followed me from room to room, naggin, naggin. I could never do right by her. For fifty years she nagged. Nagged me to death, Doc."

We were silent for a while as I palpated his abdomen: it was soft like a child's without tension or tenderness.

"You are well, Uncle Otis, but I can't believe that you're actually off your medicines."

"I jist hate to say it over and over Doc, but for fifty years she was my ulcers, and now that she's gone, I feel free again."

Indeed, Uncle Otis, at seventy-seven, was a happy man, and when he left my office he did not make a return appointment.

"I hope I won't need you anymore Doc," was the last thing he said as he glinted and slipped away.

Six months later, his name was on the books again and, of course, I worried. In medicine, nothing is what it seems to be at first glance because other truths always lurk behind the placid veil of appearance. I heard my nurse usher him into the exam room saying, "You're looking real good, Uncle Otis, and it was nice meeting you ma'am."

"It must be his daughter-in-law bringing him to the doctor," I ventured. *"Perhaps he's not driving any more."* These were my thoughts as I entered the exam room. He stood at attention as he greeted me and shook my hand with a firm grip. A sly, adolescent twinkle darted from his eyes.

"I'd like for you to meet my fiancée, Doris," he smiled. "We go dancin three times a week and we're gonna get married next month," he blushed, shining with ostentatious pride. "My boys don't like it but I don't care. I'm happy and so's she. Her husband died three years ago with cancer."

Uncle Otis sighed when he finished his exposé and a defiant sneer escaped his lips, landing on Doris's smug, half-smiling face.

"Nice to meet you ma'am." I bowed and shook her hand, to Uncle Otis's great satisfaction. "I wish you all the joy in the world."

"He's quite a man Doc," she bragged with a brisk, falsetto voice, "and says the nicest things about you."

"She's at least ten years younger and well preserved, but what a stilted form?" I mused, as I replied, "Uncle Otis and I go back a long way, ma'am."

When I looked back at him, his grin had sprawled beyond his sideburns and all fifty years of sickness-and-agony had absconded from his memory. Politely, he asked Doris to leave us and, when we were alone, he fisted his hands, furrowed his brow, and a pensive blush crimsoned his strained face.

"I'm not here because I'm sick Doc. I've been datin her for two months now and we've tried a few times but it don't work. She said she don't mind cause we're marryin for company. I don't like it, Doc. I jist don't. I wanna implant, and I wan it before the honeymoon."

"That's not simple surgery, Uncle Otis," I gasped while I wrestled hard to rein in a smile that threatened to break through my taken-aback face. I wanted to retort, *"You're pushing eighty and that surgery could endanger your life,"* but I didn't. He must have noticed my hesitation because his voice became abruptly strained as he insisted:

"I still wan'it, Doc. I know I'll do fine. I jist know it."

"Well then," I stalled, flipping through his chart as if looking for information that might delay my decision. "In that case," I said, clearing my throat, "let me discuss the issue with a urologist friend of mine and I'll get back with you."

"No Doc. You don't understand. I wan'it now, not later," he affirmed with a resolute frown. Please, don't make it any harder than it is."

"I'll try Uncle Otis," I sighed, and patted his shoulder lovingly as I ushered him toward the door. "I'll try my best. I promise."

On the way out, I heard him tell my receptionist that he wanted to book a time for Doris, that he wanted her to have a complete check-up, and that he'd like her to have it as soon as possible. These were his last words before he took Doris by the hand and marched out.

After much soul searching I acquiesced and referred him to Dr. Stone. We teamed together, taking special care of him during and after the operation. Luckily, we managed to avoid the myriad complications that commonly occur when this kind of surgery is performed on octogenarians. He surprised us both when he was ready to leave the hospital on the third day. When I came to discharge him, he thanked me with sincere gratitude and added, "I hate to be so pushy Doc, but when can I try it?"

"On your wedding night, Uncle Otis," I authoritatively asserted while keeping a straight face, "not a day sooner, and you must give me your word before I'll let you leave."

"But, that's two weeks from now," he frowned with pride. "You sure drive a hard bargain, Doc. You sure do," and his bright, mischievous eyes giggled as he went on, "I jist don't know if I can hold out that long."

In spite of his flaunted disappointment, Uncle Otis left the hospital a proud man with unshakable confidence that his failed virility had been miraculously restored to vital function.

Two months after the wedding, Doris came in to follow up on her blood pressure. Her cheerful disposition seemed a bit constrained and she wore a faint veil of melancholy over her made-up face.

"Doris," and giving her a warm hug, I asked, "Are you feeling all right?"

"Oh, yeh, I feel fine, Doc," she sighed. "I'm just tired and I'm afraid that my blood pressure ain't gonna be as good as you wan it."

Indeed, her pressure was still high even though she was faithfully taking her two medications. I checked it three times in three different positions, and each time it was high. She must have noticed my consternation because she quickly came to my rescue.

"I hate to tell you this, Doc, but it's not your fault that my pressure is still high. You see, he's exhaustin me. He wants to go all the time, wants to dance everyday, and wants to have sex two times a night. He won't let me rest or sleep and I'ma gettin real sore down there, if you know what I mean. I've talked to his boys and they've even talked to him, but he won't listen. He just bought a new Lincoln and wants to take me on a long road trip, but I don't wanna go. He's a hard man to say no to, Doc, and I'm way too old for this kind of stuff."

I tried to reassure her by saying that nothing lasts, that he would have to settle down sooner or later, and that because he must have felt deprived for fifty years, he's now on the rebound and has an insatiable need to satisfy his hungry soul. She understood, but was not sympathetic to my plea.

"I wouldn't have married him if I had known that he was gonna go crazy on me. I'm way too shrunk and shriveled down there, if you know what I mean."

I could see her point. She married for company and security while Uncle Otis married for his fifty years of lost romance. She wanted a peaceful, quiet end and he, a flaming, meteorite finale. *"Only time could reconcile this conflict,"* I thought, *"only patient time."*

Indeed, for several months after Doris's last visit, I did not hear from either of them. I often wondered about the couple and hoped that they had succeeded in working things out. On several occasions I was tempted to call, but changed my mind as I began to dial. With their prolonged silence they could be trying to hide some things from me, and my call might embarrass them. I worked and waited.

One afternoon, Amy, Uncle Otis's niece came in for a check-up. When I saw her, I couldn't restrain my curiosity and, after inquiring about her health, I asked about the newlyweds:

"Glad to see you Amy. You look well, as always. How are your husband and children doing? And, by the way, how are Uncle Otis and Doris doing?"

"Oh, you haven't heard?" She said with nonchalant face.

"Heard what?" I asked as my heart began to gallop.

"Yeh, Uncle Otis got so bad they had to put him away in a nursing home."

"Nursing home? What nursing home?"

"He's in the *New Life Home*, but there's nothing new about it. It's where they bury old folks while they're still alive. The doctor said that he had many mini strokes, one after the other, and that's what killed his brain."

"I'm so sorry to hear that," I lamented with melancholy face. "He was doing so well when I last saw him. I wonder what caused him to have so many mini strokes? Did the doctor say that he had atrial fibrillation?"

"That sounds about right," she affirmed. "I overheard the doctor telling his boys something like that."

I paused a while, standing in the middle of the examination room, reflecting on Uncle Otis's short-lived romance with life and how it ended as abruptly as it had started. Something about him was heroic, tragic, and farcical all at the same time. *"Trapped by old age,"* I thought, as I examined Amy. Then, overcoming my melancholy trance, I inquired with sympathetic tone, "So, how's Doris handling it?"

"Oh, she spends her days hagglin about money and never goes to visit him. His boys had to take her to court."

"Well," I gulped with a dry mouth. "Who's looking after him then?"

"Oh. I don't really know. The nurses I guess."

Driving home at the end of that day, I nursed an urge to visit Uncle Otis. My feelings were a whirlwind of confusion, revulsion, and denial. I was afraid of what I might find out, but I was also afraid of not finding out. Perhaps, I needed to see him one final time before I could allow myself to forget him. Stories must have an end and his story did not end with seeing his niece. It would end, I hoped, if I could see him one more time and put his memory to rest.

The words of Simone de Beauvoir spun like a rondo in my mind as I drove, with solitude sitting next to me in the passenger seat:

> *It is old age, rather than death, that is to be contrasted with life. Old age is life's parody, whereas death transforms life*

into a destiny: in a way it preserves it by giving it the absolute dimension. Death does away with time.

I had to wait for the weekend to make the drive. When my boys asked if they could go along I replied, "This is a personal matter; no one else is invited."

The *New Life Home* was a two-hour drive, but time sped, unnoticed, because my imagination was rife with myriad scenarios and visions. I arrived just before noon and walked into the long brick structure that was shaped like a cross. It sprawled over a furrowed, weed-eaten parking lot that was sparsely dotted with old cars.

There was no reception desk, just a long hall with closed doors on both sides. Starting at the head of the cross, I walked until I reached the arms. Poised in the middle of that intersection was a small desk with no one at it. *"Ring The Bell For Help,"* said the sign. When I rang, echoes rolled in all four directions, some doors opened, gray heads popped out and in, then all doors closed, leaving me standing like a lone nail in the crossing.

"May I help you, sir?" came a kind voice among shuffled steps, approaching from behind. I turned and waited until she stood before me, all smiles with bright, circumspect eyes. Her ruddy cheeks, blackened hair, and rotund waist stood in striking contrast to the stark, dim halls that stretched and yawned in all four directions. Yolanda, for that was the inscription on her nametag, was grandmotherly, buxom, rouge-lipped, and warm-hearted.

"I'm here to visit Uncle Otis."

"Are you family?" she asked with cautious smile.

"No, I'm his Oklahoma City doctor."

"Oh my," she cried, placing her manicured hand over her plump bosom. "You've come a long way, doctor, but I'm not sure he'll recognize you. He didn't recognize his own children when they visited him last Thanksgiving."

"Thanksgiving?" I gasped. "But, that was six months ago."

"Well, since he don't know no one, no one comes anymore. Let me take you to him and you can see for yourself."

I walked behind her toward the foot of the cross. She stopped at room 109, stealthily opened the door, peeped in, and then whispered, "We have to be careful. He startles easily."

I walked in behind her. The room was dark, stark, clean, and sparsely furnished. There was a wooden chair in one corner, a small side-table with a bottle of water and a glass next to the iron-framed bed, and a doorless, windowless bathroom with sink, toilet, shower, and a torn shower curtain, lounging on the faded tile floor. The drawn window blinds let faint streaks of May's sun in. Uncle Otis, fully dressed in boots-and-jeans, lay on his bed, expressionless, emaciated, and holding his stomach with both hands.

"Look who's here to see you, Uncle Otis," cried Yolanda.

He peered at us with sunken, unfocused eyes, and then turned his head away.

"Uncle Otis," reemphasized Yolanda. "Look. You have company."

The word company must have titillated his brain because he turned and looked at us again, flashed a faint smile, and then closed his eyes. I sat beside him on the bed, held his hand, and whispered, "It has been a long while since I've seen you, Uncle Otis. Do you remember me?"

He quivered, squeezed my hand, opened his eyes, and a slivered smile escaped his pursed lips.

"Oh, my," sighed Yolanda from behind. "I've never seen him smile before."

"Uncle Otis," I whispered. "Do you know who I am?"

"Yes," he whispered back, and twice nodded.

"Do you remember my name?"

"Yes," he nodded again and a proud smile crimsoned his face. "You're Dr. Hawi."

"Oh, my," sniffled Yolanda. "Oh, my God, Doctor," she sobbed and squeezed my shoulder. "Uncle Otis," she cried. "Do you know my name?" she beckoned, holding her nametag to his face.

"Yolanda," he croaked, choking on the word. Then, looking at me, he added, "She's very good to me."

Yolanda, sobbing, pulled the wooden chair from the corner and sat next to us. Her ruddy cheeks had become smudged, but her face sparkled with incredulous delight. I looked at her astonished aspect, her flickering eyes, her heaving cleavage, and asked, "What medicines is he taking?"

"He's not taking any medicines," she replied, a bit perturbed.

"Does anyone take him out for walks?"

"No. He doesn't like to leave his room."

I tugged on his hand and said, "Uncle Otis, lets go out for a walk."

He sat up, looked at Yolanda and me with wet, blinking eyes, stood up, and wobbled to the door.

We walked out from the door at the foot of the cross and were greeted by the warm, wonder-sun and fresh air. Uncle Otis walked between Yolanda and me, gazed at the green, sighing earth, the whispering trees, and the cotton-flying sky, as if he were viewing the countryside for the first time. We sat on a bench, cuddled among the tall trees, but none of us broke the silence of the shade.

Then Yolanda got up and said, "I need to go back, but you two can stay here as long as you want to."

"Can I have my lunch here?"

"Of course you can, Uncle Otis," screamed Yolanda with a blithe, high-pitched voice. "I can't believe that you're asking for food." Then looking at me, she explained, "He's hardly eaten or said anything for months. This is a real miracle, Doc. I'll be right back with his lunch tray."

Waiting for Yolanda, Uncle Otis and I gazed in silence at the nursing home basking before us. Witnessing his surprise revival, I was no longer sure that Uncle Otis was the victim of many small strokes. I reached for his wrist and checked his pulse. It was slow and regular with not a hint of atrial fibrillation. Seizing our moment's privacy, I whispered, "Uncle Otis, you were doing so well when I last saw you. You even left without making a return appointment, remember?"

"Of course, I remember," he whispered back with subdued voice.

"So what happened to you that you ended up here?"

"Same thing as before," he gulped.

"Same thing as before? What do you mean by that, Uncle Otis?"

"She started naggin, naggin, jist like my first wife. I couldn't get away from her. All she wanted was money and more money. No matter how much I gave her, she still nagged and wanted more. I couldn't get her to shut up and I was too embarrassed to confess to my boys that I had made a big mistake. They were never in favor of the marriage because they were afraid it would mess up their inheritance, and they were right. She was after my money and my land, Doc, and I couldn't see it, but they could. I jist couldn't get myself to tell them that they were right and that I was wrong."

"So what did you do?"

"My stomach started hurtin, so I stopped eatin, and I stopped talkin, and I lost all my gained weight. They all thought that I was demented and I let them believe it. I was happy when they moved me here because that kept me away from her."

"Why didn't you call me?"

"I didn't want you to find out that I had gone back to where I had started, and I was afraid you'd put me back on the damn medicines."

"How come you hate the medicines that gave you back your health?"

"No, it's not that, Doc. I jist wanted to die and I was afraid that if you'd start treatin me I would live. I'm almost eighty years old. I've had a long life, Doc, and I'm tired of livin with the wrong women."

"Why don't you get a divorce and start living again?"

"Too embarrisin to face my family, lookin like a fool. I jist can't do it."

"Oh, yes you can. Better face your family than your Lord."

When I said that, Uncle Otis's eyes flashed with terror. He gazed at Yolanda, approaching with his lunch tray, and muttered with clenched jaws, "I don't know what you mean by that."

Before I could explain, Yolanda was upon us. With a broad, rouge, enticing smile, she put the tray in front of him and said, "Now, Uncle Otis, you'd better eat all your food this time." Then, looking at me, she reminded, "He's hardly eaten anything since he came here. He just nibbles, takes a few mini bites, and leaves the rest for the dogs. You can see how much weight he's lost. This morning, he weighed 93 pounds."

While Uncle Otis eyed his food with dread, Yolanda relinquished her smile, slapped her generous hips with aggrieved annoyance, then turned to me and said, "I've got so many others to feed. Would you please take him back to his room when he's ready, and ring the bell on the desk so I'll know to come check on him."

I watched Yolanda undulate back to the home. Her brisk, determined walk evinced her inner strength. *"She's certainly the capable captain of her ship,"* I thought, as I sat back and observed Uncle Otis battle with his food. At first, he took a cautious bite and waited, as if he were testing his stomach. When the bite was not rejected, he grinned and followed it with another. It must have tasted good because his third bite was taken with no hesitation. Then, as if awaiting medical approval, he paused and looked at me with inquisitive eyes.

"You should eat it all, Uncle Otis," I affirmed, "and I'll make sure it doesn't hurt your stomach."

"But, I'm worried and afraid, Doc."

"Worried about what?"

"About what you said."

"What did I say?"

"You said, 'better face your family than your Lord,' and that frightened the dickens out of me."

Uncle Otis laid down his fork and his face re-donned that cringed, expecting-a-fist look that first introduced me to him.

"I jist can't eat when I'm afraid."

"Are you afraid that your stomach might reject the food?"

"No, I'm afraid of the Lord."

"Afraid that the Lord might reject you if you starve yourself to death?"

"That's it," he nodded with a shameful face.

"Suicide is a sin, Uncle Otis."

"I know," he gasped.

"So, why don't you start eating again? The Lord forgives those who repent."

"But, if I don't die, I might have to live with her again."

"No, you don't. You can get a divorce and have your life back."

"But, divorce is a sin."

"No, Uncle Otis. Suicide is a sin. The Lord would rather have you divorced and alive than married and dead."

"You rekin?"

"Yes, Uncle Otis, I reckon."

Uncle Otis smiled with relief, took a fourth bite, then a fifth, and said, "I can't believe I'm enjoyin eatin."

I watched his appetite grow with every bite; he ate like a starved prisoner of war, polished his plate, licked his lips with proud pleasure, and announced with resolve, "I giss I don't belong here no more."

On my way back, a calm feeling of content crept over me as I drove and the words of General Douglas MacArthur played like a record in my memory:

> *Nobody grows old by merely living a number of years. People grow old by deserting their ideals. Years may wrinkle the skin, but to give up interest wrinkles the soul… You are*

as young as your faith, as old as your doubt; as young as your self-confidence, as old as your fear; as young as your hope, as old as your despair.

My surprise visit must have resurrected Uncle Otis's interest in life, rekindled his faith, snuffed his doubt, recharged his self-confidence, discharged his fear, summoned his hope, and evicted despair from his soul. The belief in challenging life instead of surrendering to it was an ideal that he had deserted during two marriages that have devoured most of his life. I hoped, as I drove back in uplifting reverie, that he would re-espouse the belief that he had the right to live the untroubled life.

A day or two after I returned and couldn't get Uncle Otis out of my mind, I sent Dylan Thomas's villanelle to Yolanda and asked her to read it to him every morning so that he will not fall back into despair and abandon his life-challenging ideal:

*Do not go gentle into that good night,
Old age should burn and rave at close of day;
Rage, rage against the dying of the light.*

At the office, immersed in work, my mind still took short excursions to Uncle Otis. I had my hopes, but also my doubts. I had seen too many patients crash on the shores of complacency because they could not muster enough resolve.

I recalled widow Walton who could not evict the grandson that lived with her, abused her, and stole her money to buy drugs. She would complain to me every time she came, would promise to call her lawyer as soon as she got home, but never did. That theme repeated itself throughout my medical career and taught me not to trust promises made by abused souls because abuse subdues resolve.

With time, I lost contact with Uncle Otis and also lost my compulsion to revisit him. I doubted that subsequent visits would do any more good than my first. Sweltering summer came and left, redeeming fall arrived, the trees *polychromed* then danced and stripped, and old-man winter was on the gates when Uncle Otis's name appeared on the appointment book again.

With Yolanda by his side, he walked tall, had gained his lost weight, and had grown a pencil mustache. I hugged them both and waited, holding my curiosity back. He had no complaints. He had just come in to tell me that he had gotten a divorce, that he now lives alone in his country home, and that Yolanda was his salaried aid and companion. She comes every morning, takes care of the house, cooks for him, drives him around, and goes back to her home in the evening. He pays her twice more than what she was making at the *New Life Home* and they have become the best of friends.

As he talked, Yolanda beamed with pride. She said very little until he was ready to leave. It was then that she whispered in his ear.

"Oh," he chortled. "I almost forgot." He got up from his chair, stood at attention, took in a deep breath and recited to my delight:

> *Do not go gentle into that good night*
> *Old age should burn and rave at close of day*
> *Rage, rage, against the dying of the light.*

*

A year later, I received a call from Yolanda:

"Doctor," she began with feathers in her voice. "I hate to tell you this, but Uncle Otis died last week, a few days before his eighty-first birthday," she sniffled.

"What happened? Why didn't you call me?"

"I was embarrassed, Doctor. He died at my home, making love to me in the dead of night. It was hard enough calling his family, but I guess, they all knew it because they didn't act surprised."

"You made him happy, Yolanda, and I'm glad he ended his life in your arms."

"He was such a wonderful, generous, fun-loving man," she sobbed. "We were in love, Doctor, like teenagers. I just don't know what to do with myself now that he's gone."

To assuage her tears, I told her that dying in the arms of the woman who loves you is the best death that any man can hope for.

"But, that doesn't help my loneliness," she cried aloud. "I miss him so much, I could die of pain."

"You've helped him live, Yolanda. Now, live your calling by giving life to the other neglected, waiting-to-die elderly who need you to have a second chance at a meaningful life and a meaningful death."

After that call, I walked into my office, closed the door, and unleashed my thoughts. How desperately our elderly need a purpose, a love, a voice, and a good death. The words of Simone Weil (1909-1943) came rushing to me:

> *Death is the most precious thing, which has been given to man. That is why the supreme impiety is to make bad use of it. To die amiss.*

Thanks to Yolanda, Uncle Otis was rescued from loveless neglect and given a purpose, a love, a voice, a meaningful life, and a good death.

This theme, *Left-to-Die-in-Loveless-Neglect,* is an old shame that has been effacing humanity's elderly for centuries. It must have been on Alfred Lord Tennyson's mind when he penned his epic poem, *Ulysses*. It is a poem about living the full life and dying a meaningful death against, and in spite of, advancing age.

Tennyson (1809-1892) had this end-of-life theme tackled by no one else but the indomitable Odysseus who, after the sack of Troy, had spent the rest of his adulthood, adventuring with his shipmates throughout the Aegean. Addressing his then elderly mariners, Odysseus repudiates the *Left-to-Die-in-Loveless-Neglect* option and offers a meaningful *Life-of-Struggle-Until-Death* option in its place:

> *—you and I are old;*
> *Old age hath yet his honour and his toil;*
> *Death closes all: but something ere the end,*
> *Some work of noble note, may yet be done,*
> *Not unbecoming men that strove with Gods.*

Uncle Otis, First Edition, AL-HAKEEM, Journal of the National Arab-American Medical Association, Fall 2007. Revised Edition completed in October of 2016.

A Dying Man Tells

    Formative years viewed with the dimmer sight of old age are the raw materials for latter life epiphanies. It took nearly seventy years for me to understand what the poet, Dylan Thomas, meant when he framed that concept in his famous villanelle. Said the poet, in *Do Not Go Gentle Into That Good Night:*

> *Grave men, near death, who see with blinding sight*
> *Blind eyes could blaze like meteors and be gay,*
> *Rage, rage against the dying of the light.*

    Indeed, we only understand what life allows us to understand, and as we age, our only constant companion becomes our memory.

*

    In 1987, as my father lay dying of pancreatic cancer in his Beirut home, I made monthly flights to Lebanon, sat by his side, and listened to his tales, not realizing that his mind was bidding farewells by oozing stories that had been his constant companions for years. One story-laden morning—among Arabic coffee and Koranic chants that wafted through our open windows from Beirut's minaret loudspeakers—he asked, "Is there much corruption in America?"
    "Of course," I replied, failing to discern that the question was but a rhetorical introduction to a graver issue.
    "Do corrupt Americans flaunt their corruption?"
    "No, Dad. They camouflage it and flaunt righteousness instead."
    "Then, that must be the difference between your western world and our eastern world," he nodded knowingly. "I do not

know which of the two corruptions [eastern or western] is the more honest?"

"How can corruption be more or less honest?" I quizzed with an intrigued grin.

"Well," he smiled back. "If a corrupt person unwittingly admits corruption by flaunting it, would he be less corrupt than if he were to hide it and profess righteousness instead?"

Pondering the question, I took a sip of coffee then asked, "Why should it matter?"

"There's a repulsive charm in our third-world *shatarah* [our competitive cleverness in evading the law] and we hoist it with ostentatious pride, saluting it as if it were our national flag."

I paused in agreement, refilled his coffee cup, and waited, for I knew that there was more to come.

"Do you remember our friend, Habib?"

"Habib, the rich lawyer?"

"Rich lawyer, indeed," he sighed and took a sip. "A few years ago, he came in glowing with pride and couldn't wait to tell me what he had just accomplished:

"It seems that in Habib's little mountain town, a rich cousin of his built a stone wall around his home, unwittingly fencing in a sliver of government land behind his house. No one noticed except Habib, who filed an anonymous complaint with the municipality. When the municipality sent in a surveying inspector, his cousin was apprehended and incarcerated. The wife rushed to Habib for help, which was the expected action because he was the family lawyer.

"Habib visited his cousin in jail and informed him that, in view of the seriousness of his incursion, it would cost $10,000 to free him, expunge the municipality records, and save the expensive stonewall. The cousin, who was more than happy to pay the sum, was released three days later and expressed his sincere gratitude by sending an expensive gift to Habib's home.

"When I asked Habib how did he manage all that in such a brief time—a question, which he had been dying to answer—he related, with a smug smile that never left his face, that he bribed the judge with $500 to incarcerate and release Habib, and bribed the municipality inspector with $250 to expunge the municipality records by saying that his initial report was erroneous."

"And what did you say to him when he was through bragging?" I asked with unconcealed disgust.

"I asked him if he had suffered from remorse when he had the time to think about what he had done. He sneered and then declared that his *shatarah* made everyone happy. 'My cousin is happy, the judge is happy, the inspector is happy, the wall is saved, and I made $9,250 in three days,' he broadcast with remorseless ebullience. I then piqued him by asking about his younger brother, who had been fired from his post as a seaport inspector because he refused to accept a bribe from a member of the parliament, who was smuggling in a large shipment of whisky. He sneered again and said, 'My brother deserved what he got. He's now working for the Pepsi company instead, making less than half what he used to make at the port.' Then, as if to validate his corruption, he quoted from Shakespeare's *Measure for Measure:* 'Some rise by sin, some by virtue fall.' This was probably the only Shakespearean quotation he knew because it suited his devious ways."

Our conversation was then interrupted by *wellwishers* and it had to wait until the next morning's coffee before it resumed. I broached the topic by telling my father that in the U.S. one goes to jail for bribery. With downcast eyes, he explained that bribery had been the East's modus operandi during the four hundred years of Ottoman Empire rule, and that this slippery slope has gotten steeper, thanks to our civil war, which has rendered justifiable what had, until then, been unthinkable.

"Corruption is contagious," he lamented. "Once it becomes epidemic, the only vaccine that can halt its spread is mass enlightenment, which history has shown is impossible to achieve. All the prophets have, so far, failed. All societies decline with time, moving from order to disorder. The advantage of America is that it's a new world, whereas our world suffers from the relentless infirmities of old age."

He then surprised me by quoting from a poem I had penned while Lebanon's civil war raged, revealing its long, bloody fangs:

> *Yes, I have known the gentle peace of death*
> *The pain and sleepless anguish of Macbeth*
> *Have loved and hated, even leased my soul*
> *With perfect logic, softened to comply*
> *With inner whims that do not yield nor die*
> *Yes, this is I*
> *There hardly is a process, which I could not justify.*

*

That morning's conversation left me concerned, not only about the U.S., but also about the future of humanity. My morose mood was uplifted, however, by another *shatarah* story, which was as funny as it was corrupt. An exuberant Mr. Jabbour dropped in on his way to the airport. He was going back to Sierra Leone, where he had a prosperous business. After exchanging the customary salutations and circumlocutions, he presented my father with a $250,000 check.

"What's this for?" gasped my dad.

"For the orphans of our civil war. You know the honest organizations. Distribute it among them as you see fit, but do not mention my name."

Then, without fanfare or flourish, Mr. Jabbour took his leave and rushed to the airport.

"Who's this man?" I asked, astounded by his buoyant nonchalance.

"He's an old classmate of mine," began my father with a tempered smile. "After high school, he joined his father's haberdashery business in Sierra Leone, when the country was still a British colony. With time, he made friends with the natives who worked the diamond mines, and would sell them merchandise on account, which they settled when they got paid. Before long, they started selling him diamonds, which they would smuggle out of the mines for quick cash. As this trade grew, the British became suspicious and staged repeated surprise searches of his home, shop, and car, but never found anything. Their informants assured them that he was buying and hoarding stolen diamonds, but they could never tell them where the diamonds were hidden. With blatant insouciance, he hid the diamonds under the smoldering tobacco ashes of his pipe, which he kept in his mouth, especially during surprise searches.

"Periodically, he would travel to Switzerland, sell the diamonds, and deposit the money in a secret Swiss account. Aware of his *shatarah*, British customs would search him thoroughly, rip his suitcase apart, purge him with caster oil, and sift through his liquid stools, but no one ever thought of looking inside his smoking pipe.

"One busy day, an informant happened to see him put a recently purchased diamond in his pipe. When the British-customs-search-car appeared in front his shop, after having conducted a thorough surprise search only the day before, he realized that his cover had been blown, and quickly flushed the pipe's ashes into his bathroom sink. That sink's elbow became his new hiding place, but from that point on, leaving Sierra Leone with diamonds presented insurmountable difficulties.

"One day, while hunting, he fell and broke his leg. A doctor friend of his at a nearby clinic put a cast around the fracture. One week later, Mr. Jabbour booked a flight to Switzerland and, before going to the airport, had someone tip the British customs that his leg was not broken and that the diamonds were hidden inside its false cast.

"Upon arrival—eight hours before his flight in order to give the authorities ample search time—he was immediately whisked into a private room. In spite of agonizing screams, convulsive protestations, and a visibly swollen and bruised shin, his cast was pulverized. When no diamonds were found, his luggage was meticulously inspected, his suitcase was ripped apart, he was stripped, his body cavities were searched, and his bowels were purged with a double dose of caster oil. At the end, with everyone exhausted and disgusted, the British officer in charge, feeling foolish and remorseful, offered to drive Mr. Jabbour back to his orthopedist to be re-casted, and then bring him back to the airport in time to make his flight.

"This time, at the doctor's office, the diamonds were strategically placed between the layers of his new cast and Mr. Jabbour was escorted back to the airplane, as if he were a diplomatic dignitary."

"Is he still smuggling?" I asked, intrigued.
"He no longer needs to," replied my father, holding the $250,000 check in his hand.
"Is he still corrupt?"
"Yes, but he perceives himself as a Robin Hood."

When he said that, a verse from Sam Walter Foss's poem, *The House By The Side Of The Road*, leapt into my consciousness and I shared with my dad:

> *Let me live in a house by the side of the road*
> *Where the race of men go by*
> *The men who are good and the men who are bad*
> *As good and as bad as I*
> *I would not sit in the scorner's seat, or hurl the cynic's ban*
> *Let me live in a house by the side of the road*
> *And be a friend to man.*

*

My father died in July of 1987 at the age of sixty-nine. Now, I am sixty-nine and my father's stories are still young in my memory. His last dying words to me were, "No one can change where humanity is heading, Son. Just be the best you can be and remember me to your children."

Flying back home, after my father's funeral, the following verses descended upon me and I penned them in midflight:

When I shall go, I shall not leave a dent
Nor those behind me wonder where I went
I'll simply fade away with grace
Unmentioned by the tidings of the day
They will not say: "We miss his loving face."
And history will look the other way
Though I shall try, as I am passing
Just to catch his eye
Perhaps he would remember that
I was among the boys
Who lived, and loved, and made a lot of noise
Until their times grew thin
Then, seeing that they caused so little change
Have settled down with illness and a double chin.

A Dying Man Tells, First Edition, Al-Jadid magazine, Vol. 20, No. 70, 2016. Second Edition completed in October of 2016.

The Nun's Tale

"First let me tell you whence her name has sprung,
Cecilia, meaning, as the books agree,
'Lily of Heaven' in our English tongue,
To signify her chaste virginity;"

The Second Nun's Prologue
The Canterbury Tales
Geoffrey Chaucer

For a storyteller, there are always details that are too intimate, and at times too embarrassing, to relate. But without such delicate revelations I would be unable to tell my story. Therefore, I beg Reverend Mother Julia's pardon before I begin and hope that my reasons for telling would not be misunderstood.

It happened in the spring of 1985 when the delayed blossoms were just beginning to sprout out of their dead repose. Winter had been mighty that year, holding Oklahoma hostage within its icy cage until the end of March. My clinic was not too far from the convent of St. Mary's and many of the nuns including the Reverend Mother Julia had become patients of mine over the years. Indeed, the Reverend Mother and I had nurtured a unique intellectual friendship and had had many a deep discussion about the ruthless changes that were overwhelming our society and country.

My fascination with Reverend Mother Julia began years ago when I discovered her passion for Greco-Roman literature. She was an erudite lady, an avid reader of the classics, and had the uncanny gift of memory, which enabled her to quote *ad libitum* from the works of the ancient masters during seemingly ordinary conversations. Whereas I delighted at guessing the origins of her quotes, she, in turn, delighted at correcting me, and we thus thrust and parried each time we conversed.

My office knew to give Mother Julia double time when she came in for her annual examination because our discussions were irresistibly lengthy and meandered through the forbidden alleys of life. But unlike past discussions, during that April's annual examination, Mother Julia shared with me a personal concern of hers, a matter she had never broached in all the years I had taken care of her.

"We're all getting too old, Doctor," she began, "and we're no longer able to attract novices to our convent." Then she added with unconcealed grief, "I'm terribly worried about St. Mary's order. We need continuity and, unlike youth, old age cannot grow into the future."

"Why are you unable to attract youth?" I asked with restrained surprise. "You lead such peaceful lives against a tumultuous world. I thought that alone would be enough of an incentive to attract new recruits."

"Oh, we still get some young recruits, but they abscond before they take their vows. A peaceful life of contemplation and worship can no longer compete with the growing temptations of our free world."

As I struggled for an optimistic response with which to counter her disillusionment, Mother Julia took in a deep sigh and then let it out with a sudden question.

"Have you ever read *The Magic Mountain* by Thomas Mann?"

"The 1924 novel for which he won the Nobel Prize for literature?" I answered, happy at the change of topic.

"I hate to disagree with you, Doctor, but it was his 1901 novel, *Buddenbrooks,* that won him the Nobel Prize in 1929, although, according to Mann's wife, this prize would not have been accorded without the publication of *The Magic Mountain*. Be that as it may, in the first chapter of *The Magic Mountain*, Mann says: '*A man lives not only his own personal life as an individual, but also, consciously or unconsciously, the life of his epoch and his contemporaries.*' I fear that the future of St. Mary's convent, because aspiring recruits must also live the lives of their epochs, is going to become precarious. Oh, how it pains me to see my seventy-five years, most of which were dedicated to St. Mary's order, go to waste."

I was touched by the quivering concern in Reverend Mother's face, but had nothing to counter with except, "Someday, the burdens of freedom will overshadow its temptations and more young women will seek again the dedicated life."

"Oh, but no, Doctor," she quickly retorted with a sad smile. "I don't want us to become a refuge from life. We seek those young women whose calling to serve is their primary reason for joining. Life in the convent is much harder than life outside and that's precisely why most of our novices abscond."

Mother Superior's insightful words stayed with me as, day-by-day, April skillfully un-furled its seductive colors before my roaming eyes. I could see why life in the convent was harder on young women. In the spring of their lives, their urges to blossom would be more difficult to contain than those of the winter-caged flowers that were flaunting their flaming colors for all of us to see. The words of Anis Nin (1903-1977) surfaced into my consciousness as I drove to work one particularly voluptuous morning: *"... and then the day came when the risk to remain tight in a bud was more painful than the risk it took to blossom."* With great reverence to the celibate life, I concluded that it must take great strength and conviction to suppress nature's youthful urges against spring's vast awakenings.

At the tail of one busy day in early May, when that year's winter-locked Spring had finally come into full bloom, my nurse, Rebecca, walked sheepishly into my office and stood before my desk, tongue-tied and blushing, with arms behind her back. My first thought, seeing her Mona-Liza smile, was that she had come to inform me that she had finally gotten pregnant. Knowing that she had been trying to conceive for several years and that she had been taking fertility pills for the past several months, I smiled back at her blushing cheeks and ventured, "You've come to tell me that you're pregnant, right?"

"No, no, it's not about me," she stuttered.

"Well, who's pregnant then?" I quipped.

"No one is pregnant, Doc," she sighed with dismay, "but there's a lady in the waiting room who wants to make sure that she won't get pregnant."

"Is she a patient?"

"No, she's a nun."

"A nun?" I gasped. "A nun like the other nuns we take care of?"

"Yes, except this one is a very beautiful, young nun, and she wants me to give her birth-control-pill samples."

"And what did you say to her?"

"I said that I must talk to you first."

"Did she ask for an appointment?"

"That's the trouble. She said that she did not need an appointment and that all she wanted was a pack of birth-control pills."

"Did she say who sent her here?"

"Yes, Mother Superior."

"You mean the Reverend Mother Julia? Can't be right. No way." I snapped.

Feeling bewildered, I stood up, scratched my head, walked toward the door, then turning back to Rebecca, I asserted, "No, no, something is wrong with your story."

"But, Doc, I swear that's how she introduced herself to me. She said that her name was Sister Cecilia and that Mother Superior was the one who sent her here to get a pack of birth-control pills."

With Rebecca at my heels, I marched into the empty waiting room. A young nun in full habit was stiffly poised on the edge of a chair with wide-blue eyes, frozen in their sockets, staring at me. As soon as I walked toward her, she stood at attention, smiled, and held out her hand.

"Please come in, Sister," I said as I shook her sweaty palm.

"Oh, no Doctor, I don't need to waste your time. I'm not sick. I only need a pack of birth-control pills. I've just joined St. Mary's convent. I'm Sister Cecilia. Mother Superior told me to come here."

"But, Sister Cecilia, I need to check a few things before I know what kind of pill to give you."

"Oh, no, no, Doctor, just any kind will do; just whatever you can spare will be fine. Roses cannot tell the difference."

"Roses?" I smiled with intrigued aspect.

"Oh, yes Doctor. Mother Superior put me in charge of the convent's rose garden."

"I did not know that roses liked birth-control pills."

"Oh, but they do, Doctor. I dissolve one pill in a watering can and sprinkle the roses with the hormone water twice a week."

"Really?"

"Oh, yes. It gives them such brilliant colors and protects them from disease."

"I had no idea. Who taught you this trick?"

"Sister Isabella at St. Helen's. She's an organic gardener and she's the one who taught me everything I know."

I gave Sister Cecilia two packages, each containing twenty-one active pills and seven placebos. Suppressing a smile, I took the time to explain that she should discard the placebos and only use the active pills. We parted amicably but not before I promised to come see her roses in late May, when they would be in full bloom.

Before Rebecca went home that evening, she passed by my office to say goodnight, but instead of saying it from the door, as was her habit, she sat down and sighed as if she had something important to say.

"Anything bothering you?" I egged her on.

"Well, did you notice how beautiful Sister Cecilia was?"

"Beautiful?" I pretended.

"I'm jealous, Doc. Don't tell me you didn't notice her big, blue eyes, button nose, full lips, baby complexion, and figure like a Greek goddess."

"Well, the waiting room was a bit dark," I pretended again.

"What's this gorgeous girl doing in a convent?" she exclaimed with a mordant voice. "It's a real shame, you know, for someone as beautiful as she is, to hide in a convent full of old nuns."

"Maybe she's not hiding. Maybe she feels it's her calling. What's wrong with being beautiful and being a nun?" I asked, trying to seem unmoved by Sister Cecilia's striking appearance.

"Well, this just upsets me to no end, and I don't really know why?"

Having said that, Rebecca's chin began to quiver as she tried to swallow back her tears. Although I understood the reasons behind her intense emotion, I pretended not to notice and, instead, attempted to sustain the conversation with a probing question.

"Rebecca," I asked as I took off my eyeglasses, "do you feel intimidated?"

My question must have hit a tender nerve because as soon as I asked, she broke down and began sobbing. I handed her a tissue and waited in silence until she finally regained her composure. Her first words to me after she had dried her tears were, "Maybe I do feel a bit intimidated, but I don't really understand why. I'm not bad looking myself, and seeing beautiful women has never bothered me before."

"I think I can explain your quandary with a quote from Rilke."

"Rilke? Who's Rilke?"

"A Bohemian-Austrian poet considered to be one of the most significant poets in the German language."

"And what did this Rilke say?"

"He said: *'For beauty is only a step removed from a burning terror we barely sustain, and we worship it for the graceful sublimity with which it disdains to consume us.'* "

"I'm not sure I understand. What does all this mean?"

"It means that sublime beauty intimidates us because it makes us feel like we're in the presence of a deity."

"Oh, I see. That's a deep thought, too deep for me for sure. But, it does explain my crazy emotions."

Rebecca looked at me with red, pensive eyes, relieved to know that her emotional burst had a sensible explanation. She even asked me a few more questions about Rilke and the poem that contained the quote. I promised to bring her my copy of the *Duino Elegies* the next day, and when she left she was at peace.

What I did not tell Rebecca was that my Rilke explanation was contrived in order to hide the real reason behind her tears, a reason that would have been too painful to vivisect. Indeed, the truth had more to do with Rebecca's strong maternal instincts and her deep jealousy of all the young mothers around her, who flaunted pictures of their beautiful children for her to see. Sister Cecilia's choice of the celibate life—in spite of her stunning beauty and fecund youth—presented a wasteful contrast to Rebecca's aching heart. Perhaps, vicariously, Rebecca wanted Sister Cecilia to marry and bear the beautiful children, which Rebecca was not able to have. Moreover, I did not help matters by asking Rebecca, when she first walked into my office, if she had come to tell me that she was with child.

That night I slept wistfully not just because Sister Cecilia was, indeed, breathtakingly beautiful but, rather, because her birth-control-pill story was much too charming to be left untold. I felt a strong urge to write it because, among other things, it taught me that the human mind was inherently suspicious and that initial gut feelings were more often wrong than right. But how to tell her story eluded me until the time came to view the roses.

It so happened that on Friday, May 31 of 1985 a disastrous barrage of 42 tornadoes hammered Pennsylvania, Ohio, New York, and Ontario, causing 88 deaths. On Sunday, the second of June, a special mass in memory of the victims was held at St. Mary's and I was among the worshipers. The Reverend Mother Julia asked us to bow our heads, pray for all the tornado victims, and raise special prayers to Sister Cecilia's parents whose home in Kane, Pennsylvania, was demolished while they, by the grace of God, escaped unharmed.

After the service, Mother Julia, with tears in her eyes, told me that Sister Cecilia was transferred back to St. Helen's convent in East Kane where that convent's chapel had been totally demolished by the tornado.

"She's more needed there than here and she's an only child," whimpered Mother Julia. "I guess it's best that she stays close to her aging parents."

"She seemed bright and brave," I added, hoping to console with my simple words Mother Julia's dampened spirits.

"She was the only bright light among us old oaks, and kept us so entertained that we no longer felt our age. Oh, Doctor, we've lost the only blithe sapling among our geriatric ranks. Who knows if we'll ever get another one? As I told you before, very few novices take their vows nowadays."

The sadness in Mother Julia's face lingered during the silent interlude that followed. In an attempt to lighten the awkwardness, I asked her to show me Sister Cecilia's roses.

"Oh, you still remember the roses?" she said laughingly.

"Well, how could I forget? I was the one who gave her the birth-control pills. You can imagine my surprise when she asked for them and my great relief when she told me what they were for."

"Indeed, that must have been funny, Doctor. Let us go then, you and I," she said as she led the way to the convent's garden.

"Reverend Mother," I exclaimed with surprise, "you never told me that you're a T. S. Eliot fan. *'Let us go then, you and I'* is the opening line of *The Love Song of J. Alfred Prufrock*."

"All of us in this convent love poetry, Doctor. Incidentally, I heard that you've just published a new book of poems."

"I did, Reverend Mother, and I'm very proud of it."

"Perhaps you might consider sharing it with us, one evening. Poetry is the balsam of aging souls."

"In that case, I would be delighted to spend an evening of poetry with you. Just tell me when and I'll be there."

"Well, how about next Sunday evening after dinner? Would six-thirty be fine with you?"

"Do you mind if I bring Dr. Mandy along? He's a very sensitive poet and it would make the event more interesting if both of us read."

"By all means, please do extend our invitation to him; your friend is my friend."

"Reverend Mother, you have surprised me again. You've just quoted Al-Imam Ali?"

"Indeed, and I did it because I knew that it would please you."

"Do you know the entire quote?"

"Are you testing me, Doctor?"

"Perhaps, but merely because I've never heard a Westerner quote the Fourth Caliph of Islam before."

Mother Superior and I stopped by Sister Cecilia's roses. Pointing to them with her supine palm and looking at the sky as if addressing God, she quoted: *"Your friends are three: your friend, the friend of your friend, and the enemy of your enemy. And your enemies are three: your enemy, the friend of your enemy, and the enemy of your friend."*

"Reverend Mother, I'm startled. Quoting T. S. Eliot was enough of a surprise, but quoting Al-Imam Ali, and doing it verbatim, well, that to me was unimaginable."

In the moments that followed, both Reverend Mother and I admired Sister Cecilia's roses. The colors were indeed vibrant, the leaves, *blemishless*, and the stems tall and graceful. The narrow soil patch along the convent's southern wall resounded with the adolescent giggles of spring roses. Gazing at the lush gush of colors, Reverend Mother's eyes began to blink uncontrollably. Then, looking away as if the memory were too painful to endure, she inhaled the delicate aromas that fragranced the heavy air and addressed the sky with, "Oh, why did they have to take her away? She made us feel young and lit up the convent with her youthful joy. *'She had a heart—how shall I say?—too soon made glad, too easily impressed; she liked whate'er she looked on, and her looks went everywhere.'* "

"That was Robert Browning." I gasped. "It's a quote from *My Last Duchess*, Isn't it?"

"Indeed, Doctor. Bravo. And the duke killed her because she was too sweet to suit his taste. Likewise, they took Sister Cecilia away from us because she was too sweet. Now all we have are the roses, which will become neglected again. Age dulls and youth burnishes; such are the verdicts of life."

"Who knows, Reverend Mother? She might return one day," came my consoling remark.

"It would take a miracle to bring her back. They'll hold on to her as long as they can because they're all getting older over there just like we are over here."

"But miracles do happen, Mother Julia. In medicine we see them all the time."

"Indeed, Doctor, and we do too. In this vast, inanimate, cold, burning universe of ours, life on this tiny planet is the miracle of all miracles. Everything alive is a miracle, Doctor. But life without Sister Cecilia feels most sinister to us now and that, I'm afraid, is not going to change soon."

On the way home, I was able to empathize with Mother Superior's profound pain because I understood it. I was in my late thirties then, had witnessed accelerated aging in my older patients, and seen how one additional year for octogenarians impacted them like ten.

Reverend Mother had no access to youth via children or grandchildren and Sister Cecilia represented, perhaps, her only chance. Indeed, she was grieving as if she had lost her only child and her quote from Robert Browning's *My Last Duchess* was quite apropos. I knew that poem well. It tells the story of the Duke's young wife who was as sweet to everyone else as she was to her own husband. The old Duke, jealous that he was not getting any special attention, executed his young wife and then married another with a larger dowry.

Slowly, I came to understand what Mother Julia meant when she said that poetry was the balsam of aging souls. Poetry, being forever young, brings youth unto age just like a grandchild does or like Sister Cecilia did during her brief stay at the convent. That realization helped me view the upcoming Sunday's poetry reading with deeper significance. For the six remaining elderly nuns, it was not just entertainment; it was, indeed, a chance to recapture their youthful feelings, which had departed with Sister Cecilia.

All week, Dr. Mandy and I arranged and rearranged the poems we planned to read. We agreed to alternate readings and chose only uplifting topics, given the dire needs of the situation. On Friday, Mother Superior informed me that she had invited several older convent friends and that we were going to have the readings in the big living room where the Civil-War Clock stood. That clock was donated to the convent by the fourth great-grandson of Stonewall Jackson and was the convent's most prized treasure. It was a handsome, though nonfunctional, grandfather clock in a mahogany wooden case with rusty weights hanging behind its glass window. Rumor had it that the time it read, 4:33 was the time in 1863 when General Jackson surrendered his last breath. To preserve the memory, the clock had been decommissioned since then.

On Sunday, Dr. Mandy and I arrived together at six-thirty sharp. Sister Monica led us to the grand living room, which was full of shaking, gray heads awaiting our recital. Mother Superior welcomed us and introduced us to the group as the two doctor-poets who had come to share their gifts with our meager ears, a hint that we should read loud because everyone in the room was hard of hearing. It was a most solemn group and we felt like adolescents performing before our grandparents' friends.

We read with deliberately slow, loud voices and gave plenty of time between poems for discussion. The group seemed to come alive after each poem as smiles intermingled with tears and gnarled fingers clapped with muffled applause. Because I had started the reading, Doctor Mandy's time came to end it, and for the finale he chose a poem called *The Chimes*. It was a most uplifting poem about a young mother who, awaiting her husband's return from war, hung a bell above her front door and spent her years waiting for the bell to chime. One night, after she had given up all hope, the bell chimed awakening her and her three sons who rushed to the door to find their wounded father, standing at the doorstep, leaning on crutches. The poem ended with the bell continuing to *chime, chime, and chime,* long after the veteran father had walked back into his family's bosom.

When Dr. Mandy finished and the applause died down, the grandfather clock, standing in the room, began to chime. Reverend Mother and the other nuns, having never heard it chime before and knowing that the clock had been decommissioned since 1863, glared at each other with startled disbelief, knelt down on their knees, and repeatedly crossed themselves. The other guests, not understanding the significance of the chimes, seemed dumbfounded until the highly emotional Reverend Mother explained the mystery of the situation. The evening ended gloriously with the feeling that a small miracle had transpired at the convent, and we all went home with blithe, fluttering hearts.

*

Two Sundays later, after the chapel service had ended, Mother Julia approached me with an unusual smile and said, "The Lord has been good to us, Doctor."

"Good news?" I quizzed with gleaming eyes.

"Very good news, Doctor. Our roses are not going to die of neglect, after all, because Sister Cecilia is being transferred back to us."

"Oh, Reverend Mother," I blurted out with joy. "I'm so delighted for the convent and for the roses. Please do reassure Sister Cecilia that I'll always have a fresh supply of birth-control pills ready for her."

Mother Julia's eyes quivered with moisture and she hesitated as if she were about to reveal something of great intimacy. Then, overcoming her reticence, she asked:

"Do you remember the chimes of the grandfather clock the Sunday before last, Doctor?"

"Oh, yes, yes, of course I do, Reverend Mother."

"Well, I believe that the chimes were the annunciation of Sister Cecilia's return," she whispered as she wiped off her grateful tears. "That clock had not chimed for the past one hundred and twenty-two years, and no one has touched it since it was granted to us ten years ago. Bend your head in prayer with me, Doctor, and let us thank the Lord for having blessed us with yet another miracle of life."

First Edition of *The Nun's Tale, Part One,* appeared in *The Bulletin* of the Oklahoma County Medical Society, October/October 2016 Issue. Revised Edition completed in October, 2016.

The Letter

    "Doctor," he whispered as he clutched my hand. "I'm afraid."
    "But, Father Peter, you're condition," I hesitated, "is stable."
    "My abdomen seems more swollen today and it hurts worse. What if the surgery doesn't go well?"
    "Father," I sighed, clearing the lump in my throat. "You've told me the same thing before all of your other surgeries." And then, jesting, I quoted *Jesus-to-Peter* when he failed to walk on water, *"O thou of little faith, wherefore didst thou doubt?"*
    He responded by pointing to his black robe, hanging behind the door, and followed his motion with: "There's an envelope in the inside pocket of my robe. Would you please give it to her if I should not make it? She's the young student from our college whom you met yesterday. I've been her counselor for over two years now."
    Having said that, a shy gleam shimmered like a deep secret behind his eyes. Of course, I pretended not to notice, and with a stern voice that belied my surprise, I reassured, "You'll make it, Father Peter. God willing, you will."
    He must have noticed that I didn't look him in the eye when I spoke because he quickly added, "As a child, she was abused by her natural parents, out of love, they still maintain." Then, after an awkward silence, and with cheeks a bit ablaze, he shook his finger at me and reiterated, "Doctor. No resuscitation, please."
    "No resuscitation, Father. You won't need it."

    Father Peter and I became friends from the day we met. He was a robust, erudite Russian priest who, as a younger man, joined the neighboring Eastern Orthodox Monastery and College, almost 25 years ago. One day, soon after he had arrived, he was brought to the emergency room where I was moonlighting, with his first bout of intestinal obstruction. He was broad shouldered, of medium build, with ruddy cheeks, short hair, brown piercing eyes, and a kind, compassionate manner. He hugged readily, roared when he laughed, and did that often, even during casual conversation. When once I accused him of punctuating his sentences with hearty laughter, he quickly rebutted in a bold Russian accent, "I laugh because I am happy. To me, every comma is a smile and every period, a roar."

His only blemish was a clubfoot that he totally ignored, but among his literary friends it earned him the title of Lord Byronski. His most astounding trait, however, was that whenever you were with him, you always felt loved. He liked women, indeed, but no more than he liked men, and always had plenty of both in his company. That is why I did not heed when he introduced me to Miss Jenny Taylor the day before. I did remember her well, though, because of her striking appearance—tall, lean, with brown hair to the waist like a long, epic poem. Her pointed nose, green eyes, and young, tight skin stood in sharp contrast to Father Peter's pudgy, middle-aged looks. Aside from her notable aspect, I did remark that she was taciturn and, all of yesterday, sat at Father's feet, leaving the chairs beside him for others. Thus I digressed as I sat, silently holding Father Peter's hand before they summoned him to surgery. Waiting together before the gurney arrived, we felt no further need to speak. Instead, the two of us communicated at a higher orbit, in tender anguish, heart-to-heart, and soul-to-soul.

I followed the stretcher with rainy eyes until it turned around the corner. Then, hesitantly, I went back into his room and pocketed the envelope. It was sealed and addressed to me. I thought of myriad things as I slowly walked back to my office, fingering the envelope along the way:

"Could a middle-aged priest fall in love with a young student? Could that be why he was afraid? Why did she not come to see him today? Why was the envelope addressed to me instead of her? Is it safer that way? Well, does it really matter?"

Before I entered my office, perhaps for some portentous premonition, I crossed myself thrice, once for each of us, and then, almost obliviously, started to see patients.

I was expecting the surgeon's call sometime around noon. It should not take more than four hours to resect the adhesions and free the intestinal obstruction. I was surprised when he called after only one hour:

"John, this is James."
"What went wrong?"
"Nothing went wrong. He just had the black bowel syndrome."
"Dear Lord. You mean his bowels are dead?"
"Every single inch. I'm so sorry."
"What do we do now?"
"Nothing can be done. I closed him up and sent him back to recovery."

I was by his side when he awakened. His pain was so overwhelming that I dowsed him with morphine before we even had a chance to talk. After that, he couldn't speak, but his eyes clung to mine with moist, sighing odes, and I knew that he knew. A while later, and somewhat unexpectedly, he smiled with his cold, morphine lips a gray good-bye and quietly parted.

The funeral was held at the Monastery, solemn, serene, accepting. The choir, the voices, and the liturgy bridged earth with sky and suffered the grieving hearts a glimpse of heaven. Indeed, death among the faithful is a rejoining, not a departure. Standing in prayer, I recalled these words from *The Little Prince* by Antoine De Saint-Exupéry:

> *Here is my secret.*
> *It is very simple:*
> *One cannot see well except with the heart.*
> *The essentials are invisible to the eyes.*

During the service, I looked all around but couldn't find her. Father Abraham pointed her out to me afterwards. She stood alone, like a willow at sunset, gazing at the moist October leaves, her black dress wailing in the wind. I reintroduced myself, handed her the letter, then stepped back and waited.

"Oh, it's from him," she gasped. Her crimsoned, green eyes flickered as she frantically tore the envelope open.

"He asked me to give it to you just before he went to surgery," I added, while she read.

In the wind, her flowing hair flapped incessantly between the trembling pages and her tears. Then, after a drawn-out, macabre sigh, she surrendered the letter back to me and pleaded in a drowned, cryptic voice, "Would you please read it. I can't. I just can't."

It was entitled: *Gently*, and introduced with the following phrase:

"My Dearest reminder that first, I am a man, that love is ever gentle, and that ungentle love is mad."

Gently

Gently
Spring mellows winter's frown
And beckons earth un-brown
Her buried smiles

Gently
The sun redeems the night
And mountains hood their crown

Gently
We bow to years
And colors fade

Gently
You stole into my soul
And stayed...

*

Petals are whispering lips
Lucky the rose
To kiss many a breath and sight

The vines
Play crimson songs
At night

A smile is God touching
A child, God smiling
A touch, love praying

Oh
How you and I
Have prayed

Gently
You stole into my soul
And stayed.

With a half smile wrought out of a contorted face, she thanked me when I handed the letter back. I bowed and left her standing in the fall, a black spring amidst the astonished leaves and blushed horizon, blowing between the songs of death and arms of life.

The Letter, First Edition, *Al-Hakeem*, Journal of the National Arab-American Medical Association, spring issue of 2008. Revised edition was completed in October of 2016.

Murder in the O.R.

Societies advance across time's deserts, from primitive to civilized, by climbing over the jagged cliffs of oppression in pursuit of the pastoral valleys of freedom. Their bloody march, which transpires over centuries, and their fierce battles for enlightenment and emancipation from the intransigent forces of ignorance and superstition, bequeath them, at enormous cost, the liberties, which we have and take for granted today.

Constitutions, which are promulgated by free societies in order to uphold their achievements and guard them against the slippery slopes of decay and dictatorship, represent their hard-earned, collective values. Nevertheless, history has shown us that when laws are abrogated by war, societies fall back into primitive anachronism, and that in all societies, regardless of how advanced they might be, linger individuals and groups who hold onto their primitivism as if it were a glowing torch of enlightenment.

*

Our story, which derives its pathos from such historic phenomena, begins at the medical school of the American University of Beirut, when Lebanon was at peace and social harmony was playing beautiful tunes. The three decades after the Second World War had ushered-in a renaissance era, when enlightenment was a collective goal and poor families sold dear land to educate their children. But, it was also an era when family warlords levied demands on educational and civil institutions, and nepotism was the accepted modus operandi.

During our first medical year, it did not take us long to realize that one of our older classmates, Jazir, languished in a much lower epistemic orbit. Tall, handsome, powerful, charming, rich, elegant, but arrogant and ignorant, he demanded respect with force rather than worth. With skepticism we watched this primitive student plough with inimitable ease the vast fields of knowledge that stretched before us, and we all pretended not to notice when his preposterously faked grades placed him at the top rather than at the bottom of the class.

Year after year, while we negotiated the massive tides of information that ebbed and flowed in and out of our brains, Jazir, expending meager effort, was duly promoted, landed a surgical internship, and became the favored topic of operating room whispers. Stories of his incompetence, antics, and faux pas circulated among the hospital staff like viruses, causing wide concern and consternation. Nevertheless, all this transpired without any formal protest or departmental reprimand. Dr. Jazir, as if by some pontifical fiat, had been ordained infallible and no one dared question his performance.

At the end of internship, Dr. Jazir wanted to go abroad for residency, but no program would accept him because the recommendation letters, which accompanied his applications, were muffled and guarded. Nonetheless, a non-teaching, private hospital in Beirut was coerced into accepting him as a surgical resident. After spending two years under the informal tutelage of myriad local surgeons, he joined the staff of his little hometown hospital and began his surgical career.

*

Meanwhile, Riad, my best friend and soul brother, left for Germany to do a residency in Obstetrics and Gynecology, and I came to the US for my postgraduate training in Internal Medicine and Infectious Diseases. While he and I continued to communicate across the Atlantic by telephone and letters, a savage, internecine civil war broke out in our homeland and raged, like forest fire, for the next twenty years.

One day, Riad called to tell me that, in spite of the war, he was going back home to start his practice in Tripoli.

"Are you mad?" I cried.

"I think I am," he giggled.

"And what else are you planning to do?" I quizzed.

"I'm going to get married."

"To a German Fräulein, perhaps?"

"No, to a lady from Tripoli. She's waiting for me and has already found us a flat in a nice building near the port, which is sheltered by other, taller buildings from bombardment."

"Bombardment?" I gulped.

"It's the safest place she could find. She said that most surrounding buildings have received direct hits, but not that one, which is why its rents are higher than the rest."

"And, how about casualties in the area?"

"People we don't know die every day, and every now and then, someone we know dies, and that always squeezes our hearts. I received some bad news the other day."

"Anyone I know?"

"Poor Dr. Samir was sitting on his balcony, having a drink, when he received a direct hit."

"Dr. Samir, the ENT specialist?"

"Yes, he lost both legs, but he survived."

*

Several years passed before I could visit Lebanon again, and communications between Lebanon and the US became precarious due to infrastructural damage. I lost contact with Dr. Riad, but he never left my mind. Often, I would think about him and wonder how he was faring. Distance, like death, devours time, but keeps us tethered to our past.

One year, during a lull in the war, I ventured back home, more out of yearning than out of need. It was the kind of yearning that grew and swelled inside my chest, in spite of time and distance, until I could no longer bear it.

*

    The Beirut airport was an anthill, teeming with chaos. By the time I arrived at my Tripoli home, I was a flat candle, flickering with its last flame. But, the salutary powers of family love resuscitated me and I found myself reborn by the next morning.

    "What would you like us to do today?" asked my mother.
    "I would love to visit my aunts and uncles in the village."
    "You can't. The road to the mountains is not safe, and many people are being kidnapped at the various checkpoints."
    "Is Tripoli any safer?"
    "Not if you venture alone."
    "So, you mean to say that we are homebound."
    "No. Taxis are safe because they pay tribute to all the militias. Their cars are the only ones that are allowed to pass through checkpoints without inspection."

    I called Dr. Riad. His wife said that he was at the hospital, delivering a baby. I waited two hours and called again. He was still at the hospital but was about to head back home.
    "Come have lunch with us," invited Abla. "He always talks about you, and would love to see you."

*

    When Riad opened the door, our eyes glimmered with disbelief. Our youthful black heads had become peppered with gray, our lean waistlines had gathered inches, and our young faces had furrowed with concern. The words, *you've aged*, escaped in muffled whispers from each of us as we hugged. But soon, all the time and distance that had separated us vanished like a sigh, and we were back in medical school, a couple of sleep-deprived, laboring students, worried about exams.

During lunch, among the cooked *kibbi* (meatloaf with crushed wheat), stuffed grape leaves, and *fattouch* (salad with toasted bread crumbs), we reconnected where we had left ten years before and cautiously filled in the blanks of our disparate destinies. Deaths, births, marriages, divorces, and lives were mapped onto our global memories until we were back in the moment's shade, as if time had not elapsed.

When we retired to the living room, I asked, "How's your work?"

"I should have stayed in Germany," he sighed.

I sipped from my demitasse of Arabic coffee and waited.

"As you must know, we live in a little hell here," he continued. "Our tap water is polluted, pedestrians have no walking room because the pavements are jammed with parked cars, electricity comes only 4-8 hours per day, electric generators roar on every balcony, roadblocks are at every corner, hyperinflation is making us poor, airport closures and cut communication lines often surprise us, and nothing is safe or sacred."

"But, how about your work?" I asked again.

"It's dangerous because when something goes wrong, the doctor is always the one to blame."

"And how about payments?"

He sighed again. "I get paid sometimes, but sometimes, when the outcome is not good, I'm afraid to ask for my fee. If a woman begets a deformed child, or if she has to have a caesarian section, or if I have to perform a hysterectomy to stop a hemorrhage, I have to be careful in how to phrase my request for payment."

"Surely, you have many grateful patients."

"I do, but it's the bad ones that break my spirit. Last week they called me at 2 a.m. to deliver a child. I had to do a caesarian section in dim light, with only a nurse anesthetist assisting me. It was a healthy boy and the father was happy. But, when I told him that my fee for an emergency caesarian was $200, he retorted with, 'you charge $200 for 20 minutes of work? Why, that's $10 a minute. That's outrageous.'

"I lost my temper, told him that he forgot to add the ten years of postgraduate study to the 20 minutes of work, and then asked him, since he seemed to be so good at mathematics, to divide $200 by ten years plus twenty minutes. He threw the money in my face and marched away."

At the end of his little story, Riad's face beaded with sweat and his skin turned ashen. We remained silent for a while and then talked about his children, growing up in a war zone. He was worried not only about their future, but also about their worldviews.

"It cannot be good," he sighed. "We are trapped in a violent situation, which appears to have no end."

*

Attempting to change the topic, I asked, "and how is Dr. Jazir doing?"

"Dr. Jazir?" he fired back. " *'Well, heaven forgive him and forgive us all; some rise by sin, and some by virtue fall.'* "

"That's from Measure for Measure; isn't it?" I asked.

"Shakespeare would have included a Dr. Jazir character in one of his plays had he been writing today. The great bard missed a good chance at exploring a most tenebrous dungeon in human nature."

A sardonic smile surfaced on Riad's face, but was soon replaced by a bitter frown. Twice, he attempted to speak and twice he changed his mind, as if to begin telling was tantamount to breaking a woman's waters and suffering, vicariously, the travails of her parturition.

I did not probe, nor could I remain taciturn. Instead, I quoted to the air, " *'Character is destiny.'* "

"Who said that?" he asked, rejuvenated.

"Heraclitus of Ephesus, circa 500 B.C."

"Indeed, character is destiny," he reiterated, nodding his head. "How we are wired determines what happens to us."

"And who determines how we are wired?" I quizzed.

"Nature, nurture, and circumstance," he replied without a hint of hesitation.

"And how about God? Does he play a part?" I quizzed again.

"Nature, nurture, and circumstance are God's trinity upon this earth," he emphasized with a closed fist.

"In that case, no one should be blamed for what one is."

"Perhaps not," he agreed. "Perhaps we are the ones who should be blamed for empowering the unworthy and allowing them to take charge. Dr. Jazir should have been expelled from medical school. Instead, he was promoted and unleashed on an unsuspecting public, shaming our profession and defaming our calling."

At this point in the conversation, Abla joined us.

"Are you talking about the infamous Dr. Jazir?" she asked with a smirk.

"Yes, dear," sighed Riad.

A flash of anger burst through Abla's cheeks as she tried to compose herself, but couldn't.

"If you don't tell your friend what he did to you, I will," she sparred.

Riad shifted in his seat, cleared his throat, scratched the back of his head as if to excavate memories that he had laid to rest, and then began:

"Dr. Jazir has done well overall. He worked hard, was dedicated to his patients, and earned a fair reputation as a general surgeon. He operated mainly in his little hometown hospital, but, occasionally, he operated here in Tripoli, at the same hospital I work at.

"The incident happened last year when, by coincidence, we met in the locker room. I had just finished delivering a baby and he had just finished operating on a woman who had a pelvic tumor, which he presumed was cancerous. While dissecting the tumor that was ramified and attached, he accidentally cut both ureters.

"Shocked at hearing his horrific story and seeing how nonchalant he was about the whole matter, I asked him, 'So, what did you do?'

" 'Nothing,' he replied with a smirk.

" 'You didn't call in the urologist to re-anastomose the ureters?' I asked with a sharp, shocked voice.

" 'What for?' he smirked again. 'She's going to die anyway and with severed ureters she will die quicker, which would be better for everybody.'

" 'How can you be sure of that?' I screamed. 'The tumor may not be malignant. She may respond to chemotherapy. She may live a long time if she had the right kind of care. You have no right to play mighty God on a poor, unsuspecting woman who has trusted you with her life.'

" 'Listen, Riad,' he replied with fuming ire. 'If word gets out that I have severed her ureters, it would ruin my reputation. I'm going to let her die and you are going to keep your mouth shut.'

" 'I'm not going to keep my mouth shut,' I shouted back. 'I'm going to report you to the authorities.'

"Dr. Jazir pulled a revolver from his locker, cocked the trigger, grabbed me by the neck, forced the barrel into my mouth, and said, 'If you say one more word about this, I will make your beautiful wife a widow and render your two, innocent children, fatherless.'

"I was so shaken that I began to tremble, but he did not remove the barrel out of my mouth until I nodded a yes."

Here Riad stopped talking, lowered his eyes, and gazed at his feet. Abla, infuriated, took over telling the rest of the story:

"When he arrived home," began Abla, pointing her eyes at Riad, "he was a gray ghost. And when he told me what had happened, I turned red with rage, raised my voice to him, and told him that he should return to the hospital and tell the woman's family what had happened.

" 'But, I don't know the woman nor her family,' he shouted back, 'and you know that the ruthless Dr. Jazir will keep his word and will kill me.'

" 'I don't care,' I screamed back twice as loud. 'Better dead than an accomplice to an operating room murder.' "

Here, Riad picked up the thread and finished the story:

"I went back to the hospital, found the family, told them what had happened, and called in Dr. Amin, a urologist friend of mine who had trained with me in Germany. He was aghast and only asked one question.

" 'How long ago was her surgery?'

" 'About an hour or so,' I guessed, not knowing why he asked.

" 'Good. I can only save her if the ureter wounds are still fresh. Otherwise, it's a deadly mess. Have the O.R. get ready. I'll be there in 20 minutes.'

"Dr. Amin took her back to the operating room and I assisted. To the lady's great fortune, we found the ureters only nicked, not severed, which still would have killed her, but it made our job much easier. I watched in awe as Dr. Amin's dexterous fingers repaired the defects with fast, confident facility. When it was all over, my legs faltered and I sank to the floor, exhausted.

"But, oh, you should have seen Abla's face when I walked in. It was a sunrise, glowing with pride.

"Two days later, the tumor was declared benign. Of course, Dr. Jazir never returned to make rounds on the woman. He had spies at the hospital, you see."

"Have you seen him since?" I asked.

"No, but every time I attend a wedding or a funeral, I worry about running into him. He is a man of his word, you know, and more so since the woman and her family told their story to his entire hometown. Dr. Jazir, of course, said that he was the one who had called in the urologist, and was also the one who had saved the woman's life by removing the big tumor out of her pelvis."

"Perhaps, had you stayed in Germany, your medical life would have been easier," I reflected, "but then, that woman's life would not have been saved."

"Indeed, character is destiny," he murmured. "I guess I am where I was meant to be."

Murder in the O.R., First Edition, The Bulletin, Oklahoma County Medical Society, March/April 2016. Revised Edition completed in October of 2016.

Arthur VanChef

"Sir?" I raised my hand with a pressing question on my mind.

With jesting eyes, he looked around the classroom, surveyed the space behind him, and then, smirking, responded, "I see no knights around. Why don't you call me Arthur?"

That was my first encounter with this larger-than-life man who, unwittingly, conducted his class around a table, but saw himself as a minuscule speck on the smudged cheeks of humanity.

It was the first class of the fall semester of 1995, that ominous year of the Murrah Bombing and the fiftieth year since our atomic epistles to Japan. As an ex-undercover police officer, Arthur felt personally responsible for all of Oklahoma's violent tragedies, especially those that he could not prevent.

"Killing or harming innocent children is a crime against nature's renaissance, a crime, like all sins, that only an all-forgiving God can forgive, and only after absolute and complete repentance and remorse," was his opening statement, which left the class stunned. Then, as an afterthought, the experienced police officer in him added, "When a mind and soul become hardened enough to perpetrate a crime like that, repentance, while possible, is rare." With the Murrah Bombing's 168 victims on Arthur's mind, he reminded us that he would never forget the date, April 19, because April was the month of nature's renaissance, and 19 was the number of innocent children who were killed in that explosion.

At 49, I was his oldest student. He was 42 at the time, and the rest of the students were my children's ages. What I wanted to ask when I raised my hand and called him *Sir*, no longer seemed significant after his opening remarks. I later observed that when Arthur spoke, the class listened, and his opening statement always set the mood for that day's session.

Arthur did not talk much about writing. Instead, he talked about life and about writers. "I'm not here to correct your punctuation, spelling, tense shifts, or grammatical errors," he would say. "You can go to the language lab for that. My job is to make published writers out of you."

Arthur defined *writer's block* as an unconscious fear of rejection, and added that not finishing a work is an unconscious fear of rejection, and that not submitting a work is an unconscious fear of rejection. He shared with us how often he had to submit his works before they were published. "I have a rule," he said. "I resubmit my manuscripts the very same day they are returned: I never let them overnight at my place." Then he told us about the many rejections some famous works had to go through before they were finally published. "To finish a work and to stubbornly resubmit it are the two antidotes to rejection fear," he emphasized. "Publishing is a war that can only be won by fearlessly charging and recharging the enemy until the enemy runs out of ammunition."

It fascinated me that Arthur did not say much about the art of writing. "You're all good writers," he reassured, "otherwise you wouldn't be in this class. Your writings are as good or better than many of the books out there. You are writing at a professional level and much better than I ever wrote when I was your age. When I look at my first novel, I am horrified. The only reason I keep it around is to remind myself of how bad I was when I first started."

"Keep your words simple," Arthur repeatedly stressed. "Showing off your erudite vocabulary turns readers off. Remember the banter between William Faulkner and Ernest Hemingway: *'He has never been known to use a word that might send a reader to the dictionary,'* said Faulkner. *'Poor Faulkner. Does he really think big emotions come from big words?'* retorted Hemingway. *'Never mistake motion for action,'* and *'In order to write about life, you must first live it,'* are two of my favorite Hemingway sayings. But Hemingway was not perfect, either. His dialogues, long and untagged, sent me back counting to find out who was saying what. Be better than Hemingway; keep your dialogues both simple and clear. Clarity is essential for reading ease. Don't expect your readers to struggle for you; they won't."

Arthur insisted that we read our works aloud in class and, after each reading, he would open the discussion with his own critique, which was always poignant. Often, he would suggest a change of heart instead of a change of detail. "Put some love in your work," he would instruct. "A love story subplot helps the work along and keeps the readers enticed. Don't just rely on anger, hate, and action to propel your story: balance them with kindness, love, and tranquility. Such contrast will enhance the credibility and readability of your work. And, don't forget to tag your characters with memorable traits; names are much easier to forget than images. You need images and emotions to enthrall the reader; descriptions alone will not do."

Arthur was kind to us student-writers, always highlighting the good parts with positive reinforcements before pointing out the parts that required repair. "The most cruel thing you can do to a burgeoning writer is to describe his work as good when it is not. It is much kinder to be brutally honest, but do it constructively and suggest positive ways to improve the work. One can always improve a manuscript through the critical feedback of sincere readers."

Arthur taught perseverance. "Writers write every day and not just when the muses inspire them. You don't write only when you get intuition. You write because you want to write, because you can't live without writing, because you love what you're writing, and because writing is the only way you can stay in love with your art. If you can't fall in love with what you're writing, don't bother submitting it. An unloved work is a worthless one. How can anyone else love what you write if you, the author, don't love it first?"

Writers revise," Arthur would emphasize. "Your work is not finished until battle fatigue overcomes you, having given it your very best fight. Your work is ready only when you feel so proud of it that you dare submit it with no fear of rejection. And remember, it takes as much time to edit and revise a work as it takes to write it. A first draft is nothing but a fallow field: it takes the long labor of sowing and tending before it yields the ripe crop that you can sell."

But, after advocating revision, Arthur would qualify. "Revision does not mean revising your first chapter fifty times before starting your second. Many a writer, mired in endless revisions, ends up with unfinished work. You are allowed to revise a chapter once but never twice. Run along with the work as if it were a marathon, and once you cross the finish line, then go back and revise. The best revisions come after the work is finished, when the ideas are mature and the vistas are panoramically clear to your mind."

Arthur was ever eager to tell us about talent. "You're all talented," he would announce, "otherwise you wouldn't have made it to this class. Perhaps some of you are a bit more gifted than others, but, in the final run, differences in talent don't matter as much as you think. What really matters is how hard you're willing to apply yourselves, day after day, and night after night, pouring out your soul with fierce force and determined dedication. Contrary to myth, creative writing comes out of the heart and not the mind. Great writers have great hearts, hearts that pulsate with all the pains, passions, pleasures, and aspirations of life. We are a unique breed of artists: instead of ink, we dip our pens into the inkpots of our hearts and the inscrutable humors of our souls."

Detail for Arthur was the writer's garb, costume, uniform, and makeup. "Without proper appearance, you will not be taken seriously," he would reiterate. "Imagine a soldier going into battle wearing a tuxedo, or a sex worker posing at the corner of a dim alley wearing a nun's habit. Readers will not become integrated into your scenes without sufficient detail. Show us the delicate accouterments of the world you're writing about, connect us to its history and times, and make us privy to the intimate thoughts and emotions of its players. Don't just say you crossed the river. Share with us what you saw, heard, smelled, and felt while paddling across its cool, frothy currents. Don't just say you shot the deer. Share with us the type of gun you used; tell us it belonged to your grandfather; describe the *calligraphed* initials on its silver plate; make us want to hold it, aim it, and own it."

Arthur, the writer, derived his juices from his eclectic history, not just as an undercover officer, but also as a martial artist who had studied Aikido, Thai Boxing, Kung Fu, Kali, and Spanish Knife Fighting. He holds a black belt instructor rank in Okinawan Karate and a 7th Degree Black Belt in Bei-Koku Aibujutsu. He is also a Certified Bowie Knife Instructor, a Blademaster in Knife Defense, and an NRA certified firearms instructor. His favorite quote about our permissive laws comes from Friedrich Nietzsche: "*There is a point in the history of society when it becomes so pathologically soft and tender that, among other things, it sides even with those who harm it, criminals, and does this quite seriously and honestly.*"

"Enthrall us by showing us your expertise and not by telling us about it," was Arthur's proverbial maxim. "Don't ever say you just fought someone. Show us the moves, the blades of the knives, the type of bullets, and let the spent shell casings burn our fingertips, because the more you research and learn about a topic, the more believable your writing becomes. Good writers take the readers to the movies where they see a lot and are told but little. Showing makes the reader think, imagine, divine, synthesize, and take part in the action all the way to the denouement."

"Telling is boring," he would iterate. "It puts readers to sleep. Creative writing is the intricate story telling with magnificent imagery, imagery so poignant that it evokes intimate thoughts and excavates profound feelings. Think like a movie director. Use intimations to entice the readers' imaginations, and turn off all the distracting sounds and lights around your readers so that they have no choice but to focus on the panoramic, multicolored screen that you spread before their eyes. You are the articulate painters of tales; don't tell us how and with what you paint; just show us your beautiful canvases."

Arthur, a man of myriad emotions, emphasized feelings as the cardinal precedents to good writing. "You can't write about what you don't know because you can't feel what you don't know. Stick to what you know, because that's where your feelings lurk. If you feel nothing, you will write nothing, but the stronger your feelings are, the stronger your writings will be. Let your imagination conjure the feelings you need before you begin writing, and when your feelings run dry, take a break. Writing without passion is banal. Don't do it. Even though I have to give you writing assignments, I will never tell you what to write about. I want you to think of your assignments not as homework but as springboards from which you dive into the depths of imagination to discover what, otherwise, would remain undiscoverable."

    Arthur emphatically reminded us that freshness and surprise are the essential spices that make our works irresistibly delicious. "Avoid the spaghetti and meat balls of clichés. Entice with creative language; ambush the reader with innumerable surprises; keep him enthralled with magical syntax. Ensconce your surprises at the ends of your sentences, paragraphs, and chapters, but keep the biggest one for the denouement. *"On my way to town, I stopped by the donut shop and was met with the sweet smell of freshly fried bread,"* is a cliché sentence. But, *"On my way to town, I stopped by the donut shop and was met with the rancid odor of frying flesh,"* is a shocking sentence, which causes us to want to read on. *"With great passion, I kissed her succulent lips,"* is a romantic sentence. But, *"With great passion, I kissed her pale, purple lips,"* is a titillating one because it causes us to wonder. *"The pebble rippled the dormant pond,"* is a great image. But, *"The pebble surprised the dormant pond,"* is a magical portrait. Surprising the readers keeps them mystified and keeps them reading. Guard the suspense: don't ever let your readers guess what you're about to say."

    Arthur was ineffable. Describing him as extraordinary or exceptional would be too simplistic. In fact, he hated for anyone to point out that he had written more than fifty novels and books. Arthur was eccentric, esoteric, abstruse, and fascinating. His attire was a mélange of adventurer, undercover agent, cowboy, vigilante, hippie, maharaja, and rebel. He was consistently inconsistent in his metamorphic appearance, reinventing himself with each session. And he liked the girls, not as a father though, but as an admirer of the lilies of the field, seeing women as the sublime, aesthetic manifestations of God's creation.

Arthur's ferocious appearance belied his primal kindness, but not when it came to the inconsiderate, loud-mouthed students, who, wittingly or not, usurped the class's discussion time. He would tolerate such usurpers once, or perhaps twice, but then the officer in him would emerge with a roar, which would promptly restore order. When one of those usurpers asked him once, "How many men have you shot?" he pierced her with his laser gaze and hoarsely replied, "Not enough, and none lately." She blushed and never pried again.

"Don't give me your works just before the end of the semester. If you do, I will not have time to read them," he confessed. "I will give you your grades based on your efforts, but you will not benefit from my reviews and criticisms. I give good grades to all who try hard because that's the only thing that really matters. Try hard, and in time, the writing world will open its gates to you. Excellence comes of struggle, and nothing worth reading has ever been written in haste. The art of writing involves the transformation of clamorous mental chaos into orderly music, and that always takes a great deal of time. There are no shortcuts in art."

"There is only one thing worse than bad, unloved, hasty, dutiful writing," he would declare while shaking his finger. "The only thing worse than the worst writing, is not writing. Writers write, and those who think about writing but do not do it are mere dreamers. Bad writing can be bettered with time but what is never written can never be improved."

Through almost twenty years of continuous class attendance, I have witnessed many students join Arthur's ranks with shaky pens and graduate with sanguine resolve. Many have had their works published. Many continue to drop in for an occasional visit to the class that was their crucible. And many continue to regard their teacher as the friend who always insisted that he had taught them nothing. "You, the students, are the individual reagents," he would point out, "and you, the group, are the chemical reactions that transform these simple elements into complex compounds. I am merely the catalyst who facilitates your transformation."

"But, Sir," I raised my hand in protest.
"What is it, Sir Lancelot?" he quipped.
" *'A teacher affects eternity; he can never tell where his influence stops.'* "
"Who said that?" he teased. "Was it Merlin, perhaps?"
"Oh, no, Sir," I reparteed. "It was an American journalist, historian, academic, and novelist who used the pen name of Frances Snow Compton, but is better known to us as Henry Adams, the grandson of President John Quincy Adams.
"I see," he nodded. "Well, perhaps I am a teacher, but y'all are the real teachers because I have learned a lot more from you than you have learned from me."

"The chief event of life is the day in which we have encountered a mind that startled us," said Ralph Waldo Emerson. I never understood what that meant until I encountered Arthur VanChef. After that first class in the fall of 1995, I went home and penned the first chapter of my first novel, and I have not stopped writing since.

Two Miracles

After coming to the US in 1971 I vowed never to lose contact with my Lebanese roots, as so many immigrants do. Keeping my promise, I flew back to Lebanon, year after year, to visit my family. There were seven of them at the time and they all lived in Amioun, our family's hometown in the northern mountains. Over the years, my father, two of his brothers, and one of his sisters died, reducing my visitation stops to only three homes: my mother's, Uncle Ibraheem's, and Aunt Jenefief's.

When Aunt Jenefief broke her hip, she was 87, and even though the surgery was successful, she spent most of her remaining time in bed. Widowed and unable to do her own housework, she hired a live-in maid, Sumayya, who became her devout companion.

I first met Sumayya in 2000 when she opened the door for me. She was a bright-eyed maiden in her late teens, lean, vibrant, witty, beautiful, and articulate. She came from Abikar, a small farming town, and was the eighth sibling of a farming family of twelve. Working as a live-in maid with all her expenses paid, she earned $300 a month, which she willingly gave to her father. It was an equitable arrangement.

Opening the door at the first ring, Sumayya surveyed me carefully before she said, "Welcome, you must be the doctor who has just arrived from America."

"Yes," I stuttered, taken aback by her biting beauty. "I'm Salem Hawi, Aunt Jenefief's nephew."

"Please, do come in. She's expecting you."

While Aunt Jenefief and I visited, Sumayya brought us Turkish coffee, asked me if I would try some of her lentil soup, and insisted that I should have a piece of *baklava* that had just arrived from Al-Hallab, the oldest sweet shop in Tripoli, established in 1782 when Lebanon was under Ottoman rule. Then, satisfied that I had been well served, she quietly sat in the corner on the other side of

Aunt Jenefief's bed, and resumed reading in her used, paperback copy of Charles Dickens's *Great Expectations*.

"She reads all the time," whispered Aunt Jenefief, "and spends all her pocket money on books.

"She's reading English," I observed with thrilled eyes.

"She reads French too," came my aunt's proud response, "and buys lots of books from the used bookstore near St. George's church."

As I quietly conversed with my aunt, curiosity eroded my propriety and I found myself peeking at Sumayya each time a conversation lull afforded me the opportunity. Knowing that she came from a small, farming town with only one elementary school, I wondered how this teen-aged girl managed to educate herself in spite of the demanding farm labor, which must have consumed her entire family. Besides, most of the houses in her town were two-room stone homes, which meant that all twelve had to sleep, huddled, without privacy, let alone the luxury of a reading lamp.

When my visit ended, Sumayya walked me to the door and, with a sunrise smile, wished me well and went back to my aunt's bedside. While my thoughts were still on Sumayya, I climbed the lone street up to Uncle Ibraheem's hilltop home for my second stop. It was summer and the hill's breeze provided respite from the summer's heat as my uncle, his wife Salam, and I sat on the large veranda overlooking the vast olive plain below.

Sipping lemonade and sampling Uncle Ibraheem's almonds, the conversation meandered among Amioun's happenings, marriages, births, funerals, and St. George's icon of the Virgin, which had cried tears of oil.

"Tears of oil?" I gasped.

"Yes," asserted my uncle and followed it with, "and you need to go visit St. George before you return to the States."

"*She* started crying oil tears when Father Elias incensed her during last Easter Sunday's service," came Salam's quivering words. "The first to notice it was Sumayya, who cried at the top of her voice, 'The Virgin is crying.' Hearing Sumayya's cry, everyone in church closed in and, with incredulous eyes, viewed the Virgin's oily tears. Father Elias interrupted the service and made an urgent call to the bishop who, in spite of his busy schedule, drove up to Amioun to check things out that very same afternoon.

"The entire town followed him into the church, but when he stood before the icon, it did not cry. He lifted it above his head and walked with it round and round the church while chanting *'Christ has risen from the dead and has stepped upon death with death.'* It was during the third round that Sumayya whispered in Jenefief's ears *'She's crying again,'* but the bishop couldn't see it because he was holding the icon high above his head. However, when the entire congregation suddenly fell to their knees, he lowered the Virgin till he could see her face and cried with all the might in his lungs, *'Oh, Jesus, heave mercy on us all,'* then dropped to the floor, shivering with chills."

I waited until Salam finished drying up her tears. Then, after her sighs had died and enough silence had passed, I ventured cautiously into the conversation with, "Who is Sumayya?"

"Jenefief's maid," came Salam's calm reply.

"I was just there; why didn't they tell me?"

"Neither Jenefief nor Sumayya like to talk about it," interjected Uncle Ibraheem in a deep, monotone.

"But why not?" I quizzed.

"Because after news of the miracle were circulated by the media, loads of busses started coming to Amioun from all over Lebanon, Syria, Jordan, and even Cyprus. They would visit the church and then would go to Jenefief's home wanting to talk to Sumayya because she was the first to witness the miracle. The constant harassment frightened both of them, so they closed their door and vowed never to speak about it again."

I gazed at the vast olive plain in the valley with hamlets surrounding it upon the hills. In the supervening silence, the tranquil scene appeared like the Lord's cup, brimming with green bounty. I inhaled the joyous spirit of the view and while still enthralled by the conjured image of *a holy grail brimming with green bounty,* I whispered my rhetorical question into the warm summer air.

"What was the Virgin crying about?"

After several whimpers, Salam crossed herself thrice and murmured, "May God have mercy upon Amioun."

I waited until the fear in her eyes subsided and then looked to Uncle Ibraheem's pensive face for explanation.

"This question has occupied Amioun ever since last Easter," he said with a hoarse voice, grave with concern. "Some say that the Virgin cried tears of oil because God's wrath will rain brimstone and fire on Amioun like it did on Sodom and Gomorrah. Others say that She cried tears of oil because we're going to suffer seven years of drought, which will kill all our olive trees. We're all so frightened by these interpretations and it has become taboo to discuss the matter. Only God knows why She cried and that's what I told everyone at the last town meeting."

Realizing that I had unwittingly choked the air with apprehension, I attempted to redirect the conversation toward lighter topics. Unwittingly, again, the next question that came out of my mouth was, "And what was Sumayya doing in church? Isn't she a Muslimah?"

"She takes your aunt to church every Sunday. Ever since her hip replacement, Jenefief has been unsteady on her feet and is afraid to use her walker, unless Sumayya is by her side."

"So what does Sumayya think of the miracle?"

"She won't utter a word to anyone, but we think she has been changed by it."

"Changed? In what way?"

"She could barely read Arabic before and used to ask for Jenefief's help while deciphering the morning paper headlines. But since the miracle, she has been reading Arabic, English, and French and spends all her pocket money on books. Her father swears that she dropped out of school before she finished sixth grade because they needed her help at the farm."

Being a man of science, it was hard for me to accept what I had just heard, but I was open-minded enough not to discount miracles. I wanted to know more before I formed my opinion, but I was afraid to ask for fear that I might provoke more apprehension.

I lapsed into a pensive trance and hardly stirred until Salam cracked the shell of silence with, "How about some chilled grapes?"

"Grapes," I gasped. "Do you have any *Durbali*?"

"I also have figs and *clementines*," she added with eager eyes.

While Salam was fetching the bowl of fruits, I asked Uncle Ibraheem my last question.

"How many times has the Virgin cried?"

"Only twice and both times during last Easter. You can still see traces of the oil on Her cheeks. They had to put Her behind glass, though, because too many tourists tried to touch her."

"Does the church door stay open?"

"No, they've been locking it for fear of thieves. You'll have to call Father Elias to open it for you."

The next day, I made a late afternoon appointment with Father Elias. We entered St. George, the town's all-stone, heathen temple, turned church under Roman rule. Cautiously, we walked on out tiptoes until we stood before the virgin, crossed ourselves, and prayed. Then, as if I had come from another planet, Father Elias looked at me with grinning eyes and asked, "Has anything like this ever happened in America?"

"Not that I know of, Father," I replied with lowered head.

"Do Americans believe in miracles?"

"Oh, yes, they do, Father," I responded with reassuring tone.

As soon as I said that, the smirk left Father Elias's face and was replaced by a deep, reverent expression. Then, after some solemn silence, and with eyes still on the Virgin, he continued his polite interrogation.

"What kind of miracles do you have over there?"

"Ah, apparitions, healing of the sick, saving souls, and answers to prayers," I fidgeted.

"Have you ever witnessed a miracle, Son?"

"No, Father," I confessed. "The only miracles I've witnessed were medical, and they've all had scientific explanations."

A week later, the day before I left for the US, I stopped by Aunt Jenefief's to say good-bye. Bright-eyed Sumayya opened the door and welcomed me in with her usual, blithe manner. While my aunt and I visited, Sumayya sat in the corner and read *Le Petit Prince* by Antoine De Saint-Exupéry. I desperately wanted to ask Aunt Jenefief about Sumayya's reading skills before and after the miracles, but my good sense prevented me because I knew that they did not wish to talk about the issue. But, when I spied Sumayya underlining in her book, I seized the moment and inquired,

"What did you just underline?"

With effortless French she replied, *"Voici mon secret. Il est très simple: on ne voit bien qu'avec le cœur. L'essentiel est invisible pour les yeux."* (*Here's my secret. It's very simple: We cannot see well except with the heart. What's essential is invisible to the eyes.*)

As we conversed, among fruit and tea, the doorbell rang. Sumayya's eyes glittered with expectation as she hurried to the door with flushed face. I heard whispers, giggles, and finally Sumayya's pleading voice came through the bedroom door as if she were dragging someone.

"You have to come in and say hello. He's Aunt Jenefief's nephew. He's a doctor. He lives in America."

A handsome young man in his twenties sheepishly followed Sumayya into the room. They stood facing us, brimming with passion and squirming with embarrassment. I stood up and extended my hand.

"Hello, I'm Salem Hawi."

"I'm Anthony Ghantous, the son of your friend, Nadeem."

"Oh, your dad and I spent most of our youth together. How's he doing?"

"He's fine. You should drop by and say hi before you leave."

"Is he home now?"

"He's sitting on the veranda, having a drink with my mother," giggled Anthony as he and Sumayya flashed eyes and scurried out.

I had not seen Nadeem Ghantous for several years. When I walked in, he and his wife met me with smiles and hugs as if time had not elapsed. A thought hit me as we sat on the veranda, reminiscing. *"The only thing that can halt time is friendship. It seems to resume at reunions as if interim time had been suspended."* That was how it was with Nadeem and me. We turned into adolescents and resumed from where we had left as if no time had transpired. When I told him that I had seen Anthony at Aunt Jenefief's and that he was the one behind my surprise visit, Nadeem's face dropped and he choked on silence, as if his tongue were a locked door, holding back his words.

Knowing that I must have trespassed on forbidden grounds, I held my breath and quietly sipped coffee while my eyes wandered away among the olive trees. After that stretch of awkward silence it was Nadeem's wife, Linda, who resumed the conversation.

"He and Sumayya are madly in love and they're talking marriage," she sniffled.

"You know that she's a Muslimah and her family is very upset at the prospect of a Christian marriage," added Nadeem.

"But Christians and Muslims have been intermarrying for decades," I protested. "My cousin Hala married a Muslim and has a wonderful marriage. So why is it so different in their case?"

"We're fine with it," added Nadeem "but they're not. Your cousin married an enlightened man, but in Abikar, people are still tribal and resist intermarriage because of ignorance. Religion is just their excuse, but Christians can be just as ignorant: remember when the priest's son in Kfarzoor murdered his sister because she eloped with a Muslim musician."

"But tribal is a desert term? We don't have nomadic tribes in Lebanon, so what on earth did you mean by tribal?" I queried with disbelief.

"You've been gone too long, Salem," he protested. "Ancient tribal traditions still survive in certain remote towns and still prohibit Muslim women from consorting with any man, Christian or Muslim, and from marrying against their fathers' wishes. If either should transpire, the woman's family is shunned by the tribe until the dishonor is cleansed with blood. Her father has already threatened that his family would disown her if she were to marry my son, but she doesn't seem to care."

"She's a rebel then," I exclaimed, feeling thrilled at her defiant stance.

"She wasn't always that way, you know. Her transformation came about after the miracle."

"Really?" I feigned surprise.

"She could hardly read before, but now she reads French and English books and has all these modern ideas about life and freedom, which her family regards as blasphemous. She's also teaching herself German because her oldest brother works in Germany and she's planning to surprise him the next time he comes to visit."

"So, when's the wedding?" I grinned.

"Whenever the couple decide," came Nadeem's dry reply.

On my way back to the US, I mused upon Sumayya and Anthony's dilemma, but spent most of my travel time pondering the two miracles. Why did the Virgin cry tears of oil on Easter Sunday? Why did She only cry twice on that same day and not again? Why was Sumayya the first to notice Her tears on both occasions? And how did the Virgin's tears of oil transform Sumayya from near illiterate to a polyglot? By the time I landed in Oklahoma City, I had decided that the transformation of Sumayya was, indeed, the more important miracle of the two.

For some arcane reason, however, I could not tell my wife and children. Perhaps I feared that they might ridicule me or that they might gossip about it to their friends. There was something sacred about the matter, something solemn and sublime, something Eastern and numinous that I feared might be diminished by Western misconceptions. That year, I had many a dream about Sumayya and Anthony. Something about the couple intrigued me. I even considered flying in for their wedding, but I didn't.

My next visit to Lebanon came about during the summer of 2002. By then, Sumayya and Anthony were no longer on my mind and I had shelved the two miracles in the remote recesses of my unconscious. My brother met me at the airport and together we drove to Tripoli where my mother and sister awaited us.

"Two years between visits is a long span for an octogenarian," reproached my mother as I embraced her. She then followed it with, "At eighty-six, two years represent too large a percentage of the rest of my life."

"I couldn't possibly come last year," I mumbled.

"Were you too busy to come see your mother?"

"I had neck surgery and was not allowed to travel."

"You had major surgery and didn't tell me," she reproached again. "I could have prayed for you and lit a candle under the Virgin's icon."

As soon as she said that, the two miracles flashed back into my consciousness and I was seized with intense urgency. I wanted to know how Sumayya and Anthony were doing, and if Sumayya's family had accepted her Christian husband. But, intuition warned me not to broach the topic at dinnertime. I held my tongue and resolved to make discovery during tomorrow's visit to Amioun.

Next morning, I drove to Amioun and started my visitation routine at Aunt Jenefief's. This time, another maid opened the door, which did not surprise me. Again I introduced myself as Jenefief's nephew and was promptly shown into her bedroom where she met me with wide-open arms and a broad, welcoming smile. We talked about her health issues, her worsening unsteadiness, and her inability to make it to church anymore. I wanted to ask about Sumayya, but never could find the moment. Instead, we talked about the upcoming presidential elections and about the devaluation of the olive oil prices because of fierce Syrian competition.

My second stop at Uncle Ibraheem's was equally unrevealing because, again, I was uncomfortable broaching the topic of Sumayya and Anthony for fear of rekindling yet another portentous reaction. It was as if some intuitive force were preventing me from asking, a force which I had been well acquainted with since childhood, and which I had learned to fear, trust, and obey.

Next, I resolved to visit my friend, Nadeem Ghantous, because I knew that he, being Anthony's father, would tell me everything. It was in the late afternoon when the sun was subsiding into the sea that I found them, cooling off on the veranda. Linda was dressed in black and Nadeem seemed subdued. I half-waved at them from the street, but they did not wave back. Instead, Nadeem rose to his feet, motioned for me to come in, and ambled down the stairs to open the door.

"Thank you for coming, Salem," he greeted as I entered.

"Why the thanks?" I asked, surprised.

Standing in the foyer, we gazed at each other with knowing eyes. I could tell that something had gone awry and he could tell that I did not know.

"Let's sit here for a moment," he whispered as he ushered me into the living room. "Linda need not hear this again."

"Hear what?" I frowned and held my breath.

"Hear what I'm about to tell you," he fidgeted. "It happened last year," he rubbed his eyes, "just before Easter."

I watched Nadeem's eyes brim as a pale shiver quaked his face. He sighed twice then with a moist, stuttering whisper began his story:

"They were such a joyful couple. None of her family came to the wedding, which we held at St. George's. She was three months pregnant when her father showed up at our door, said that her brother had come back from Germany and wished to see her. Knowing how opposed her family was to the marriage, she told Anthony that she'd better go alone and promised she'd be back before dark.

"When she did not return we all became worried because she was punctual. Anthony called her cell phone several times and left messages, but she never responded. At about nine o'clock, Anthony and I drove to Abikar. We asked around until we found her father's home. He opened the door as if he were expecting us and said that she had gone back by taxi just before dark. Anthony asked to see her brother, the one who had come from Germany, but the father said that he had already left.

"We called Amioun to see if she had shown up and were told that she hadn't. Not knowing what else to do, we returned home with heavy hearts and waited till morning to alert the authorities. At eight o'clock, the first thing we did was to report her missing at the *Saraya* (government building). The head detective, Jamil, who is a good friend of mine sat us down and questioned us. He asked if she had gotten pregnant before the wedding and we told him yes. He then asked if her family had known about the pregnancy and we said that she never hid anything from them, especially from her mother. Then he asked if any of her family or friends showed up at the wedding and we said no. For the longest time, he held his head with both hands. Then he suddenly stood up and said, 'Let's go. I think I know what happened and I think I know where to find her.'

"We rode in his military Jeep back to Abikar. We showed him her father's home but he did not stop there. Instead, he drove through town, up the hill, parked along side the cemetery, and asked us not to leave the car. He walked up and down between the rows until he found a fresh, shallow, unmarked grave. It was then that he motioned for us to join him. As we stood there, he asked Anthony to dial her cell phone. We both thought that he had gone mad until we heard the ring from underneath the dirt.

"The shock was more than we could stand. Before Jamil could fetch a shovel from the Jeep, Anthony had already dug her out with his bare hands and was holding her to his chest while mumbling incoherently. She had been shot in the heart.

"Jamil made a few calls and we took her back home. All of Amioun met us at the *Saraya*. We buried her next to my mother and father. The day after the funeral Anthony took his shotgun, said he was going hunting, went into the olive groves, and shot himself. We had two funerals that week. His mother is inconsolable. I think that she'd like to see you. Let's join her on the veranda."

Later on I learned that the Lebanese law makes allowances for honor crimes and hands perfunctory sentences to family members who commit them to cleanse the family's shame. Sumayya's brother received a six-year sentence in absentia and the government made no attempts to extradite him from Germany. Sumayya's father was not charged as an accomplice. Her mother wore black for one year. All of Sumayya's books were donated to the Amioun library.

That summer, I returned to the US a wiser man. I was glad I hadn't told my wife and children about the Amioun miracles, which I finally understood, but only with my heart. Antoine De Saint-Exupéry was right when he said, *"We cannot see well except with the heart. What's essential is invisible to the eyes."*

Indeed, I surmised that what the Virgin had cried about was Sumayya's fate, which was why She gifted her so many more lives by rendering her literate in so many languages. And indeed, Sumayya did live and enjoy all the lives in all the books she had read that year.

Love, which conquers all, is the mightiest force within us and the only force brave enough to transcend all human barriers. It's God's most venerable gift to humanity, His strongest antidote to violence, and His holiest road to peace.

Mighty Love, humanity's spiritual pastor, soul *sublimer*, art teacher, desire kindler, passion igniter, beauty beholder, joy granter, meaning maker, and arch hunter of hearts has but only one, fierce predator: Ignorance.

Life From Under the Knife

"Come, Salem. Come quickly."
"Oh. What happened?"
"Mom has fallen ill."
"What?"
"She's in the hospital."
"Why?"
"She's had a stroke. Her right side is paralyzed. She's babbling, 'Life. Knife. Fingers.' No one understands. We don't know what to do. Everyone is waiting for you."
"Okay, Sis. I'll be on my way."

My schedule swelled with appointments like a bookshelf, with books stacked back to back. The names, silent like book titles, filled the waiting room. I motioned to Cathy to follow me into my office. She hesitated, trying to disengage from a conversation she was having with Mrs. Stitchmaker who stood at the window with questions about her bill.

"So, why did they deny..."
"Myrtle..."
"They paid only $3.25 on the EKG..."
"Myrtle, I'm sorry..."
"And they paid nothing on the urine..."
"Myrtle, the doctor is calling me..."
"And here they say you overcharged me $1.25..."
"Myrtle, please, lower your voice and have a seat. I'll be back in a minute."

Exasperated, Cathy hurried in, her eyes on the flashing telephone line tolling its fourth ring.
"This poor woman is driving me crazy and everyone can hear her."
"Norma, I need to leave right away."

"Leave, with a waiting room full of patients."

"My mother has had a stroke. Lamia just called."

"Oh, my. I still remember when they called about your dad and you had to leave right away. Would you like me to drop everything and work on your tickets?"

"Please. I'd like to leave today. And write off Mrs. Stitchmaker's balance and tell her that her insurance paid it in full."

While Cathy worked on my tickets, I saw my afternoon patients with my usual alacrity, and not one of them noticed my worried mind or my anxious eyes. As I ushered my last patient out, Cathy stood suspended next to my desk, with a shuffle of papers in her hands.

"I can have you in Beirut tomorrow evening if you can be at the airport in two hours. You'll fly American Airlines from here to London and Middle East Airlines from London to Beirut. By the way, your patients all noticed that you seemed distracted and, one after the other, have asked me if anything was wrong. What would you like me to say?"

As I examined the tickets, I thought, *"How transparent I must be, even when I think that I am faking it well. These last minute fares are steep. They prey on the desperate. Well, I have no choice."*

The words of a poem I had written many years ago surfaced out of my unconscious, began drumming within my chest, and racing with my heart:

> *The east wind calls my name*
> *I know that I must go*
> *The wind may never call again.*

I handed Cathy my credit card, organized my unwritten charts into three delinquent piles, took off my white coat, packed my brief case, and, as I walked out, Cathy gave me a shuddering embrace and whispered into my shoulder, "Please be careful. They're still fighting over there. This morning, there was a battle in Sidon between the army and a new rebel group."

"The battle was north of Sidon, my dear, at the refugee camp by the river. Mother is in the Soha Hospital on the other side of town. I'll call you as soon as I get there. I don't know when I'll be back. Call Drs. Hooper and Michael. Ask them to please cover for me while I'm gone."

In gray October skies, the airplane buffed against cotton clouds and swooned down lurking air pockets, as it arched its way from our windy city to the other one, which embraces Lake Michigan. It then hopped to the world's crucible of hospitality, marred by its two absent towers, arriving half an hour late. My connecting time was just enough to make the transatlantic leg. In the takeoff distance, floated the lit mirage of Bartholdi's colossus, and in my heart echoed the words of Emma Lazarus on the Statue's pedestal:

Give me your tired, your poor,
Your huddled masses yearning to breathe free,
The wretched refuse of your teaming shore,
Send these, the homeless, tempest-tost to me:
I lift my lamp beside the golden door.

Heathrow was awakening when we landed, and the un-thronged passport lanes yawned in the misty British sunrise.
"How long are you staying in London, sir?"
"I'm transiting to Beirut."
"Business or pleasure?"
"Neither, sir."
"Oh?"
"My mother has had a stroke."
"I'm sorry, sir. Have a safe trip."

The crowded Middle East Airline left on time with knee-room-only seats; no one crossed legs during the four-and-a-half-hour flight. The Lebanese hors d'oeuvres and belly-dance music, however, tempered our imprisonment and ameliorated the backaches that groaned with failed attempts to shift positions. Over Beirut, I could see smoke arising from distant fires and rubble-riddled streets that, as a student, I had sauntered through and frequented their loud, politically hot cafe's. When we touched down, a communal sigh breathed relief throughout the cabin, and knees felt assured that freedom was imminent. As I walked out, having cleared customs, my brother stood waving in the distance. He managed a smile as we hugged before he whisked me to Sidon.

Along the serpentine, seashore highway—bedecked with towns, resorts, restaurants, and shallow seawater bins lined with salt sacks—we broached sundry topics. We talked of Syria, Israel, Hezbollah, Muslims, Christians, Jews, the recently assassinated son-of-Sidon, Senator Hilu, and the upcoming olive harvest in Kafr Az-Zaitoon. We even talked about the weather, the early snows, and the failing economy. We talked about everything except about Mother.

At the hospital, a crowd stood in front of her room. Aunts, uncles, cousins, friends, and distant relatives, one by one, kissed me on both cheeks and mumbled unintelligible phrases ending with the divine word, *Allah*.

In the room, Mother's shadow lay motionless and a slow-dripping IV line snaked underneath the white sheets into her left arm. Those in the room stood back, as I approached and began stroking her forehead. She started to breathe faster when she felt my hand, then her eyes opened and wandered about the room until they fell on me. A smile lit up her face as she attempted to articulate my name, "Sa, Sal, Salem" and, at the same time, reached with her right hand and clasped mine.

Murmurs and whispers behind me got louder and louder, turned into cheers, and the outside crowd long-necked into her door. The words, "She said his name and moved her right arm," echoed from one to another and many eyes teared over quivering cheeks. It took me a while to apprehend that Mother had been in a coma until that very moment.

On the third hospital day, barely leaning on my arm, she walked down the hospital hall and on the fourth day, we took her to our home in Sidon. In our mountain town, Kafr Az-Zaitoon, rumors frenzied about her sudden recovery and reached Father Elias who hurried down to Sidon for a visit.

"They are saying that you woke up for your son who came from America to see you. They are saying that you woke up as soon as he touched your forehead. They are saying that he has a healing hand. You have to come with him to St. Nicholas this Sunday. Lots of sick people are planning to come to be healed by his hand. Through him Christ has performed a miracle. Praise God. Praise the mighty Allah."

"Father Elias, I'm leaving tomorrow," I reminded. "I have patients and appointments that cannot wait until next week."

"I'll come in his place, Father," interjected my mother. "Christ does not need my son's hand to heal the sick. We'll all pray together this Sunday."

"Inshallah, Inshallah, Doctorah. May God bless you all. Too bad Dr. Salem will not be coming up to Kafr Az-Zaitoon with you. A lot of people will be disappointed, but it must be God's will that he return to his own patients in America."

That night, my mother talked and I listened. "They killed my son, the one I brought to life from under the knife."

"What do you mean mother?"

"I have never told a soul, but I may tell you now since Dr. Babandi and all his children have died. You cannot repeat this to any one because people still remember and it will shame the Babandi family. Do you promise?"

"I promise, Mother."

"It happened in 1944, after the Great War. I had just finished my Obstetrics and Gynecology residency at the American University of Beirut and came to Sidon to work with Dr. Babandi at the Babandi Hospital. I assisted him on surgeries, and there were lots of them because he was the most famous surgeon in all of South Lebanon. One day, he was operating on a spinster who had an abdominal mass and couldn't eat. When we opened her up, we found the mass to be a pregnant uterus.

"He asked me what should he do and I said, *'Close her up and get out.'* He did not agree and thought that, for the reputation of the woman, he would do a hysterectomy, tell everyone that he took the mass out, and that she was cured. I said, *'No, you cannot kill an innocent fetus. When God gives life, no one may take it away.'* He insisted as the chief surgeon, with knife in hand, on going ahead with the hysterectomy. I covered the woman's uterus with my gloved hands, looked him straight in the eyes, and before his stunned operating room crew, I shouted into his masked face, *'You will have to cut my fingers first before you kill this innocent child.'* He looked around, paused for a moment, threw his knife into the air, and walked out of the operating room mumbling, *'You close her up then, and you go explain things to her waiting family.'*

"I closed her up, told her parents that she was pregnant, that she should relocate to another town, and that she should dedicate her life to raising her child because, as of that moment, her child should become her most pressing responsibility. After leaving the hospital, she married the father of her child and left town in a storm of bitter gossip. Sixty years later, that boy became Senator Hilu, who was recently assassinated. Shhh. No one knows this story but you. The operating room crew, Dr. Babandi, the woman, her husband, and her parents have all died. I am the only one left from that era. When you reach ninety-five, you will have outlived all your generation. Have a safe trip home, Son. I will light a candle for you this Sunday at St. Nicholas and pray for your healing hands."

When I returned to work, I told Cathy the story but camouflaged the names and places. Her eyes filled up with tears and she cried, "Stop writing poetry. Stop writing novels. This is the one story you must write for your mother's memory. That's why, when she was in a coma, she lay mumbling, *'Life. Knife. Fingers.'* Don't you see? It was the only memory that floated above her coma. *Life From Under The Knife.* That's what you need to call that story."

Life from Beneath the Knife, First Edition, AL JADID Vol. 18, no. 67, 2013-2014. Second Edition completed in October of 2016.

Frédéric Chopin's Four Ballades

*"... and then the day came when the risk to remain tight in a bud
was more painful than the risk it took to blossom."*
Anaïs Nin (1903-1977)

Monday: *Ballade #1 in G Minor*

"What's going on, Doc?"
"Nothing. Just working."
"Lately, even when you're with us, you seem alone."
"Too much to do and much more to worry about."
"I'd better leave you to your work, then."
"Goodnight Rebecca."

Charts float before my eyes as she closes the door and walks into the night. I stare at her calves—full, firm, purposeful, and comfortably cuddled inside her pantyhose like a newborn twin. The door shuts. I close my eyes and sigh. Why didn't I ask her to sit down for a minute? She can see through me as clearly as I can see through the gossamer of her pantyhose. Only she does not know that I gaze at her legs whenever she's not looking—or, maybe she does? Women always know more than men suspect.

Chart after chart swims before my eyes. It's late but I like my office better than I like my home. Here the charts keep me company. At home, not even a poodle or a cat greet me at the door. Still, each night, I race home as if someone I love is waiting for me. She, on the other hand, has a real husband who waits for her, and children who live close by.

I turn off the lights and walk towards the door, briefcase in hand, unsure of foot because I'm going nowhere. I look for her in the hall, in the parking garage, and all along the roads that take me home. I should have asked her to sit down for a minute. We could have had a little talk. What I feel for her frightens me but, instead of avoiding it, I fantasize about it. Loneliness is a dangerous state; it mars wisdom with folly and beguiles the mind with siren delusions.

Tuesday: *Ballade #2 in F*

Work is heavy. I steal a glance at her calves each time I get a chance. Patients come and go. I give them kindness, compassion, listen to all they say until their throats are emptied, and then I ask my questions: how long, when, where, how often, why, and why not? I have to extract the answers out of their wombs by forceps. Patients do not know the difference between vital and trivial information.

The charts grow taller upon my desk. I look at the piles after the last patient leaves. Three hours, I mumble. It'll take me three hours to write all the notes and answer all the phone calls. I won't be able to leave till after eight. But why the hurry? I remind myself. I'm going nowhere.

"Goodnight, Doc."
"Oh, you're leaving, already?"
"It's almost eight."
"Eight? I had no idea. Look at all these unfinished charts."
"Can't you leave some till tomorrow?"
"Tomorrow will bring its own charts with it."
"You're looking thin, Doc. Your cheeks, I mean…"
"You mean I'm looking old?"
"Oh, no. I just meant that I needed to start feeding you lunch."

I avoid her eyes by eyeing my charts. She starts to leave. I should ask her to sit down and visit for a minute. She walks away slowly, as if to allow me time to say, *goodnight Rebecca*. I gaze at her calves. They stop at the door and then begin to turn around. I drop my eyes. I can't let her know that I love her legs and the way her waist undulates with each rhythmic stride. She's a married woman with children. I pretend not to notice that she's back in my office, and when she speaks I feign surprise.

"Ah, you're back."
"What would you like for lunch, tomorrow? I can run and get you something or can bring you a sandwich from home."
"I never eat lunch, Rebecca."
"Well, Doc, you need to. You're looking pale and thin."
I want to ask her to sit down, perhaps she would cross her legs and I would get to listen to the rustling of her hose and steal a gaze at her sculptured knees. She sees through me, as I blush a bit, trying to suppress my sensual thoughts.
"A penny for your thoughts, Doc."
"Oh, no." I gasp. "I could not possibly tell you what I'm thinking."

My blush deepens because she caught me in the act of thinking about her legs. Sweat beads sprout over my forehead, but I do not wipe them off. She just stands and watches me swelter under her gaze while I pretend to study the chart before me. The longer she stands the more I sweat. My fountain pen makes a spreading smudge of ink in the note I'm writing, but I continue pressing it to the paper with my clenched fingers. She turns to go. I think I offended her because I refused to look up. She walks away with half determined steps and stops at the door. I'm afraid to gaze at her calves lest she be looking at me from behind her shoulder. I keep my eyes on the spreading blotch of ink before me. The door opens and closes without a goodnight. I quietly finish my work and again race back home as if someone is awaiting me. I look for her in the streets. I regret that I did not gaze upon her calves when she was walking out with half determined steps.

Wednesday: *Ballade #3 in A Flat*

"Doc. Here's your sandwich. Just pause for a few minutes and eat."
"Won't you sit down?"

"I have to answer the phone."

As I take a bite I realize that I had asked her to sit down when I knew that she couldn't. But at least I did it. I feel smug. It wasn't that hard. Perhaps I can do it again tonight. My heart races; my mouth goes dry; I have trouble swallowing the sandwich. I wrap it back in its wax paper and throw it in my wastebasket. She won't notice that I didn't eat it. She's too busy answering the phone.

The afternoon marches on, I run between rooms, and I give more time to some because they need to cry. I fall behind and the waiting room fills up with vacant eyes. One cannot rush patients. It's going to be another after-eight day. Rebecca catches me between rooms. I look at her fallen face and ask, "What's wrong?"

"Mr. Alpert died. His wife just called, crying. She's going to call us back about the funeral arrangements."
"Why didn't you let me talk to her?"
"You were in the exam room and you've been running behind since you let Lisa cry on your shoulder for half an hour."
"I'll call her when I finish seeing our last patient."
"I've already told her that you will."

The evening stretches like a snail and crawls across the setting sun. Mr. Alpert smiles at me each time I think about him. It was almost two years ago when I told him that he had pancreatic cancer. "I know where I'm going, Doc." he said with a smile. His wife hid her face behind her hands and left the room.

One more patient and I'll be able to start writing notes. I wish I could go to the restroom, but Mr. Hale has been waiting a long time. He needs his back injected. His wife and daughter are in the room with him and they have a list of questions: "He's no longer able to control his urine. Is that related to his back?"

I ask him to give me a urine sample and it takes him a long while to give it. On the microscope, his urine is full of infection. I tell his wife that the antibiotic will cure his incontinence. She's relieved; and he's relieved that he was able to straighten up his back after the shots. They leave happy and I go to my desk.

"I'm sorry I have to leave early, Doc. My grandson is in a play."

I'm relieved because I don't have to fret about asking her to sit down. I watch her rhythmic calves march out and I do not tell her that the hem of her dress is up-folded, revealing her sinews.

Thursday: *Ballade #4 in F Minor*

"How was your grandson's play?"
"He wet his pants on the stage."
"Just like Mr. Hale."
"What on earth do you mean by that? It was very embarrassing for the entire family."

She tried to conceal her affronted tears as she handed me my first chart, sighed, and added:

"Mrs. Wilmot was snooty to me when I reminded her that she has an unpaid balance. She's refusing to pay for her EKG because she says that we didn't do one. I made a copy of the EKG from her chart, with her name *lasered* on it, and handed it to her. She just put it in her purse, smiled, and walked away."

Mrs. Wilmot is delusional. Thirty years ago she was sharp and beautiful; now she's slightly demented and thinks we try to cheat her. Her husband died and when she was cleaning up his closet she discovered that he had been a life-long homosexual. Throughout their forty-five-year marriage, he made love to her only a few times, and only once on their honeymoon. They adopted a son who died of AIDS.

The day unfurls patient after patient and question after question. I manage to stay on time because there were no long stories waiting in the throats. I resolve, after I get to my desk, to ask her to take a seat when she comes in to say goodnight. I prepare my face for the right expression, I rehearse my words, and I begin charting. Six o'clock, seven o'clock, and she's still on the computer entering charges. Then I hear her back up and signoff, and I know that the moment is nigh. Once more, I prepare my face and rehearse my words.

"Well, Doc, if you don't need me, I need to head home. There's a storm coming."

"I'm sorry to have made fun of your grandson's incontinence."

"He does that whenever he's afraid."

"Why don't you sit down and tell me about it."

"Oh, there's not much to say except that he started doing it after my husband left."

"Where did your husband go to?"

"I've filed for divorce and the kids are having a hard time accepting it."

My ears begin to ring like bells, and words refuse to fly off my tongue. I choke on joy and cough until I turn red in the face.

"Are you all right?"

I clear my throat, wipe my eyes, and lace my voice with a hint of remorse.

"I'm so sorry to hear that, Rebecca. Please do sit down. I've been meaning to ask you to sit and visit for quite a while but, for some reason, I couldn't get myself to do it till now."

Her chin begins to quiver as she eases herself into the chair facing my desk and crosses her legs. The rustling of her pantyhose vibrates in my bones and rushes into my chest, causing me to gasp.

"What's wrong Doc.? Are you okay?"

Stealing a look at her sculptured knees, I smile and pretend that I feel nothing. Then I summon my courage and ask, "When will your divorce be final?"

"In two weeks."

"I went through it last year; remember?" I reemphasized.

"Did it cause you to feel all alone?"

"Desperately so. How about you?"

"It's suffocating me. The loneliness, I mean. Does it ever get better?"

"Only if you find love again?"

She stands up.

"I'd better be going, Doc. It's getting late."
"Going where?"
"Home, of course."
"And is there anyone waiting for you at home?"

She does not answer and starts to walk away. I look at her furtive calves and say to my self, *carpe momentem*. I stand up and walk towards her. She hears me approaching, stops, but does not turn. I tag her on her shoulder and whisper, "Let me finish my charts and we can go have dinner together."

"No, it's too soon. What will people say?"
"Please come back, sit down, and let me finish my charts."
"Oh, no Doc. I really need to leave."

I let her shoulder slip away, escort her calves to the door, and go back to my desk to finish my pleading charts. Close to nine o'clock I walk to my car, the only car left in the parking lot. As I get in, my cell phone rings.

"Doc, you know there are no open restaurants at this hour except Othello's in Edmond."
"Oh, Rebecca, what, why, ah, from where are you calling?"
"From Othello's."
"What in heaven's name are you doing there?"
"Waiting for you."
"And what would people say if they see us together at this late hour?"
"Frankly, my darling, I don't give a darn."
"Rebecca," I chortle as I race to her, "Anaïs was right after all."
"Anaïs? Who's Anaïs?"

"Anaïs Nin."

"And what did this Anaïs Nin say?"

"She said: *'And then the day came when the risk to remain tight in a bud was more painful than the risk it took to blossom'*."

Four Ballads, First Edition, Journal of the Oklahoma State Med Association, Vol. 105, No. 7, July 2012. Revised Edition, Frédéric Chopin's Four Ballads completed in October 2016.

Love's River

"Who lives way up there?" I asked our guide, Muneer, as I gazed beyond the snow-laden cedar trees, floating in the fog.

"His name is Sanneen," answered the guide with a half smirk.

"But, that's the name of a mountain," I protested.

"That's the name the locals gave him because he lives alone, on top of that Cedar Mountain. No one knows his real name."

"Is he a monk?"

"You could say that. He lives in total solitude and when he comes to town for supplies, he uses very few words."

"Did he build this log cabin?"

"No. He just lives in it. It was built by the Turks at the start of the First World War as an observation station. It lay abandoned from when the Ottoman Empire was dismantled in 1918 until he rented it from the municipality about two years ago."

The guide led us into the lobby of Cedar Hotel where writhing flames from a massive fireplace warmed our shivering bodies before any hot tea touched our lips. After we became comfortable, the guide announced that it was too cold and foggy to proceed up to the Cedar Forest and that we would be better off if we would descend down to Bisharri, Gibran Khalil Gibran's hometown, and spend our entire time visiting Gibran's tomb and museum.

No one protested as the three of us raced back to the van. My two American guests, Kristin and Angela, somewhat disappointed that they could not visit the Cedars of Lebanon, engaged the guide in conversation.

"What was that mountaintop observation station supposed to observe?" asked curious Angela.

"The Turks, at the start of the First World War, became fearful of Christian rebellion, which would detract their armies from the front. To starve the mountain folks, who were mainly Christians, they blocked all supply routes from the fertile Beqaa Valley, causing half the population to die of famine. That observation station was built to scan for mule caravans, attempting to smuggle food to the mountain folks."

Visiting Gibran's museum and tomb consumed the remains of that day. Exhausted, we proceeded back to our Beirut hotel with Kristin more elated to have visited Gibran's museum than the rest of us. "Gibran is my hero," she announced as we descended. "He fills me with joy every time I read him."

Angela, on the other hand, was disappointed. She had traveled across the Atlantic and Mediterranean in order to visit the biblical Cedars of Lebanon and was thwarted by bad weather.

"Can we go back to the Cedars?" she pleaded. "For some reason, I feel an emptiness inside of me. I can't go back home feeling that way."

"This is our last day," I lamented. "Tomorrow we cross the border to begin our tour in Syria."

My answer provoked Angela's tears. With hand on chest, she quietly sobbed and spoke no more.

After spending a week in Syria, we were on our way back to Beirut when Angela approached the guide and asked if he would be willing to take her up to the Cedars, alone.

"We have one day in Beirut before we leave for the US," she reminded. "Couldn't you take me to the Cedar Forest on a private tour?"

The guide looked to me for an answer because Angela and her sister were in my custody.

"Why not?" I grinned, which brought a glowing smile to Angela's forlorn face.

"I want to go along," said Kristin. "I have seen enough of Beirut. Seeing the Cedars would be the climax of our trip."

The next day, the three of us climbed up the Cedar Mountain in Muneer's fifteen-year-old car, a 1985 Mercedes Benz.

As the dizzying road writhed upward, the plateau below shrank, the seashore thinned, and the sea became a shimmering turquoise jewel. It was a clear, sun-loved winter day.

At the entrance to the Cedar Forest stood a uniformed unit, wearing helmets. The Lebanese Armed Forces had set up a checkpoint and were turning cars away.

"Go back to where you came from," said the lieutenant who peered at us through the driver's window.

"My guests came all the way from the US to see the Cedars," I protested.

"Come back tomorrow."

"They fly back to the US tomorrow," explained Muneer.

"Let them come back next year, then," barked the lieutenant.

"What if we just want to pass on to the Beqaa Valley," argued Muneer.

"If you're just passing through, back up and use the alternate road," said the lieutenant, pointing to our left. "Beyond this point, this road is not safe and we suspect that the Cedar Forest has been mined."

The alternate road was a narrow, old road forged by the French Army during the French Mandate days after the First World War. Viewing it from below conjured awe for it snaked up the steep slopes like a long, black serpent.

"Let's go back to Beirut," sighed Kristin. "I smell trouble and I don't want any part of it."

"Let's go up to the little log cabin," retorted Angela with a rebellious, voice.

"What for?" cried Kristin with a tired moan.

"I want to visit the monk who lives in it," replied adventurous Angela.

"He's not a monk. He's just a recluse."

"We've made it this far," snapped Angela. "I'm not going back until I've visited the hermit at the top."

"What if he's not there?"

"He's always there," reassured our guide as he turned around and spurred his car up the indomitable slope.

The old Mercedes groaned as it climbed like a beast of burden, huffing, and puffing, and billowing smoke from its thundering muffler. Midway, Muneer stopped at a bend, and addressing Angela and Kristin, pointed to the Cedar Forest below.

"At least, when you return to the US, you can tell your college friends that you have seen the biblical Cedars of Lebanon."

We gazed in awe at the green patch of *Cedrus lebani* basking in the distance, a lush island bursting out of a gray mountain, a stretch of history frozen in time and place, chronicling millennia of lives and strife. I glanced at Kristin's visage glowing with wonder at this sub-heavenly sight, at Angela's chin quivering with awe, and at Muneer's face beaming with pride. The silence of the mountains hissed against the high winds and an azure halo of God's love hovered above, calming our hearts with its sunny bounty.

"Stop," cried Angela as we reached the top. On our left stretched the fertile Beqaa Valley, on our right basked the deep, green lips of the Mediterranean Sea, and at a short distance up the mountain stood the lone log cabin, like earth's navel, submerged in snow.

Angela, as if compelled by some numinous force, stepped out of the car and with resolute steps marched up to the cabin. The rest of us preferred the cuddled warmth of the car to the uninvited visit to a recluse. Angela knocked with her fist. The cabin's door moaned as it opened. Angela stepped in and disappeared from view.

We looked at each other with furrowed brows. A thousand what-if's shot out of our gaping eyes, but none of us said a word. With trepidation we tried to understand that all of this was perhaps meant to be because the azure halo of God's love was hovering above, and His splendid spirit was suffusing the limpid air, the silent snow, and the vast vistas that solemnly recited his psalms. *"Beauty can make believers even out of stone-hearted atheists,"* I thought.

Muneer kept the engine running to keep us warm. In our cocoon of silence we waited as time snailed by. But Angela did not return. We all thought that we should go after her but none of us moved or spoke. *"He could have harmed her. He could have assaulted her. She's a trusting, pretty girl. She shouldn't be alone with a man she does not know, high in these lonely lands."* These very thoughts played over and over in our minds and aimlessly roamed among our heavy hearts. Yet, still, Angela did not return.

I, being her Lebanese host, began to feel personally responsible. I had promised her mother, Cathy, to bring them safely home. I remember how my invitation came about, spurred by certain conversation fragments that escaped Cathy's lips.

We were having dinner, their mother and I, when they rang the doorbell.

"And what are you two honeymooners doing, chirruped Angela as she walked in, followed by Kristin."

"We were discussing where to take you two college girls during Christmas break."

"This is your first Christmas as a married couple. What's wrong with staying home," broke in Kristin with a meek voice.

"Because my Lebanese husband had promised to spend Christmas with his aging mother, long before he asked me to marry him," explained Cathy. "When I said yes, he told me that we would have to celebrate this Christmas with his mother. When I said that I couldn't leave my girls alone, he offered to take you along. So, as it stands, we're all going to Lebanon for Christmas."

But, circumstances were neither lenient nor permissive. After we had purchased our tickets and were set to leave, Cathy fell and fractured her hip. While at rehab, she insisted that we go without her.

"This is a unique chance for my girls to visit Lebanon. Take them and go, but bring them back safe and sound," she insisted, as we were discussing cancelling our trip.

These snippets of conversation echoed in my ears as we waited for Angela to emerge from that lone log cabin, issuing plumes of smoke from its gnarled chimney.

How long it took Angela to emerge cannot be estimated in time units. In life units, however, it took hundreds of sighs and thousands of heartthrobs.

When at last she emerged, there were tears on her cheeks and a quivering smile on her lips. Approaching us with a stately, equine gallop, she held a letter to her chest as if it were a newborn babe.

In the car, with letter still on her chest, she sobbed, holding her breath between sighs that sounded like whoops. Down the mountain we drove in sad silence, back to Beirut. No one dared intrude on Angela's solitude. We knew that she would tell us when she was ready.

It was on the way back to the US that Angela told her story. She spoke with shimmering eyes, flushed cheeks, and a furrowed brow. "He is a beautiful man," she began, "a most sensitive, grief stricken, inconsolable soul. While at college in the US, he had fallen in love with an American girl and poured out his love to her in his *Poems to Nancy*, which she relished, savored, and saved. But, when it was time to leave, her Christian parents stood strong against a Muslim man who planned to take their daughter back to turbulent Lebanon. He had made up his mind to return home and it was time she made up hers. 'Go back home without me,' she at last told him. 'We're not destined to unite.'

"In Lebanon he buried himself in work, but could not forget her. He consorted with other women, but could not forget her. He drowned himself in alcohol, but could not forget her. His parents were after him to marry, but he could find no one else who attracted him like Nancy. After five years of distraction and indecision, he resigned from his well-paying job, rented the log cabin, which he had admired during his skiing days, and decided to spend the rest of his life as a recluse.

"One day, his father came up to the cabin and handed him a letter from Nancy. She had gotten married to someone who pleased her parents, had two children by him, divorced him, and bitterly regretted not having married her Lebanese love. She ended the letter with, 'call me and I shall come; my children are your children; we could have more children together; we are still young; I love you and want to live between your arms until I die.'

"Mustafa, for that's his name, told me that he wrestled with his emotions for seven months, unable to decide. 'There's no going back,' he confided. 'If we go back, we will foster a tragic reunion. The children will suffer. She and I will suffer. I know that I have been doomed to eternal grief, but she might find a second life. America is a big, free country, free of bitter social taboos. In Lebanon restraints lurk at every bend, stifling freedoms and fostering misery.'

" 'Why don't you go back to the US,' I asked him. " 'You have shared your grief with a stranger. Why not share it with her? It might bind your hearts tighter than ever.'

" 'There's no going back,' he repeated. 'Love is a river. The water that flows downstream is forever gone. We have been apart for seven years now. Seven years of our lives have flowed down love's river and drowned into the sea.'

" 'But, what's going to happen to you?' I asked with a grief-riddled voice.

" 'I shall become a lesser person, a diminished replica of my former self, a loveless candle that slowly consumes itself as it continues to give light until it is no more.'

" 'Is there anything I can do?' I ventured.

" 'You can mail this letter to her when you return to the US. My answer is in it. If you talk to her, tell her that I would gladly die for her, but I cannot live for her or with her anymore. I can only live with my solitude, alone, away from love's river, with memories as my only companions. It's all in the poem. You may read it if you wish. For some arcane reason, I have not dared to seal the envelope.' "

When Angela finished telling her story, she placed the letter on her chest and said, "My emptiness has been filled."

"What emptiness," retorted Kristin.

"The emptiness I felt inside of me when we couldn't visit the Cedar Forest. Remember when I said that for some reason, I have an emptiness inside of me and that I can't go back home feeling that way?"

"And what is it that filled your emptiness," I asked, intrigued.

"The poem," she replied. "When he read it to me, we both cried and I was filled with gratitude for having been allowed into this man's noble soul. That's when my emptiness was filled. It was filled with a unique sense of purpose, filled from love's river, the river that forward flows and never waits."

"Are you saying that lovers should never wait?" I quizzed.

"You and my mother faced a similar situation," she replied with a smug smile. "If you had procrastinated as they had, you would not have married, none of this would have transpired, and I would not have been baptized in love's river."

"Amen," I nodded. "Are you going to read us the poem?"

"I'll read it when we see my mother," she replied as she tucked the letter deep inside her purse.

At the rehab center, huddled in joy, Angela and Kristin spoke of their adventures and told their stories. Then, when all was told, Angela stood up, and with a moist, quivering whisper, announced that she was going to call Nancy and tell her to pack and travel to Mustafa's little log cabin. When we all protested saying that it was none of her business, she surprised us with, "I'll even go back with her, if I have to. I'm not leaving them alone until they're reunited. His poem has filled my emptiness with a sense of purpose and I, in return, shall fill his."

"If you go back with Nancy, I'll go back with you," cried Kristin, "so I can read to him what Gibran said about love." Then, with a joy-filled voice, she quoted:

"And think not you can direct the course of love, for love, if it finds you worthy, directs your course."

Hearing that, Angela gave Kristin an emotional hug, pulled out the envelope from her purse and, with a defiant smirk, read to us the hermit's letter:

*

My Dear Nancy, December 2010

There is no going back once we have exited the gates of love. Love's river forward flows, and even though we may travel upstream again, we will never find the same waters we had sailed from. From the Cedars of Lebanon, please accept this poem as my answer to your request.

<u>*Love's River*</u>

The snowflakes tremble in the dimming light
And it is cold, and sad, and very white
A melancholy stillness lulls the wind to sleep
And bids the setting sun goodnight.

With memories, a little wine, and fate
On winter nights like these I hibernate
Away from man, my loneliness and I
Where peace is vast like death and intimate.

I saved my sweetest dreams for you before
But since I left, somehow, I dream no more
Instead, I die each night then resurrect
And walk by day in order to forget.

I placed my life in savings at the bank
I spend it wisely and I always thank
My banker, though he gives no interest
Nor does he tell me how long I have left.

How much I hunger for your love and yearn
Ignite you in my bed and with you burn
But then I fear the shattering of dreams
Upon a fossil past that can't return.

So, stay away, I need my memories
Of all the lusty wine and dusty cheese
That still I taste upon your gasping lips
On cold and lonesome winter nights like these.

I love you,
Mustafa

The Holy Quakes Of Malula

When beliefs violate borders, lightning is forked. Most of us suspend our lives in worldviews we had absorbed during the impressionable stages of our childhoods. We remain, indeed, the copyrighted properties of our times and places unless we revolt against this ancestral, intellectual incarceration. Only then, after enduring the chastisements of severance, do we dare become emancipated thinkers. This is a tale for all of us who were inculcated with a certain worldview at a time when our mental defenses were weak and our ancestral loyalties were strong.

<u>Travel</u>

"Are you sure Lebanon is a safe country?" cried my wife. "I am an American blonde, who will stand out among your Arab throngs. They could kidnap me and deliver me to ISIS. I don't want to end up on the six o'clock news."

Warm, trembling tears tumbled down Cathy's cheeks. Her lips puckered and her chin quivered with the anguish of a frightened soul about to be delivered to the land of violent unknowns.

I paused until her sniffling ceased. Then, I held her hand to my lips and whispered into her pale palm, "Darling, you are my bride. You need to meet my family. They are expecting us. Do not let worry creep into your angelic soul. My potentate brother will ensure our safety."

"How do we escape if trouble erupts and they close the Beirut Airport? It has happened before, you know. I still don't understand why you didn't let me obtain Syrian visas?"

"Because we were pressed for time, Darling, and if you were to send our passports to the Syrian Embassy in Washington, we would run the risk that they may not be returned on time."

After a long silence, Cathy walked away and returned, dragging her empty suitcase behind her. I wanted to say that she was the only woman on earth, who packed just before it was time to leave, but I refrained from comment for fear that, in her apprehension, she might misconstrue my compliment as effrontery.

"What kind of weather should I expect?" she sighed with trepidation. "What clothes should I take? Is it safe to wear jewelry or short sleeves? Is the water safe? Is anything safe over there?"

The suitcase, unzipped and open-faced, endured a hundred put-ins and take-outs as I loaded mine and, like a patient packhorse, waited without uttering a word. *"Fear is not amenable to reason,"* I reminded myself as I avoided her crestfallen face while eyeing the clock that chewed the seconds with chilling speed. *"Perhaps I should just intimate that time was running out,"* I thought, but refrained from reiterating the obvious, lest it increase her perturbation and cause further delay. *"I'd better wait until the taxi driver rings the doorbell,"* I decided as I slipped out of the bedroom to open the garage door.

"Where are you going?" she pleaded. "I need you to stay with me?"

"I'm just going to open the garage door, darling. The taxi should be arriving any minute now."

"You're never going to leave me and wander away when we get there, are you? Remember, I don't speak the language."

"Of course not, my love. I shall always be by your side."

The doorbell rang. She zipped her suitcase. Then, leaving me behind with the two suitcases, she marched out, burst into tears, and shouted into the empty living room, "You've been in this country for forty years and I'm still not sure if you're an American or a Lebanese?"

Dragging the suitcases behind her, I whispered, "I am both, darling. I have the fortune and the misfortune of being a Lebanese American, whereas you are only American because your ancestors came to this land more than a hundred years ago."

"And none of them ever looked back or ever went back," she muttered, without turning her head.

On the way to the Will Rogers World Airport, the power lines were blackened with fluffy, feathered creatures, all beaks pointing in one direction. Cathy watched the spectacle with brimming eyes and sighed repeatedly, as though the season of black, migratory birds—wafting like swirling dervishes, peppering earth, dust-deviling the sky, and perching in haughty files along power lines—portended a *voyage noir*.

The variegated vistas of autumn leaves quivering in the scented air were passed, unnoticed, as Cathy's eyes hung on the black, orderly lines that marked the sky. Then, stunning the ominous silence, she heaved a Poe poem:

> *Open here I flung the shutter*
> *When, with many a flirt and flutter*
> *In there stepped a stately raven*
> *Of the saintly days of yore...*

"Darling," I reassured, clasping her moist, unresponsive hand. "You will have the time of your life."
Still gazing out the window in detached solitude, her fingers surprised my palm, and her resonant voice intoned:

> *And the raven, never flitting*
> *Still is sitting, still is sitting*
> *On the pallid bust of Pallas*
> *Just above my chamber door...*

"Don't be a raven dear," I whispered. "You are my white pigeon, remember?"
Cathy's gaze relinquished the black birds lining the power lines; her hand clutched mine with firm resolve; and she capitulated with a melancholy sigh. I said nothing more. From that point on, silence became our conversation.

Arrival

Twenty-six hours after we had left home, we touched down at the Beirut International Airport. Deep furrows, exhaustion, and worry frayed Cathy's face. Awakening to the reality that we had entered an eastern culture zone, she clung to my arm and whispered, "Why's everyone standing up when the seatbelt sign is still on?"

"Welcome to chaos, Sweetheart. You've just entered the Middle East."

"Oh, dear," she gasped. "The airplane is still taxiing and they're already pulling down their carry-on bags. What if…"

"Culture shock, Darling. In the US, orderly lines. In Lebanon, disorderly crowds. Better get used to it."

At customs, Cathy stood aghast, watching people squeeze and elbow into the fat, writhing lines.

"Good God," she murmured as she squeezed into me. "You could have at least warned me. You said Lebanon was a beautiful country."

"But, this is not Lebanon, darling."

"Oh? What is it then?"

"It's the airport."

At the baggage belt, a solid wall of passengers blocked our access and our view. Making use of that time, Cathy pulled a hand mirror out of her purse, took a look at her face, fluffed her hair, and as if talking to herself, uttered the famous, self-deprecating cliché, "I look awful. Your family's going to think that you've married an old woman."

When we walked out with our luggage into the arrival hall, anthills of *welcomers* with flailing arms and joyful screams charged, overwhelming their loved ones with triple kisses and tearful embraces. As Cathy's gaping eyes were absorbing the scene, I searched for my brother, who was supposed to meet us and whisk us out of Beirut up to our mountain town where the family was waiting. In spite of the many bobbing, intervening heads, I was able to spot him standing behind the throng, looking at us with calm, smiling eyes.

"This is Cathy, my bride," I introduced.

Without a word, Samir pulled Cathy into his arms, rocked her from side to side with dancing moves, and giggled like a tickled child. Ambushed, Cathy burst into strained laughter until her eyes fell on my brother's bodyguard, standing behind him with a handgun bulging from his waist.

"Welcome to Lebanon," chanted my brother, unaware of Cathy's abrupt pallor.

"Nice to finally meet you," she responded with a parched voice, her eyes still locked on the bodyguard's belt.

"This is Ali, my bodyguard and my driver. Let him take charge of your luggage," added Samir after he released Cathy from his gregarious arms.

When Ali approached, Cathy, with eyes still locked on his belt, dropped her luggage and took a step back. I held her hand and we followed my brother and his driver to the car.

"Why's she afraid?" asked my brother in Arabic, without turning back to look at us.

"Because she watches the news," I replied in Arabic, hoping to escape Cathy's scrutiny.

"What did you two just say?" whispered Cathy as she tightened her grip on my hand.

"He asked why are you afraid and I told him because you watch the news."

"How did he know that I was afraid?"

"Because he saw your gaping eyes lock onto his driver's belt."

"Oh. I had no idea I was that transparent."

"You'll get used to it."

"Get used to what?"

"Get used to Lebanon."

"You think?"

"Yes."

"Yes what?"
"Yes, I think."
"Yes you think what?"
"I think, in time, you'll get used to Lebanon."

The Road

Passing through Beirut's honking, concrete jungle with five-lane traffic in two-lane roads must have reminded Cathy of the fat, writhing lines at the airport. She broke the silence with, "How come they don't stay in their lanes?"

"The Lebanese may become individually civilized but, collectively, they are primitive and behave like domestic herds," smirked Samir.

"And why do they all honk?"

"Because they are frustrated by the congestion. It can take up to two hours just to get out of Beirut."

"Is that how long it's going to take us?"

"Perhaps. But, Ali knows some shortcuts."

We had been travelling for 26 hours and adding two more hours just to get out of Beirut rekindled existential dread in Cathy's heart. Nothing that Samir or I said succeeded in appeasing her. Perched on the brim of tears, she grew taciturn and the incessant honking added startle to her already alarmed state.

Samir, attempting to entertain her, discoursed on Lebanese politics. "Lebanon is now a stable country because the dominant factions are demographically equipotent. The Shi'ites, Sunnites, Druze, and Christians are governed by their warlords and coexist amicably. Two thirds of the population is now Muslim and one third is Christian. One hundred years ago, the Christians were two thirds and Lebanon, at that time, was regarded as the only Christian Arab country."

Growing more nervous as roads became more congested, Cathy coughed the exhaust fumes that had accumulated in her throat, and with a hoarse voice that betrayed her tension, asked, "What about the government?"

"What about it?"

"If each faction is ruled by its own warlord, what does the government do?"

"It merely oversees the institutions. We are a warlord democracy, which means that our elections are decided by our warlords and so are all government positions. Democracy, which means rule by the people, ignores the reality that most peoples are too primitive to rule."

After a period of silent hesitation, Cathy coughed again and blurted out the question, which must have been nagging at her mind:

"And what about ISIS?"

Samir did not act surprised nor did he trivialize the issue. In his calm, politically seasoned manner—for he had served as an elected member of the parliament twice—he reassured her with, "At present, there is a tacit détente between those who assist and those who resist ISIS. Both sides have agreed that Lebanon should be left alone because interference with its sovereignty would prove too costly for all sides involved, especially for ISIS."

"How come?" asked Cathy with a hesitant tone.

"Because of our civil war, all the Lebanese are armed to the teeth, have highly trained militias, and will unite in violent resistance against any ISIS incursion."

Cathy coughed again, but no further questions exited her exhaust-polluted throat.

Midway between Beirut and our mountain town, Amioun, the road began to clear, the blue sea shimmered on our left, and charming little towns rolled past our right side windows. I half glanced at Cathy and was pleased to see her face relax as she absorbed the scenery. On one side, the whispering waves of the mild-tempered Mediterranean Sea, and on the other side, the green-skirted, mighty mountains dancing in the distance. *"Natural beauty, like children, brings smiles to the faces,"* I thought as I savored the now clean air that was beginning to refresh our moods.

"Before long, we'll be home, darling," I chanted.
Cathy, for the first time, smiled.
"Oh, look. We're now passing through Biblos."
"Why's the name familiar?" she asked.
"Because it gave its name to the Bible. From this port, long before Christ, Phoenicians exported Egyptian papyrus to the Aegean from which the Greeks made *biblia*, books. The Greek word *biblion*, book, was later imported into English as Bible and the word papyrus, as paper."
"This is an ancient land, Cathy," added Samir, happy to see the faint glint that lit up Cathy's face. "Soon, we will be leaving the shore and taking the mountain road, which passes through Amioun on its way to the Cedars."
"Cedars? THE Cedars?"
"Indeed. The historic Cedars of Lebanon from which King Solomon built his temple."
Cathy gasped. There was so much for her eyes to absorb but so little time to do it, now that the car had picked up speed.
"What is that?" She said as she pointed.
"It's just another castle," teased Samir. "We have so many of them that we, as natives, no longer notice them."
"Steep cliffs surround this one from all sides," she exclaimed. "How do they get to it?"
"There's a tiny foot road carved into the rock that admits only one person at a time."

Soon after, the road bifurcated and we took the steep, mountain road. Cool air with the fresh scent of white-mountain herbs wafted through our open windows. Up and up we climbed in awe, along the hems of cliffs that grew steeper the higher we climbed. With her back turned to me and her eyes looking out the window, Cathy groped for my hand and clasped it without saying a word. Overtaken by the wild beauty of the white clay mountains, deep valleys, the sea behind, the snowcapped mountains ahead, replaced her existential dread with the awe of worship.

In response, I quoted from a poem I had penned upon visiting the Canadian Rocky Mountains:

> *I stood and stared, and stared, and gazed*
> *And gazed and could not stop*
> *Devouring each darting slant*
> *And every haughty top.*
>
> *These never-ending chains of crowns*
> *Lips and faces, smiles and frowns*
> *Engulfed me in their magic maze*
> *I could not help but gaze.*

The Reception

When we reached our Al-Kourah district, the high plain burst into full view like a green lake of olive trees, surrounded by hills. On top of the hills stood ancient hamlets with Syriac names, which derive from Aramaic, the native language of Jesus Christ. From Kfarhazeer we could see Amioun, basking atop a long, rocky ridge like a watchful mountain lion, its haughty beauty both charming and disarming.

"Here it is," I announced as I pointed.

Cathy's startled gaze roamed like a searchlight in the silent night. The car reached the base of the ridge and began the steep, winding climb. Again, she reached into her purse, pulled out her small mirror, and began touching up her face and tidying up her hair. Near the top, the car left the highway and took a steeper side road lined with thick cedar trees.

The engine groaned. We heard voices. Our house broke into view. A gratulant crowd rushed at us. The car stopped. The women exploded with ululations. I jumped out, ran around, opened Cathy's door, and gave her my hand. When she stepped out, arms went up into a clapping frenzy and ululations turned into welcoming chants. Cathy's face quivered, her eyes vacillated, her feet froze, and a cold smile seized her lips. That was when a deluge of merciless, triple kisses engulfed her and swept her away.

Inside the house, my mother conducted the show. "Please speak English," she admonished each time the conversation took an Arabic bend. "Our beautiful bride does not speak Arabic," she announced while holding Cathy's hand. The house buzzed like a beehive while hors d'oeuvres and wine circulated among the insatiable crowd, stretching the night into the late night. Then, as the darkness deepened, one by one, the guests *farewelled* us and left.

Huddled together in the quietude after the storm, my mother, brother, and sister, sat with us for our first family meal. Slowly, Cathy's features relaxed and, as she interacted with her new family, spontaneous smiles began to shimmer over her tired face. Love hovered like a halo around our first supper. At home and safe, the violent conflicts of the land seemed as distant as stars.

When we retired to our bedroom, Cathy took off her high heels and walked barefoot around our bridal bed, ornamented with two overlapping jasmine wreaths.

"I feel at home now," she announced as she flung herself onto the bed. The jasmine wreaths giggled as they wafted their sensual scent about her head. Then, as if the jasmine aroma reminded her of earth, she rose with a musical sigh and pleaded, "Take me out for a little walk."

"It's dark and cold, darling."

"Just a tiny, little walk," she beckoned.

"But, it's after midnight."

"Oh, well. That shouldn't matter, should it?" She giggled, as if tipsy.

"We've had such a long day, dear. Aren't you tired?"

"No. Let's go."

"Okay," I acquiesced, then looking at her bare feet added, "put on your shoes."

"No."
"You're not going out barefoot, are you?"
"Yes I am."

Hand in hand we stole out the front door. The moon smiled and the stars began to gossip when they saw us. Cathy walked to the ancient olive tree basking in the front lawn.

"You and I are one, now," she whispered.
"Indeed, we are, my love."
"I wasn't talking to you," she smirked.
"Whom were you talking to?"
"I was talking to the olive tree."
"What on earth do you mean?"
"On earth, that's what I mean."
"What earth?"
"Lebanon's earth. I have, with my bare feet, touched Lebanon's earth, just like this olive tree. Now, she and I have become one."
"And what about me?"
"Take off your shoes and join us."

I did. Holding hands under the olive tree, Cathy leaned her head onto my shoulder and cooed, "I've lost all my fears. I feel that I am one with the land. Have you any idea how emancipating that feeling is?"

The Consultation

The morning arrived at noon. We awakened to the sun, burning in the sky. The snow-mountains laughed in the east. The sea sang in the west. The green hills around Amioun stretched with feline satisfaction. Dogs barked, chickens chuckled, but the roosters held their silence for they had already delivered their early morning arias. In Amioun, roosters don't falsetto at noon.

Lunch awaited us with a table-full of family. For the first time, Cathy ate raw *kibbi*, the Lebanese version of steak tartar.

"No, no. Not with the fork," instructed my aunt. "We use the fork just to furrow the kibbi. We then fill the grooves with olive oil and use our pita bread to shape the bites. Wrap a bite of the kibbi with a piece of bread, like this," she demonstrated, "and then eat it with a green onion."

Cathy, at first, ate with caution. But, after a few bites, she lost all hesitation and ate with gusto.

Then, my mother put a pile of *hindbi* on her plate.

"I love greens, but what is it?" asked Cathy, gazing at the verdure before her.

"It's *hindbi*," replied my mom.

"So, what's *hindbi*?"

"In America you call it dandelion."

"You eat dandelion?"

"Try it just like you tried your *kibbi*. Wrap it with a piece of bread and eat it with a green onion."

"Really?"

"It's twice cooked; don't worry. First we boil it and then we fry it."

We all watched Cathy mouth the dandelion with calculating caution. An approving nod followed. Then, we heard a delectable hum as Cathy, again, cleaned her plate.

"She must be hungry," whispered my cousin in Arabic.

"She's happy," said my mother in English, "and happiness brings all kinds of appetites with it."

The afternoon was full of visitors. Arabic coffee came in cups on a tray each time a new group arrived. Some brought flowers, some chocolate, some fruits, some vegetables, and some, their children. We exercised by standing up, shaking hands, and sitting down, all the way into the evening. Cathy began to look fatigued, but never lost her smile. When the last group left, we sighed and huddled quietly around my mother.

"There's someone at the door," announced Beatrice, my mother's live-in helper.

"They've come all the way from Beirut," I noted, as soon as I saw the car.

"Who are they," asked Cathy, slipping on her high heels.

"Friends from my college days."

It soon became obvious from their faces that they had come on serious medical business. They and I moved to an adjoining room. Coffee was served. Then Mahmood's son, Hussein, said: "My father is scheduled to have cardiac surgery on Friday."

"What kind of cardiac surgery?" I asked with alarm because Mahmood and I were the same age."

"His arteries are blocked," replied Hussein.

"I'm going to have a quadruple bypass this coming Friday," announced Mahmood with a resigned voice.

"Do you have symptoms such as chest pain or shortness of breath?" I interrogated.

"No, I feel fine, but the heart catheterization showed blockage."

"Why did they do a heart catheterization if you had no symptoms?"

"Because my father died of a heart attack when he was my age, fifty-five. I was the one who asked for the cath."

"Did your father smoke? Was he overweight?"

"No, but he had diabetes, high cholesterol, and high blood pressure."

"Have you been checked for these things?"

"No, because I never saw a primary care physician. I merely asked a cardiologist friend of mine to do the heart cath. They did check my blood pressure before the procedure, though, and told me that it was normal."

Shocked at his negligence, I asked Mahmood to do the necessary blood tests, which he did the next morning and brought them to me in the afternoon. Based on the results, I started him on a daily aspirin, atorvastatin for his cholesterol, metformin for his diabetes, and asked him to walk one hour every day.

"Do I need to go ahead with the surgery or can I wait?" He asked with blinking eyes.

"Are you afraid of having the surgery?" I quizzed.

"I'm not just afraid," he confessed. "I'm petrified. I think that it will kill me."

"In that case, because you have no symptoms and because you have great fear, I think that the risks of going through with the surgery outweigh the risks of waiting. Fear is a major risk factor that should never be underestimated."

Fear left Mahmood's eyes as soon as I said that, and was replaced by resolve.

"When do you think I should repeat the heart catheterization then?"

"In one year, if you continue to have no symptoms."

Mahmood left a happy man and we agreed to revisit the problem when I returned next year. His goodbye was gleeful and he made a point of thanking Cathy for allowing me to spend the needed time with him.

"What did you do to your friend?" asked Cathy as we escorted their car with our tired eyes.

"What do you mean?"

"When he walked in, his eyes were gaping and his face was furrowed with concern. When he walked out, he was smiling."

"I took away his fear."

"And how on earth did you do that?"

"By putting his bare feet back on earth, darling."

The Escape

Friday, instead of bringing Mahmood to surgery, brought Mahmood back to Amioun.

"Are you all right?" I gasped when I opened the door.

"Yes, yes, I'm all right, but trouble is on its way."

As soon as she heard that, Cathy joined the conversation.

"What trouble?" she quizzed.

"At the mosque today, the sheikh informed us that violent riots are expected and that the Beirut airport has been closed."

"How do we escape if the airport is closed?" blurted out Cathy.

"We will go to Syria and you will fly out from the Damascus Airport."

"And how do we get into Syria without visas?" I asked, trying to seem calm so as not to further agitate Cathy.

"I know a general who can order the Syrian customs to give you visas."

"Mahmood is Syrian," I explained to Cathy, whose face by then had turned ashen green.

"So when do we leave?" she stuttered.

"Right now," pressed Mahmood, "before the rioters block the roads with burning tires."

In the bedroom, as we hurled our clothes into our suitcases, Cathy asked, "Can you trust a Syrian? What if he surrenders us to ISIS?"

"Syrians have been protecting Christians for centuries," I reassured, "and Mahmood has been my friend since high school. Besides, the riots are political, not religious."

"I hope you know what you're doing, darling," she retorted. "I have a very bad feeling about all this."

When we came downstairs with our suitcases, my mother was waiting at the door.

"It only takes four hours to get to Damascus. Would you please call me as soon as you can after you pass through Syrian customs," she pleaded after she kissed us goodbye.

We bid her a quick farewell, got into Mahmood's car, and took off. Only after we had been on the road a while did I notice that our driver was Ali, and that we were in my brother's SUV. I said nothing, hoping not to provoke further alarm. But then, Mahmood, who sat next to the driver, asked Cathy if she remembered Ali. His innocent question shocked Cathy out of her trance. She struggled for words, emitted an acknowledging hum, and then hid back behind her silence.

"Ali was with me when the Sheikh broke the news to us at the mosque," added Mahmood. "We hurried together to Samir who loaned us his car and insisted that Ali should be the one to drive us, being both armed and experienced."

"Armed and experienced?" muttered Cathy. "Are we about to pass through a war zone?"

"I doubt it, but it pays to be prepared."

"And why are you fleeing with us?" she asked.

"Because I know Syria well and I can make sure that you get back home safely."

Sitting in the back, Cathy and I held hands as the car drove on. There was hardly any traffic going toward Tripoli, but all the cars coming from the opposite direction flashed their lights at us to indicate that there was trouble ahead. The air grew denser when we began to see smoke rising from the roads ahead. Ali, who was from Tripoli, decided to take a peripheral road through the ghettos. We managed to get into the bowels of town without meeting with roadblocks, but getting out of the ghettos proved most difficult. Each time we tried to get out and onto the highway, we encountered angry, armed men blocking the road with burning tires. Utilizing their guns as if they were extensions of their arms, they would wave for us to turn back. But, when we tried to turn back, we were blocked by the line of cars behind us, which further entangled us into a seemingly inescapable traffic web. The entanglement repeated itself with each new road Ali tried. As time ran out and the situation deteriorated, we began to hear shots and explosions all around us. Ambulance sirens echoed and frightened screams choked on the smoky air. Holding hands, I could feel Cathy's heartbeats, pounding in my palm. *"Cathy's intuition was right,"* I surmised. *"Lebanon is not a country to which one honeymoons his bride,"* I admitted with profound regret.

Unable to exit shantytown, we stopped in front of a small house in a crowded street with a Vespa parked in its doorway. Ali knocked at the door and asked the man who opened for directions. The man, raisin-skinned, long-haired, white-bearded, and weather-worn, limped out to the car and greeted us with grandfatherly compassion. Then he explained that the rioters had blocked all roads to the highway because they wanted to trap as many hostages as they could.

"There is only one small dirt road behind the mosque, which I use to get to my orange grove after attending the Friday prayer," he whispered. "It's a rough tractor road, but I think it will let your car pass."

A sudden nearby explosion followed by a barrage of shots shattered our whispering conversation. The man ducked and shouted, "Put down your heads and follow me."

"Just give us directions," beckoned Mahmood, noting the man's frailty.

"You'd never find it," replied the man while his eyes roamed round and round like a seasoned spy. "Just follow me and I'll get you through."

The man—who did not know us, and whom we did not know, but to whom we felt tethered by a primal bond—started his Vespa and we followed him through the winding intestines of Tripoli from one narrow street to another and another until we reached the mosque. There, he waved for the crowd to let us through, calling *"Allahu Akbar"* at the top of his feeble voice. The crowd parted, chanting back *"Allahu Akbar"* with fists raised high above their heads.

The dirt road, which lay like a curved tail behind the mosque, meandered through the orange groves, grew narrower, but never too narrow for our vehicle to pass. At times our wheels ran tight along its steep edges because watering canals were along both sides. When the passing got difficult, the man slowed and when it got easier, he sped. Deep in the groves, we could barely see the sky. It felt like we were passing through a long, narrow, *arbored* tunnel, which had no end in sight.

After about an hour in this meandering maze, we began to hear road noises. Here, the man waved for us to stop while he went on and disappeared from view. We waited in abject silence, afraid to move, but kept the engine running. The buzz of the Vespa faded as the man drove away and, when we could no longer hear it, Mahmood ordered Ali to turn off the engine. With windows open, we harked for the return of the Vespa, without which we would not dare move.

Cathy was the first to whisper, "I think he's coming back."

We listened for the buzz. It seemed too distant at first, but became louder the closer it got. For a while, we could not be sure if there were another car behind it, and that ominous suspicion launched our worry into a higher orbit. But, when at last he burst into view, he drove straight to the driver's side and said, "The road is safe and the highway is near. Just drive slowly so you would not make much dust."

Then, at a cautious pace, he drove ahead of us until we saw the highway, speeding into the distance. Without stopping, he waved a goodbye, turned around, and disappeared into the orange grove.

Back on the paved road, Ali took off like a rocket, leaving a trail of smoke behind him. Mahmood tapped him on the shoulder and reiterated what Sir Winston Churchill had once said to his driver.

"Slow down, Ali. We're in a hurry."

The Pass

At Lebanese customs, Ali asked us to stay in the car while he took our passports and went in with Mahmood. One of Ali's cousins was employed there, and even though Lebanon allowed Americans to exit without visas, Ali wanted to expedite our crossing. While awaiting Ali and Mahmood's return, we saw a crowd of fleeing Syrian workers, detained behind an iron bar. Many of them made surprise charges, attempting to cross into Syria without passports, but they were all seized by the customs soldiers and dragged back, under arms, to where their comrades stood.

After several small groups had made failed attempts to escape into Syria, the entire group stampeded in, overwhelming the soldiers. Machine gun fire hailed over their heads, which caused the mob to duck and hit the ground. Regaining control of the situation, the customs soldiers led the humiliated workers back and ordered them to sit down on the dirt.

"If I see anyone stand up, I will shoot him," threatened the officer in charge. "You will be allowed to pass only after your passports have been stamped."

Later on, we learned that the workers, threatened by the breakout of violence in Lebanon, wanted to get back home before they were inadvertently trapped and killed in the fighting.

At the Syrian customs, Mahmood went in alone with our passports. The scene was crowded but orderly because there was a strong military presence. Hoping that he would succeed in getting us through by orders of his friend, the general, we waited in the car, still shaken by what we had witnessed on the Lebanese side.

"Nothing goes like it's supposed to," declared Cathy, interrupting the solemn silence. "What if the general forgot to call? They could send us back to Lebanon or else arrest us and throw us in jail. I have read about the brutality of Syrian prisons."

Nothing that I said succeeded in making Cathy feel any better. Rubbing her sweating palms against her jeans, she believed that the worst was yet to come, and her agonies increased by the minute as she sat frozen in her seat, staring at the customs entrance. But, to her happy surprise, Mahmood and Ali finally emerged with triumphant faces.

"The orders to let you pass were awaiting us when we checked in but, because of the crowd, it took a while to get to the window, " announced Mahmood with smug satisfaction.

We said very little after we crossed into Syria, remaining tense all the way to Damascus because we still could not believe that we were safe. But, when we arrived and checked into the hotel that Mahmood had reserved for us, our distress quickly dissipated and we all became suddenly hungry. The cool Damascene air was inviting, and ISIS was too far away to be of concern.

At dinner we planned the next day's activities. We would first go to a travel agent and book the earliest possible flight back to the US. Then, depending on how much time we had, we would visit certain important historical sites located within a reasonable radius.

Sleep was swift and sweet but, unlike Amioun, the morning was not ushered in by dogs barking and chicken chuckling. Instead, it was Mahmood who awakened us to say that it was time to visit the travel agent, who was located in the hotel's lobby. We hurried down and in one hour we had our tickets. We were to leave the next day at noon, which meant that we had a full Saturday to explore the sites.

"Drive us to Malula," said Mahmood to Ali.
"What's in Malula?" asked Cathy.
"An ancient shrine carved into a giant rock."
"Is it safe?"
"Yes. It's under Syrian Army control."

We drove for two hours and were pleased to see orchards and groves instead of burning tires and armed men. When we arrived, the only edifice was a massive rocky cliff with nothing visible on top. Led by Mahmood, we walked along the base until we reached the pass.

"Here," Mahmood said, pointing to the pass, "began the legend of the king's daughter who converted to Christianity against her father's wishes. The father became doubly enraged when she would not recant and decreed that she be thrown to the lions. The lions were starved for a week before her execution day, but when she was thrown into their den, they curled around her feet like loving dogs. Then the angry father ordered her burned at the stake, but, as soon as the fire was lit, a rain cloud put it out. Frightened by her powers, the guards in charge arranged her escape.

"When the king found out that she had absconded, he ordered a cavalry regiment to chase her and bring her back. With the army behind her and this rock before her, she realized that her end was nigh. Awaiting the cavalry's imminent arrival, she closed her eyes and prayed for Jesus to have mercy on her soul. When she opened her eyes, the earth quaked, the rock split, and she was able to escape through the pass. When the regiment arrived, however, the rock had become a solid wall again and it remained so until the king died. At his death, another earthquake reopened the pass and it has remained open ever since.

"The king's daughter spent the rest of her life on top of the rock where she founded a church and preached the word of God to all who came. When she died, she was buried underneath the church. After death, her fame spread and the church became a holy shrine, visited by pilgrims from all over the region."

With brimming eyes and shivering voice, Cathy asked, "Can we visit the church?"

"Yes, of course, my dear. That's why I brought you here," replied Mahmood with a broad smile. "We're going to walk through the sandy pass, which will take us to the other side of the rock. Then we're going to climb up to the top, where the church sits. How are your knees?"

"My knees are fine," affirmed Cathy with her eyes gazing at the precipitous cliff, "and I can climb like a goat."

The Cave

The four of us, Mahmood at the helm and Ali at the rear, trod the narrow, sandy pass. The high rock walls on each side provoked a weird sense of awe, causing us to whisper instead of talk. Cathy began to look transformed, her face shone with a numinous light, and she crossed herself as she hesitated before every turn, for the pass was silent, winding, and dark.

At one jagged, narrow turn, Cathy stopped.
"What is it, darling?" I asked with a hushed voice.
"I don't know, but all of a sudden I feel afraid."
"Have you had a change of heart?"
"Oh, no. I want to visit the church, but my feet seem to be refusing to move."
"Would you like me to take you back?"
"No. I don't want to turn back. I just feel mired."
"Why don't you take off your shoes like pilgrims do and walk barefoot on the cool sandy ground. Become one with earth, as you did in Amioun."
"Of course, my shoes," cried Cathy as she took them off.

With one hand holding her shoes and the other holding my hand, Cathy and I tiptoed silently as if we were the only creatures around. Out of respect, Ali kept his distance behind while Mahmood walked ahead without glancing back. When we arrived at the clearing, Cathy sighed with relief, put her shoes on, and, without a hint of hesitation, led us up the rock.

"She is a goat," declared Mahmood as we followed Cathy's long, confident, strides.

At the top, like a sleepwalker, Cathy wandered around in a daze. She visited the little church, dipped her fingers in the courtyard fountain and smeared a cross on her forehead, broke holy bread with the nuns at the convent, and then, by happenstance, wandered into a cave where a thousand candles burned. There, she stood like a statue while the rest of us sat around the fountain in the courtyard.

"Did you feel it?" asked Mahmood with alarm.
"Feel what?" I replied.
"The earthquake."
"What earthquake?"

"Just now. The whole rock shook."

"I felt nothing," I asserted. "Are you sure you felt an earthquake or did you, perhaps, have a vertigo attack?"

Mahmood looked around at all the meandering pilgrims who, like me, did not seem alarmed. Then, turning to the driver, asked, "Ali. Did you feel an earthquake?"

"Earthquake?" repeated Ali with raised eyebrows. "What earthquake?"

Turning pale, Mahmood walked away from us, sat on a stone, and held his head between his hands. At that very same moment, breathless and equally pale, Cathy emerged out of the cave, and without acknowledging Ali or me, went straight to Mahmood.

"Are you all right?" she asked.

"I don't know? I felt an earthquake that nobody else felt. Did you feel anything when you were inside the holy cave."

"Holy cave?"

"The cave you were in is a holy cave."

"Oh. I mean yes. I mean I did feel a shudder. It felt like the walls trembled. Then the candle flames flickered. Then I heard a pounding in my chest, like distant drums, which startled me. I looked at the pilgrims standing beside me, but none of them appeared aware of what was happening.

"At that point, I realized that I was having a religious experience, that I was being blessed, that every worry was being lifted, and that the Holy Spirit was entering into me. Then, filled with the Holy Spirit and at peace with the world, I gave thanks, crossed myself, and walked out, feeling buoyant and uplifted."

"So I've not gone mad, then," declared Mahmood, looking at Ali and me with relief. Then, turning to Cathy, he murmured, "I'm going in."

We watched him take off his shoes, step into the cave, and stare at the candles for the longest time, as if he were hypnotized.

When he walked out, he also seemed transformed and his visage glowed with meek, affable warmth.

"Did you feel anything?" asked Cathy.
"Yes," he gleamed.
"What did you feel? Tell me, please."
"I felt a warm swelling in my chest. But it was a good swelling, like a morning sun, like a full moon, like a newborn life."

On the way back to Damascus, we exchanged little conversation. Somehow, silence seemed the better language, melancholy, the better mood, and the holy earthquake of Malula, the ineffable thought.

Sunday morning broke with Mahmood's call.
"It's airport day for you, and Beirut day for us," he chimed. "The riots have quieted down and it is safe to return."

At the Damascus airport, we thanked Ali, who had to stay with the car. Mahmood, on the other hand, remained by our side until we were ticketed. After hugs and held-back tears, as we started to walk away, he said, "See you next year, Cathy."

To my utter befuddlement, Cathy looked back and said, "See you next year, Mahmood."

The Return

When we flew back the year after, Cathy seemed fearless and asked my brother, who picked us up at the airport, "Where's Mahmood?"

"He's having his heart catheterization today, otherwise he would have come with me. But, he plans to visit you in Amioun this coming Sunday."

Cathy did not seem to notice Ali's firearm, bulging from his waist. When he took charge of our luggage, she did not step back, nor did she cough when we passed through the smoggy Beirut streets. On the way to Amioun, her eyes were busy observing the many sites and scenes that she had not noticed the year before.

"I don't remember seeing this," she exclaimed, "nor that, nor all these other things. Oh, my. How blind I was, and how much beauty I've missed."

In Amioun, she embraced and triple-kissed all her *welcomers*, and spent a loving time with my mother. When we retired to our room, she took off her high heels, unpacked, and said, "Let's go."

"Go where, honey? It's midnight and we haven't slept for 28 hours."

"Come on, Darling. Don't be a wuss. Don't you want to be with me when I stand barefoot under the olive tree?"

"Oh, yes, of course," I replied with sleepy eyes. "We must never forget Lebanon's good earth."

The Epiphany

Sunday lunch was a grand family affair but Mahmood did not come. After lunch, Cathy asked Samir, "Where's Mahmood? I thought you had invited him."

"I did and he promised to come. Something must have delayed him. I've called him twice and he didn't answer."

"That worries me," squirmed Cathy. "Can't you send Ali after him? Maybe he had an accident."

"He's so punctual and always calls if he's going to be late," reflected Samir, "but if he doesn't show up in another thirty minutes, I will send Ali after him."

"Did his heart catheterization go well?" I asked.

"I don't know. We haven't talked since."

As we sat with coffee and conversation, Cathy paced and eyed the window with restless gaze. My mother and several family members asked me what was wrong to which I replied, "She's worried about Mahmood."

Waiting and pacing, Cathy's worry grew until it became intolerable. She walked up to Samir and announced, "I fear something has happened to Mahmood."

    With shaky hands, Samir laid his coffee down, got up, called Ali, and said, "Let's go find him."

    "Cathy and I will go with you," I volunteered.

    "No, brother. You and Cathy need to stay with your guests. Besides, we have no idea how long we will be gone."

    We escorted Samir to his car, stood out in the cool afternoon, and watched him disappear down the winding, cedar-lined road. Then, Cathy walked to the olive tree, took off her high heels, and stood there, with feet bare, praying. I refrained from joining her because, seeing her closed eyes and *vespering* lips, I surmised that she wanted to be alone.

    All of a sudden, a car honked from the steep, *cedared* road beneath the house. Cathy stopped praying and opened wide her eyes. Then, Samir's car returned and parked, but Samir and Ali, who seemed to be involved in conversation, did not acknowledge Cathy or me. Cathy's eyes filled up with questions. As I gazed at her quivering face, Mahmood's car, like a sudden gush of wind, burst into view. Cathy let out a cry, threw her shoes into the air, and rushed to Mahmood.

    "What took you so long," she screamed. "You had us all worried."

    After a long, tearful embrace, Mahmood explained:

    "I went to the Malula holy cave to give thanks. Being Sunday, it was crowded, with hardly room to stand. I sat on the edge of the fountain and waited for the crowd to dissipate. I did not realize that my cellphone had slipped out of my back pocket, into the water, until I reached for it after I had given thanks."

    "Why on earth did you go alone to Malula?" blurted out Cathy with perturbed eyes.

    "Muslims don't usually pilgrim to Christian shrines," answered Mahmood with a wry smile. "But, I returned to give thanks because my heart catheterization revealed that my arteries had become totally clean."

"What?" I gasped with disbelief.

"The cardiologist could not believe it either. He kept comparing last year's catheterization to the present one, shaking his head, and saying, *'That's just not possible.'*

"Then, with consternation, he asked me if, during the past year, I had done anything differently. I told him that I had been taking my metformin, my atorvastatin, my aspirin, and walking one hour a day.

" *'That can't do it,'* he disagreed. *'We never see such rapid resolution, regardless of treatment. No, you must have done something else. Think hard because what ever you did could help others. What else did you do?'*

"I told him about Malula, but he brushed it off as a silly superstition. *'Science does not believe in miracles,'* he smirked, *'nor in the holy quakes of Malula. No, perhaps unwittingly, you've done something different, something, which if you could remember, could be used to help so many others.'* "

Leaving the rest of us spellbound, Cathy, with a calm, compelling voice, reached for Mahmood's hand and said, "Take off your shoes and follow me."

We left them under the olive tree and went into the house. As I watched them through the window talking, laughing, fidgeting, and dancing with bare, buoyant feet, my soul was filled with ineffable joy.

A transmutation had taken place before my incredulous eyes, an exorcism of fear, a graft of faith, a descent of hope, a grant of courage, and a flood of love, which overflowed the winding banks of humanity.

Crisis

And feel, who have laid our groping hands away;
And see, no longer blinded by our eyes.
Rupert Brooke (1887-1915)

It happened so fast it took me by surprise. Later on, however, I did ask myself pressing existential questions and managed to conjure suffocating answers. One solemn incident, which endured for only a few minutes, occupied my thoughts for days. How blind is the *Homo sapiens*' perception of reality, and how microscopic, I mused.

Standing in the checkout line at Walmart, I said nothing to my wife as she glared at me, wondering what should she do. I just nodded twice, dropped my eyes that I may no longer see what was happening, and directed my gaze instead at the boy's boots, banging against the rotisserie chicken in our cart. After a shard of embarrassing silence, I heard my wife furtively ask the disgruntled checker, "How much more does she owe?"

"Six dollars and thirty-three cents," grumbled the checker.

Trembling, my wife's hands reached into her purse, pulled out a ten-dollar bill, handed it to the checker, and—trying to avoid the woman's eyes—looked at the boy instead and playfully inquired, "Do you like chicken?"

"I only like nuggets," he flirted.

The checker handed my wife the three dollars and sixty-seven cents, which she promptly handed to the mother of the boy, saying, "This is for his piggybank."

The mother took the money, smiled a thank you, pulled the cart with groceries and son in it, and, as she turned around to leave, screamed at the top of her voice, "Stop kicking before I kick your ass."

Everyone in line froze as they watched the woman take off in a huff and head toward the door.

We walked back to our car, carrying our groceries, holding hands, yet somehow avoiding each other. Neither of us was able to break away from that silence that held us behind its barbed wires. We drove into the evening as if distance were time, night were space, and the way home was the road to peaceful oblivion. It was at the first stoplight, in the dead wait of urban order, when my wife spoke.

"She only had a few items in her cart—just food, no beer, no cigarettes."

"Her boy seemed happy," was the only response I could muster before the light turned green and we drove into the barbed silence again. Something about red lights makes us talk, I thought. It must be easier to drive in silence than to wait in silence. As car lights flashed into my eyes the words of George Eliot flashed into my mind:

If we had a keen vision and feeling of all ordinary human life, it would be like hearing the grass grow and the squirrel's heart beat, and we should die of that roar which lies on the other side of silence.

At the next red light my wife reflected, "The two checks she endorsed must have been very small."

"She seemed surprised when they weren't enough," I added.

"Oh, she wasn't just surprised; she was also embarrassed."

"You were quick, darling, handing the money to the checker just before she began returning some of her items."

The green light suddenly intruded on our sour conversation and we again drove into the silence. Why didn't we give her more? I thought. Ten dollars are hardly enough. What if she needed gas money? What if she couldn't pay her rent? What if her son needed medicines? Another red light stopped us, but this time neither of us spoke. It took two more lights before my wife mumbled, "Did you hear her scream at her little son?"

"She didn't scream at her son."

"Oh, yes she did. Everyone heard it."

"No dear, she screamed at poverty."

"Poverty?" She exclaimed with eyes wide with surprise.

"Poverty was what she screamed at, darling. Her dry tears just came out as screams at her little son."

My wife must have had an epiphany because she sighed and closed her eyes. Her chin twitched and officious tears came to her cheeks as the light turned green. She sniffled and busied herself with looking inside her purse for a handkerchief, which she never found. Her repudiated tears, un-wiped, fell onto her chest. Time groaned, the road dimmed as we neared home, but neither of us felt the hoped-for relief, even after we had arrived and carried our groceries in.

"You know she was pregnant," murmured my wife, still sniffling.

"I thought she was just fat."

"That too," she snapped. "You men don't notice things."

"What would you like for dinner, dear?" I distracted.

"I'm not hungry. I'm going to bed."

"It's only eight," I protested.

"It's already midnight for me."

I watched her drop the groceries on the counter, turn around, and gallop upstairs without a goodnight. I calmly stowed the purchased items, went into my study, picked up my bible, flipped to Matthew 25:29 and read:

For everyone who has will be given more, and he will have an abundance. Whoever does not have, even what he has will be taken from him.

Was that divine justice that punished the poor with more poverty or was that an observation upon humanity? I wondered. We are given our brains, bodies, families, times, places, experiences, and coincidences—and none of these givens ever come under our control. Yet, it is these seven pillars of fate that hold up our temples and destine our lives. As I laid my bible down, a stanza from a poem I had penned in youth re-visited me:

> *Coincidence*
> *She wears green shadows intertwined with dreams*
> *Lurks unforeseen, in silence plots and schemes*
> *At times she hurries matters to profound extremes*
> *Delights in rolling fortunes in reverse*
> *Coincidence*
> *She sways the universe.*

I picked up my bible again, flipped to Luke 12:48 and read: *"From everyone who has been given much, much will be demanded; and from the one who has been entrusted with much, much more will be asked."*

Reading that, I felt ashamed because I realized that my wife and I do not give enough of what we have been given. Lucius Annaeus Seneca's (4 B.C – 65 A.D) aphorism cried loud between my ears:

> *What is your greatest failing, you ask? False accounting. You put too high a value on what you have given, too low a value on what you have received.*

She was not the first poor, pregnant woman I had ever seen, I thought, so why am I in crisis? Perhaps it was because I had to look her in the eyes and experience her as a fellow human being with deeply hurt feelings. Or perhaps because I have never had to look poverty that close in the face before. Or perhaps it was the contrast between my fully paid credit cards and her empty purse. Or because I did not reach into my wallet to give her the two one-hundred-dollar bills I always carry on me for emergencies. Or could it be because I had failed to discern that both her poverty and her shame were, indeed, my very own emergencies? I had not only failed a less fortunate human being, I admitted; but I had also been doing it all of my life, without notice. That, indeed, was why I was in crisis, I surmised.

Where do I go from here? I pondered. It is too late to find her, but never too late to find others. The world is full of what Epictetus called: *"Poor souls burdened with corpses."* And we, who have roofs and toilets, don't ever look them in the eyes. They are out somewhere, on the margins of life, like picture frames that nobody notices because we only look at the featured themes.

To escape my burdensome thoughts I plowed into the *Meditations* of Marcus Aurelius (121-180), the first self-help book ever written on how to attain inner peace. I read through the parts I had underlined from previous crises until I found the quote I was looking for:

Observe how man's disquiet is all of his own making, and how troubles come never from another's hand, but like all else, are creatures of our own opinion.

I acknowledged that I was, indeed, the sole source of my own, miserable guilt, but I also understood that I could not help it.

I next went to Meister Eckhart (1260-1328) and read: *"I further maintain that sorrow comes of loving what I cannot have."* Indeed, my sorrow did come of loving my inner peace, which I was unable to attain at that moment. Then I read:

I much prefer a person who can love God enough to take a handout of bread, to a person who can give a hundred dollars for God's sake.

Was I the one trying to give a hundred dollars for God's sake? I asked. And was she the one who loved God enough to take a handout of bread? It must be far more painful to take than to give, but if that were so, why then am I still in pain? I wondered.

It was getting late but my eyes were dry with turmoil. I turned to *The Prophet* by Gibran Khalil Gibran (1883-1931) and went straight to his chapter on giving:

You give but little when you give of your possessions. It is when you give of yourself that you truly give.

Perhaps I am in crisis because I had not given enough of myself, I thought. I felt compelled to read on as if I knew that down the lines some epiphany awaited me:

There are those who give with joy, and that joy is their reward. And there are those who give with pain and that pain is their baptism. And there are those who give and know not pain in giving, nor do they seek joy, nor give with mindfulness of virtue; they give as in yonder valley the myrtle breathes its fragrance into space. Through the hands of such as these God speaks, and from behind their eyes He smiles upon earth.

This is it, I sighed. The pain of not giving enough is the same as the pain of giving with mindfulness and both are baptisms in suffering. I need to become a myrtle instead and give of myself unaware, I surmised, and as I did, a white veil of peace dropped down on me. I closed my books, turned off the lights in my study, and ran up to my wife, who lay awake, reading.

"What were you doing, all this time?" she asked, closing her book.
"I was thinking."
"Thinking about what?"
"About, about, '*How ludicrous and outlandish is astonishment at anything that happens in life.*' "
"I recognize the quote. You've been reading Aurelius again."
"He wasn't enough this time. I had to go to Eckhart and then Gibran before I found my peace."
"Gibran, your countryman?"
"Yes. I thought you liked him."
"You read his piece *On Giving*, didn't you?"
"I did. You're very perceptive."
"You know, he plagiarized it from Aurelius." She smiled.
"Gibran Plagiarized? No way." I protested.

"You were the one who pointed it out to me on our first date, remember?"

I stood stunned, trying to remember the conversation of our first date. "It happened so long ago; how could you remember it so clearly? Are you in crisis too?" I quizzed.

"You've conveniently forgotten, didn't you? Why don't you go get me the *Meditations* and I'll show you where you had marked the page."

I ambled down to my study, pulled the Meditations out of the shelf, crept back upstairs, and defiantly handed her the book. She flipped through it until she found the marked page and, without acknowledging me, read the quote I had underlined thirty years earlier:

There is a type of person who, if he renders you a service, has no hesitation in claiming the credit for it. Another, though not prepared to go so far as that, will nevertheless secretly regard you as in his debt and be fully conscious of what he has done. But there is also the man who... has no consciousness at all of what he has done, like the vine, which produces a cluster of grapes and then, having yielded its rightful fruit, looks for no more thanks than... a bee that has hived her honey.

I lowered my head as I raised her hand to my lips and whispered between her clenched fingers, "Gibran plagiarized Aurelius as Aurelius plagiarized Christ."

"No he didn't," she protested. "You're making that up."

I ran downstairs, brought back my bible, opened it to Matthew 6:3 and read:

So when you give to the needy, do not announce it with trumpets, as the hypocrites do...to be honored by others. Truly I tell you, they have received their reward in full. But when you give to the needy, do not let your left hand know what your right hand is doing, so that your giving may be in secret...

"Don't read anymore, please," she interrupted. "I get the point. There are no new ideas under the sun."

"And poverty has been with us since eternity." I added.

"And since eternity, humanity has never given enough?" She affirmed.

"Giving does not erase poverty." I patronized. "It often makes it worse."

"Worse? Now why's that?"

"Because it teaches complacency."

"So, what's the solution, then?"

"Teach the poor new skills, give them security and opportunity, and improve whatever you can of their seven pillars of fate."

"Oh, stop philosophizing, please."

"What would you rather I do, darling?"

"Turn off the lights and just hold me."

There are times when a simple incident forever changes our lives. That woman was unaware of her giving—like the myrtle, which breathes its fragrance into space or the vine, which produces a cluster of grapes. Yet that poor, pregnant woman gave us a seminal lesson in humility and charity, which we should hope to emulate. It finally came to me that Meister Eckhart, indeed, was talking about the likes of her when he proclaimed, *"I much prefer a person who can love God enough to take a handout of bread, to a person who can give a hundred dollars for God's sake."*

To give unaware is not to know that one is giving, so that the receiver may not receive with gratitude but rather with reverence to life's bounty. I learned all that from a poor, pregnant woman who took a handout of bread for the love of God. As it turned out, she was the unaware, true giver, and we, the ever-grateful receivers.

Crisis, First Edition, The Journal of the Oklahoma State Medical Association, Volume 107, February 2014, Pages 61-63. Revised Edition completed in October of 2016.

Odysseus

"I have your ticket."
"I'm not going."
"It's my aunt's funeral. She was last of my father's sisters."
"I'm sorry, Dad."
"But why?"
"Have you forgotten?"
"But, that was twenty years ago. Things are different now. We do not have to land in Damascus, the Beirut Airport has been operational for years, the twenty-year Civil War is over, and Lebanon is safe and at peace."
"I'm sorry, Dad. Lebanon is your country, not mine."

"Children grow away from their parents just like parents grow away from their children," I thought, as I slid my cell phone back into my pocket. *"Growing away might be nature's way. But, how about dying away? If growth scatters us, shouldn't death gather us? Isn't that why funerals are reunions?"*

Basking alone above the transatlantic clouds, my mind resounded with childhood memories of my aunt, but then they turned into worrisome thoughts when darkness shrouded my view.

Two hours at the Oklahoma City Airport, two hours to Chicago, three hours of layover, ten hours to London, four hours of layover, five hours to Beirut, and a two-hour drive before I arrive at our family home in our mountain town, Amioun, where everyone will be waiting for me except my aunt. A twenty-eight-hour journey and when I arrive, everyone will ask: *"But, where is your son?"* And I will confabulate: *"He couldn't come because his wife just had back surgery. He wanted to come, of course, but it was not possible because he had to take care of their three children. His heart is with us, though, and he sends his love to everyone."*

To explain my son's fear, after twenty years, would have been culturally embarrassing.

My aunt, like the rest of us, has been dying for years. But, unlike the rest of us, her memories have also been dying alongside his fading form. Her mental attrition, which began at eighty-five, escalated like a river's rapids before the waterfall. And when she reached the precipice, she dove unaware and was gulped by the infinite intestines of munificent death.

As soon as they called me, I purchased two tickets, and then called my son. We are the only two fruits that have fallen far from the family tree. The rest of the family huddles within our mountain town's corral, and they were all waiting when I walked in.

After hugs, triple kisses, utterings, and sniffles, we all sat in solemn silence, gazing at the carpet, which framed our human rectangle. No one spoke because there was little to say. We were all relieved at her well-deserved rest, yet none of us was willing to verbalize it because it would have been disrespectful. But, when the prolonged silence started to suffocate the group, some began to fidget. Mercifully, at that most hypoxic of moments, Arabic coffee was served, someone coughed, another sighed, and a third one lit a cigarette and suffused the room with second-hand smoke. Then, a hoarse voice cracked the silence with, "Where's your son?"

"He couldn't come because his wife had just had back surgery," I said with automatic words.

"*Salamitha,*" (safe recovery,) many muttered, stripping their rosary beads with restless fingers.

"He wanted to come, of course, but it was not possible because he has three children to take care of."

"Your aunt, may God rest her soul, would have understood," croaked the one who had popped the question.

"He sends his love to everyone," I added, putting an end to that intrusive interlocution.

"What would we do without clichés?" I thought, as I stood in line, after the services, accepting condolences in the *stoa* of our

prehistoric church. All that day's utterings, including mine, were comforting, cultural clichés. *"Traditions recapitulate a people's history, alongside language codes and inherited beliefs,"* I surmised.

Being bicultural, living in the US while still tethered by family and friendship ties to Lebanon, gave me unique, atavistic insights. I understood that one can not grow deep cultural roots on demand, that whatever roots one already has partly define one's identity, and that one's emotional bonds are far more formidable than one's biological codes. My son, born and raised in the US, did not share my ethnic sentiments, and that proved painful to explain to my Lebanese family.

The night before I returned to my US home, sipping Arabic coffee among my childhood friends, the name Shamdas came up. I had heard that he had been detained in Syria some thirty years ago and so I asked, "How long was he in confinement before he was released?"

"He was never in confinement," asserted George.

"I must have heard wrong, then," I sighed with relief.

"We still have no idea what happened," chimed in Waleed.

"You mean..."

"After he drove you and your son to the Damascus Airport, he disappeared for a few weeks and then returned to Amioun with a new Mercedes Benz. When we inquired about what had happened, he simply said that he had a mission to accomplish before he could return."

"When was the last time you saw him?" I inquired, attempting to sound neutral.

"He relocated to Beirut a few years ago and none of us has seen him since. I'm surprised, however, that he did not show up for your mother's funeral, given his strong, historic ties to your family."

For some arcane reason, when I heard the phrase, *his strong, historic ties to your family,* dark memories from our trip to Damascus welled up in my mind and I was seized with visceral dread. My heart almost leapt out of my chest, sweat beaded my forehead, my mouth went dry, and I was gripped by nausea. My friends noticed my pale, clammy aspect and one of them rushed me a glass of water. Then, during the ensuing, inscrutable silence, they understood that I knew things, which they did not know, and that they knew things, which I did not know. It was at that memory-laden watershed, vivid with frightful transference, that George told me their part of the story:

"For several weeks, after he drove you and your son to Damascus, we tried to find out what had happened to him, using all the political connections at hand, but no facts were uncovered. We became so worried, especially because the roads between here and Syria were sputtered with dangerous checkpoints manned by vicious militias. Indeed, that was the real reason why Shamdas had insisted on driving you and your son to the Damascus Airport in his personal car. Even more worrisome, the Syrian government denied that he was ever detained and had no record of him entering or leaving the country. We worried, given his dark political colors, that he might have been liquidated, or as Nizom had metaphorically put it, 'interred at the bottom of the Bosporus, Ottoman style.' "

"Ottoman style?" I gasped, half afraid to find out what was meant by that.

"That's what the Ottomans used to do to freedom fighters. They would blindfold them, bind them with heavy iron shackles, take them for a boat ride, and drop them into the middle of the Bosporus, rendering them untraceable."

Here, Nizom blurted out a famous poem penned by that era's freedom writer, W. D. Yakan:

> *In one night's shrouded firmament*
> *As if its sun was forced to set*
> *A free man who was one of us*
> *Was dropped into the Bosporus*
> *When next day's sun redeemed the skies*
> *His widowed home was wet with cries.*

I hesitated awhile, but words scratched at my throat like a dog wanting to get out. My friends noticed my conflicted expression and glanced at each other with roaming eyes. It was Nazeeh, the lawyer, who finally began my interrogation with, "So, Salem, how did that drive to Damascus go?"

"It went well," I sheepishly replied.

"Well?" mimed Nazeeh with raised eyebrows.

"Shamdas got us safely to the airport and we flew out on time."

"Was it a smooth ride?" He crosschecked.

At that turn in the conversation, I realized that the time had come to tell them my side of that thirty-year-old story, which I had refrained from telling during my subsequent trips to Lebanon for fear of endangering Shamdas. In spite of multiple visits to Amioun, Shamdas and I never crossed paths again, perhaps because he was intentionally avoiding me, thinking that if I did not run into him, I would be less inclined to recall and relate the events of our Damascene experience. With that mental strain gnawing at me, I surveyed my friends' expectant faces and, after a reflective pause, began my story:

Had the Beirut Airport not been closed due to the Civil War, my son and I could have entered Lebanon with our American passports. But, to be permitted to land in the Damascus Airport, we had to obtain visas from the Syrian Embassy in Washington D.C. When the embassy's application questioned if we wanted single or multiple-entry visas, unwittingly, I chose single, and that proved to be a deadly error.

On our way back to the Damascus Airport, we passed through the Lebanese customs without incident. Upon arriving at the Syrian border at 3 a.m., we presented our passports to the officer in charge. After flipping though our documents, he nonchalantly informed us that we did not have re-entry visas into Syria. We had unknowingly used our single entry visa to enter Syria at the Damascus airport when we first arrived. Now that we needed to fly out of Damascus, we needed another visa to re-enter Syria, which we did not have. I tried to explain to the officer that it was an honest mistake, that I had patients waiting, that my son had to be in college, and that we were transit passengers with Syrian Airlines tickets. The officer was firm. He wanted us to return to Lebanon and obtain new visas from the Syrian Embassy in Beirut. That meant that we would miss our flight and be delayed for several days.

All that time, Shamdas stood at a distance, merely observing. My son turned pale at the realization that his college debut was going to be postponed. I looked to Shamdas for help, but he cautiously pointed his eyes toward the exit and walked out. We followed him to the car, a large Mercedes-Benz that roared like a bulldozer. He asked us to get in, sit in the back seat, and slide down so that our heads would not be visible through the rear window. Without asking why, we obsequiously obeyed. Dread hovered as my son and I looked at each other with awe, for we knew that Shamdas was a military man of fearsome repute, that he had led our hometown's defense against invasion by the upper-mountaineers, and that he was revered as Amioun's saving hero.

Shamdas drove slowly until we reached the armed sentry standing by the barrier gate.

'Raise the bar and let us through,' he commanded with a calm, confident voice. 'Here are my papers. I am an officer in the Syrian Secret Service and I command you to let us through.'

When the sentry asked to see our papers, Shamdas retorted, 'They're my responsibility, not yours.'

When the sentry refused to raise the bar, Shamdas rolled back the car about thirty feet, turned off all lights, revved the engine and, taking off like a missile, shattered the barrier bar and sped into the tenebrous night.

Bullets crashed into the trunk, right behind the back seat, and into the rear window, right above our heads, but none of them went through.

'It's bullet proof,' muttered Shamdas, driving as if nothing significant had happened.

My son and I, our heads below our knees, were afraid to sit up until Shamdas, half sneering, whispered, 'You may sit up now. He didn't see your faces nor did he see my license plate.'

We dared not look at each other, and silence hissed until we reached downtown Damascus. There, Shamdas hailed a taxi and told us that it would be safer for the taxi to take us to the airport. Before he retrieved our luggage, we stood in awe, glaring at the bullet imprints on the car's trunk and rear window. There were several of them and each formed a burst of rays, like a splash of paint onto a canvas.

'He was a good marksman,' I quipped.

'He was doing his job and I'm glad he did,' said Shamdas with somber sincerity.

'What do you mean by that?' I quizzed with livid lips.

'If he hadn't shot and hit me, he would have been severely punished.'

'How are you going to traverse the borders, back to Amioun, with this bullet-riddled car?' I asked as an afterthought.

'After you leave, I'll report the incidence to the authorities, get clearance, and then head back to Amioun.'

My son, who had not spoken a word until then, asked with a quivering voice, 'Will you be all right, Sir?'

'I've done worse things and managed,' he smiled. 'You don't need to worry about me.'

After reassuring us, Shamdas handed the taxi driver our luggage and closed his bullet-riddled trunk. We thanked him with forced smiles and drove off, hoping that we would not be arrested at the airport. The taxi driver was friendly and unsuspecting, but we remained taciturn because many taxi drivers are also secret service men.

At the airport the lines were long, but we snailed on, furtively scanning the crowds. At check in, our hearts almost sank *when the ground steward inspected our passports, glared at our blanched faces, and then walked away, leaving us suspended at the tip of a long line of passengers. The few minutes it took him to return brought grumbles from the passengers behind us, but neither my son nor I dared look back. When he returned, he handed us our passports, processed our luggage, gave us our boarding passes and, smiling knowingly, said, 'Have a safe trip.'*

At the gate, we stood in line, staring at the ground crew, afraid to glance around or talk. After we boarded, we kept our eyes to our laps, ostrich style. When the airplane took off, we both gazed at the diminishing landscape with sighing gratitude. We refused all food and drinks, maintaining our grave silence until we landed at London Heathrow. Only then, when we safely stood on British soil, did my teenaged son speak.

'Dad.'

'Yes, son.'

'I would like a hamburger, French fries, and a large coke, please.'

Hearing my story, my friends froze and became pensive. Then, slowly, the dense air gave way to sighs of relief.

"He certainly is an indomitable, inscrutable man," said the lawyer Nazeeh. "He left us with so many inexplicable unknowns. I bet the ground steward who took your passports knew exactly who you were. And I bet Shamdas had the authorities call the airport to facilitate your exit even though you had no re-entry visas stamped on your passports. And perhaps, in return for that favor, he was asked to accomplish some secret mission, which he must have accomplished rather well, otherwise he would not have been rewarded with a new Mercedes Benz."

"How did your son handle it?" asked Nizom, trying to move the conversation away from our mysterious hero.

"Not well," I sighed.

"Is that why he did not come to his Taita Katreen's funeral?" asked George.

"It is," I confessed. "Years do not erase fear. It hides in the darkest crevices of our minds, deploying like dynamite when sparked by a cue. In medicine we call it the post-traumatic-stress-disorder syndrome."

"You were afraid too, but, in spite of that, you have managed to return on several occasions," observed George.

"I was raised here, where danger and fear came with our daily bread. He was raised where life is a bountiful river. Our youth formats our mental codes and colors our personalities. No one can fly away from his roots. We remain forever tethered to our formative experiences, and what we become is what life allows us to become."

"Was it not Tennyson who said, '*I am a part of all that I have met*?' " asked George, who was an English major.

"Indeed, he did say that in his famous poem, *Ulysses*. Perhaps in our story, Shamdas is the fearless, indomitable Odysseus, whose wooden-horse intrigue helped win the Trojan War and who, after it was all over, taunted giants, resisted sirens, led his men through unforgettable adventures, and kept on moving restlessly from one deadly mission to another."

Easter in Naxos

The colors of faith had never appealed to my eyes: I had taken my own colors from the spectrum of the rainbow and never felt the need to gaze beyond the sky. The metaphysical realms were not dimensions into which I could levitate without invoking myths. Mythology, the collective art of historic imagination, did not captivate my intellect as much as did the hard, scientific evidence of reason. I must have been so constituted because I favored reality in spite of its thorns and resisted the temptations of imagination in spite of their rich rewards. Thus, I must have been pre-wired from birth and indelibly programmed thereafter by life's tireless fingers. Indeed, for better and for worse, we are what we are until something startles our mind and forever changes us. This is the story of one such startling moment.

Ever since awareness troubled humanity, fate and faith have sat on opposite poles of the human soul. Whereas fate evoked fear, uncertainty, despair, and capitulation—faith conjured courage, confidence, hope, and resolve. It was this balance between fate and faith that edified the human spirit throughout the ages and scattered humanity along the bell-curved spectrum between imagination at one end and reality at the other.

During that fateful year, the tenth year of the second millennium, reality's thorns were excruciatingly sobering. Several of my colleagues and friends had been stricken with cancer, a few had died, and some were teetering on the precipice of finality with myriad, incurable diseases. I found myself writing posthumous poems filled with guilt and shame at their demise:

> *I felt shamed to see the glow*
> *Of nature's raging firestorm*
> *Consume to ash*
> *The beautiful and kind*

The starlit mind
The smile that caught the sunrise
The heart that held the sunset.

I felt ashamed, my friend
Ashamed of my youth
Ashamed of my health
Ashamed of my luck
Ashamed that I have come too late
To mitigate your fate.

Indeed, during that death-of-peers year, I began distancing myself from reality's thorns and taking refuge at the other end of humanity's bell curve in the sublime realms of imagination, singing along with Ghalib:

I keep a certain distance from the reality of things
It's the same distance between me and utter confusion.

Feeling that I was about to reach my boiling point, my wife and I took an Easter respite from the practice of medicine and flew away to Greece for a sunny time in the Aegean archipelago. I had always thought that the word archipelago meant a group of islands but when I bought my Greek-English dictionary in Naxos, I was surprised by the etymology: arkhi- *'chief'* + pelagos *'sea'*. This prevalent malapropism must have occurred because the Aegean Sea is remarkable for its large number of islands.

Naxos, our first stop, is the island where Zeus, the father of all the gods, was brought up. In his honor, the inhabitants named the island's tallest mountain Zas. On the top of Zas, an eagle granted Zeus thunder, which gave him power over Olympus, the home of the gods. When Zeus fell in love with Semele, the daughter of the king of Thebes, the jealous goddess Hera enticed Semele into asking Zeus to reveal his stunning, divine splendor to her. When he did, pregnant Semele became overwhelmed and died of shock. Zeus, though unable to save Semele, was able to save their unborn child by stitching the embryo into his thigh.

Dionysus—the god of wine (known to the Romans as Bacchus), patron of agriculture and theater, and liberator through wine's ecstasy—was born in Naxos out of Zeus's thigh and because the people of Naxos worshiped him, he blessed their island with rich vineyards.

    Trying to forget about my two best friends who were teetering on the precipice of finality, my wife and I treated ourselves to long walks along the Island's shores, listened to Greek music in *tavernas*, and ate feta cheese with tomatoes, peppers, and onions cooked in terracotta pots. Still, the pale specter of death wafted through my mind like an inescapable apparition, wearing the frightened visages of my two friends. To appease my angst, I made several overseas calls, which had the opposite effect. Things were getting worse instead of better, and in spite of my deliberate distance, I was becoming more troubled than when I was near.

    When we returned from one particularly arduous walk the Saturday afternoon before Easter, we noticed the hotel was abuzz with alacritous activities. Maria—the sunny face of the place with the charm of spring and the warmth of summer—explained that they were hosting a traditional Easter-Sunday lunch with live music and dance. Eleven lambs were to be grilled on spits and served with local varieties of Dionysian wine, *raki*, and ouzo. They were also planning to serve a traditional lamb-intestine soup after today's Midnight Easter Mass.

    Having been raised in the Greek Orthodox Church during my youth, I felt an irresistible urge to attend the midnight mass with my Catholic wife who had never attended Orthodox services before. The Byzantine chant, *"Christ has risen from the dead,"* had enchanted me as a youth and my sorely soured spirits needed its uplifting powers more than ever. The faces of my two dying friends flashed in and out of my consciousness throughout the evening as we readied ourselves for the Midnight Mass at the neighborhood's *Pendanassa* Church of Naxos.

    Hoping to get good seats, we began our walk toward the church a little after eleven. The *tavernas* and cafés were brightly lit and waiters scurried about, making preparations for the post-midnight-mass throngs. Music, church bells, and firecrackers sputtered the quiet night air while candle-carrying crowds with festively arrayed children converged on the *Pendanassa* church from the spidery maze of narrow streets that sprawled around it. One could feel the fever suffuse the eager night air as the resurrection hour approached. Exactly at midnight, the Byzantine chant will hail:

> *Khristos Anesti Eknekron—*
> *Christ has risen from the dead*
> *And has stepped upon death with death*
> *And has granted life unto those in the graves.*

When we arrived, the old, stone church was already full of worshipers, lined along the walls because there were no available seats. The sanctuary wall was decked with ancient, colorful icons, painted over centuries by the island's artists. The stone arches and glass-stained windows told Byzantine tales from a Greco-Roman era that had left its indelible stamp upon the region. The archpriest wore a large, bejeweled crucifix upon his chest, was arrayed in magnificent robes embroidered with gold and silver, and swung an incense censer, suffusing the supplicating worshipers. The Byzantine chanters, all men with deep voices, *madrigaled* the Easter prayers into the incensed air as the priest made preparations to lead the congregation out of the church, into the churchyard, where the pronouncement, *"Khristos Anesti Eknekron—Christ has risen from the dead,"* will announce the awaited moment of resurrection.

We noticed that when the local worshipers entered the church, they always headed straight to the icon *easeled* beneath the altar, kissed it, crossed themselves, and then found their standing place. From our vantage point, my wife and I could not discern the details of the icon, obscured by the glare from its glass cover.

The suspenseful expectation of resurrection rose by the minute when close to midnight the archpriest, holding the silvered Bible high above his head, led the huddled congregation through the narrow-arched, side-door into the churchyard. A lighted platform awaited him and his chanters, and near it hung a massive bell with a rope tethered to its pendulum—a festive addition, no doubt, to the smaller bell hanging from the belfry. Young men lined the surrounding roofs with ready fireworks and the boisterous throngs drowned the Byzantine chants in a storm of supplicating locutions. I clasped my wife's hand, as we made our way toward the lighted stand, so we would not be separated by the tug of bodies pushing and elbowing us from all directions.

The huddled faithful hung their eyes upon the priest's lips and awaited the midnight moment when he would pronounce the fateful, proverbial words: *"Khristos Anesti Eknekron—Christ has risen from the dead."* As the awaited instant drew nearer, a pulsating pressure began to throb behind my eyes and my head started to tremble uncontrollably in the crescendo of expectation. Struck by the moment, I became imminently aware that something startling was happening to me. It felt like a premonition, a life-altering event, an out-of-body experience, or something frightfully numinous and horrifyingly fateful. Without understanding why, I was moved to close my eyes and worship. Unable to formulate words, I began praying for my two dying friends by conjuring blissful images of grace and vitality. It was while my eyes were closed, my *glossolalic* lips, mumbling unintelligibly, and my head, swirling as if I were free-falling from some unearthly height—that the resurrection occurred.

As soon as the archpriest began the *Khristos-Anesti-Eknekron* chant, the night exploded with fire and sound. The two bells began their salvos, powered by the youthful arms of their eager ringers. The fireworks upon the roofs split the womb of the sky with showers of meteors. And the jubilant throngs, in unison, burst the night with their *Khristos-Anesti-Eknekron* voices. As I joined in the chanting, the pulsating pressure, throbbing behind my eyes, exploded with unstoppable tears. I covered my face with both hands as I began my out-of-control sobbing. Not wanting my wife to see my childhood tears, I turned away, squeezed toward the gate, and waited for her to follow. When she caught up with me, I was surprised to see that her face was equally besmirched. Without uttering a word, we understood that we had shared the same, numinous experience. When the chanting ended, we clasped hands and, like a pair of wings, floated out of the clamorous churchyard back into the deep, silent night.

Easter Day was festive with music, dance, and roasted lamb. By mid morning, eleven lambs were roasting on spits in preparation for the grand lunch event. At noon, hotel guests began gathering around the swimming pool where tables were set with colorful flowers and colored eggs. Ouzo, *raki*, and local wines filled the toasting glasses while the live *bouzouki* music flooded the sunny, Sunday air with merriment and motion. Dancers, holding hands, danced in rings to the Greek tunes and invited the guests to join in. Moved by the din, I joined the twirling rings and danced to the beat with merry abandon and reckless disregard to group synchrony. It mattered not to the natives that I could not dance, but it mattered a lot that I was happy to participate. Other guests joined in when they saw that my clumsy, dissonant moves were bringing smiles instead of sneers.

That afternoon, after the festive lunch celebrants had dispersed, my wife and I took a long walk along the Naxos shore. As we walked, I found myself nervously fingering the cell phone in my pocket as if I were expecting an important call. Un-calmed by the halcyon rhymes of waves, I unwittingly hastened my pace, without knowing why, causing my wife to protest. The cycle of slowing down and speeding up, again and again, reproduced itself throughout our walk. It was something I could neither control nor understand. It took my wife's intuitive insight to unravel my marching mystery.

"You're worried about your friends," she announced.
"Am I?"
"You're unable to relax."
"But I don't have anything on my mind."
"Oh, yes you do. Why don't you get it over with, call them, and find out how they're doing."

"It's too early to call; we're eight hours ahead."
"No it's not; it's already eight in the morning in Oklahoma."
"Well, let me wait a couple of hours and then I'll call."

Two hours later, from our hotel, I called both hospital rooms where my two friends lay. Neither of them answered. One was getting a stem cell transplant and the other his final cycle of intensive chemotherapy. After calling several times without getting a response, I called the nurses stations but they refused to give me any information. Something was wrong and I was not privy to it. I felt the isolation deep in my heart and was too remote to do anything about it.

The next afternoon, I called again and was able to talk to the wives. Both friends were septic because the chemotherapy had killed all their white cells. They had high fevers, were on multiple antibiotics, had trouble maintaining normal blood pressures, and were in the intensive care unit. I felt this eerie synchrony of fate squeeze my breath away as I confessed to my concerned wife that they could both die at any minute because of septic shock. Pretending to ignore the tears in my eyes, she said, "Let's walk back to the *Pendanassa* church. It's our last day in Naxos and I'd like to visit it one last time before we leave."

I did not move nor did I answer. My mind at that precarious moment was mired in a murky haze of fear and my heart felt utterly helpless, faithless, and abandoned. I ignored her plea to return to the small, empty church, lay on my bed, closed my eyes, and surrendered my thoughts to hopeless doom. My friends' lives tumbled before me, free falling from a high cliff into a bottomless pit where a tenebrous finality awaited them both.

"Salem darling, did you hear me? I'd like us to go back to the *Pendanassa* church one last time before we leave," reminded my wife with musical tone.

I felt her soothing, warm hand stroke my brow and her lips kiss my cheeks with ineffable tenderness.

"Darling, where are you?" She whispered, perhaps smiling, while my sight was still shrouded in darkness.

Resignedly, I took her hand, kissed it, and then, like an obedient child, stood up and murmured, "Let us go."

Holding hands, we walked without words. The churchyard was vacant, the massive bell still hung near the silent platform, and a solemn stillness suffocated the place. The church door was open but no one was there. We crossed ourselves and tiptoed in until we stood before the icon, which during the Easter services, all the natives went straight to, kissed, and then crossed themselves. It was an old painting framed behind glass with a faded image of an exhausted Christ, moments before he was nailed to the cross.

I had seen many a painting of Christ on the cross, or dragging his cross, or covered with a shroud and surrounded by weeping women, or lying dead in his mother's lap. What was unusual about this particular painting was that He was lying on the ground, reclining on both elbows, looking utterly exhausted, gazing at His cross, and calmly awaiting His crucifixion. He and His cross were the only subjects of the painting; the soldiers and the multitudes were not depicted, not even in the background. He appeared thoughtful, resigned, lethargic, contemplating the moment of his fate with deep, knowing eyes.

As we stood before the icon, I saw images of my two friends, lethargic, pale, resigned, reclining on their ICU beds, contemplating the moments of their dying. The harder I tried to lose my friends' images in order to regain that of Christ's, the farther Christ's image receded until the only subjects I could see in the frame were my two friends. I felt a sudden urge to emulate what the islanders had done last night. To my wife's surprise, I kissed the icon, crossed myself, and then fell to my knees in supplication. She placed her trembling hand upon my head and solemnly waited until I had finished praying.

I must have appeared drenched and exhausted when I stood up because she rushed me to the nearest bench and laid me down. When I was able to stand up again, I cautiously approached the icon and peered into it again. The image of an exhausted Christ—reclining on the ground, awaiting his crucifixion—was back, and the images of my two friends, reclining on their ICU beds, were no longer there. For some unfathomable reason, I felt a cool mist startle my face and slowly tremble down my body all the way to my feet. Refreshed and buoyant, I clasped my wife's hand, walked out of the church and back to the hotel, all the time pretending that nothing significant had transpired.

I slept well that night, un-assailed by sinister thoughts, and the next day we were moved by ferry to *Santorini*. The island floated like a fragmented ring around a bull's-eye of lava. Its steep cliffs surrounding the *caldera* gave it the appearance of a cup, half-full of seawater, floating in the middle of the Aegean with a lump of licorice in its midst. For some inscrutable reason, the word *caldera* intrigued me and sent me straight to my Greek-English dictionary. *"Caldera, a large volcanic crater, typically one formed by a major eruption leading to the collapse of the mouth of the volcano; from caldaria meaning boiling point."* I was intrigued by the etymology but had no idea why. Perhaps something about the setting held a deep significance to me even though I was unable to discern it. Again it took my wife's insight to remind me that we came to Greece because I was about to reach my boiling point.

After three days of Santorini sun, my wife and I took a boat ride to the mound of lava in the center of the *caldera*. As we climbed to the top of this black mountain, our guide explained that the Santorini volcano erupted several thousand years ago, collapsing most of the island into its mouth, drowning it into the sea, and leaving only the fragmented rim-of-cliffs that remain today. It erupted again out of the sea some five hundred years ago and caused the mountain of lava that we were standing on to rise like the tip of an iceberg into the middle of the *caldera*.

Instantly, the image of a resurrected Santorini captured my imagination, perhaps because Easter was still vivid in my mind. When my wife and I reached the top, I told her that we were standing on Christ's head and that the cliffs of Santorini that surrounded us were his crown of thorns. I must have offended her religious sensibility because she demurred.

"Please don't talk like that," she snapped as she put her hands to her ears. "I don't care to hear this of kind talk."

"But, Sweetheart, what's wrong with conjuring a holy image out of nature?"

"Standing on Christ's head isn't exactly a holy image. Find yourself something more pleasant to imagine."

"I'm sorry, Sweetheart, but I can't help how this place makes me feel. Deep in my heart, I believe that the volcano we are standing on does represent the resurrection of Christ."

"And I can't help but think that the thin mountain air has gone to your darling, little head."

"Well then, if that's the case, let's go back to base and see if my head will clear."

Having said that, I started my descent but noticed a few steps later that she had not moved from her place. Surprised, I looked back at her and inquired, "Aren't you coming down with me to see if my little head will clear?"

Smiling with sky-full eyes, she held out her hand and giggled, "Let's not go down just yet. For some reason, I like it up here."

I walked back to where she was standing, peered into her glowing eyes, and whispered, "And what do you like about being up here, Sweetheart?"

"I don't really know. I guess it makes me feel rejuvenated."

"Rejuvenated?"

"Yes, rejuvenated, and don't you be making fun of my feelings again."

"But rejuvenate is a compound word derived from Latin where *re* means *again* and *juvenis* means *young*."

"So why's that significant?"

"Well, to become young again is to grow up again, or to rise again into youth."

"You're making fun of my feelings again. I don't want to hear anymore."

"But, Sweetheart, don't you see, the word resurrection comes from the Latin verb *re-surgere*, which means *rise again*. Feeling rejuvenated is very close to feeling resurrected. Something about the volcano has touched your soul just like it has touched mine and it cannot be the thin mountain air."

"And how do you know that?"

"Because the cliffs of Santorini where we are staying are higher than this mountain top."

She did not reply. Looking away, she sniffled, wiped her cheeks, eased her wet, trembling fingers into my hand, and, for the longest time, *tranced* into the vast, blue dome of heaven, sighing repeatedly as she gazed.

After our heart-to-heart dialogue, my wife and I were quiet as we descended back to base. We were both feeling rejuvenated by the resurrected island and that must have caused us to become even more pensive on our way down. There was a peculiar sadness about leaving the top, and we both felt it when we arrived at the base. Waiting to board the boat, my wife looked at me with remorseful eyes and said, "You haven't checked on your friends for several days now. I think you should call and find out how they're doing."

"I am afraid of bad news," I explained. "That's why I haven't dared to call."

"And are you still afraid after having stood on the head of a resurrected Christ?"

Feeling reproached, I paused for breath, thought of the cool mist that rejuvenated me when I stood before the *Pendanassa* icon, looked into her deep, green eyes over-brimming with hope, pulled the cell phone out of my pocket, and called my first friend.

"Salem. It's so good to hear from you. My fever broke two days ago. I'm off antibiotics and am making white cells..."

"When will you go home?"

"They're talking about the day after tomorrow. I've been here three weeks and two days, and most stem-cell transplants are not allowed to return home before at least four weeks..."

I took in a deep sigh and called my second friend.

"Salem, I thought you were in Greece. Are you already back?"

"No, I'm calling you from Santorini's volcano. How are things going?"

"Going quite well and better than anyone had expected. I just received my bone marrow results. My oncologist thinks that I've gone into remission."

"How about your PET scan?"

"It's clean and they might let me go home tomorrow..."

My wife's eyes lit up when I threw my cell phone high into the air for her to catch. Rushing into my arms, she screamed, "They both made it; didn't they?"

"They're both going home this week."

"And you thought that they were dying."

"They were, Sweetheart."

The boat blew its horn into the silent sky.

"Darling, the boat is ready to leave. Let's not miss it."

"I'm staying here, Sweetheart. Let's wait for the next one."

"But why, Darling? We've seen it all and there's nothing more to see."

"Because I want to climb to the top of the volcano one more time for the same reason that you wanted to visit the *Pendanassa* church one more time."

"And why's that?"

"Because I want to stand on Christ's head for one last time and scream into the sky dome, Christ has risen from the dead and has brought my two friends back with him. *Khristos Anesti Eknekron.*"

Back in Oklahoma, I never told my two friends about Christ's icon in the *Pendanassa* church, nor about the out-of-body experience I had, praying for their resurrection while kneeling in front of it, nor about the cold mist that rejuvenated me, nor about standing on Christ's resurrected head and screaming into the sky dome, *"Khristos Anesti Eknekron."* But ever since that time, I have come to see resurrection in everything around me:

In flowers rising out of the inanimate soil to give us beauty
In faith rising out of our divine natures to give us solace
In clouds rising out of the salty seas to give us water
In prayers rising out of our faith to give us miracles
In foods rising out of the dead earth to give us life
In love rising out of our hearts to give us meaning
In hope rising out of our despair to give us joy
In bells that raise their dins into the skies
In chants raised to the skies in gratitude
In moments that startle us into loftier realities
In tears that rise out of our souls to ease our pains
In cold mists that rise out of icons to rejuvenate our bodies
In mighty spirits that rise out of loved ones' deaths to relay life
And in islands that rise out of the sea to rekindle our imaginations.

The last few stanzas from Samuel Taylor Coleridge's *The Rhyme Of The Ancient Mariner*, which I had never quite understood before, finally became clear to me because I understood them with my heart instead of my mind. They were uttered by the mariner who had shot the innocent albatross with his crossbow, causing the ship to be cursed and all his shipmates to be parched to death. Nevertheless, after much suffering, and with the albatross still hanging from his neck, he was redeemed and his shipmates resurrected because he regained his ability to pray—thus making prayer, redemption, and resurrection, the central themes of this epic poem.

The Mariner says:

The selfsame moment I could pray;
And from my neck so free
The albatross fell off, and sank
Like lead into the sea.

The Wedding

When I picked up the phone that Monday evening in August of 2011, I thought I was hearing the voice of my hero, Ghalib, Mirza Assadullah Khan (1797-1869) *oboing* across the half-night: *"Ghalib, I think we have caught sight of the road to death now. Death is the string that binds together the scattered beads of the universe."*

I gazed at the rouge Oklahoma sunset hovering between the day and night and thought: *"In the East, that very same sunset is a sunrise, poised between the night and day. How confusing is relativity? How can the same thing be two different things at the same time?"*

My brother's voice across the time-space wilderness resounded in my head. *"Another echo of confusing relativity,"* I thought. *"How can we dialogue, ear to ear, from two dissonant times and places?"*

"Brother." he said, "Can you hear me?"

"What's wrong?" I gasped. "Your voice portends a heartache."

"Uncle Ibraheem gifted us his years."

"Oh. When? When's the funeral?"

"Whenever you arrive?"

"If I leave tomorrow morning, I can be there Wednesday evening."

"Good. I'll tell Father Elias to set the funeral for Thursday afternoon."

Another of my hero's sayings scrolled before my burning eyes: *"O Asad, don't be taken by the delusion of existence. The world is but a ring in the web of thought."*

Uncle Ibraheem was the baby, the last of my father's eight siblings, the only one who did not remember his father. His father, Priest Nicholas of Amioun, died at eighty-two when Ibraheem was only five months old and his mother, Grandma Khouryieh, was fifty-two. The saga of this frail woman—who, singlehandedly, raised eight good children between the Two Great Wars and died at the age of 102—is an unsung Odyssey. Lebanon was under French mandate then, having been extricated by forceps from the womb of the dying Ottoman Empire.

Flying east across eight time zones confounds the brain's circadian rhythm and spins vertiginous thoughts around the half-awake mind. Looking from above the clouds, I thought that I could see eternity's dome bending under the weight of time. My thoughts grew wings. *Homo sapiens* originated in Africa about 200,000 years ago, out of a planet that is four-and-a-half-billion years old, I mused. And, throughout that entire time span, no one had ever experienced air travel until the 1930s. That was when *Homo sapiens* first travelled against time. I felt privileged as I recited to myself lines from John Gillespie Magee's *High Flight:*

> *Up, up the long, delirious burning blue*
> *I've topped the wind-swept heights with easy grace*
> *Where never lark, or ever eagle flew —*
> *And, while with silent, lifting mind I've trod*
> *The high, untrespassed sanctity of space,*
> *Put out my hand, and touched the face of God.*

Beirut airport was abuzz with immigrants returning from the circumferences of earth to their little hometowns in Mount Lebanon, where awaiting them were all the loving arms and brimming eyes of relatives and friends.

"What is the purpose of your visit?" asked the officer as he examined my American passport.

"A wedding," I replied.

"Oh, congratulations. Who's getting married?"

"My uncle."

He eyed me with consternation as he took a second look at my birth year, 1946. Then, as if it were his duty to investigate this sexagenarian oddity standing before him, he held the passport stamp in midair—to indicate that he was not going to stamp my passport until I had answered his questions—and wryly inquired, "How old is your uncle?"

"Eighty-eight," I replied, with a matter-of-fact face.

"Is it going to be a big wedding?" he teased.

"A very, very big one, indeed." I nodded knowingly.

"And how old is his bride?"

"Four-and-a-half-billion years," I smiled.

He grinned—as if to say that he understood that I did not wish to divulge the bride's youthful age—and muttered, *"Alf mabrouk."*[4]

Then, with automatic disregard, he stamped my passport, handed it back to me, and yelled, "Next Please."

Amioun, our hometown, stretched like a sly cat atop the long, rocky ridge that framed the olive plain below it, its nightlights in the distance glowing like a halo around a golden crown.

At my uncle's home, family and friends were sitting on the cool, long veranda and all women were dressed in black. His wife, Aunt Salam, walked towards me as I was pulling my suitcase out of the car. She was smiling when we started hugging but her smiles turned into tears over my shoulder. I kissed my five cousins, their spouses, and their ten children before I sat next to my aunt and asked, "Did he suffer?"

"He went peacefully and quickly. We were all with him. He smiled at us before he took his last breath. Pneumonia was his friend."

The funeral services were held at St. George's Orthodox Church, one of the oldest in continuous use in the world: it used to be a heathen temple, dating back to about two thousand years before Christ. One could see the different strata of stones carved during different eras to rebuild its walls after myriad destructions by war and nature. The floor, the walls, and the arched ceiling were all of ancient stone. It could only hold in its bosom my uncle's

---

[4] A thousand congratulations.

family, his close friends, and the local community. The rest of the attendees hovered around the church like a belt of pilgrims, and savored the siren tunes of the Byzantine mass as it crept into their ears out of anachronistic loudspeakers.

"No hand shaking or kissing, please," announced Father Elias, as he ended the mass and led the family into the condolences hall. There, we all stood in an arch while the masses of *condolent* faces passed us with bowed heads and uttered, *"Allah yirhamu."*[5] The passing endured close to four hours, causing our eyes and feet to surrender their stamina to accruing fatigue. It was not possible for some to remain standing—my mother at ninety-five, my aunt at eighty two, and the many others who had frail joints—all sat down after the first hour or two and escorted the long line of melancholy faces with their tired eyes.

It was deep into the night before we could retire back to Uncle Ibraheem's home for a huddled family time. Faces were relieved at the closure of an eighty-eight-year life that was filled with love and smiles. We talked of simple matters, admired all twenty boisterous grandchildren, and memorialized with endless tales a generation whose last ambassador had just bid us farewell.

The following three days were equally grueling. Visitors filled the condolences hall on Friday, Saturday, and Sunday and we all took turns in sitting and standing up. They came from remote corners with faces that had aged along with mine. I renewed contacts and friendships with many I had not seen since I left Lebanon, forty years earlier. We made covenants with each other and promises, which we knew we could not possibly keep, but which felt sincere at the moments of making: "Let us get together soon. Come visit us, please. We'll call you when we visit the US. We have so much to talk about."

During these few days, I said so many goodbye's to so many old faces that I might never see again. Lines from a poem, *'How Do*

---

[5] May God bless him with mercy.

You Say Good-Bye', which I had written to a departing friend a long time ago, floated before my gaze:

> *Let us wander to the tavern at the corner of the street*
> *Share a jug of frothy spirit, something warm to eat*
> *Watch the many faces of a lazy afternoon*
> *Exit together in the dimming light*
> *And then, pretending we shall be together soon*
> *Depart on separate ways into the night.*

Back at the airport, a high school friend and classmate shouted my name above the throngs. We hugged after forty years as if we had never been apart, sat in an isolated corner, and began reminiscing. Then, as if seized by an afterthought, he looked at me and said, "I'm sorry about your uncle. I saw the pictures in the paper. *'It was a massive funeral,'* said the reporter who wrote the article."

"Do you happen to have a copy?" I asked, wanting to return with something to show my Oklahoma family.

"No, I'm sorry."

"Never mind. I'll get one from one of my cousins."

"He must have been a very rich and famous man, judging by the thousands of people who showed up to pay their respects."

"Uncle Ibraheem? Rich and Famous? He was anything but that." I smiled.

"Well? How come such a massive funeral then?"

"He was a kind man who spent his entire life glowing with joy. It was his joy, his indelible smile, and his tireless readiness to help anyone in need that touched all those who knew him."

"Does he have children?"

"Five, and they're all like him."

"You mean kind, helpful, and glowing with joy?"

I smiled and nodded. I did not tell him that my ordinary uncle and aunt raised five highly intelligent, educated, and very successful children. Relative to kindness and joy, such attributes seemed perfunctory at that moment.

Back among the clouds, between East and West, it suddenly came back to me that funerals are weddings just like sunsets are sunrises. Feeling smug at my startling discovery, I picked up the new book I had planned to read on my way back, David Hume's *A Treatise Of Human Nature* and began browsing. A group of lines that contemplated death clung to my eyes. *"We all were part of the inanimate for four-and-a-half-billion years. Then we all experienced miniscule specks of sentient existence, which we came to call life. Why then, when we are returned to our primary state, do we so protest?"*

"Funerals are not just weddings," I thought. "Indeed, they are also reunions." We are returned to our original home, to be what we had forever been, wedded to earth. Two thousand years ago, the Stoics had it figured out: *"The goal of life is to live in agreement with nature, which is to live according to virtue. For nature leads to virtue."*

And Epictetus (55-135), not Hume, was the one who said it best: *"Never say of anything, 'I have lost it'; but 'I have returned it.' Is your child dead? It is returned. Is your wife dead? She is returned."*

The Wedding, First Edition, Al-Jadid Vol.16 No. 63 Marsh 2012. Revised edition completed in October 2016.

The Curly Black Hair

Mysteries become mysterious only when we don't know enough. Magic becomes magical only when we cannot see enough. And secrets remain clandestine only if we are not privy to them. But, in the end, all is revealed because human nature abhors gaps, vacuums, and unknowns.

Such is the tale of our curly black hair, which traveled the planet, passed through the most secure of checks, tormented the brilliant minds of seasoned physicians, made fortunes for exploitative charlatans, and maintained invisibility under the microscopic eyes of circumspect inspectors.

Mr. Red Truffitt, our protagonist, was larger than the Acropolis, richer than Rome, more magnificent than Taj Mahal, more determined than Caesar, and more stable than the Pyramids. He squeezed life with a gentle grip, elaborating potent potions hitherto unknown to humanity. As a born entrepreneur and natural leader, he felt *minusculed* when life, all of a sudden, diminished him to a meek follower and despairing seeker.

All was going well in Mr. Truffitt's expansive life when the cough visited him at church, one glorious Sunday morning. Like a furtive cat, it snuck into his throat, disappeared inside its crannies, and began irritating its membranes with the nimbleness of a spider.

Holding his handkerchief to his mouth while sitting bent over in his pew may have made his incessant whoops and hacks less audible, but not less noticeable. He considered leaving in the middle of the sermon but, fearing that with his colossal figure and red head he might arouse more attention, he stayed and prayed.

Prayers unanswered, his cough persisted in spite of the many throat lozenges that found their way to him across the aisles and pews. His wife, Martha, feeling embarrassed, nudged him and whispered, "Let's leave. You're disrupting the whole church with your coughing."

The Pastor nodded and with fatherly forbearance held his sermon. Embarrassed, Mr. and Mrs. Truffitt got up and scurried out, escorted by the curious gazes of countless, sympathetic eyes.

"What's happening to you?" asked his alarmed Martha as soon as they were out.

"I wish I knew, honey, but it began right after I scratched my ear, and it got worse the more I fought it."

"And what on earth moved you to scratch your ear?" asked Martha while Red coughed his way to the car.

"Because it itched, dear," he gasped between coughs.

"Should we go to the emergency room, then?" she asked.

"Don't be silly," snapped Red with unrestrained exacerbation. "Just take me home and make me some tea."

Mr. Truffitt coughed all the way home, and then spilled the tea twice when coughing disrupted his cautious sipping. His wife made him swallow a spoonful of honey, which helped. Exhausted, he reclined in his Lazyboy and fell asleep.

The following week was clear of cough but, when Sunday arrived, he felt overcome with dread.

"Honey. I don't think I'm going to church," he told his wife as he watched her get ready.

Martha stopped dressing, gave Red a discombobulated look, walked up to him, placed her hand onto his forehead and inquired, "Are you feeling ill?"

"No. I just don't feel like going to church."

"But, that's so unlike you, Darling. What caused you to change your mind?"

"I'm afraid the cough may come again during the sermon."

"Oh, don't be silly. Sermons don't cause cough."

"It's not the sermon I'm worried about, Dear. It's just that what ever happened last Sunday, may happen again."

"You're being superstitious. Instead of letting a cough, which is no longer there, keep you at home, let's go to church and pray for your continued good health."

It took much convincing plus a spoonful of honey before Red was able to overcome his fear. But, the closer they got to church, the more he became aware that his fear was returning. Several times, he cleared his already clear throat and almost turned back but, not wanting to disappoint Martha, he made it to the church's parking lot.

Hand in hand, he and Martha walked in, but instead of going to their usual pew, Red pointed towards the back. Martha understood and led Red to an aisle seat on the farthest pew. Martha also understood when Red's hand started to sweat as it clutched hers. They have always held hands during the service, but sweat had never wetted their closeness before. Hoping to soften Red's angst, Martha squeezed his sweating palm, smiled, and whispered, "And don't scratch your ear, dear."

The sermon was apropos that Sunday because Father Stephan talked about the healing powers of faith. He discoursed on physical and emotional healing, quoted multiple examples from the New King James Version, and ended with Luke 22:50-52:

"And one of them struck the servant of the high priest and cut off his right ear. But Jesus answered and said, 'Permit even this.' And He touched his ear and healed him."

As soon as he said that, Red's incessant cough returned. The pastor pretended not to notice and went on with his sermon. Red and Martha hastily got up and left.

"I'm taking you to the emergency room, declared Martha as she took the driver's seat. Unable to respond due to his relentless coughing, Red nodded, "Okay."

In the emergency room, the doctor, after examining Red, acted worried. He ordered a CAT scan, blood tests, inhalation therapy, and then declared, "I suspect asthma, but it could be other things. We are seeing some adult whooping cough and I'm going to treat you for that without waiting for lab confirmation, which may take up to ten days."

After a long, anguished wait, the doctor reappeared, wearing a worried face, and told Martha and Red, "I'm puzzled. His CAT scan shows no masses, or infiltrates, or pulmonary emboli. His blood tests are normal. He did not respond to two inhalation treatments. I can find nothing on his physical examination. But, regardless of cause, this kind of persistent cough can have serious health consequences and must be stopped."

Red spent four hours in the emergency room before his cough was stopped. Martha kept asking the doctor to give him a spoonful of honey but he gave him morphine instead. When his cough finally stopped, the doctor sent him home on a narcotic cough syrup, 10 days of erythromycin, and referred him to a pulmonologist.

While awaiting the pulmonologist's appointment, the cough continued, came in protracted spells several times a day, woke him up at night, and reduced him to a retching wreck of his former self. Martha tried organic honey, essential oils, herbal teas, had his spine manipulated, and even took him to an acupuncturist. By the time they saw the pulmonologist, Martha had become an accomplished Internet researcher. Based on her research, she had a long list of questions for his lung doctor and certain suggestions pertaining to treatments that she had not yet tried.

Dr. Bruce was seasoned. He answered her list of questions, discussed the lack of science behind her treatment suggestions, and embarked on a complex course of investigations and therapeutic trials.

He started with a sinus CAT scan then followed it by a neck MRI, bronchoscopy, ENT and cardiac consultations, and when he couldn't make a diagnosis, he even gave Red a course of cortisone.

At their last visit, Dr. Bruce told Martha and Red that he had done all he could and advised them to go to the Mayo Clinic if they wished to pursue further diagnostic efforts.

When Red and Martha arrived at the Mayo Clinic, Red had become dependent on narcotics and was no longer able to work. Another thorough investigation yielded no definitive results and none of the treatments tried succeeded in controlling the cough. Defeated, Red and Martha returned home with new appeals to their prayer group. "If it started in church, then it must be healed in church," declared Martha.

After a year of no improvement, Martha and Red traveled to France, then England, then China, then India, all because of tips they had received from friends and church members. They returned exhausted, and on the advice of their pastor, Father Stephan, they decided to accept reality and search no more. Working part time and seeing his family physician for narcotic refills was all that Red was able to do from that point on. But, within a few months after that relative stability, his family physician, Dr. James, retired.

Trying to find another doctor who would give Red his monthly narcotics proved most vexing. Exacerbated and frustrated, they turned to Father Stephan for suggestions.

"A fine, young doctor has just joined our church," he informed them with hopeful eyes. "He comes to us from Egypt. His family is under persecution as are most members of the Coptic Church over there. He's trying to bring them here and we hope to be able to help him."

"I'm a close friend of Senator Willington," declared Red. "He's on the presidential refugee committee and wields great influence in Washington."

"May the Lord bless you and heal you," replied Father Stephan. "We are collectively appalled by the persecution of Christians and it is our duty to do all that is in our power to help them."

When Red and Martha first saw young Dr. Suleiman, he listened to their story and agreed to provide Red with the needed narcotics.

"Narcotics are addicting and I hate to give them long-term," he declared, "but, they do allow you to work part-time, and that's a worthy goal."

Dr. Suleiman did not share his Egyptian family's predicament with the Truffitts nor did Red inform him that he had an influential friend in Washington. It seemed inappropriate and premature to delve into politics that early in their acquaintance. Besides, Father Stephan knew that he could count on Red's help when the time was right.

After taking Red's detailed history, Dr. Suleiman declared that he wouldn't attempt to find the cause of Mr. Truffitt's cough.

"I'm not half as good as all the other doctors you've seen. Let's just call your cough *idiopathic* and go from there.

"What does *idiopathic* mean?" asked Red with some hope in his voice because it was the first time that his cough had been given a name.

"*Idiopathic* means of unknown cause," replied Dr. Suleiman with downcast eyes.

Red sighed as he took off his shirt and got on the examination table. Dr. Suleiman started his exam by taking Red's blood pressure.

"This is such an important measurement," he instructed. "That's why I don't trust anyone else to do it for me."

He then inspected Red's skin for moles and said, "Always wear sunscreen when out in the sun. Being fair-skinned makes you much more vulnerable than me."

Martha observed how Dr. Suleiman began his detailed physical examination. Using a bright light, he first inspected Red's mouth and throat. Then, with an otoscope, he looked inside Red's ears, stopped, looked again, and asked, "Which ear did you scratch?"

Seeing that Red did not understand what he meant by the question, he rephrased it.

"When your cough first began, you were at church, right?"

"Oh, yes, Martha and I were sitting together when it first started."

"You told me that it began right after you scratched your ear."

"Yes, yes, that's exactly how it started."

"Which ear did you scratch?"

"Oh. I'm not really sure, Doc. But, Martha always sits on my right, though, and we always hold hands. It must have been my left ear, then, because we were still holding hands when the cough began."

Martha nodded in agreement and then asked, "Is that an important fact, Doctor?"

"I think it could be," replied Dr. Suleiman with a pensive face.

"Of all the doctors we've visited, not one has asked me, which ear I scratched," added Red, half intrigued and half smiling.

"Well, probing ears to remove wax often triggers a reflex cough," explained Dr. Suleiman. "In your left ear, there's a curly, black hair, burrowing into your eardrum. May I pluck it?"

"You think it has something to do with my cough?" asked Red with incredulous tone.

"I don't know, but it's a suspect."

"By all means, Doc, let's get rid of this curly suspect."

Dr. Suleiman opened a sterile kit, took out a pair of long-nosed tweezers, and then told Martha, "I need you to hold this light like so, please."

As Martha's unsteady hand shone the otoscope light into Red's ear, Dr. Suleiman pulled the external ear upward and backward to bring the ear canal into full view. Then, after redirecting Martha's hand, he introduced the tweezers deep into the ear canal, seized the curly hair firmly, and with one deft motion, plucked the suspect out.

Mr. Red Truffitt's eyes bulged as he commenced a most violent and uncontrollable coughing spell that lasted several minutes, leaving him tearful, flushed, panting, and exhausted.

With grateful eyes, Dr. Suleiman and Martha watched the cough slowly die down. When, at last, Mr. Truffitt stopped convulsing, the first words he uttered were, "Praise the Lord. I think I've been saved."

As the news stormed the congregation, Red's story rolled over tongues at lightening speed; the church paper featured the story; and his prayer group rejoiced at hearing the good news:

Mr. Red Truffitt is healed. He's gotten off narcotics. He's back to fulltime work. He's helped bring in Dr. Suleiman's family from Egypt. Father Stephan has arranged for a special reception to welcome Dr. Suleiman's family into the church.

Father Stephan's homily at the reception was as brief as it was potent:

"We are blind to the myriad miracles that surround us and seem to notice only the exceptional ones, like Mr. Red Truffitt's miraculous healing by the plucking of a hair. But, Mr. Truffitt's healing is no greater than every one of you who lives, loves, works, and serves. Nor is his miracle greater than any flower, or green blade of grass, or tree, or animal, or insect, or the innumerable stars that bedeck our heavens.

"What I have learned from Mr. Truffitt's painful journey, and what I hope you too have learned, is that we need not wait for miracles to witness God's bounty. God's great miracles surround us and come into us with every breath, smell, taste, sight, sound, touch, feeling, and thought. Nothing mundane is ordinary. Every thing in this creation is miraculous. Let us keep our hearts and eyes open to our vast, majestic universe."

The Curly Black Hair, First Edition, The Bulletin, Oklahoma County Medical Society, May/June 2016. Revised Edition completed in October of 2016.

Forbidden Fire

"Heroism is for the young and wisdom, for the old," he sighed, and then added, "I wouldn't do it now, but at the time, it felt like the right thing to do."

"I wish I were there to witness its domino effects," I lamented.

"You were *behind bars* at a boarding school in Tripoli," he reminded.

"The mystery, which had lain under the dust for fifty years, is now burnished," I clapped with joy.

"You're the only one I've ever told," he frowned, and then downed the remains of his Samuel Adams beer in one mighty gulp.

The young waitress at the Prudential Tower Bar approached us and, with a heavy accent, inquired, "Vood you gentlemen carre for anazarr rround?"

"You must be a student," I quipped. "How long have you been here?"

"Ziss izz my first samastarr at MIT."

"Do you like Boston?"

"Much more zan Munich," she smiled and, collecting our two empty glasses, quaintly re-enticed, "Anazarr rround, perheps?"

"Sure, another round," said Nizom, sending the waitress excitedly away.

"Now that you're one sea and one ocean away from home, may I write your story?" I beckoned.

"One sea, one ocean, and fifty years away," he added with unconcealed relief. "Here comes the beer," he grinned, took a gulp, and licked the froth off his lips. "I guess the time has come to tell, but let me take a look at the piece before you publish it."

When, after three beers of reminiscing, Nizom and I were about to part, each back to his faraway life, I quoted from a poem I had written at an earlier time, lamenting the profound impact of distance upon friendship:

> *And if we say, Goodbye*
> *Who would supply*
> *The spirit here?*
> *The conflict, and the magic, and the fear?*
> *And every now and then, a cold and frothy beer?*
> *And if we say, Goodbye*
> *Who then would suture time together every year?*

For the next three years, Nizom in Boston and I in Oklahoma City hardly communicated, and the demands on my time snuffed my writing flame. But, when Nizom sent me an invitation to his daughter's wedding, my fire was rekindled. After collating all the shredded bits of 1961, that ominous year that forever changed our lives, I carved up enough time to write Nizom's story and presented it to Katy as a wedding gift. Since she had never been to Lebanon, I introduced the setting so that she would comprehend the significance of what had happened. I then retold Nizom's story as he had told it to me over beer, in the Prudential Tower Bar, three years earlier.

Dear Katy,

This letter is your real wedding gift because it is going to tell you things about your father that you do not know. What you know about your father is that he came to Boston as a student, studied engineering, worked very hard, became a highly successful chief engineer, and raised a wonderful family. You know him as a bright, loving, dedicated family man. But, you do not know the intimate details of how he grew up and what he accomplished during his Lebanese adolescence.

Your father and I grew up together in Amioun, Lebanon. His mother was a wise, resourceful homemaker and his father, the town's beloved tailor. These were the days when, in Lebanon, there were no readymade clothes. When men needed pants, jackets, or suits, they went to your grandfather, Sami, chose the fabric, and got measured. They returned in a week for the fitting, and after alterations, returned in another week for the ready garment. Until I left Lebanon in 1971, your grandfather made all my clothes. Amioun, the Christian Orthodox capital of the Arab world and the municipal capital of the Al-Kourah district, was then an olive-and-grape growing town where most people struggled to eke out a living.

Your grandmother gave birth to eleven children. Of her seven boys, four became engineers, a remarkable feat for a family of that size during these frugal times. All her children married and raised successful, highly educated families. All this from the tireless labors of a town's tailor and the wise resourcefulness of a fecund mother.

Before your grandfather saved enough money to build the family home, your grandparents with all eleven children lived in a two-room, stone house whose roof was made of white mud and straw. The front room served as living room by day, dining room during meals, and bedroom at night. The furniture was comprised of one long bench 'dashak' along the wall. Meals were served on a low table 'tablieh' around which the family sat on wooden stools or cushions.

Food was proportioned according to rank, with your grandfather and your father getting prime portions: your grandfather because he was the breadwinner and your father because he was the strongest cock in the coop. Feeding thirteen mouths was a daily challenge, and there were times when there was not enough food to satiate everyone, but there was always enough conversation and love to assuage the half-full bellies.

At night, the children slept on soft mattresses laid on the floor. Come morning, the soft mattresses were folded and put away. There was a wooden divide with a curtain door, separating the big front room from the smaller back room where your grand parents slept.

Cooking was done outside on a wood-burning stone stove 'mawadi'; bathroom facilities were in yonder nature; and baths were taken in a round brass tub 'lakan' into which the water was poured over the head with a ladling cup.

Your father, from his inception, was a charismatic leader. He was tall, handsome, smart, kind, cheerful, considerate, and a very good student. He loved Arabic literature and introduced us to the major writers of the day. As adolescents, we would spend hours listening to him read to us poems and poignant writings. We all looked up to him, loved him, were influenced by him, and felt a great vacuum when he left us and flew to Boston to finish his studies. Because so many of his Amioun friends wanted to accompany him to the airport to bid him goodbye, we hired a big bus. When we returned, the bus driver would not accept payment. "That's the least I can do for Nizom," he announced as he opened the door and let us out into the lugubrious night.

All this has been an introductory setting to the story I am about to tell you, a story which began on New Year's Eve of 1961. My father, who had promised to spend the night with us in Amioun, said he had to go back to Beirut on urgent business. Spying the moist, goodbye glances he exchanged with my mother worried me. I was fourteen then and your father was fifteen. It was around nine o'clock and the village was dark because there were no municipality lights. I ran to your father's home and together we went for a walk in the bleak December night of sleepy Amioun.

"What's wrong?" he asked when we were at a safe distance.
"I don't know, but I do know that something ominous is going to happen."
"Ominous? That's a very strong word," he remarked.
"My father went back to Beirut instead of spending the night with us."
"So, what's ominous about that?"
"He and my mother shared worried looks—looks I have never seen before."

"What kind of looks?"

"The kind of looks one evinces when overcome with great worry—looks that reeked of danger and fear."

"I wonder if your father's political party is planning a coup d'état?" came your father's poignant response. "In his last speech, which was published in the papers, he blatantly proclaimed, 'We do not ask to share in governing; we want to govern.' "

We walked the town until midnight and then sat by the fat radio in your father's home, awaiting the early morning news broadcast. After the national anthem, the broadcaster's hoarse voice announced: "An evil band of rebels attempted to seize power and were promptly extinguished."

Your father and I parted at daybreak. Soon, armed forces flooded Amioun. I and my brothers were taken away and incarcerated in a boarding school, my mother was incarcerated in a hospital, and half of the Amioun men were arrested, among them your grandfather, Sami. Weeks of trepidation followed as the secret police suspected, arrested, interrogated, tortured, and killed with reckless disregard. Everyone in Amioun was suspect and everyone went to sleep afraid. Rumors spun and circulated at alarming speed. One of the rumors was that my brothers and I were starving because we had no money to buy food.

One February day, your father suddenly appeared on the playgrounds of our school, looking for me. I don't know how he managed to travel from Amioun to Tripoli, forge his way into our high-walled, well-guarded school, and find me—without inquiring from anyone about my whereabouts. At that time, the mere asking about me would have made him a suspect. Spies lurked everywhere and I was not allowed visitors.

"How are you doing?" he smirked at my astonished face as we walked around the soccer field.
"I'm fine, but my classmates are avoiding me."
"Are they feeding you?"
"We eat in the cafeteria?"

"Do you have any pocket money?"
"No."

Your father reached into his pocket, pulled out a wad of liras, which he had saved, and sneaked it into my pocket. Then, furtively, he scanned our surroundings and whispered, "I have to leave before anyone sees me. My father was just released from prison and if they find out that I have visited you, they will re-incarcerate him and will interrogate me under pressure until I confess to something I did not do."

"Have they executed my father yet?" I stuttered.

"No, but he's in solitary confinement and they don't allow him visitors."

Your father left as stealthily as he had entered and no one found out that he had visited me. After him, I lost contact with the outside world until my mother was released in March and came to school to collect my two brothers and me. We found the front door of our home broken and the house ransacked. No one came to visit us because the secret police interrogated everyone who dared come to our door. One weekend, I asked to go to Amioun to see my friends, but my mother did not allow me because, "Conditions were not safe in Al-Kourah ever since the fires of the first of March," she explained.

"What fires?" I asked.

"The first of March is the birthday of the founder of your father's political party who was executed in 1949 because of his political views. Before the coup d'état, his birthday was commemorated with bonfires all over Lebanon. But, since the coup, the government has warned that anyone who kindles a bonfire on the first of March will be severely punished.

"So, who kindled the fires, then?"

"No one knows and no one has been accused yet, but the secret police are actively interrogating suspects."

"Was there more than one fire?"

"The whole Al-Kourah lit up after someone started a huge bonfire on the highest hill in Amioun. The army was incensed because the fire was inaccessible to the fire trucks and could only be reached by foot. It burned defiantly for hours and could be seen from everywhere, which is why it instigated a chain of fires on all the hills surrounding the olive plain."

"Who did it?"

"I told you, no one knows, but the government is very angry at Al-Kourah and is ruthlessly interrogating party supporters everywhere. That's why we have to wait until things cool down before you start reconnecting with your Amioun friends."

As a political family, our life was preoccupied with the military trials of the party members, which began soon after. We were not allowed to visit my father until later that year because he was still in solitary confinement. During our first visit, I related with enthusiasm the story of the March fires. He smiled and told me that the story had already reached the prisoners, lifted up their fallen morale, and rejuvenated their esprit de corps. "Who ever did it was brave beyond fear," was his last comment to me before our time was up.

Rumors raged about Amioun's incendiary hero. Some said the fire was accidental because no one in his right mind would dare defy the authorities with such a blatant act of disobedience. Others said that some party members journeyed from Beirut, started the fire, and fled back hoping that the authorities would not think of interrogating someone from Beirut about a fire in Amioun. Others blamed some nomadic shepherds who started the fire then migrated away. But, the fact remains that no one claimed responsibility and no one was ever indicted.

Permit me now to jump fifty years forward—from 1961, when your father was only fifteen, to 2011 when he was 66 years old. We were having a heart-to-heart talk at the Prudential Tower Bar when he decided to tell me a story. What brought it to his mind was our conversation about Dahr Al-Shurah, the highest hill in Amioun, where as children we used to play and where my father dreamt of building the family home. I was telling your dad that, *fifteen years after my father had died, my mother fulfilled his dream and built the family home on the highest point. From there, one can see the olive plain like a green sea cupped by a series of hills, where upon each hill smiles an ancient, charming hamlet.*

My description of our high-point playground must have ignited a deeply interred memory, a memory that he had tried to forget for fifty years. Placing his clenched fingers on his forehead, he gazed into his beer as if it were a mirror of his adolescent soul and said, "Heroism is for the young and wisdom, for the old. I wouldn't do it now, but at the time, it felt like the right thing to do."

"Nizom," I murmured. "What in heaven's name are you talking about?"

"The Dahr Al-Shurah fire of March 1, 1962."

"You mean the mystery bonfire that incited a ring of fires, which lit up all the hilltops around the olive plain?"

"Yes. This is what I mean."

"You did it?" I gasped with disbelief. "How can a fifteen year old boy manage such a grand conflagration? The hill is a massive rock with nothing that burns on top, and there's only one, small, winding foot road that leads up to it."

"I used tires."

"Car tires?"

"No. Big bus tires."

"Where on earth did you find big bus tires?"

"From Al-Badawi, the owner of the bus who, in 1966, took us all to the Beirut Airport."

"Did he help you carry them up the steep hill?"

"He didn't know I took them. They were old, discarded tires behind his house. I stole one tire a day for twelve days. Each day, I would sneak out of the house at midnight, steal a tire, and roll it all the way from the Al-Badawi home to the top of the hill. Often, the tire would slip and roll back down, but I would chase it and roll it back up to the top. Each trip took about two hours and left me exhausted. But, by March the first, I had four layers of bus tires

stacked one on top of the other, arranged in a triangle to keep them stable. When I stacked the fourth layer, the pile stood as tall as I was at the time and I had to build stone steps to reach its top."

"No one helped you?"
"I didn't want others to help me because it would endanger them."
"No one saw you?"
"Are you kidding? In the winter, Amioun goes to bed early. My main fear was my mother because she has keen hearing. I had to jump out of my bedroom window because our front door squeaked; and I had to use gloves so that I would not have to wash my hands when I snuck back in. And I also wore my hunting clothes because they were too dirty to show tire marks."

"Wasn't it cold?"
"It was freezing and rainy and slippery, but that didn't stop me. I couldn't let the memory of the party's founder pass unnoticed."
"How did you light the tires?"
"I filled the insides of the three lower tires with straw, dowsed them with kerosene, gave them a match, and raced back home. When I got home at about ten, the fire was raging and everyone was watching it. Soon after, other fires began to sprout on top of the hills surrounding the olive plain. Fire trucks, army trucks, and army jeeps soon arrived, but they could not reach the hilltop because there were no roads. The few who climbed to the hilltop on foot quickly realized that the fire was un-extinguishable. The twelve big, bus tires burned and burned throughout the night while everyone smiled and watched."

"And, what happened the next morning?"
"They arrested and interrogated a lot of people, but had to release them because they had no information. They even tortured several men, but were unable to extract confessions out of any of them. I was the only one who knew, but because I was fifteen, I was never a suspect."

"What happened to the other villagers?"

"All I know is that no one from Al-Kourah confessed, which caused the secret police to suspect that an organized band from the party drove from Beirut, lit the fires, and went back before they could be detected."

"How did all that make you feel?"

"I felt scared and kept my mouth shut when others discussed the fires. They would have arrested and tortured my father had they found out. Nonetheless, I kept the fires ablaze in my mind's eye. I can still see them as vividly now as I did fifty years ago."

"You are an unsung hero."

"No, I was an adolescent fool."

"You helped lift the morale of all party members, prisoners, and sympathizers."

"I also endangered my family and so many innocent others."

"Are you regretful?"

"No. I think it needed to be done. The way they summarily tried and executed the party's founder, three days after his arrest in 1949, made a rebel out of me. I was never a party member, but I have always sided with justice against injustice."

"You also happen to share the same birthday," I added.

"Why on earth would you remember that?" he asked with wide-open eyes.

"How can I ever forget that the party founder and you share the same birthday? Perhaps, in some subliminal recess of your mind, you were also lighting your own birthday candle."

Your father grinned at the suggestion, got up, and said, "It's getting late. Let's go home."

I left your father that night with a bonfire in my heart, and I resolved to tell his story. Singlehandedly, a fifteen-year-old boy from Amioun ignited Al-Kourah, on the night of March the first, 1962 because he believed that he was fighting for justice. How much courage and endurance it must have taken to fight the fear and frustration he must have experienced—rolling these big, bus *tires up the hill, night after night, and rolling them back, again and again, each time they slipped down to base, until he had completed his Sisyphean task.*

In Greek mythology, Sisyphus was the absurd hero through both his passions and his torture. His scorn of Gods, his hatred of death, and his passion for life earned him the proverbial, underworld punishment of rolling a stone up a mountain and endlessly repeating the task each time the stone rolled back down. For some, he symbolized the sun, repeatedly rising from the east and setting in the west, giving light and life just like your father's bonfire.

In his philosophical essay, The Myth Of Sisyphus, Albert Camus (1913-1960) introduces the concept of the absurd, which represents man's futile quest for meaning, truth, and value. To overcome this proverbial futility, man must revolt against it, which is the only way to render life meaningful. Life acquires meaning through struggle, he implied, regardless of the final outcome. Camus imagined Sisyphus happy because he led a life of struggle, rolling the stone, again and again, up the mountain only to watch it roll back down.

One of Camus's famous sayings is, "Fiction is the lie through which we tell the truth." In the same vein Fyodor Dostoyevsky (1821-1881) said, "We must embellish the truth to make it believable." And in that same vein, I have rewritten your father's story to tell the truth about a most daring young boy who grew up to become a most remarkable man.

Batman Kindness

An act of kindness, like an act of mercy, *"is twice blessed,"* to use the Bard's words. *"It blesseth him that gives and him that takes..."*

But, which comes first? Do we become merciful because we are kind, or do we become kind because we are merciful? Where does kindness rank on the Decalogue tablet of virtues? Can it have dangerous consequences like honesty? Can it be hurtful like love? Can it be abused like freedom? Is it the redeeming child of cruelty? Or is it our apotheosis because it is un-corruptible, rejects violence, and does not go to war like love and passions do.

Should it, like all virtues, have limits and be vouchsafed only to those deserving? Or is it the soul's taproot, *nourisher* of all virtues, and spark of the divine that causes our hearts to strum with compassion and resonate with the love of humanity? What comes first, love or kindness? Can love survive without kindness? Can kindness reach out without love? Does joy commit suttee when kindness dies? Are *Kindness*, *Love*, and *Joy* the humane trinity?

It happened when the autumn leaves, yellowed by November sun, still clung to their mothers' arms with frail fingers. *"Soon gravity and wind will win,"* I mused, as I drove to Braum's with *labni* on my mind. Our nine grandchildren were coming home for Thanksgiving and I had to start making yogurt two days before, drain the whey a day later, and harvest the *labni* spread on the third day. I was not sure if our grandchildren came to visit us for love or for *labni* and I did not care to find out because, in stark contrast to their electronic gadgets, their communion with *labni* made them interactive, kind, and well behaved.

"Get me a milkshake while you're at it, please, and don't forget to buy an 8 oz. cup of plain yogurt for starter," came my wife's pressing request as I got out of the car and walked towards Braum's sliding door. My numerous past attempts at making *labni* had failed miserably because the myriad yogurts I had tried as starters did not contain the live lactobacillus bacteria. But Braum's plain yogurt did, and with it I was able to refine my *labni* making into an art, with which I was able to snare our grandchildren.

At the checkout stand, with a gallon of milk in one hand and a cup of plain yogurt in the other, I asked the sales lady to add a milkshake to my bill and then reached for my wallet.

"Oh, I'm so sorry," I gulped, with hand still in my empty back pocket. "I'll have to run back to the car to get you the money."

The checkout lady rolled her eyes, shoved the brown paper sack to the side, and croaked, "Next please."

"Where's the milk?" asked my wife as I got back into the car, empty-handed, "And what happened to my milkshake?"

"Do you have your purse with you?" I pleaded.

"No, I left it at home," she frowned, with confused concern. "What happened to your wallet?"

"It's at home with your purse," I smirked. "Hand me the little coin sack in the glove compartment and let's hope it has enough in it to save the day."

After Jenny and I finished counting all our pennies and decided that we had just enough money to pay for the milk and the yogurt but not for the milkshake, I carried my handful of coins back to the checkout lady and sheepishly asked her to cancel the milkshake order. Instead of taking my prized coins, she handed me the brown paper sack and said, "It's been paid for."

"Paid for? Paid for by whom?" I asked, sounding a bit miffed.

"By the gentleman who stood behind you in line."

"And where's that gentleman now?" I quizzed, scanning the place.

"I don't know," she nonchalantly replied. "He paid your bill and his and then walked away."

I carried the loaded paper sack to the car and, handing my wife our prized coin collection, I related to her what had happened.

"We need to find him and get his name and address," she emphatically decreed. "We have to thank him and pay him back," she added, her chin quivering with gratitude.

"It's too late for that, dear," I said, starting the car.

"What did he look like?"

"He was young, stocky, freckled, and red-headed," I replied, as I rolled the car out of its parking space, "but I'm not sure that I would recognize him if I were to see him again."

As the car began to arc towards the exit, a young, red-headed, stocky man burst out of the store and ran towards us screaming, "You forgot your milkshake."

"That's him," I cried as I stopped the car and rolled down the passenger window.

I watched him hand my startled wife the milkshake, smile, and then take off, refusing to be engaged in conversation.

"Please, tell us your name," she cried, as he was about to re-enter the store.

"It's Batman," he smiled back, and then disappeared behind Braum's sliding door.

Astonished, we drove back home in silence, my wife, sipping her milkshake and I, watching the yellowed leaves cling to their mothers' arms with frail fingers, unmindful of what was about to come. *"Perhaps, kindness is why trees relinquish their leaves, mothers bid their children farewell, and smiles flood the joyful hearts,"* I thought. *"Perhaps, kindness is the unsung force that binds together the blithe faces of seasons. Perhaps, joy is the song of kindness, and love, the dance of kindness, and giving, the arms of kindness, and forgiving, the tears of kindness, and Christ, the sun of kindness, suffusing with His light the darker sides of humanity."*

When, close to home, I shared these thoughts with my wife, she nodded approvingly and added, "I was thinking about the very same things but was struggling to find the right words."

"It's hard to think without words," was the last thing I said before I opened the garage door.

At home, my wife went straight to the study, sat at her desk, and began writing. I knew not to bother her because she seldom writes, but when she does, it's always deep and soul rending. Quietly, I brewed her favorite tea, placed a steaming cup by her side, then stole away unsure that she had noticed.

When the afternoon languished into evening, I began preparing dinner: meatloaf, mashed potatoes, and curly endive salad. Twice I heard her leave the study to use the bathroom and when the darkness deepened, she got up and turned on the lights.

That night I ate alone and left a note in the kitchen that said, "Your dinner is in the refrigerator. Wake me up when you're ready to eat. I can't wait to hear what you've written."

It was close to midnight when she crept into bed and tapped on my head. "Darling," she whispered, "I finished it."

"I'm sorry," I yawned. "I couldn't keep my eyes open."

"Do you want to hear it?"

I sat up, rubbed the sleep out of my eyes, and said, "Did you see my note?"

"What note?" she asked, turning on the light.

"Never mind the note," I said, realizing that she had forgotten to eat. "Let's hear it."

Her stomach growled, she hesitated, and then said, "I hope you'll like it."

"Go ahead dear; I've been waiting a long time for this moment."

Her chin quivered and her face assumed a most profound expression. She sighed, cleared her dry throat, glanced at me with tired eyes, held the piece of paper to the light, and read:

Thoughts upon Kindness and Love:

Kindness is the spirit of God within us
For without God there can be no kindness
And without kindness there can be no God.

If we cannot be kind, we cannot experience love
And without love, we cannot experience joy

For joy is sickened by selfishness
Which lies with unhappiness.

Love without kindness is harsh with ruthless passions
And whereas love can be without kindness
Kindness itself cannot be without love
For it needs a heart to nest in.

Without kindness
> *Love cannot heal*
> *Mercy cannot act*
> *Compassion cannot touch*
> *Shame cannot cry*
> *Anger cannot die*
> *Vengeance cannot forgive*
> *Faith cannot conquer*
> *And humility cannot be genuine.*

At this most inopportune of moments, a few minutes beyond midnight, the telephone barked, cracking our shell of intimacy.

"*Let me not to the marriage of true minds admit impediments,*" I sang with the Bard before I answered. It was the emergency room informing me that Mr. Davide Renault had come in, complaining of shortness of breath, and that the family was waiting for me. With paper still in hand, my wife's tired eyes gazed at me as if I were a receding apparition plucked by an untimely intrusion.

"I have to go dear," I mumbled apologetically.
"Is it bad?"
"Good and bad, I suspect."
"What does that mean, darling?"
"I'll tell you when I return. Dinner is in the refrigerator; eat a bite and try to get some sleep. I have no idea when I'll return."

When, at 3 a.m., I stole back into bed, my wife woke up from her half-sleep and whispered, "How was it?"

"Both happy and sad," I muttered.

She sat up, turned on the light, and yawned, "Good and bad; happy and sad; are you going to tell me what all that means?"

"Isn't it too late for stories," I beguiled.

"It's never too late for stories," she admonished.

Realizing that sleep was not on her mind, I sat up and told her all about Mr. Davide Renault:

Four years ago, at age 70, Mr. Renault developed colon cancer and was treated aggressively with surgery and chemotherapy. For the next three years, at his annual examination, I could not detect any cancer recurrence and we all thought that he was cured. This year, his abdomen felt doughy and he had lost twenty pounds, which caused me to suspect that his cancer had relapsed. I ordered the necessary blood tests and a CAT scan of his abdomen, both of which came back normal. I called Mr. Renault and congratulated him, but asked him to return for follow up in a month instead of a year. He became frightened and asked me if I thought that he was a dead man walking. I answered that the evidence thus far did not support the diagnosis of a cancer recurrence. He sobbed as he told me that his oncologist had said that if his cancer should relapse, it would not be treatable.

In the emergency room, a repeat CAT scan showed his lungs to be full of cancer. When we compared the new CAT scan with the old one, it became obvious that the cancer was present earlier but was too subtle to be seen. Before I could tell him the truth, Mr. Renault turned blue before our eyes. We were unable to oxygenate him using 100% oxygen. He arrested, and CPR proved useless.

After a polite pause, my wife's comment came out like a long, lugubrious drone, "Good and bad. Happy and sad. Now I understand."

"God was kind to Mr. Renault," I interjected. "He granted him a good life and summoned him back without much suffering."

"God is always kind, darling, but we don't always understand the kindness of his ways."

"Why don't you finish reading your piece, dear," I said, stroking her hair.

"Its 3:30 a.m. Isn't it too late for pieces?" she smiled.

"If it's never too late for stories, it's never too late for pieces," I quipped. "I have to hear the rest of it before I sleep."

With a solemn face, she picked up the piece of paper and read from where she had left:

And just as anger begets anger
So kindness begets kindness and more
It begets love, sweetened and tame.

But alone, love cannot beget love
Because it needs kindness to light the way.

And whereas love can only talk to the heart
Kindness visits the soul.

And love, in the name of love, can go to war
Whereas kindness only strives for peace.

And love concerns itself only with those it cares to reach
Whereas kindness reaches out to all humanity.

Kindness is the great mother of life
And love, her beautiful child.

And whereas love is an attribute of the heart
Kindness comes of the spirit of God
He grants it only to those whose souls are worthy.

And whereas love mainly dwells inside of us
Kindness is like the sun
It shines everywhere, giving warmth and light
Without discrimination.

And those who are blessed with kindness
Continue to bless and touch, deep into the future
Where no one else can reach.

When she was through, I took the paper out of her hand, reread it twice, and said, "This is a religious vision, dear, that is too deep for thought."

"It took me so long to write so little," she sniffled.

"The longer the easier, and the shorter the harder," I reassured.

"Why's that?" she asked, wiping her tears.

"Because to excavate deep thoughts takes a lot of digging, and to condense life into one sentence takes a lifetime of trying, and to make a little diamond takes many centuries of pressure. 'Brevity is the soul of wit,' said the Bard in Hamlet."

"Do you agree with what I wrote?"

"Which part, dear?"

"With the concept that kindness is the spirit of God in us because it is not corruptible, whereas love is easy to corrupt."

"Are you saying that *God is kindness*, instead of, *God is love*?"

"Did I say that?" she cried, covering her mouth with her hand.

"Well, not exactly, but yes, you did," I responded, trying to sound reassuring. "You implied that if God were not kindness, he could not love earth's ever-corrupt humanity?"

"It doesn't sound as good to hear it as it did to think it," she lamented. "Perhaps I should change it back to God is love."

"I think it sounds fine the way it is," I reassured. "It's your own religious vision; cling to it."

She had nothing to say after that remark except, "I feel very tired, but I no longer feel sleepy."

"It's hard to sleep on an empty stomach," I reminded.

"Oh, I forgot to eat."

"Dinner is ready, dear. I just have to reheat it. I'll sit with you while you eat."

"Why are you always so kind?" she smiled, rubbing her stomach.

"Only God is always kind," I replied. "The rest of us have God only to the extent that we have kindness, which is never all the time."

"So, are you saying that when we're unkind, we lose God, and when we're kind, we gain God back?"

"Yes, dear. We can measure our progress with God by measuring our kindness or our lack of it."

"Is that your deep thought of the day or your religious vision of the moment?" she teased as we walked towards the kitchen.

"It's neither, dear," I said as I pulled her dinner out of the refrigerator and placed it in the microwave oven.

"What is it then?" she pleaded.

Silently, I pulled her salad out of the refrigerator, waited for the microwave oven to beep, pulled out her warmed-up meatloaf and mashed potatoes, and said, "Here's your food."

"Really, what is it? I'm not eating until you tell me."

"Tell you what?" I pretended.

"Tell me where your revelation came from?"

"Revelation?"

"You said: *'We can measure our progress with God by measuring our kindness or our lack of it,'* and I want to know where that phrase came from."

"It's a quote from the thirteenth century German preacher, Meister Eckhart. I just took out the word *peace* and replaced it with the word *kindness.*"

"How does the original quote go?"

"I'll tell you after you've had your first bite."

She eyed me impatiently while I waited until she took her first bite, followed by a second, and a third.

"Now, would you please tell me what this Meister Eckhart said?"

"He said: *'For you will have peace to the extent that you have God. Anything that is at peace has God in it to the extent that it is at peace. Thus you may measure your progress with God by measuring your peace or the lack of it.'*"

"Hmm. I don't agree with that," she said, shaking her head. "I feel closest to God when I'm in turmoil."

After eating a few more bites, she tweaked me with, "And what else did this Meister Eckhart say?"

"He also said: *'I much prefer a person who can love God enough to take a handout of bread, to a person who can give a hundred dollars for God's sake.'* "

When I said that, she gasped as if struck by an epiphany. Then, pushing her plate away, she gazed through me with dry, distant eyes and murmured, "And did we love God enough today to take a handout of bread?"

"What do *you* think?" I hesitantly asked.

"I feel we did," she sighed, lowering her head onto my shoulder.

Then, after a protracted, pensive pause, she added, "Perhaps that's why I've been in turmoil and why, just now, I suddenly feel redeemed."

"Such is the mystery of receiving," I said, stroking her neck.

"Dear God," she murmured. "Oh, what delicious pain."

Valediction

Given to my patients when I retired from medicine.

<u>Beirut, Lebanon, 1971</u>

As a medical intern, scurrying up and down the long corridors of the American University Medical Center in Beirut (AUB), I had made up my mind that after graduation, I would stay for three more years of Internal Medicine residency before going to the States for Infectious Disease sub-specialization. But, since the unexpected is more likely to occur than the expected, coincidence changed my life course, as it does everyone's.

> *Coincidence*
> *She wears green shadows intertwined with dreams*
> *Lurks unforeseen, in silence plots and schemes*
> *At times she hurries matters to profound extremes*
> *Delights in rolling fortunes in reverse*
> *Coincidence*
> *She sways the universe.*

"Salem," called Professor Aladin as I was about to enter room 404, where convalescing, lay a powerful politician who had been stabbed in a bar brawl by a Saudi Arabian prince.

"Yes, Professor Aladin," I waved, as I turned back and hurried to my caller.

"What are your plans for next year?" he asked, the gleam in his eyes betraying his pretense.

There are no secrets at the AUB, I thought, as I prepared my answer. "I am staying here for three years of Internal Medicine residency, after which I plan to go to the States for a two-year Infectious Disease fellowship."

"Hmm," he cooed, obliviously stroking his goatee. "How many years have you already spent at the AUB?"

"This is my eighth, Sir."

"And you wish to stay here for three more years?"

"Yes, Sir."

"Don't you think eleven years in one place is a bit too long?"

I lowered my gaze so as not to meet his, and did not respond.

"Why don't you go to the States for residency and fellowship?"

"Because I like it here."

"Have you no desire to find out how other medical centers teach and think?"

"I do, Sir, but I don't like traffic jams, crowded cities, street gangs, and tiny apartments."

"Nonsense. There are great American medical centers in clean, friendly cities."

"Oh?"

"I did my PhD in microbiology at the University of Oklahoma Health Sciences Center in Oklahoma City. It's a friendly town with a large Lebanese community."

"But, isn't it too late to apply now?"

"Nonsense, again. Why don't you come to my office, fill out an application, and I'll write you a recommendation."

And so it was, until six months later when my mother paged me on the overhead while I was admitting a Damascene diva, yellow with hepatitis.

"Salem."

"Yes, Mother. Anything wrong?"

"Not exactly, Son. But, a telegram has just arrived at my clinic from the University of Oklahoma Health Sciences Center in Oklahoma City informing you that you have been accepted in their Internal Medicine Residency program. You never told us you applied!"

"Oh, dear," I gasped. "I only sent one application just to appease Professor Aladdin, and then I forgot all about it."

"But, we've already told everyone that you're staying here for your Internal Medicine residency. When did you change your mind?"

"Right now. This very minute."
"So what do you want me to do?"
"Wire back: '*I will be there on time.*' "

That year, 1971, the graduation ceremony at the American University of Beirut was canceled because of smoldering political fires. My classmates and I quietly took the Hippocratic Oath in the dean's office, received our diplomas, and scurried back to our homes under the shroud of fear and gloom of uncertainty. The angry voices of violence and the visceral dread of death bellowed like smoke along the busy streets and scuttled with bloody talons across the dim, narrow mazes of silent alleys.

Close to home, I heard three shots followed by a burst of wails and screams. I stopped, peered into the worried eyes in the street, and feeling overcome by sudden heat, took off my necktie. A few steps further, my jacket began to feel heavy, and my right hand, which held my diploma, started to sweat. I took off my jacket, moved the diploma to my left hand, and hugged the wall as I hastened my pace down Bliss Street among hurrying, circumspect faces.

When I turned the corner, I saw the dead man, sprawled on the sidewalk, smudged in a fresh pool of blood. The crowd of stunned eyes and whimpering wailers stood at a distance, on the other side of Joan d'Arc Street.

I learned from the mourners that he, the bridegroom, was my age, 25 at the time, and that he was shot by the brother of the woman with whom he had eloped a week earlier. That very same brother had also shot the bride, his sister, earlier that day, to cleanse his family's honor. *"Honor can only be cleansed with blood,"* was the proverbial, espoused belief of tribal clans. In Lebanese jurisdiction, honor killings are not classified as murders, and the killers are given reduced sentences, if they are ever apprehended.

As I pressed my way back home, with the dead groom's bloody image dripping from my eyes and his bride's white apparition floating over my head, an implacable anger pounded in my heart, fueled by the abject disillusionment at historic defeat. Human nature, which throughout history has effortlessly confounded all the messengers of God, had yet again prevailed by misinterpreting the holy texts of Christianity and Islam. The bride and groom were of different religions, and that was cause enough to kill them both.

A poem, which I had written, began to recite and re-recite itself, against my silent lips:

Yes, I have known the gentle peace of death
The pain and sleepless anguish of Macbeth
Have loved and hated, even leased my soul
With perfect logic, softened to comply
With inner whims that do not yield nor die
Yes, this is I
There hardly is a process that I could not justify.

My medical diploma, now in my left, sweaty palm, began to feel useless. When I left the dean's office, I carried it with pride, like a badge of honor achieved after an eight-year struggle. But, after witnessing that bloody scene, it began to feel heavy and burdensome, like a useless brick carried over a *stoneless* desert. Perhaps I was a fool to think that, singlehandedly, I could change the world. Perhaps, only fools like me could write a disillusioned poem like this one:

Sometimes I wonder
Will the Homo sapiens brute
Decline, destruct, or evolute
Into a nobler institute than we
Where love might be a little less dilute
And where there is a place for fools like me
Fools who are simple, nonetheless, diverse
Who with compassion for their universe
Reach out to mend the future with a verse

Untouched by fashioned thoughts or views
Inclined to meditate and muse
Who seldom read the press or watch the news.

When, with these visions and disillusions barking at my mind, I walked into our home, my furrowed face was assailed by a host of family and friends who, on queue, burst into a *gratulant* clamor as my father popped a bottle of Champagne. "To our new doctor," they all toasted, clinking their glasses against my blinking eyes. I tried to pretend that all was well with the world, that my achievement was a singular source of joy, and that this long-awaited moment had, in fact, arrived. But, my pretense, which was thwarted by what I had just seen, betrayed me. Many of the guests asked if anything was the matter. Of course, with bloody disappointment ringing in my ears, I appeased them by saying, "It's merely the sadness of joy."

I could not wait for the guests to leave, which they slowly did, one after the other, like a long line of snails. It was close to midnight before my father, a surgeon, my mother, a gynecologist, and I found our quiet moment, which I had longed for all evening.

"Well, I'm finally a doctor," I sighed, interrupting the moment's quietude.

"No, you're not," broke in my father with a kind, but knowing tone.

My mother, unsurprised, smiled and stroked my back. I was too tired for banter so, I merely reiterated what my father had said, "So, I'm not a doctor?"

"No, you're not," repeated my father, but this time his tone was more deliberate.

"So what am I, then?" I asked.

"You are now a certified, life-long student of medicine."

"And when do I become a doctor?" I inquired, unable to hide my perturbation.

My father smiled, looked at my mother, and said nothing. My mother patted my hand, cleared her throat, and answered, "It will take a very long time, at least ten years, before you become a real doctor, my dear. Your father is right. All you are now is but a certified student of medicine."

"So, this M.D. means nothing then?" I protested, holding my diploma high above my head.

"It merely means that you have now earned the right to spend the rest of your life in the pursuit of medical knowledge," chimed in my father.

"But, why do I need this degree then? Anyone can choose to spend his life in the pursuit of medical knowledge."

"No, Son. In the pursuit of medical information, perhaps, but not in the pursuit of knowledge, which comes only from the experience of working with patients, day after day, and year after year. Your degree gives you the right to work with patients, but it is your patients who grant you the knowledge."

I sighed and so did my father. Then, as an afterthought, he added, "You should read *The Rock*, by T. S. Eliot.

"Why?" I nervously snapped.

"It's a wise, soul searching poem, which may help you think deeper.

"Do you remember any of it?" I asked in a softer tone, having realized that *The Rock* was not a long work of prose.

He grinned, and looking me straight in the eyes, quoted:

"Where is the wisdom we have lost in knowledge?
Where is the knowledge we have lost in information?"

I was silent awhile. My mother gleamed and nodded approvingly. My father repeatedly tapped his foot on the floor to indicate that the discussion was not yet over. It was after midnight, and I could have chosen to bid them goodnight and retire. But some restless hunger for more caused me to further probe into my parents' collective medical experience of more than half a century.

"So then, after ten years of dedicated study, working with patients, and gaining knowledge, I would at last become a real doctor?" I asked with a tired expression.

"No, Son. I wish it were that easy," murmured my dad.

At that point, my exacerbation escalated into shear anger. I took my diploma out of my lap and tossed it onto the vacant living room chair next to me as if it were a perfunctory document. My parents' aspects changed, but they remained silent. Regret crept into my mind when I saw their downcast eyes. I took in a deep breath, apologized, and then begged with a hoarse, supplicating voice, "So, if ten years of studying and working with patients do not make me a real doctor, what does?"

Before he answered, my father's eyes brimmed with unshed tears, perhaps because he could see how seriously I took my vocation. Then, after a long, stuttering pause, he said, "You will become a real doctor only when, after ten years of tireless pursuit, you will succeed in loving all your patients as if they were your very own family—as if they were your own sisters, brothers, daughters, sons, cousins, uncles, aunts, and grandparents—as if they were us."

In a rueful act, I picked up my diploma from the vacant living room chair, held it to my chest, and waited, for I could tell that he had more to say. My mother gulped and gazed at my father with pride.

"Medicine is a divine calling, Son," he began. "The power to heal illness, ease suffering, reassure anguish, inspire hope, improve quality, save and prolong life, is a terrifying responsibility. Power corrupts. Beware not to let hubris overcome your native humility. Think of yourself as a medical missionary, embarking on a long, humanitarian crusade. Put your patients ahead of yourself; be fearless in defending them against disease; and above all, love them with all your heart, for without love you will become naught but a medical technician."

I slept well that night and it was not a fitful sleep. Rather, it was a deep, restorative sleep, full of promising dreams and high-minded ideas. I could feel the weight of the cross over my shoulder, could see the long, uphill road awaiting me, and I felt fit and ready. I woke up to find that all my fears had dissipated—and only after my fears had left me did I realize how frightened I was, frightened to the bone of the massive weight of responsibility that awaited me.

Before I left for the States, my parents invited my favorite professors to dinner. Three were American and three were Lebanese with American wives. The conversation was mainly about Oklahoma because one wife was from Tulsa, one from Muskogee, and one professor was from Lawton. After dinner, while sipping Arabic coffee, the professor from Lawton, who had earned his M.D. from the University of Oklahoma Health Sciences Center at Oklahoma City, said, "Once you get used to Oklahoma, you will not want to leave it."

"Oh, no." I retaliated. "I have been offered a faculty position in the Section of Infectious Diseases at the AUB and I do plan to return and serve right here, where I am most needed."

My father, a staunch patriot, nodded approvingly and my mother added, "Lebanon needs his educated children to return and play an active part in rebuilding the country. America has plenty of good doctors, but Lebanon does not."

Oklahoma City, 1976

When I finished my residency and fellowship, I began making preparations for my return to the AUB. While at my office at Children's Hospital, for I was then the director of the Adolescent Medicine Program, my patriotic father called me from Beirut.

"Father? Any thing wrong?"
"Yes."
"What is it?"
"A civil war has begun, and it may take twenty years before peace can be regained."
"What are you saying?" I gasped, afraid to ask what he meant.
"I am saying that you should stay where you are. Lebanon is not what it used to be, and I cannot afford to lose another son."

"Another son," I reiterated with a failed voice, shaken by the recall that my brother Nadir was shot and killed by a sniper on his 28th birthday, only a few months ago."

A longsuffering pause intervened while we both sniffled.

"Your mother and I insist that you to stay where it is safe."
"But, what about my faculty position at the AUB?"
"All the AUB professors are trying to leave. Lebanon is committing suicide. It is at war with itself. Schools are closed. The government is shut down. This is not the time to launch a career or start a family. And, I repeat, I cannot afford to lose another son."

I sat down among surprise, anger, and despair. Anger at the senseless loss of my brother Nadir, despair at having lost my Lebanon, and surprise at hearing my patriotic father admonish me against returning home. I wanted to grieve, but could not. Some strange, numinous life force egged me to go on, to accept my new destiny, and to love what I had suddenly become, a Lebanese American immigrant.

And so it was. In my little Adolescent Medicine office at Children's Hospital, my identity metamorphosed in one seismic instant from visitor to citizen.

My secretary, Sandra, buzzed me on the intercom, cracking my solitude shell.

"Yes?" I asked, startled.
"Don't forget, Doc. You have a lecture to give in five minutes," came her reminding voice.
"Oh, yes." I stuttered. "Life must step upon death and forward march."
"What was that?" she giggled.
"Nothing. I was just saying that I'd better go give my talk."

Oklahoma City, 1982

As my father had predicted, Lebanon was still at war with itself, profusely bleeding from its multiple wounds. Of my three boys, all born in Oklahoma City, the older two were already going to school. I had become an American citizen, but suffered from an identity crisis, a bicultural identity crisis unshared by my three boys. Am I a Lebanese-American or an American-Lebanese, I obsessively asked myself? As always, poetry came to my rescue. Transmuting a strong emotion into verse was how I had always diffused my anguish.

> *Because I have two hearts*
> *Because I straddle oceans*
> *Because I am both banks of life*
> *The froth, the currents in between*
> *The dissonant emotions*
> *I see beyond the mighty walls of time*
> *Beyond the eyes, the made-up lips, and faces*
> *Beyond the borrowed sentiments and faint laces*
> *Because I have two hearts*
> *My soul is vagabond*
> *It camps in many places.*

Oklahoma City, 2014

I began seeing private patients as an assistant professor at OU in 1975. I joined the Mercy clinical staff and began my private practice in 1977. After two score of active service, fatigue has come to dwell among my crowded years. My body is informing me that my time to retire has arrived. My heart, on the other hand, is repudiating the verdicts of my graying reality and piling grief upon my soul.

I have loved you all and given you my best work and best years. You have honored me with your trust and requited my love. Oklahoma has long been my home away from home and you, my family away from family. I will suffer from this timely termination far more than you will because I am readily replaceable, but you are not.

Familiar faces
Let us not pretend
Though life may decimate and send
Our unsuspecting souls across
Uncharted times and unfamiliar places
Wherever we are loved, we end.

As soon as I close my door and walk off into the sunset, I shall become a memory, denied the daily interactions with my family of patients whose friendship I have long cherished and whose love I have solemnly revered. My retirement will estrange me from you all and will leave an echoing vacuum in my soul, a vacuum that for the past forty years has been filled with the ineffable joy of service and the weariless pursuit of excellence.

I take my leave content that I have dedicated my life to a worthy cause, *You*. I have served with passion, comported myself with honor, and loved all the smiles and tears that have seasoned my forty years of *physicianship*.

Above all, I thank you for your love, which was the chief reason why I made Oklahoma my home. Perhaps, if my father were still alive, he would have knighted me with the title of *Real Doctor* for I have continued to view myself as a life-long student of medicine, have honorably served my term, have always done my utmost best, and have loved everyone of you as much as I have loved my very own family.

Adieu.

Valediction, First Edition, OSMA Journal, Volume 107, Number 7, July 2014. Revised Edition completed in October of 2016

The End

Ten Books by Author at: amazon.com

Poetry—Revised Editions:

    1. Loves & Lamentations of a Life Watcher
        (1961-1987: 133 pages - 43 poems)

    2. Vast Awakenings
        (1987-1990: 154 pages - 60 poems)

    3. Familiar Faces
        (1990-1993: 149 pages - 46 poems)

    4. Four and a Half Billion Years
        (1995-2001: 204 pages - 78 poems)

    5. When You Happened to Me
        (2005-2015: 275 pages - 117 poems)

Novels—Revised Editions:

    *6. **The Mighty Weight of Love*** tells the story of a widowed Lebanese immigrant who falls in love with a victimized American divorcée. The couple and their children struggle against interred fears, indelible biases, cultural dogmas, and biological inertia. Mental illness, which distorts relationships and throws a macabre shroud over eyes, is defied by ferocious love that refuses to yield. It is set in the era of the 1995 Oklahoma City Bombing.

    *7. **Letters: A Love Story*** is about a Lebanese-Christian immigrant who leaves behind, in Beirut, a Muslim girlfriend, but they continue to communicate by letters because they could not *un-love* one another, even after they had married and had children on two different continents. The story is written in letters, stretches across forty years, 1961 to 2001, takes place in several countries, intertwines the children of the couple, and swings back-and-forth between the freedom-riddled West and the religion-riddled East. Also available in Hardback as *Epistole*.

8. Back from Iraq tells the story of a soldier, who returns traumatized, becomes a misfit, and watches his life fall and shatter into sharp shards on the concrete surfaces of fear, confusion, and tradition. To pick up the scattered pieces, rebuild his life, and save his five-year-old daughter, he had to overcome his fear with love, and fight, single-handedly, his battle against Al-Qaeda. It is set between Oklahoma City and Iraq in 2006. Also available in hardback.

9. Twenty Lost Years: A Story in A Diary is about a fourteen-year-old Christian fugitive who, after his mother's death, escapes his father's abuse and takes refuge in Tripoli, falls in love with a veiled Muslim girl, joins *Les Troupes Spéciales* under French Mandate, and, after twenty years of action and adventure, returns to his village to become the town's drunk, healer, teacher, and protector of its children. It is set among Lebanon, Syria, and France, and spans the forty tumultuous years between 1926 and 1966. Published in Beirut by Kutub, in beautiful hardback, as <u>The Diary of Aziz Al-Mitfi</u>.

10. Both Banks of Life: Forty Short Stories is a series of fictionalized, autobiographical stories, through which life unfolds, layer-after-layer, revealing truths hidden in its deeper-and-deeper hearts. The tales meander between life's somber tragedies and its blithe comedies, refreshing tears with laughs and resurrecting lost innocence with memories. The stories are set in Lebanon, Saudi Arabia, and Oklahoma, and take place between 1950 and 2014.

Web Page
Almualif Publishing
at: *saadah.net*

Made in the USA
Coppell, TX
27 February 2023